ANITA BLAKE™

VAMPIRE HUNTER

Guilty Pleasures

ANITA BLAKE™
VAMPIRE HUNTER
Guilty Pleasures

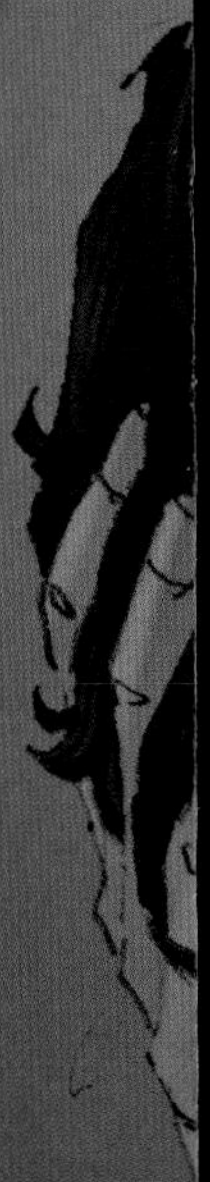

Writer: Laurell K. Hamilton

Adaptation: Jess Ruffner-Booth

Artwork: Brett Booth & Ron Lim

Colors: June Chung

Letters: Bill Tortolini

Assistant Editor: Jordan D. White

Editor: Mark Paniccia

Cover Artists: Brett Booth & Ron Lim

Collection Editor: Cory Levine

Editorial Assistant: Jody LeHeup

Assistant Editor: John Denning

Editors, Special Projects: Jennifer Grünwald & Mark D. Beazley

Senior Editor, Special Projects: Jeff Youngquist

Vice President of Development: Ruwan Jayatilleke

Senior Vice President of Sales: David Gabriel

Book Design: Spring Hoteling

Editor in Chief: Joe Quesada

Publisher: Dan Buckley

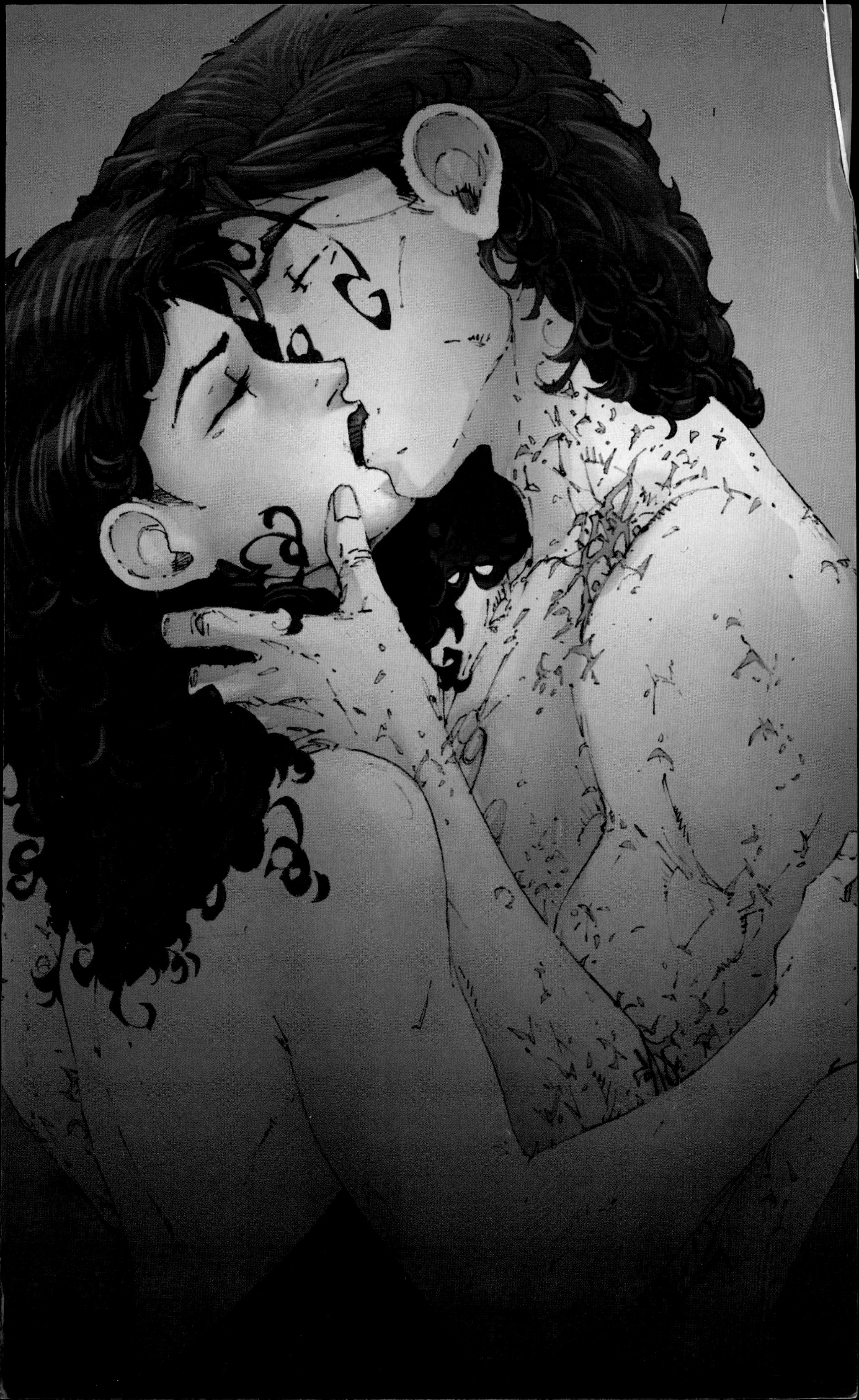

ANITA BLAKE™
VAMPIRE HUNTER
Guilty Pleasures

Anita Blake is the Executioner. She raises the dead and kills vampires. So you would think that vampires would avoid her like the proverbial plague. But there's something out there they fear even more, a killer targeting the most powerful vampires in the city. The Master Vampire of St. Louis makes her an offer she can't refuse: if she wants to save the life of her best friend, the Executioner will join forces with the very creatures she would rather kill.

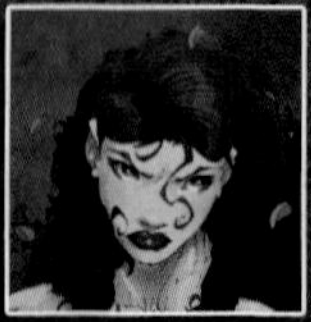
ANITA BLAKE

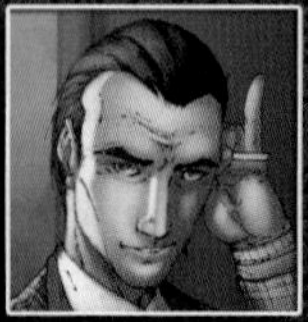
WILLIE

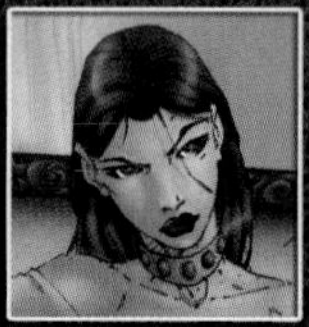
THERESA

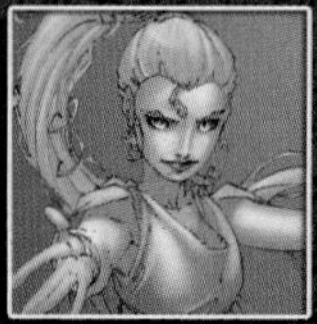
NIKOLAOS

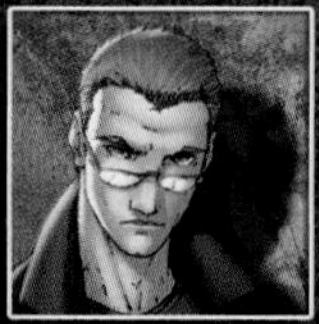
EDWARD

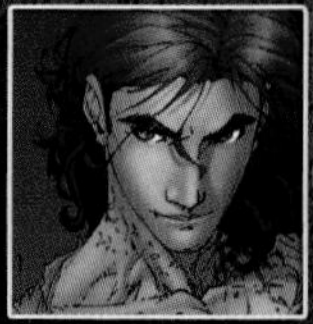
PHILLIP

PREVIOUSLY IN ANITA BLAKE: VAMPIRE HUNTER GUILTY PLEASURES...

Acting on her only available lead, Anita has accompanied vampire junkie Phillip to a freak party, where vampire-obsessed humans can meet up with the objects of their desire and give themselves over to the vampires' dark appetites. All of the killer's victims thus far were regular fixtures in the freak party scene.

To allow Anita to blend in, Phillip has told the other freaks she is his lover. Now Anita finds herself in the uncomfortable position of having to keep up this cover story as lust-filled eyes peer on...

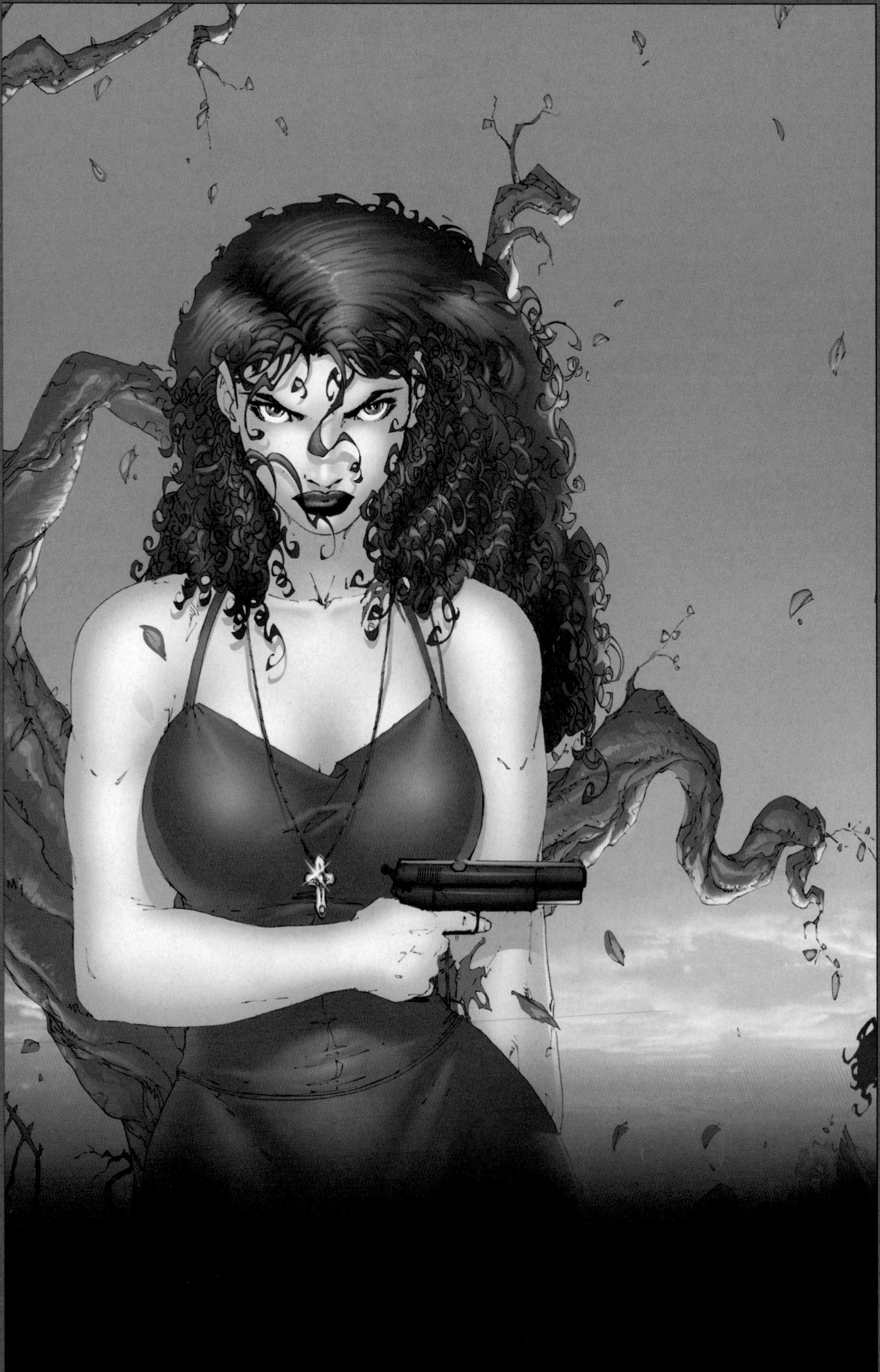

[#7]

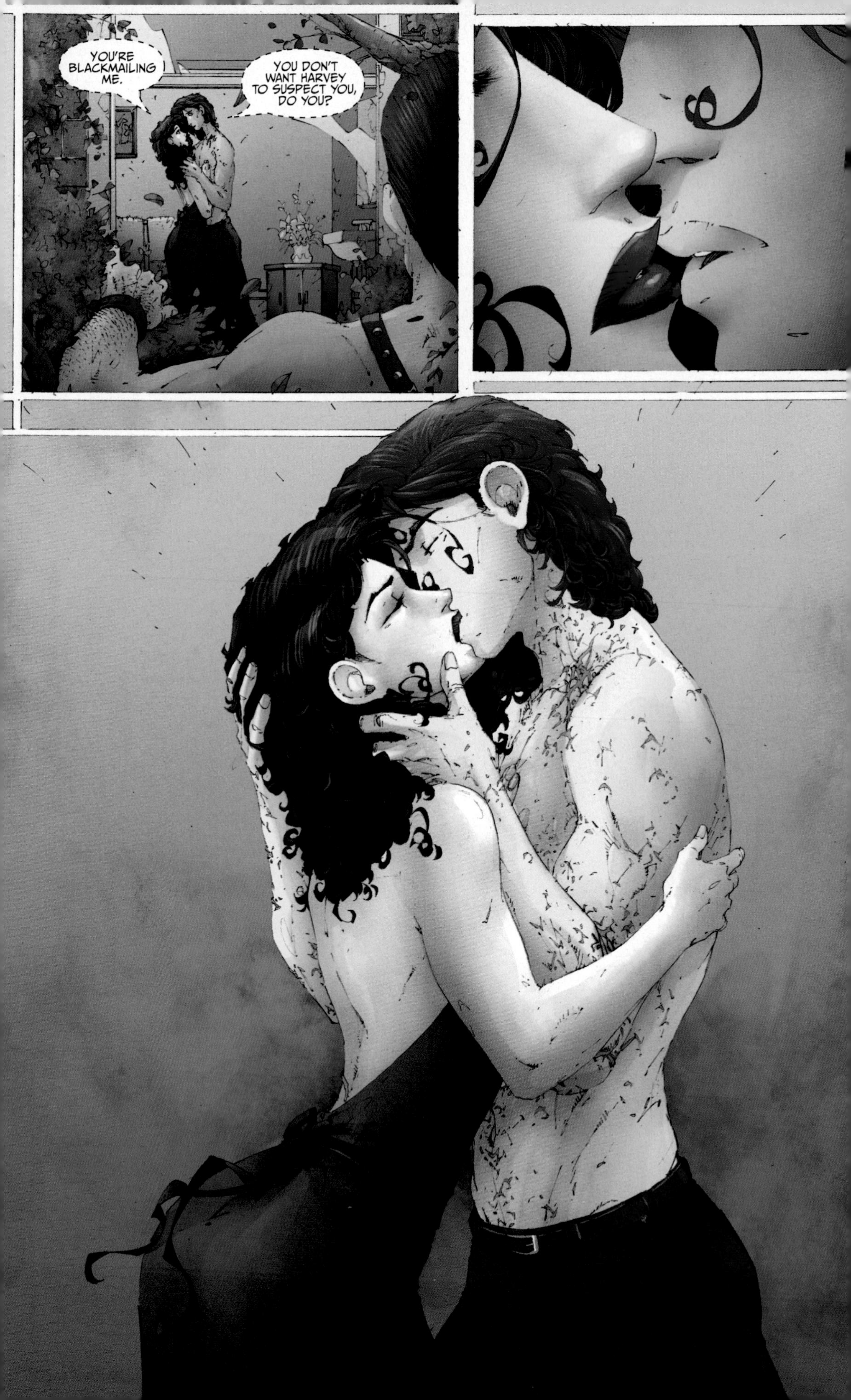
YOU'RE BLACKMAILING ME.
YOU DON'T WANT HARVEY TO SUSPECT YOU, DO YOU?

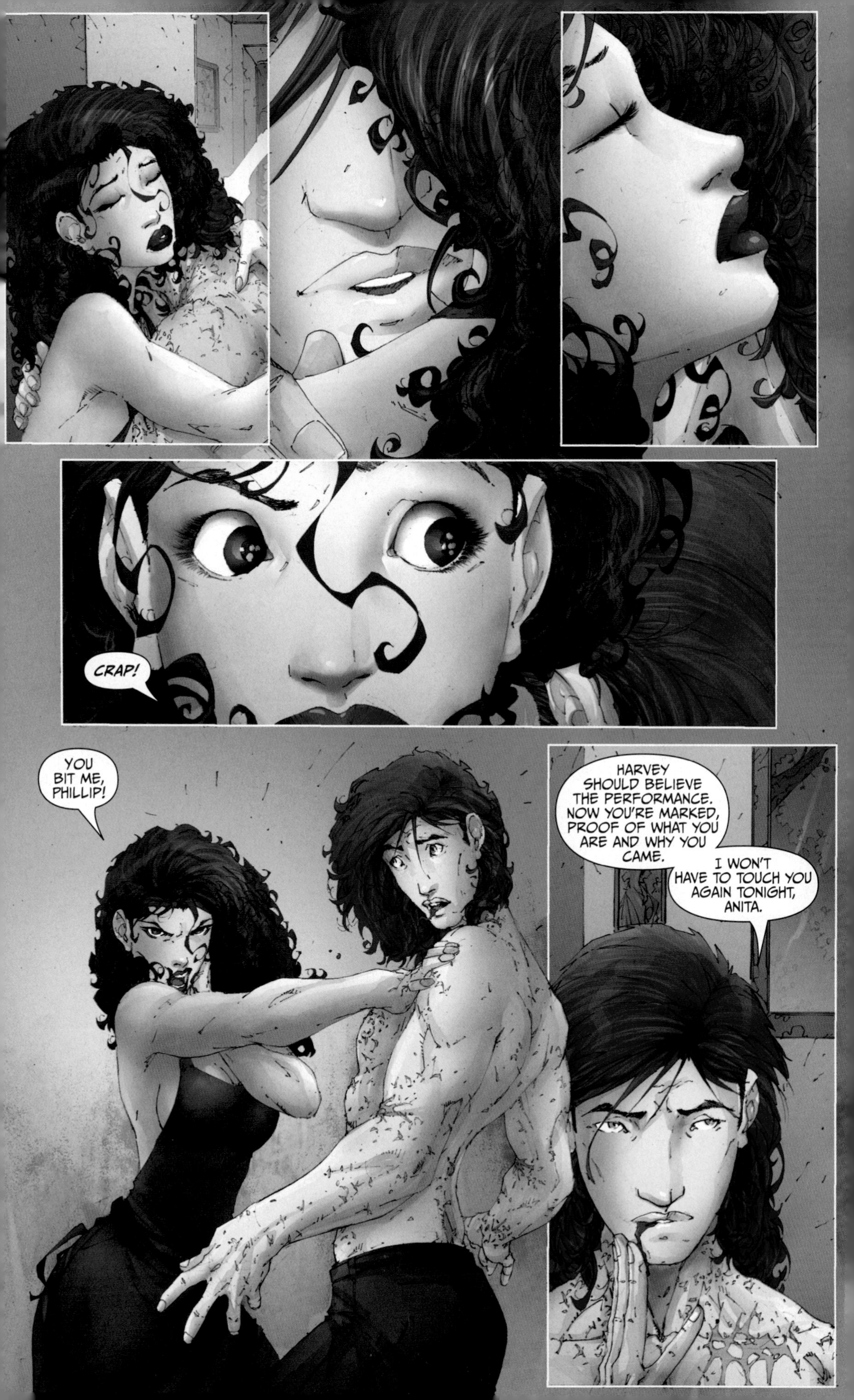
CRAP!
YOU BIT ME, PHILLIP!
HARVEY SHOULD BELIEVE THE PERFORMANCE. NOW YOU'RE MARKED, PROOF OF WHAT YOU ARE AND WHY YOU CAME.
I WON'T HAVE TO TOUCH YOU AGAIN TONIGHT, ANITA.

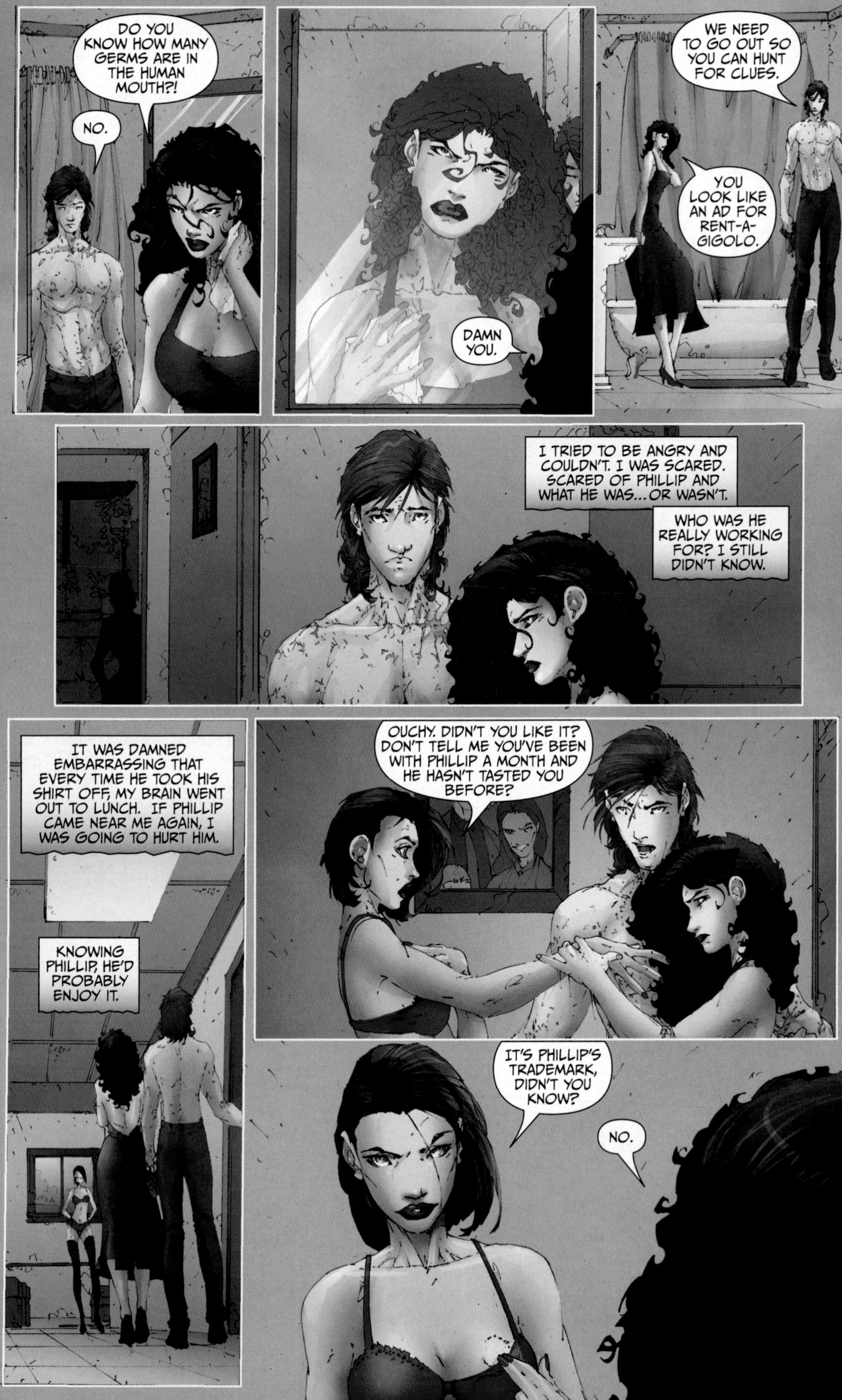

DO YOU KNOW HOW MANY GERMS ARE IN THE HUMAN MOUTH?!
NO.
DAMN YOU.
WE NEED TO GO OUT SO YOU CAN HUNT FOR CLUES.
YOU LOOK LIKE AN AD FOR RENT-A-GIGOLO.
I TRIED TO BE ANGRY AND COULDN'T. I WAS SCARED. SCARED OF PHILLIP AND WHAT HE WAS... OR WASN'T.
WHO WAS HE REALLY WORKING FOR? I STILL DIDN'T KNOW.
IT WAS DAMNED EMBARRASSING THAT EVERY TIME HE TOOK HIS SHIRT OFF, MY BRAIN WENT OUT TO LUNCH. IF PHILLIP CAME NEAR ME AGAIN, I WAS GOING TO HURT HIM.
KNOWING PHILLIP, HE'D PROBABLY ENJOY IT.
OUCHY. DIDN'T YOU LIKE IT? DON'T TELL ME YOU'VE BEEN WITH PHILLIP A MONTH AND HE HASN'T TASTED YOU BEFORE?
IT'S PHILLIP'S TRADEMARK, DIDN'T YOU KNOW?
NO.

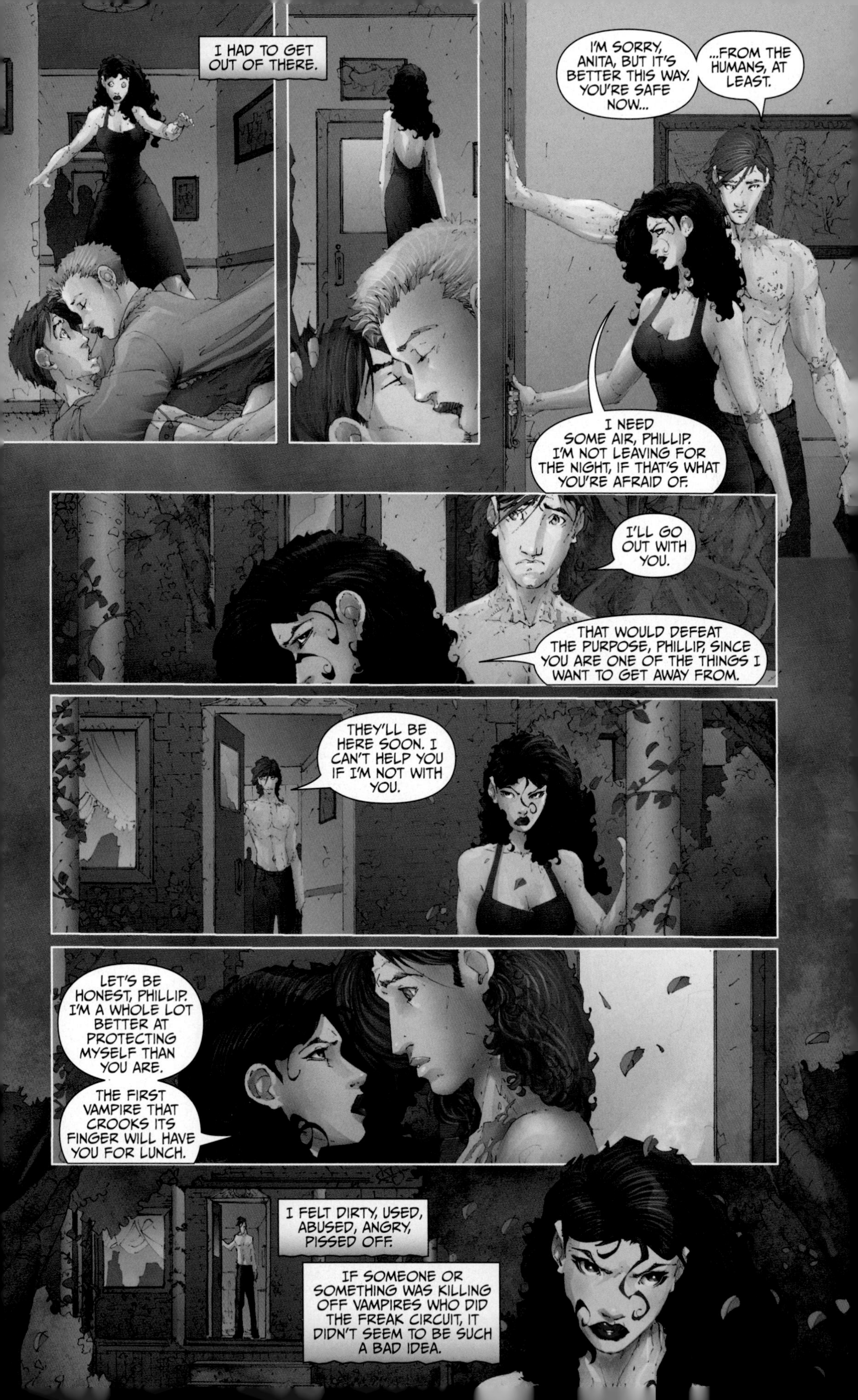
I HAD TO GET OUT OF THERE.
I'M SORRY, ANITA, BUT IT'S BETTER THIS WAY. YOU'RE SAFE NOW...
...FROM THE HUMANS, AT LEAST.
I NEED SOME AIR, PHILLIP. I'M NOT LEAVING FOR THE NIGHT, IF THAT'S WHAT YOU'RE AFRAID OF.
I'LL GO OUT WITH YOU.
THAT WOULD DEFEAT THE PURPOSE, PHILLIP, SINCE YOU ARE ONE OF THE THINGS I WANT TO GET AWAY FROM.
THEY'LL BE HERE SOON. I CAN'T HELP YOU IF I'M NOT WITH YOU.
LET'S BE HONEST, PHILLIP. I'M A WHOLE LOT BETTER AT PROTECTING MYSELF THAN YOU ARE.
THE FIRST VAMPIRE THAT CROOKS ITS FINGER WILL HAVE YOU FOR LUNCH.
I FELT DIRTY, USED, ABUSED, ANGRY, PISSED OFF.
IF SOMEONE OR SOMETHING WAS KILLING OFF VAMPIRES WHO DID THE FREAK CIRCUIT, IT DIDN'T SEEM TO BE SUCH A BAD IDEA.

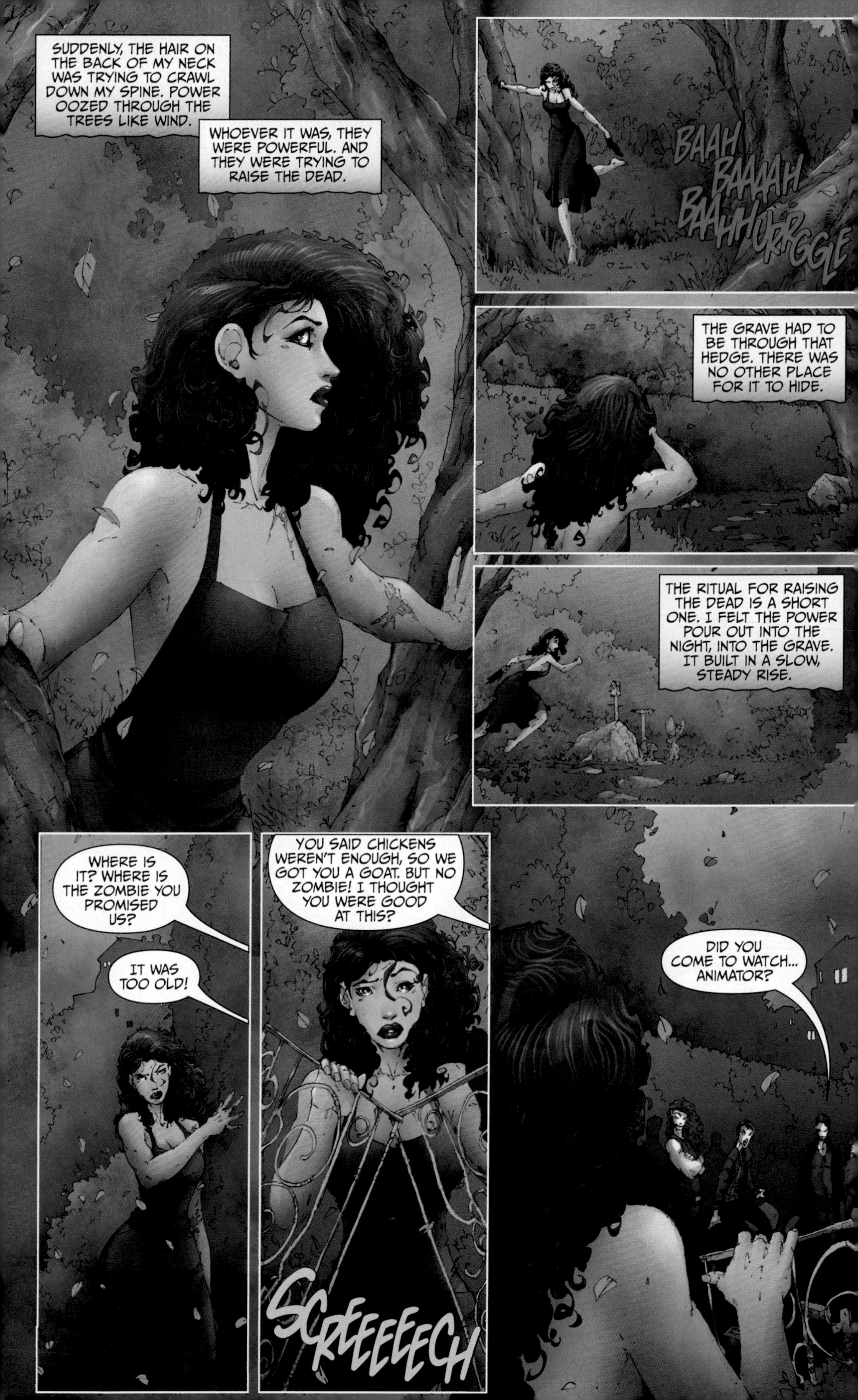

SUDDENLY, THE HAIR ON THE BACK OF MY NECK WAS TRYING TO CRAWL DOWN MY SPINE. POWER OOZED THROUGH THE TREES LIKE WIND.
WHOEVER IT WAS, THEY WERE POWERFUL. AND THEY WERE TRYING TO RAISE THE DEAD.
BAAH BAAAAH BAAHHURRGGLE
THE GRAVE HAD TO BE THROUGH THAT HEDGE. THERE WAS NO OTHER PLACE FOR IT TO HIDE.
THE RITUAL FOR RAISING THE DEAD IS A SHORT ONE. I FELT THE POWER POUR OUT INTO THE NIGHT, INTO THE GRAVE. IT BUILT IN A SLOW, STEADY RISE.
WHERE IS IT? WHERE IS THE ZOMBIE YOU PROMISED US?
IT WAS TOO OLD!
YOU SAID CHICKENS WEREN'T ENOUGH, SO WE GOT YOU A GOAT. BUT NO ZOMBIE! I THOUGHT YOU WERE GOOD AT THIS?
SCREEEEECH
DID YOU COME TO WATCH... ANIMATOR?

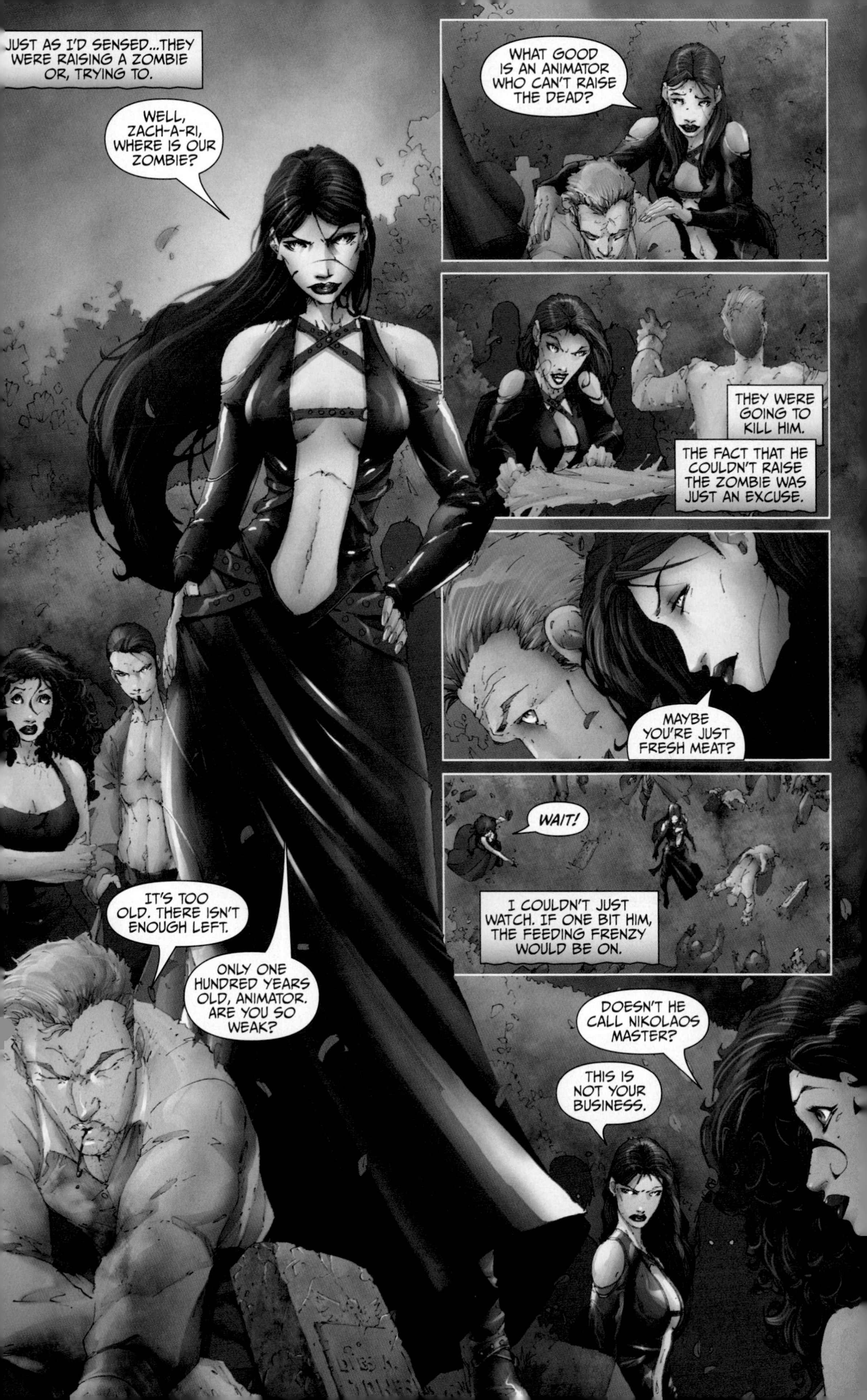
JUST AS I'D SENSED...THEY WERE RAISING A ZOMBIE OR, TRYING TO.
WELL, ZACH-A-RI, WHERE IS OUR ZOMBIE?
IT'S TOO OLD. THERE ISN'T ENOUGH LEFT.
ONLY ONE HUNDRED YEARS OLD, ANIMATOR. ARE YOU SO WEAK?
WHAT GOOD IS AN ANIMATOR WHO CAN'T RAISE THE DEAD?
THEY WERE GOING TO KILL HIM.
THE FACT THAT HE COULDN'T RAISE THE ZOMBIE WAS JUST AN EXCUSE.
MAYBE YOU'RE JUST FRESH MEAT?
WAIT!
I COULDN'T JUST WATCH. IF ONE BIT HIM, THE FEEDING FRENZY WOULD BE ON.
DOESN'T HE CALL NIKOLAOS MASTER?
THIS IS NOT YOUR BUSINESS.

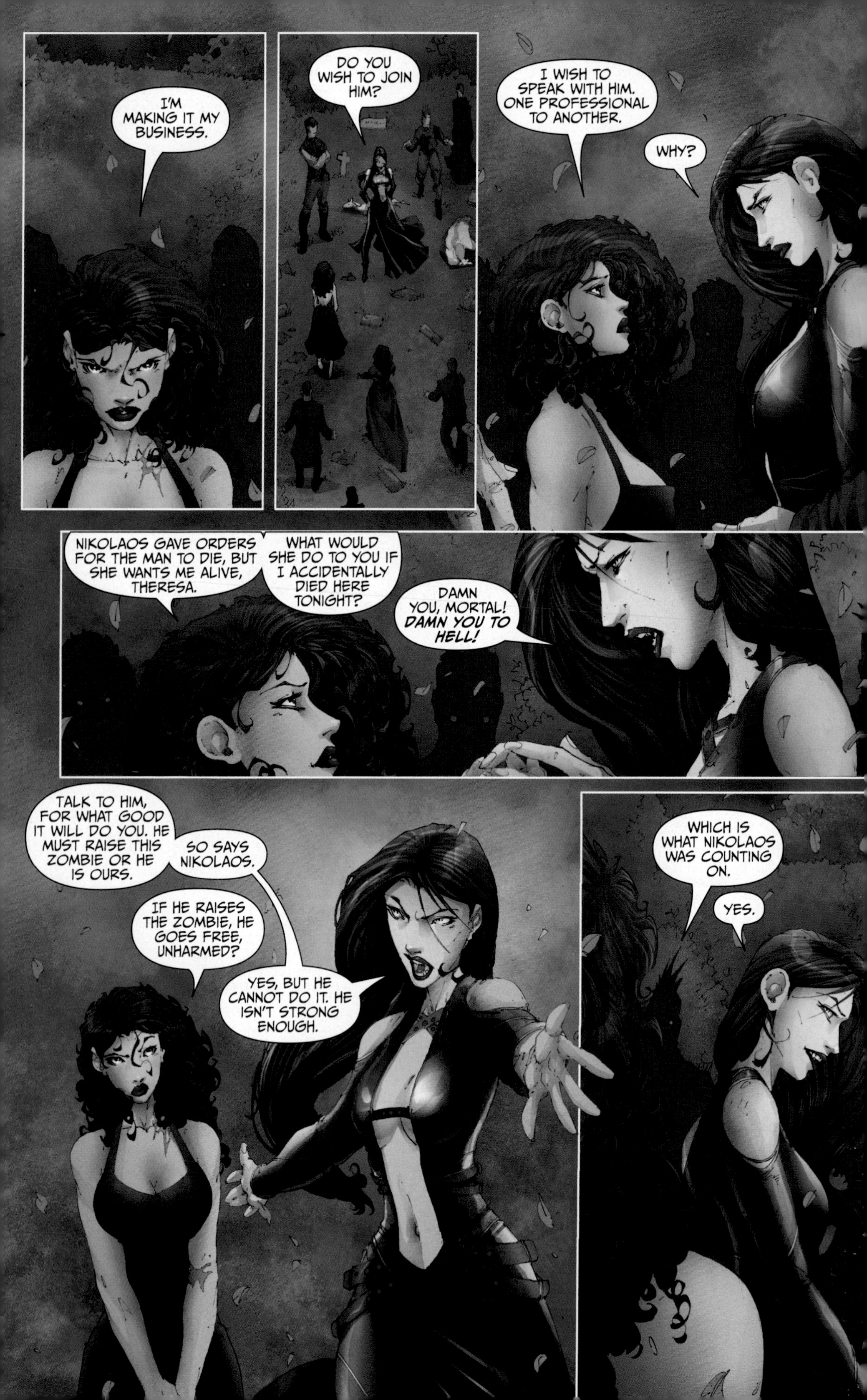
I'M MAKING IT MY BUSINESS.
DO YOU WISH TO JOIN HIM?
I WISH TO SPEAK WITH HIM. ONE PROFESSIONAL TO ANOTHER.
WHY?
NIKOLAOS GAVE ORDERS FOR THE MAN TO DIE, BUT SHE WANTS ME ALIVE, THERESA.
WHAT WOULD SHE DO TO YOU IF I ACCIDENTALLY DIED HERE TONIGHT?
DAMN YOU, MORTAL! *DAMN YOU TO HELL!*
TALK TO HIM, FOR WHAT GOOD IT WILL DO YOU. HE MUST RAISE THIS ZOMBIE OR HE IS OURS.
SO SAYS NIKOLAOS.
IF HE RAISES THE ZOMBIE, HE GOES FREE, UNHARMED?
YES, BUT HE CANNOT DO IT. HE ISN'T STRONG ENOUGH.
WHICH IS WHAT NIKOLAOS WAS COUNTING ON.
YES.

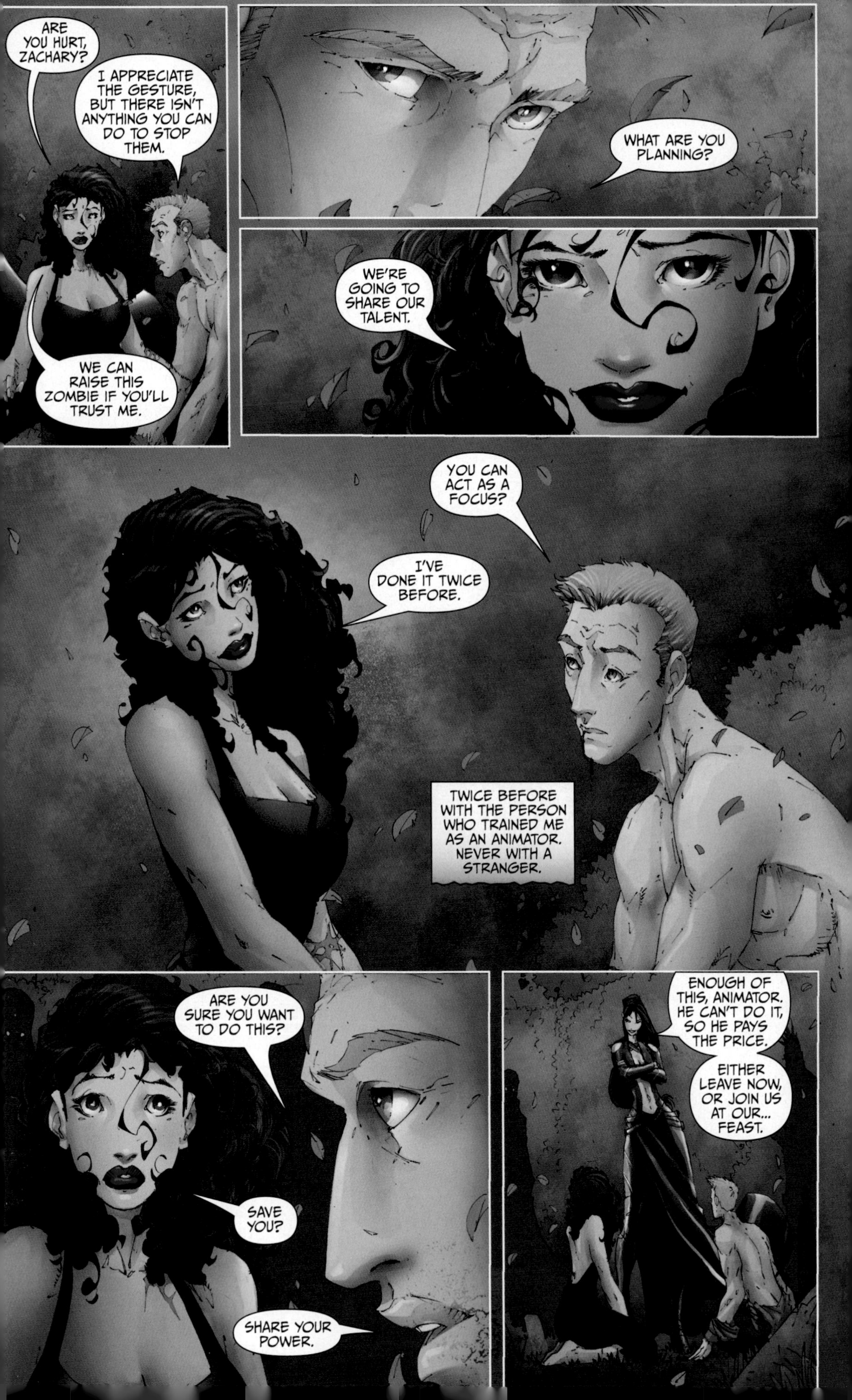
ARE YOU HURT, ZACHARY?
I APPRECIATE THE GESTURE, BUT THERE ISN'T ANYTHING YOU CAN DO TO STOP THEM.
WE CAN RAISE THIS ZOMBIE IF YOU'LL TRUST ME.
WHAT ARE YOU PLANNING?
WE'RE GOING TO SHARE OUR TALENT.
YOU CAN ACT AS A FOCUS?
I'VE DONE IT TWICE BEFORE.
TWICE BEFORE WITH THE PERSON WHO TRAINED ME AS AN ANIMATOR. NEVER WITH A STRANGER.
ARE YOU SURE YOU WANT TO DO THIS?
SAVE YOU?
SHARE YOUR POWER.
ENOUGH OF THIS, ANIMATOR. HE CAN'T DO IT, SO HE PAYS THE PRICE.
EITHER LEAVE NOW, OR JOIN US AT OUR... FEAST.

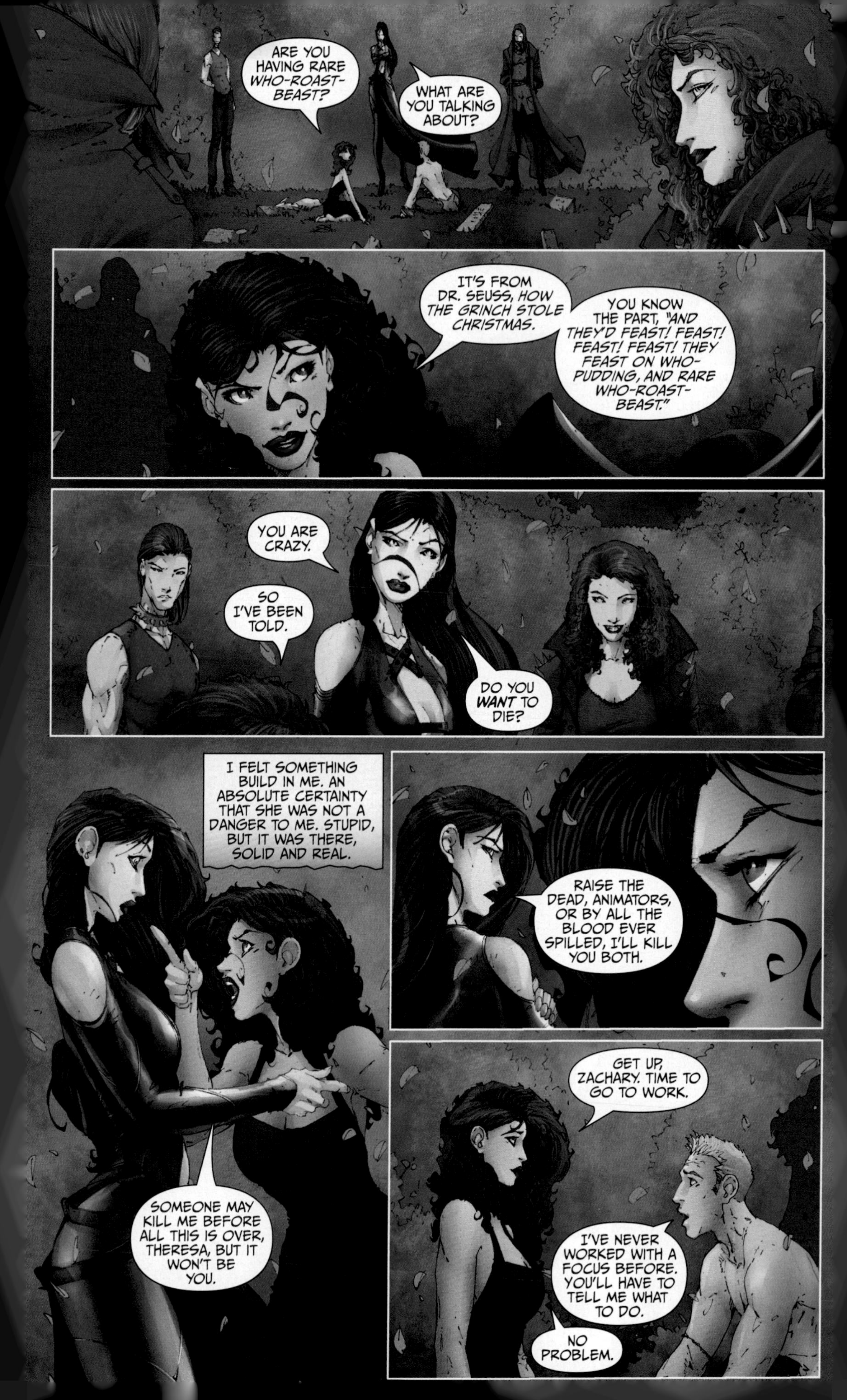
ARE YOU HAVING RARE WHO-ROAST-BEAST?
WHAT ARE YOU TALKING ABOUT?
IT'S FROM DR. SEUSS, HOW THE GRINCH STOLE CHRISTMAS.
YOU KNOW THE PART, "AND THEY'D FEAST! FEAST! FEAST! FEAST! THEY FEAST ON WHO-PUDDING, AND RARE WHO-ROAST-BEAST."
YOU ARE CRAZY.
SO I'VE BEEN TOLD.
DO YOU WANT TO DIE?
I FELT SOMETHING BUILD IN ME. AN ABSOLUTE CERTAINTY THAT SHE WAS NOT A DANGER TO ME. STUPID, BUT IT WAS THERE, SOLID AND REAL.
SOMEONE MAY KILL ME BEFORE ALL THIS IS OVER, THERESA, BUT IT WON'T BE YOU.
RAISE THE DEAD, ANIMATORS, OR BY ALL THE BLOOD EVER SPILLED, I'LL KILL YOU BOTH.
GET UP, ZACHARY. TIME TO GO TO WORK.
I'VE NEVER WORKED WITH A FOCUS BEFORE. YOU'LL HAVE TO TELL ME WHAT TO DO.
NO PROBLEM.

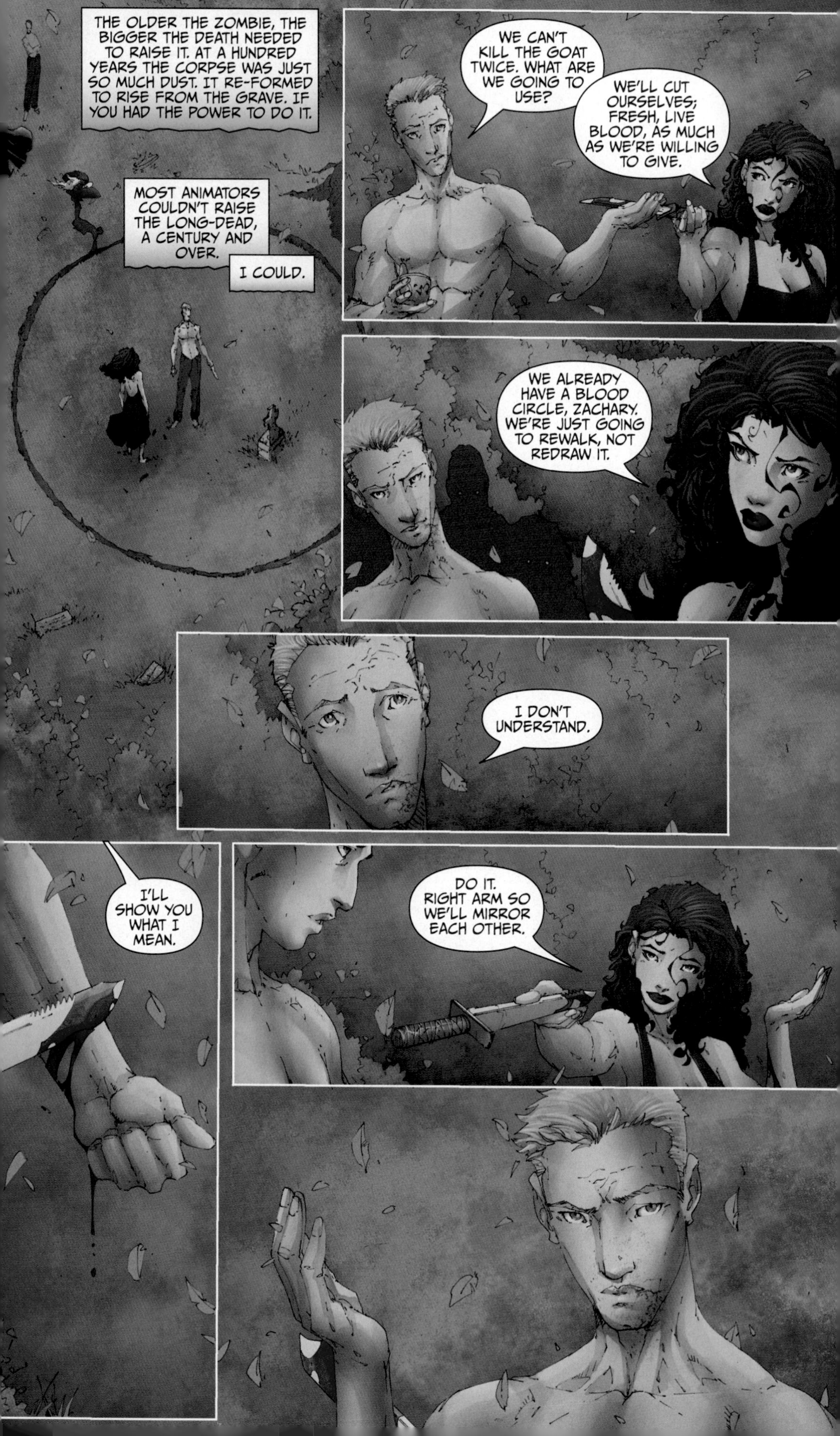

THE OLDER THE ZOMBIE, THE BIGGER THE DEATH NEEDED TO RAISE IT. AT A HUNDRED YEARS THE CORPSE WAS JUST SO MUCH DUST. IT RE-FORMED TO RISE FROM THE GRAVE. IF YOU HAD THE POWER TO DO IT.
MOST ANIMATORS COULDN'T RAISE THE LONG-DEAD, A CENTURY AND OVER.
I COULD.
WE CAN'T KILL THE GOAT TWICE. WHAT ARE WE GOING TO USE?
WE'LL CUT OURSELVES; FRESH, LIVE BLOOD, AS MUCH AS WE'RE WILLING TO GIVE.
WE ALREADY HAVE A BLOOD CIRCLE, ZACHARY. WE'RE JUST GOING TO REWALK, NOT REDRAW IT.
I DON'T UNDERSTAND.
I'LL SHOW YOU WHAT I MEAN.
DO IT. RIGHT ARM SO WE'LL MIRROR EACH OTHER.

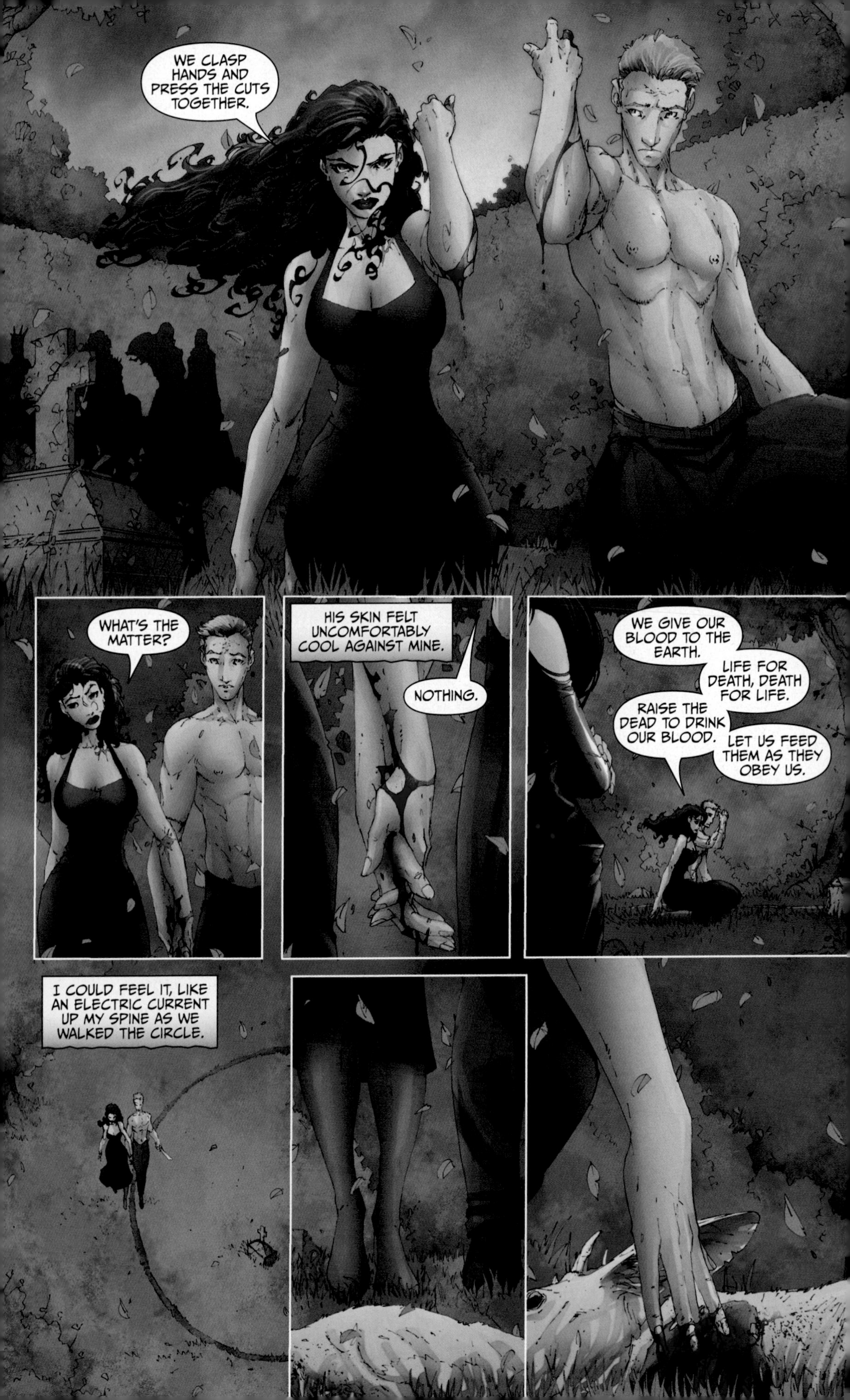
WE CLASP HANDS AND PRESS THE CUTS TOGETHER.
WHAT'S THE MATTER?
HIS SKIN FELT UNCOMFORTABLY COOL AGAINST MINE.
NOTHING.
WE GIVE OUR BLOOD TO THE EARTH.
LIFE FOR DEATH, DEATH FOR LIFE.
RAISE THE DEAD TO DRINK OUR BLOOD.
LET US FEED THEM AS THEY OBEY US.
I COULD FEEL IT, LIKE AN ELECTRIC CURRENT UP MY SPINE AS WE WALKED THE CIRCLE.

THE GRIS-GRIS NEEDED BLOOD--I COULD FEEL THAT--BUT NOT GOAT BLOOD. TIME TO WORRY ABOUT ZACHARY'S PERSONAL MAGIC LATER.

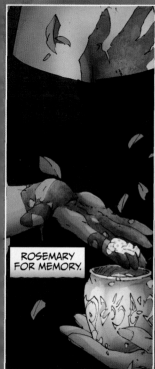

ROSEMARY FOR MEMORY.

CINNAMON AND CLOVES FOR PRESERVATION.

SAGE FOR WISDOM.

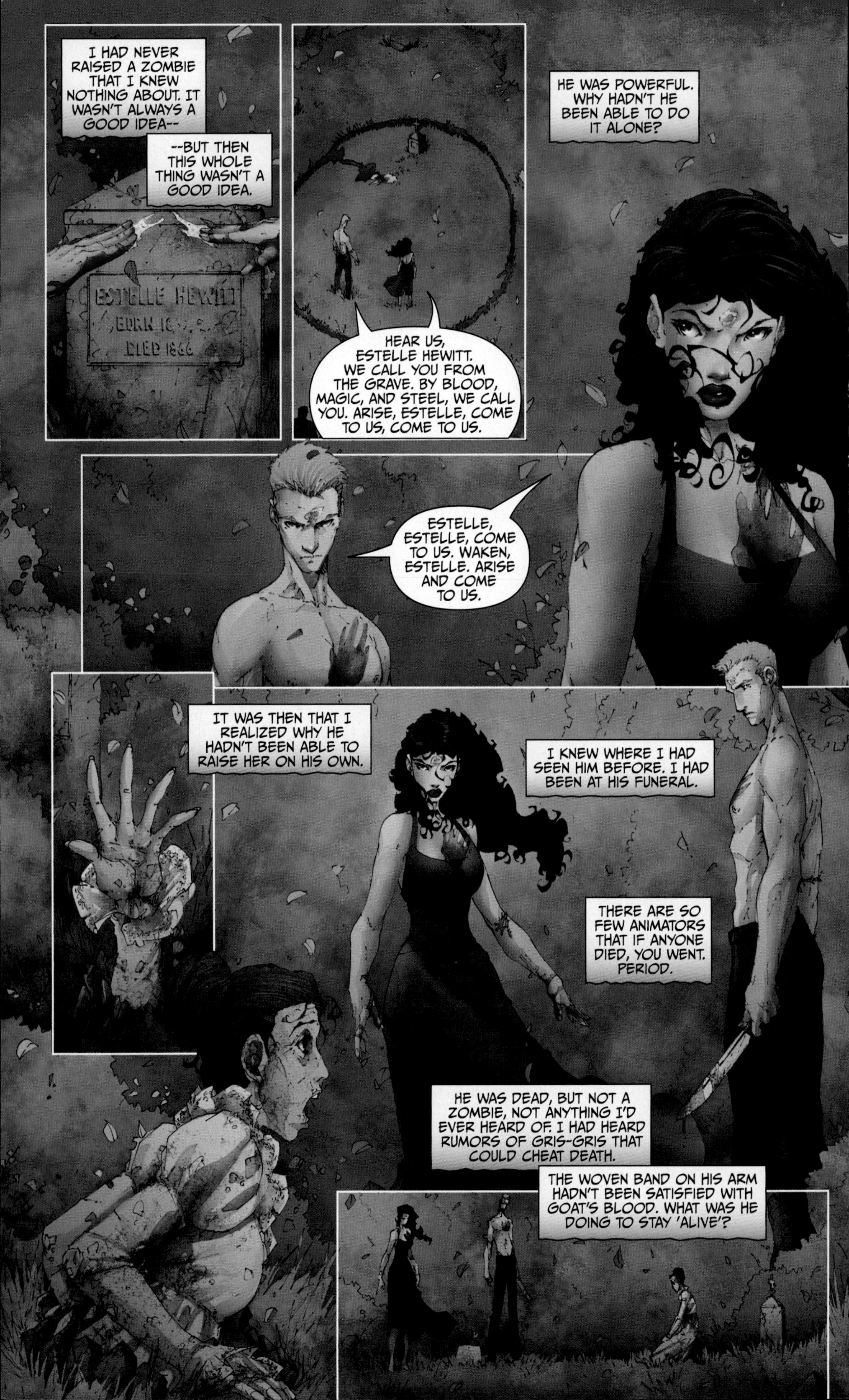
I HAD NEVER RAISED A ZOMBIE THAT I KNEW NOTHING ABOUT. IT WASN'T ALWAYS A GOOD IDEA--
--BUT THEN THIS WHOLE THING WASN'T A GOOD IDEA.
ESTELLE HEWITT
DIED 1866
HEAR US, ESTELLE HEWITT. WE CALL YOU FROM THE GRAVE. BY BLOOD, MAGIC, AND STEEL, WE CALL YOU. ARISE, ESTELLE, COME TO US, COME TO US.
HE WAS POWERFUL. WHY HADN'T HE BEEN ABLE TO DO IT ALONE?
ESTELLE, ESTELLE, COME TO US. WAKEN, ESTELLE. ARISE AND COME TO US.
IT WAS THEN THAT I REALIZED WHY HE HADN'T BEEN ABLE TO RAISE HER ON HIS OWN.
I KNEW WHERE I HAD SEEN HIM BEFORE. I HAD BEEN AT HIS FUNERAL.
THERE ARE SO FEW ANIMATORS THAT IF ANYONE DIED, YOU WENT. PERIOD.
HE WAS DEAD, BUT NOT A ZOMBIE, NOT ANYTHING I'D EVER HEARD OF. I HAD HEARD RUMORS OF GRIS-GRIS THAT COULD CHEAT DEATH.
THE WOVEN BAND ON HIS ARM HADN'T BEEN SATISFIED WITH GOAT'S BLOOD. WHAT WAS HE DOING TO STAY 'ALIVE'?

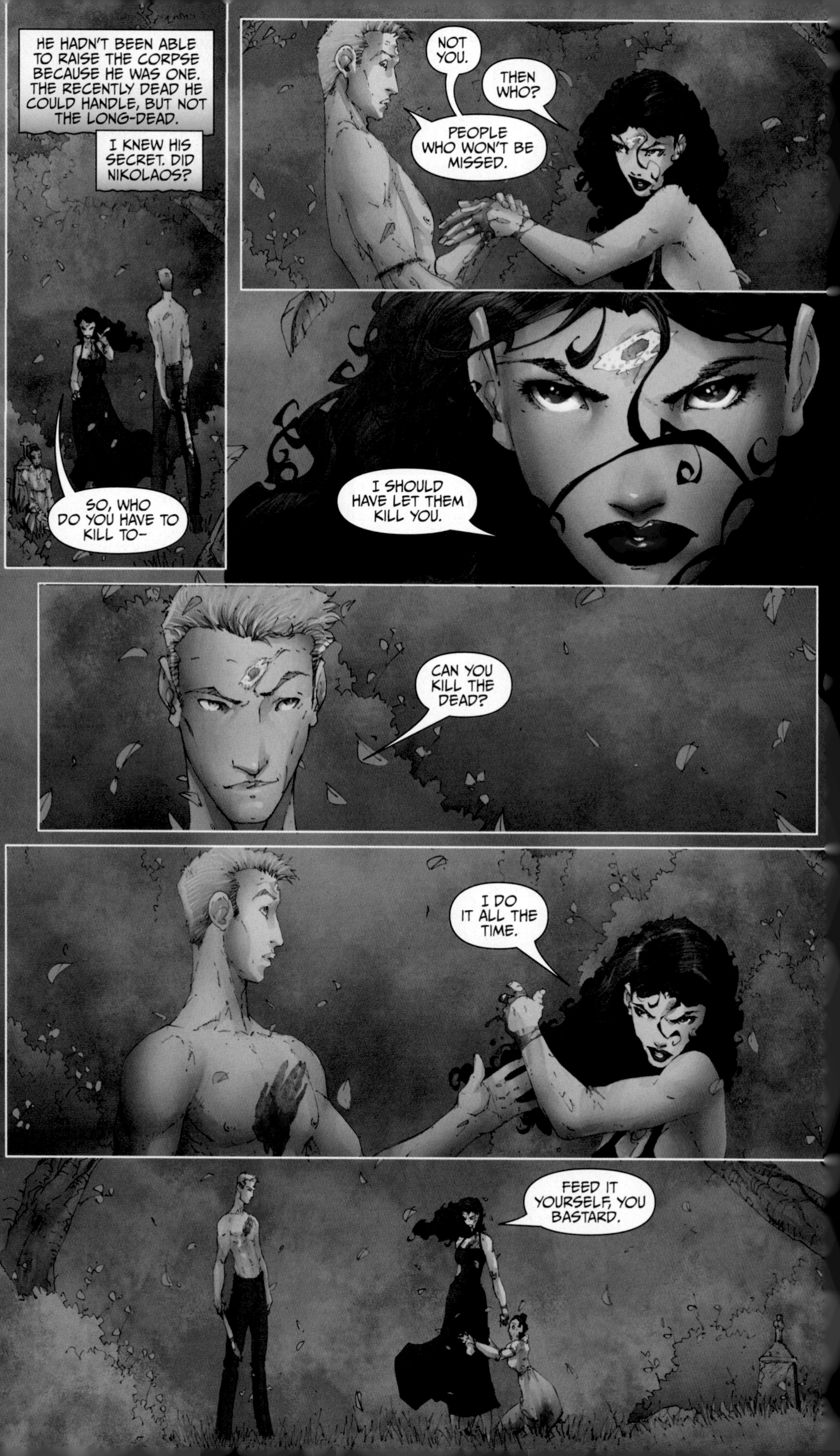
HE HADN'T BEEN ABLE TO RAISE THE CORPSE BECAUSE HE WAS ONE. THE RECENTLY DEAD HE COULD HANDLE, BUT NOT THE LONG-DEAD.
I KNEW HIS SECRET. DID NIKOLAOS?
SO, WHO DO YOU HAVE TO KILL TO-
NOT YOU.
THEN WHO?
PEOPLE WHO WON'T BE MISSED.
I SHOULD HAVE LET THEM KILL YOU.
CAN YOU KILL THE DEAD?
I DO IT ALL THE TIME.
FEED IT YOURSELF, YOU BASTARD.

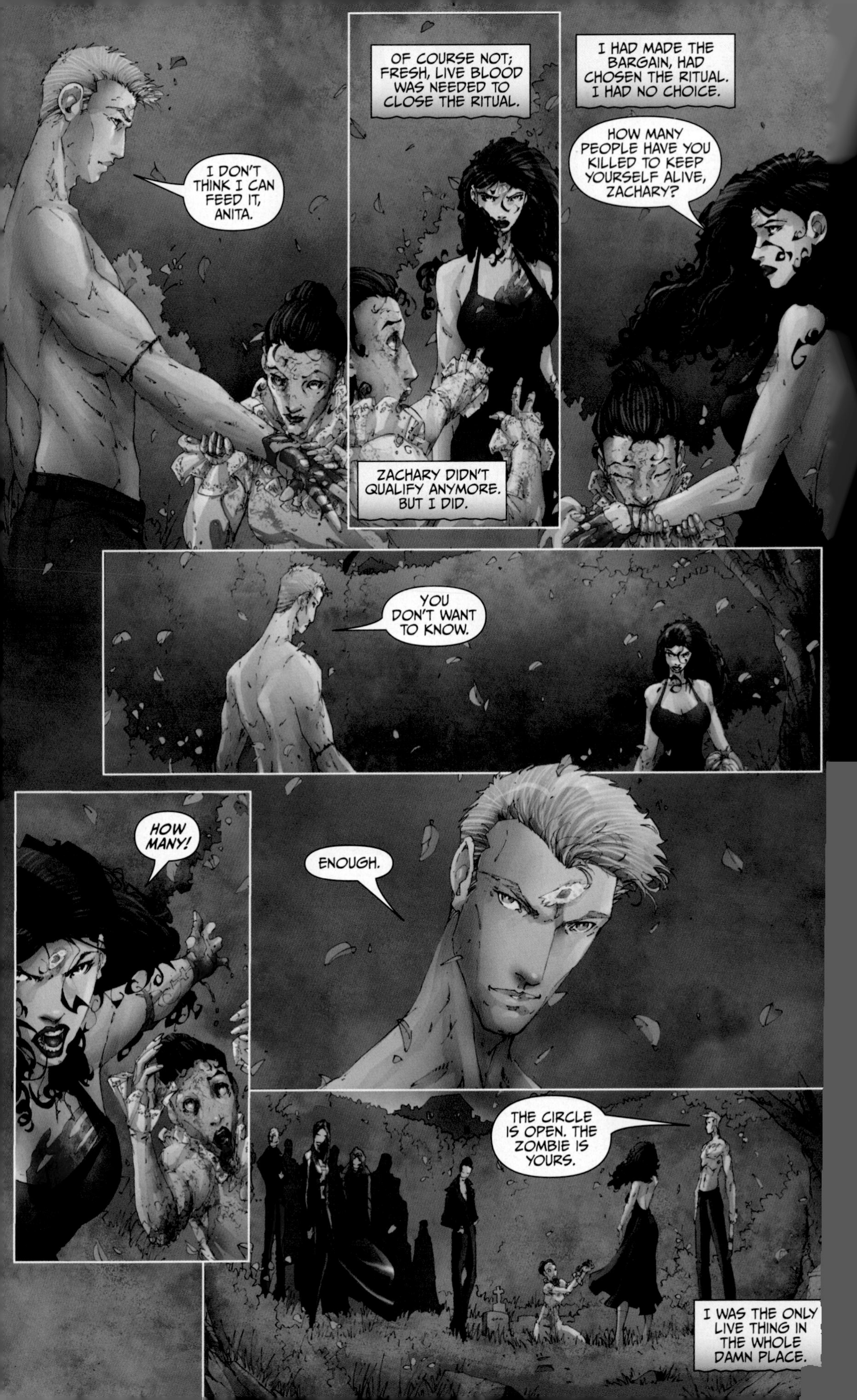
I DON'T THINK I CAN FEED IT, ANITA.
OF COURSE NOT; FRESH, LIVE BLOOD WAS NEEDED TO CLOSE THE RITUAL.
ZACHARY DIDN'T QUALIFY ANYMORE. BUT I DID.
I HAD MADE THE BARGAIN, HAD CHOSEN THE RITUAL. I HAD NO CHOICE.
HOW MANY PEOPLE HAVE YOU KILLED TO KEEP YOURSELF ALIVE, ZACHARY?
YOU DON'T WANT TO KNOW.
HOW MANY!
ENOUGH.
THE CIRCLE IS OPEN. THE ZOMBIE IS YOURS.
I WAS THE ONLY LIVE THING IN THE WHOLE DAMN PLACE.

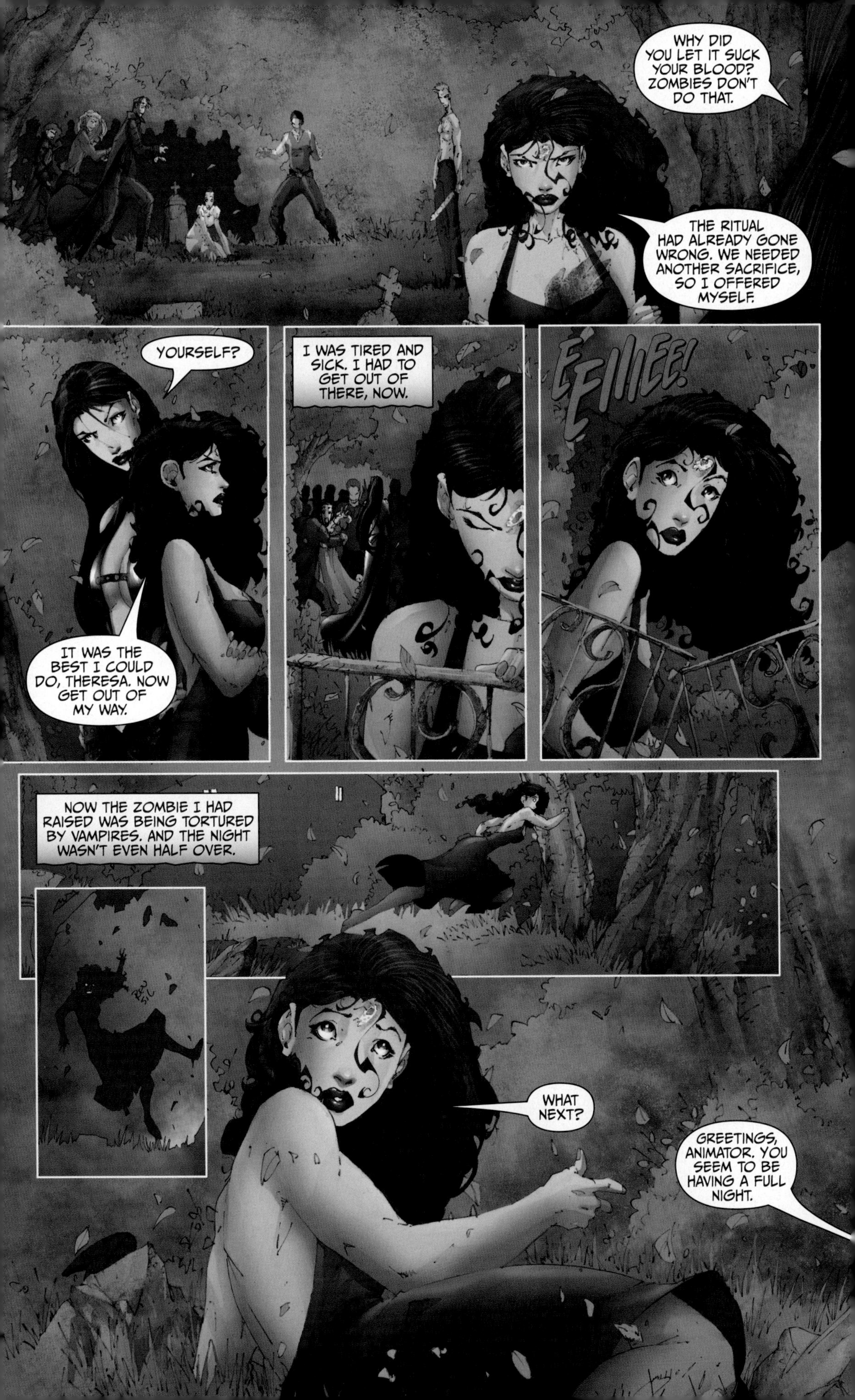

WHY DID YOU LET IT SUCK YOUR BLOOD? ZOMBIES DON'T DO THAT.
THE RITUAL HAD ALREADY GONE WRONG. WE NEEDED ANOTHER SACRIFICE, SO I OFFERED MYSELF.
YOURSELF?
IT WAS THE BEST I COULD DO, THERESA. NOW GET OUT OF MY WAY.
I WAS TIRED AND SICK. I HAD TO GET OUT OF THERE, NOW.
EEIIIIEE!
NOW THE ZOMBIE I HAD RAISED WAS BEING TORTURED BY VAMPIRES. AND THE NIGHT WASN'T EVEN HALF OVER.
WHAT NEXT?
GREETINGS, ANIMATOR. YOU SEEM TO BE HAVING A FULL NIGHT.

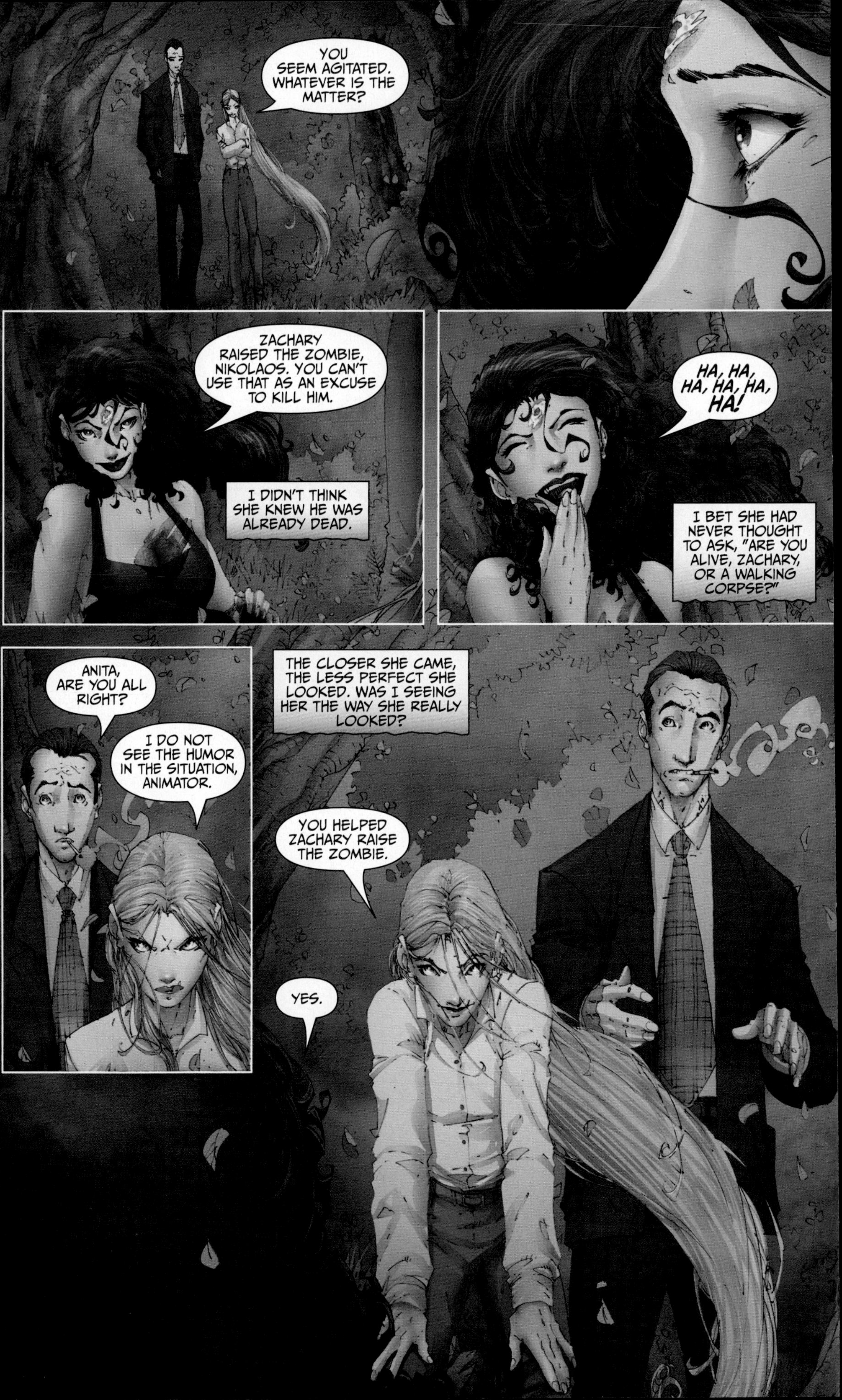

YOU SEEM AGITATED. WHATEVER IS THE MATTER?
ZACHARY RAISED THE ZOMBIE, NIKOLAOS. YOU CAN'T USE THAT AS AN EXCUSE TO KILL HIM.
I DIDN'T THINK SHE KNEW HE WAS ALREADY DEAD.
HA, HA, HA, HA, HA, HA!
I BET SHE HAD NEVER THOUGHT TO ASK, "ARE YOU ALIVE, ZACHARY, OR A WALKING CORPSE?"
ANITA, ARE YOU ALL RIGHT?
I DO NOT SEE THE HUMOR IN THE SITUATION, ANIMATOR.
THE CLOSER SHE CAME, THE LESS PERFECT SHE LOOKED. WAS I SEEING HER THE WAY SHE REALLY LOOKED?
YOU HELPED ZACHARY RAISE THE ZOMBIE.
YES.

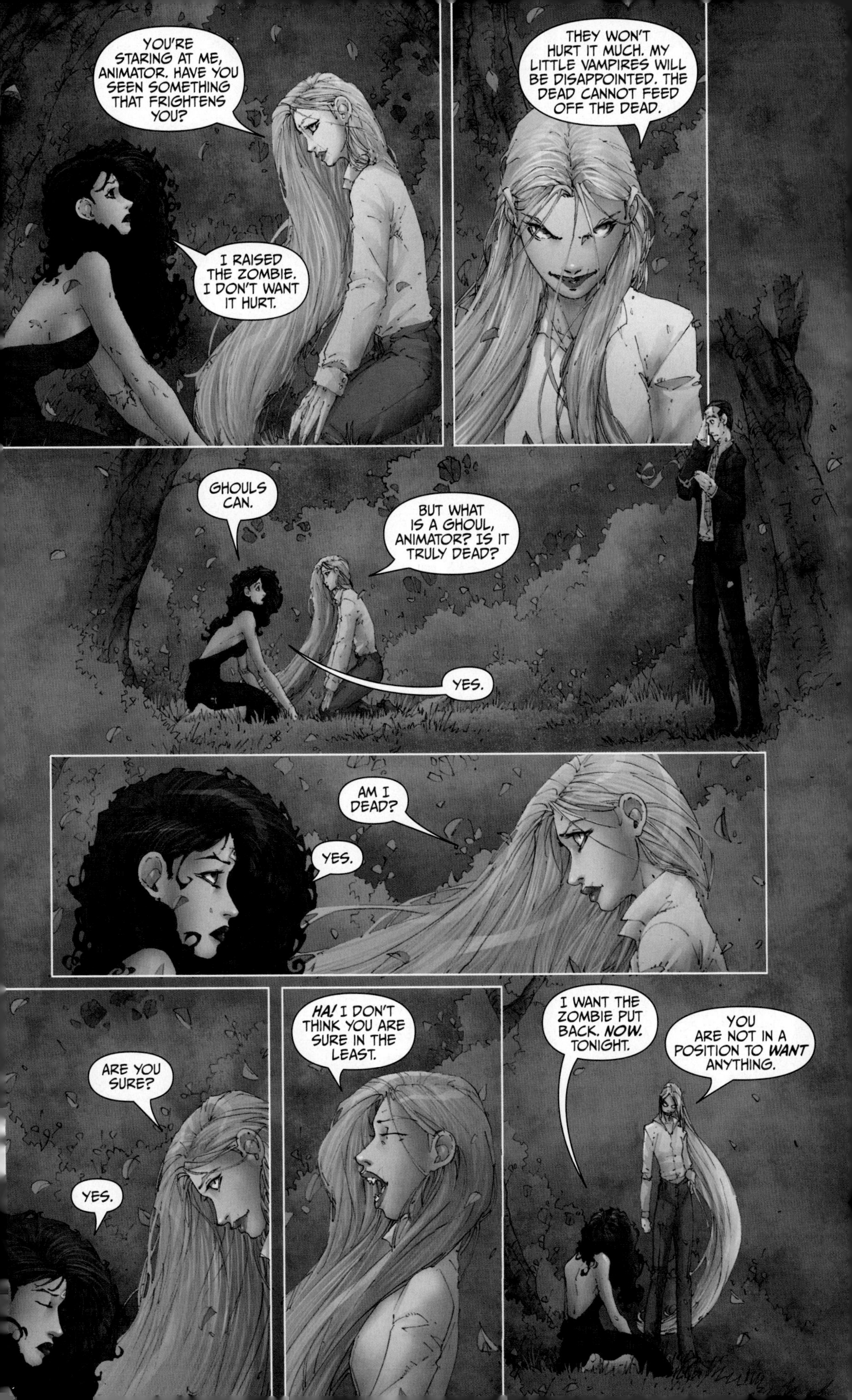
YOU'RE STARING AT ME, ANIMATOR. HAVE YOU SEEN SOMETHING THAT FRIGHTENS YOU?
I RAISED THE ZOMBIE. I DON'T WANT IT HURT.
THEY WON'T HURT IT MUCH. MY LITTLE VAMPIRES WILL BE DISAPPOINTED. THE DEAD CANNOT FEED OFF THE DEAD.
GHOULS CAN.
BUT WHAT IS A GHOUL, ANIMATOR? IS IT TRULY DEAD?
YES.
AM I DEAD?
YES.
ARE YOU SURE?
YES.
HA! I DON'T THINK YOU ARE SURE IN THE LEAST.
I WANT THE ZOMBIE PUT BACK. NOW. TONIGHT.
YOU ARE NOT IN A POSITION TO WANT ANYTHING.

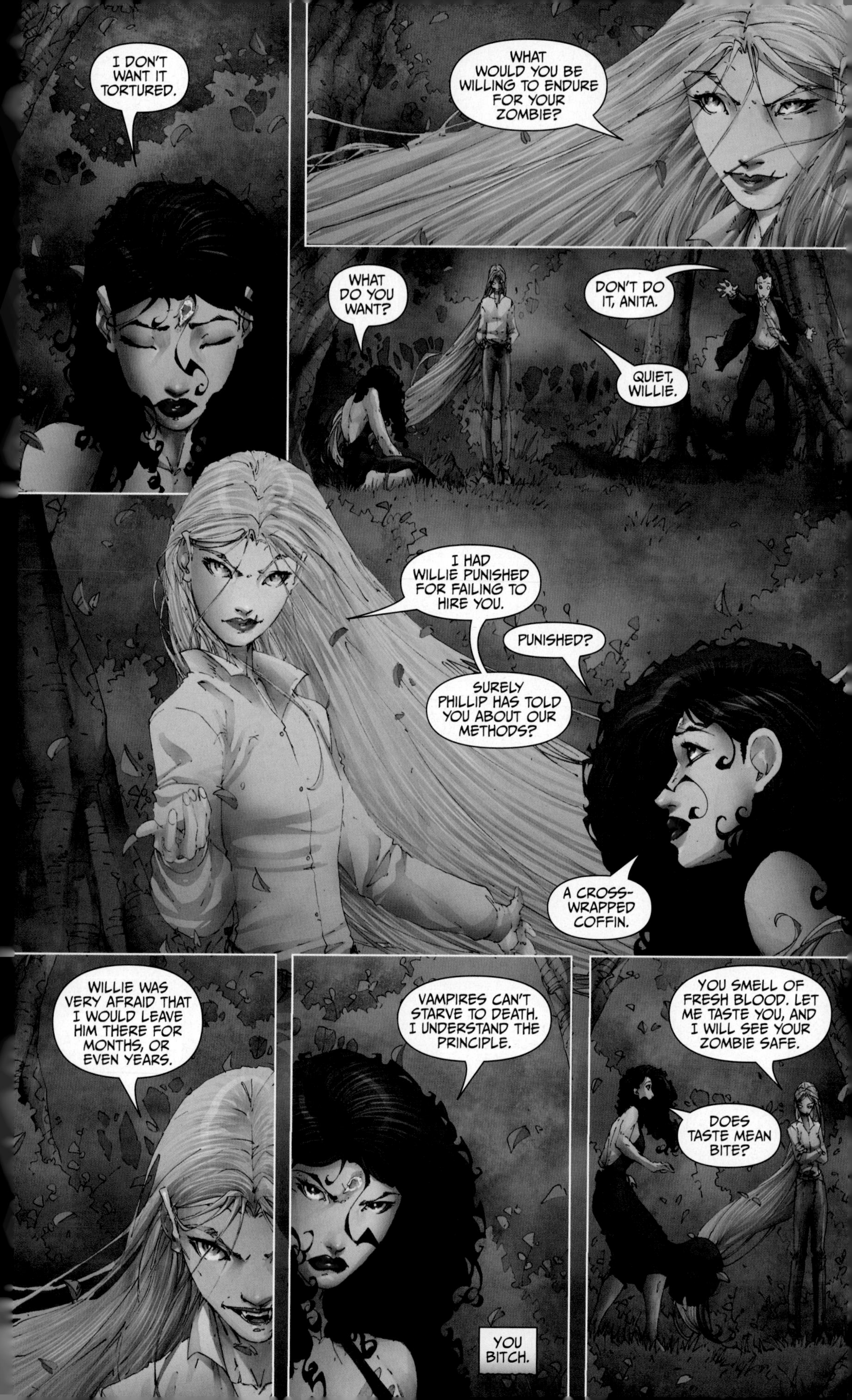
I DON'T WANT IT TORTURED.
WHAT WOULD YOU BE WILLING TO ENDURE FOR YOUR ZOMBIE?
WHAT DO YOU WANT?
DON'T DO IT, ANITA.
QUIET, WILLIE.
I HAD WILLIE PUNISHED FOR FAILING TO HIRE YOU.
PUNISHED?
SURELY PHILLIP HAS TOLD YOU ABOUT OUR METHODS?
A CROSS-WRAPPED COFFIN.
WILLIE WAS VERY AFRAID THAT I WOULD LEAVE HIM THERE FOR MONTHS, OR EVEN YEARS.
VAMPIRES CAN'T STARVE TO DEATH. I UNDERSTAND THE PRINCIPLE.
YOU BITCH.
YOU SMELL OF FRESH BLOOD. LET ME TASTE YOU, AND I WILL SEE YOUR ZOMBIE SAFE.
DOES TASTE MEAN BITE?

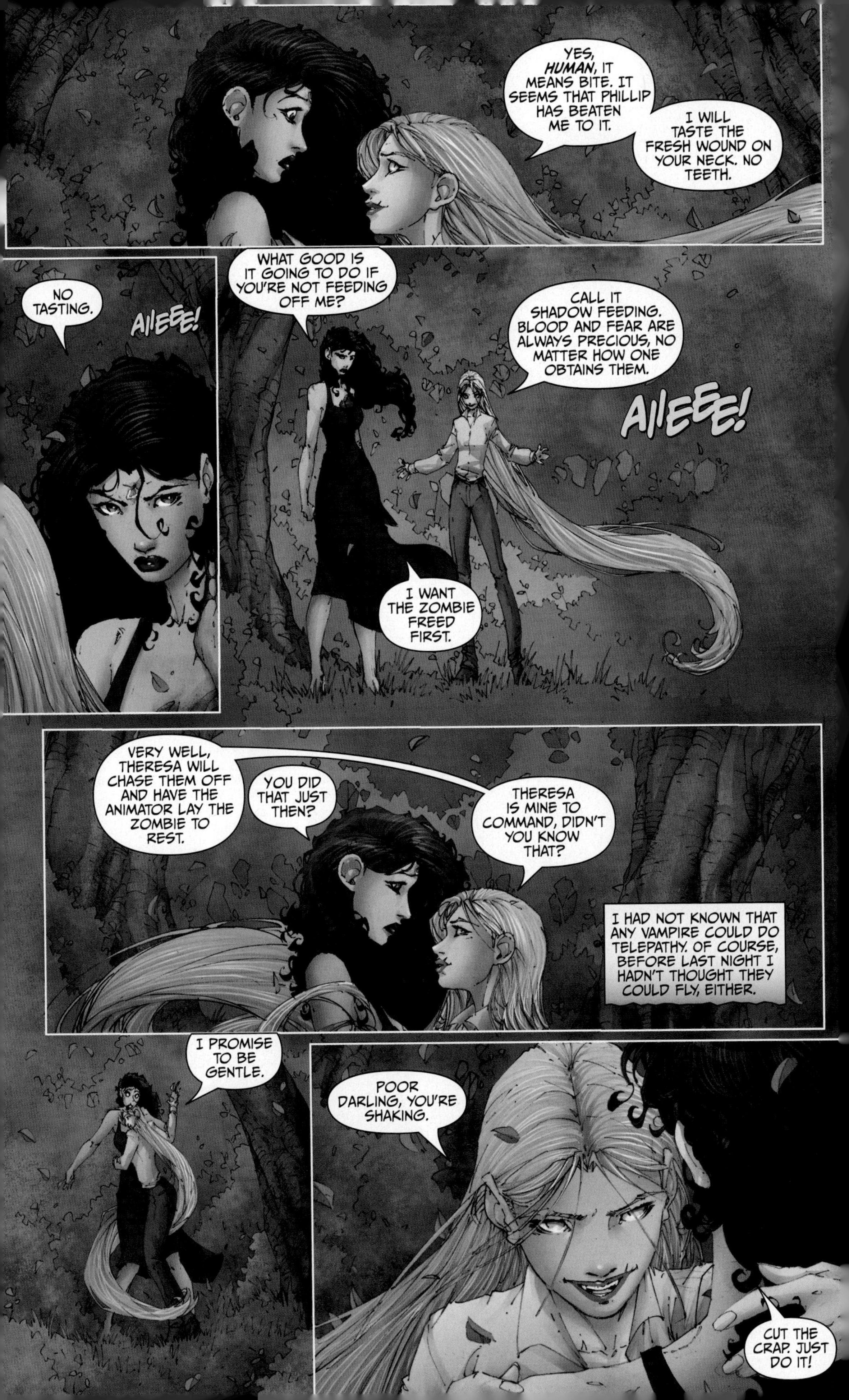
YES, HUMAN, IT MEANS BITE. IT SEEMS THAT PHILLIP HAS BEATEN ME TO IT.
I WILL TASTE THE FRESH WOUND ON YOUR NECK. NO TEETH.
NO TASTING.
AIEEE!
WHAT GOOD IS IT GOING TO DO IF YOU'RE NOT FEEDING OFF ME?
CALL IT SHADOW FEEDING. BLOOD AND FEAR ARE ALWAYS PRECIOUS, NO MATTER HOW ONE OBTAINS THEM.
AIEEE!
I WANT THE ZOMBIE FREED FIRST.
VERY WELL, THERESA WILL CHASE THEM OFF AND HAVE THE ANIMATOR LAY THE ZOMBIE TO REST.
YOU DID THAT JUST THEN?
THERESA IS MINE TO COMMAND, DIDN'T YOU KNOW THAT?
I HAD NOT KNOWN THAT ANY VAMPIRE COULD DO TELEPATHY. OF COURSE, BEFORE LAST NIGHT I HADN'T THOUGHT THEY COULD FLY, EITHER.
I PROMISE TO BE GENTLE.
POOR DARLING, YOU'RE SHAKING.
CUT THE CRAP. JUST DO IT!

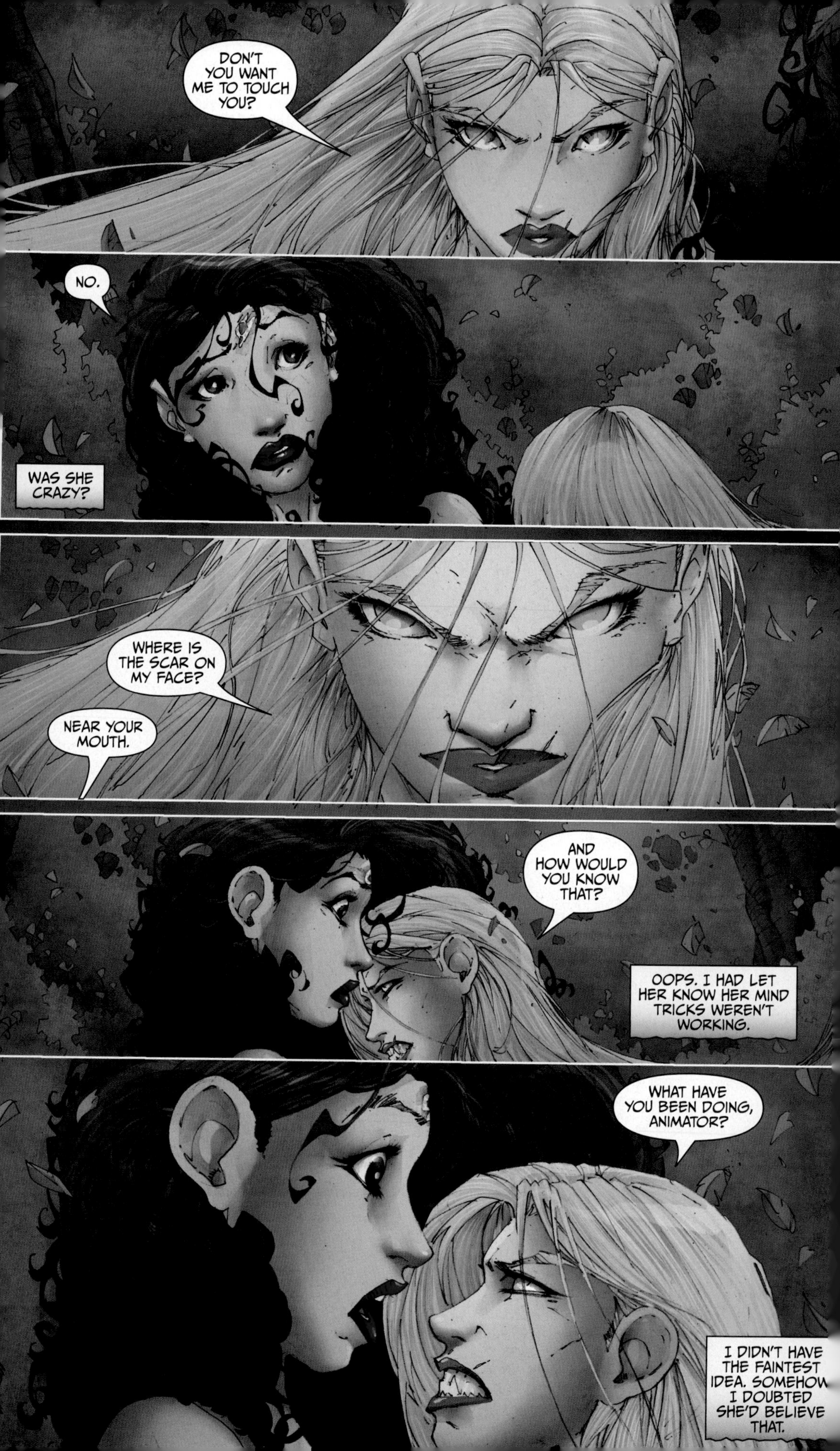
DON'T YOU WANT ME TO TOUCH YOU?
NO.
WAS SHE CRAZY?
WHERE IS THE SCAR ON MY FACE?
NEAR YOUR MOUTH.
AND HOW WOULD YOU KNOW THAT?
OOPS. I HAD LET HER KNOW HER MIND TRICKS WEREN'T WORKING.
WHAT HAVE YOU BEEN DOING, ANIMATOR?
I DIDN'T HAVE THE FAINTEST IDEA. SOMEHOW I DOUBTED SHE'D BELIEVE THAT.

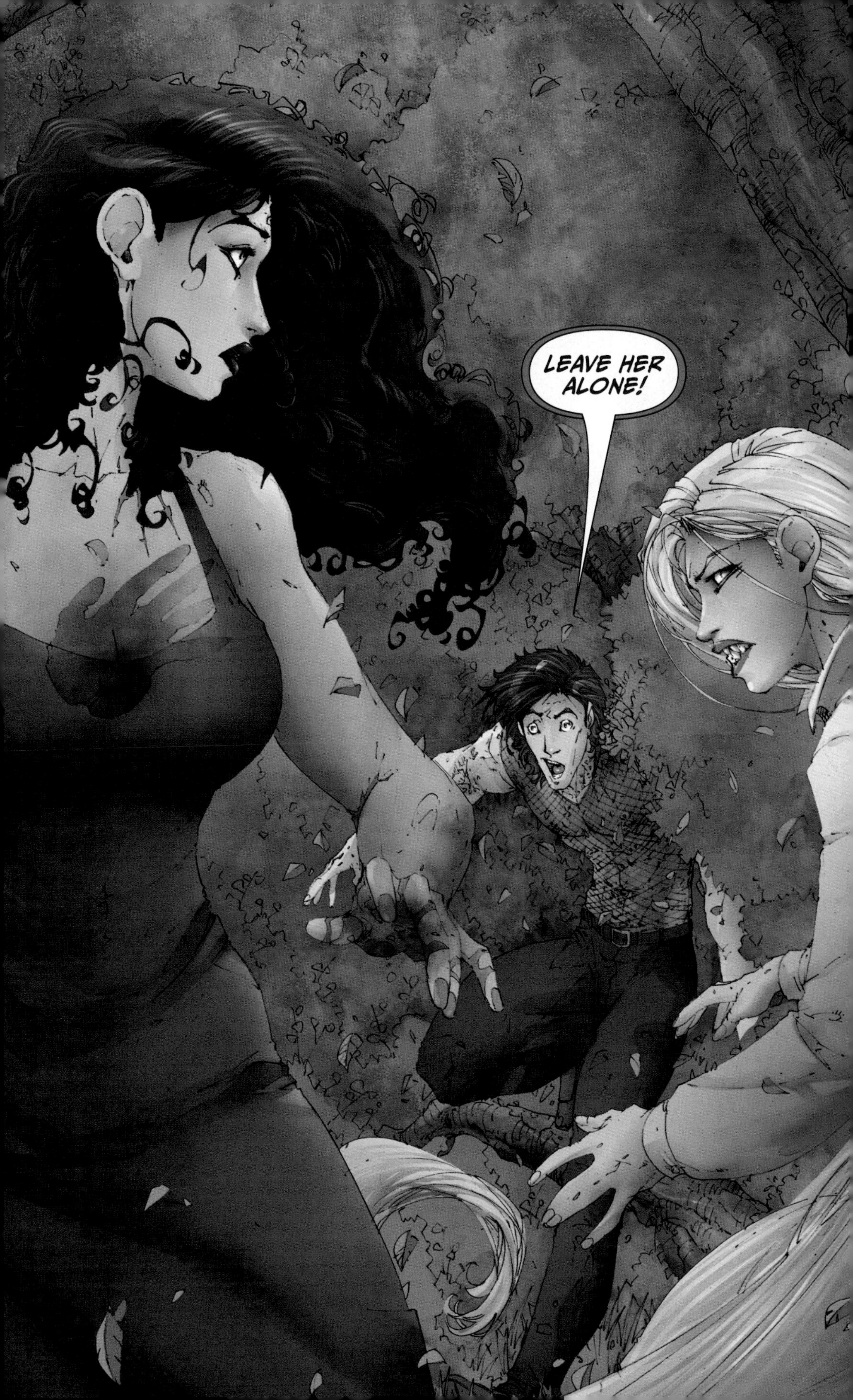
LEAVE HER ALONE!

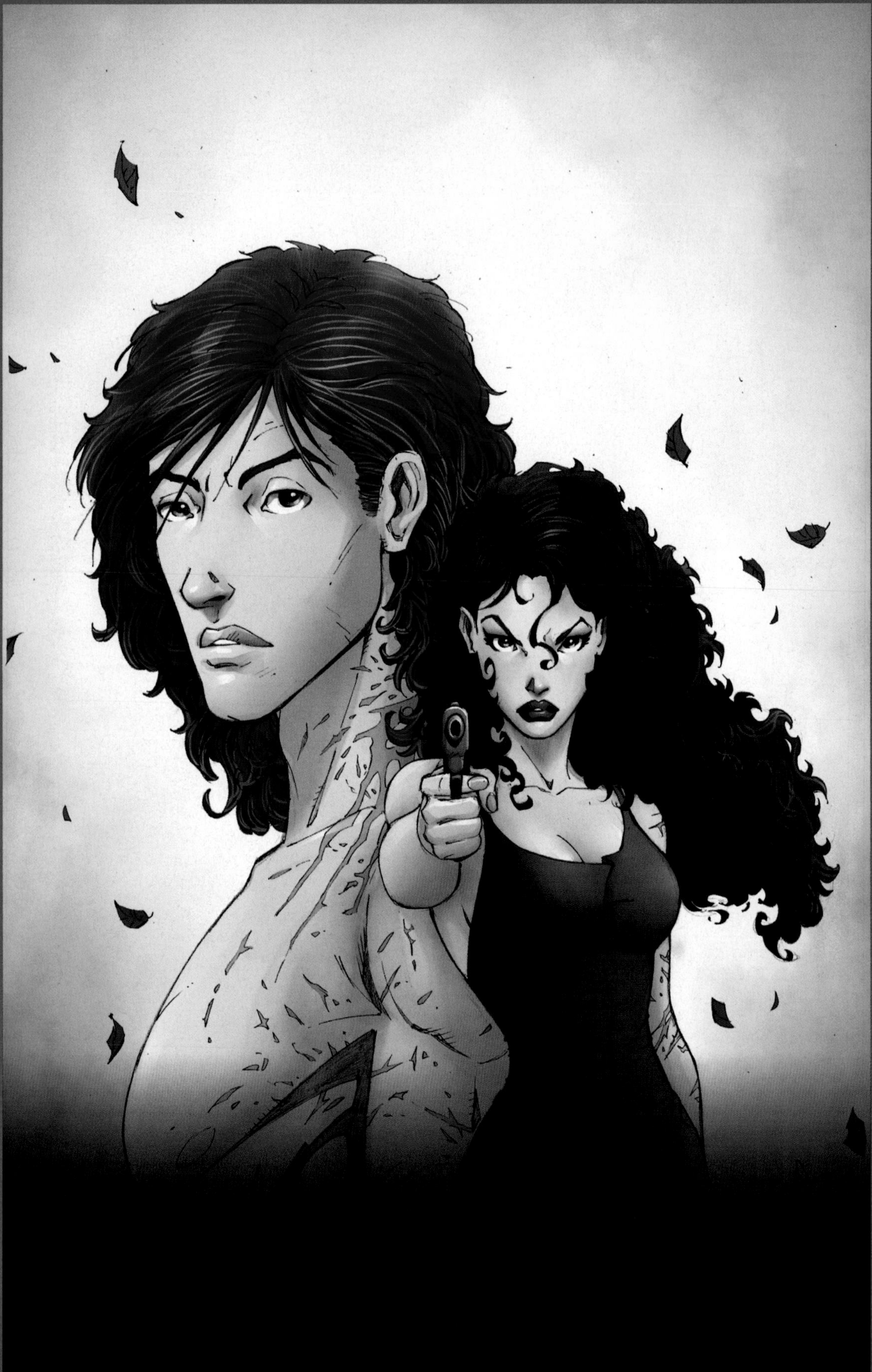

[#8]

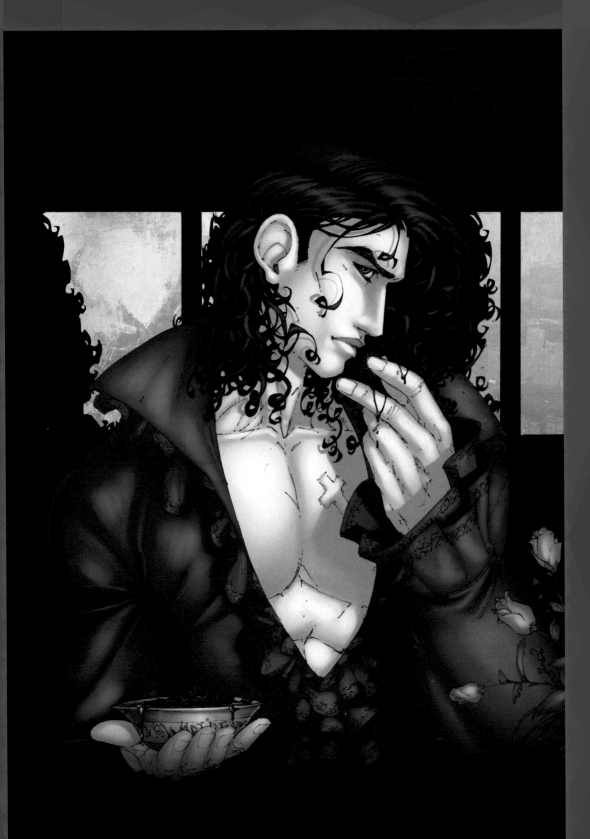

[#8 variant]

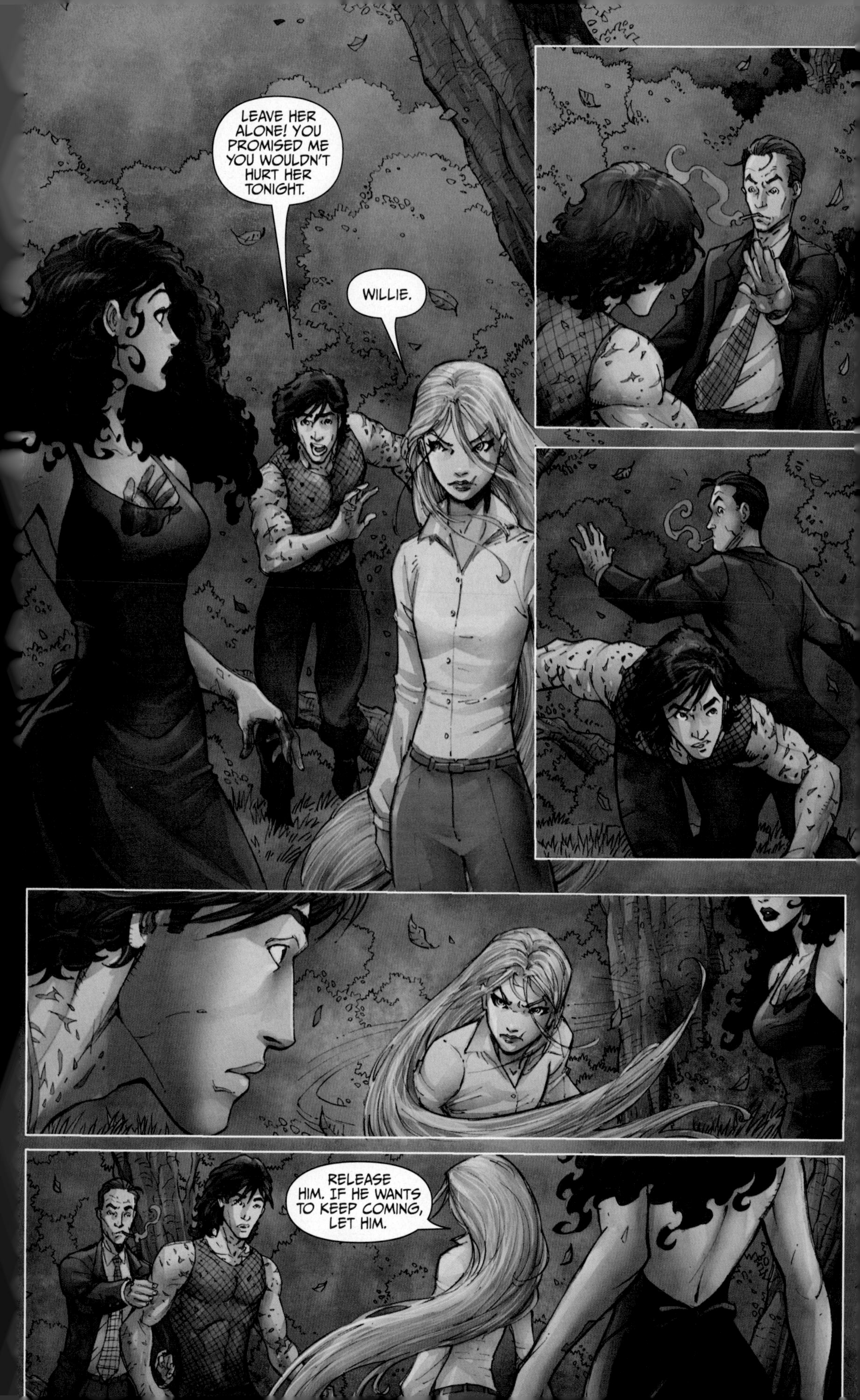
LEAVE HER ALONE! YOU PROMISED ME YOU WOULDN'T HURT HER TONIGHT.
WILLIE.
RELEASE HIM. IF HE WANTS TO KEEP COMING, LET HIM.

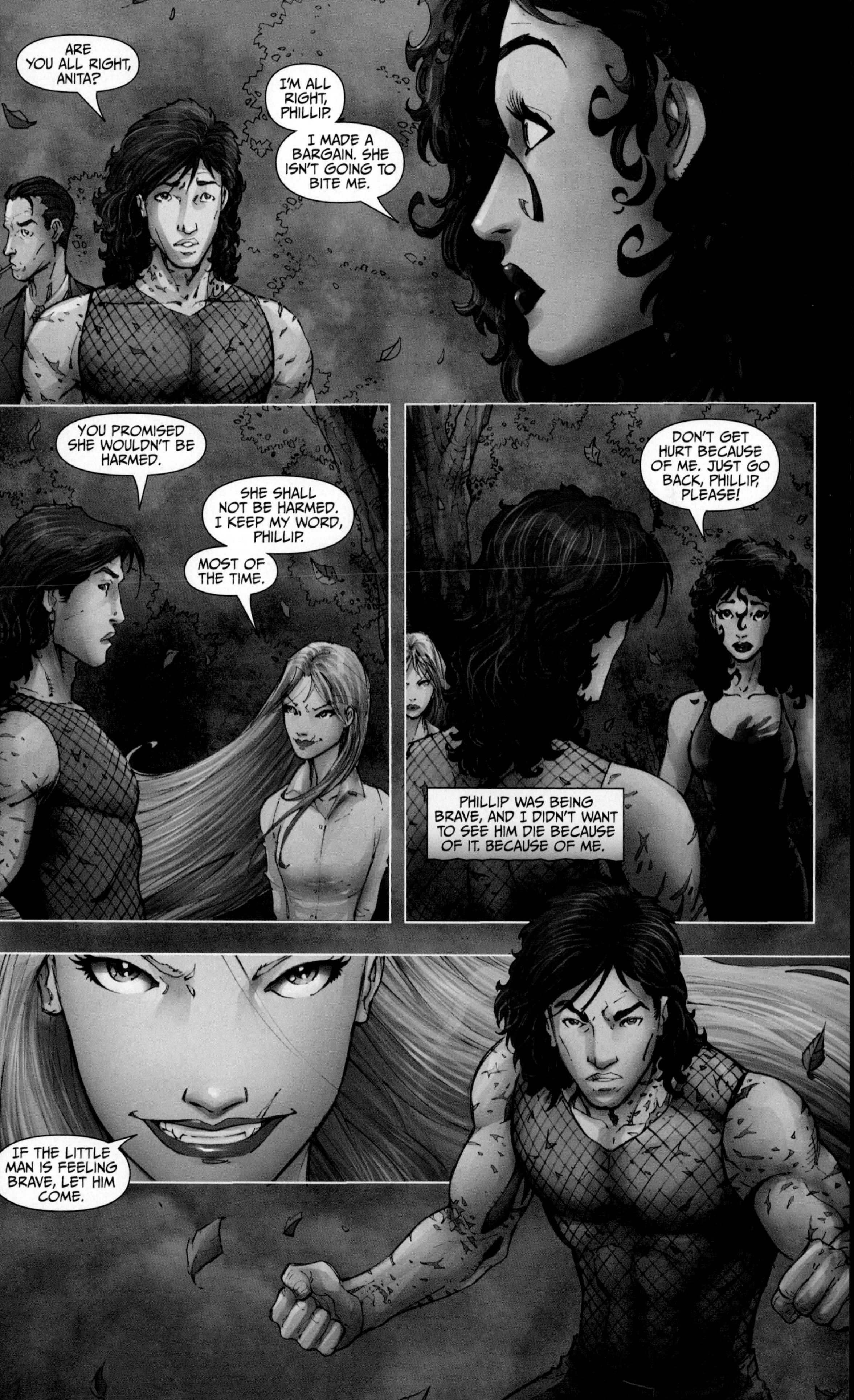
ARE YOU ALL RIGHT, ANITA?
I'M ALL RIGHT, PHILLIP.
I MADE A BARGAIN. SHE ISN'T GOING TO BITE ME.
YOU PROMISED SHE WOULDN'T BE HARMED.
SHE SHALL NOT BE HARMED. I KEEP MY WORD, PHILLIP.
MOST OF THE TIME.
DON'T GET HURT BECAUSE OF ME. JUST GO BACK, PHILLIP, PLEASE!
PHILLIP WAS BEING BRAVE, AND I DIDN'T WANT TO SEE HIM DIE BECAUSE OF IT. BECAUSE OF ME.
IF THE LITTLE MAN IS FEELING BRAVE, LET HIM COME.

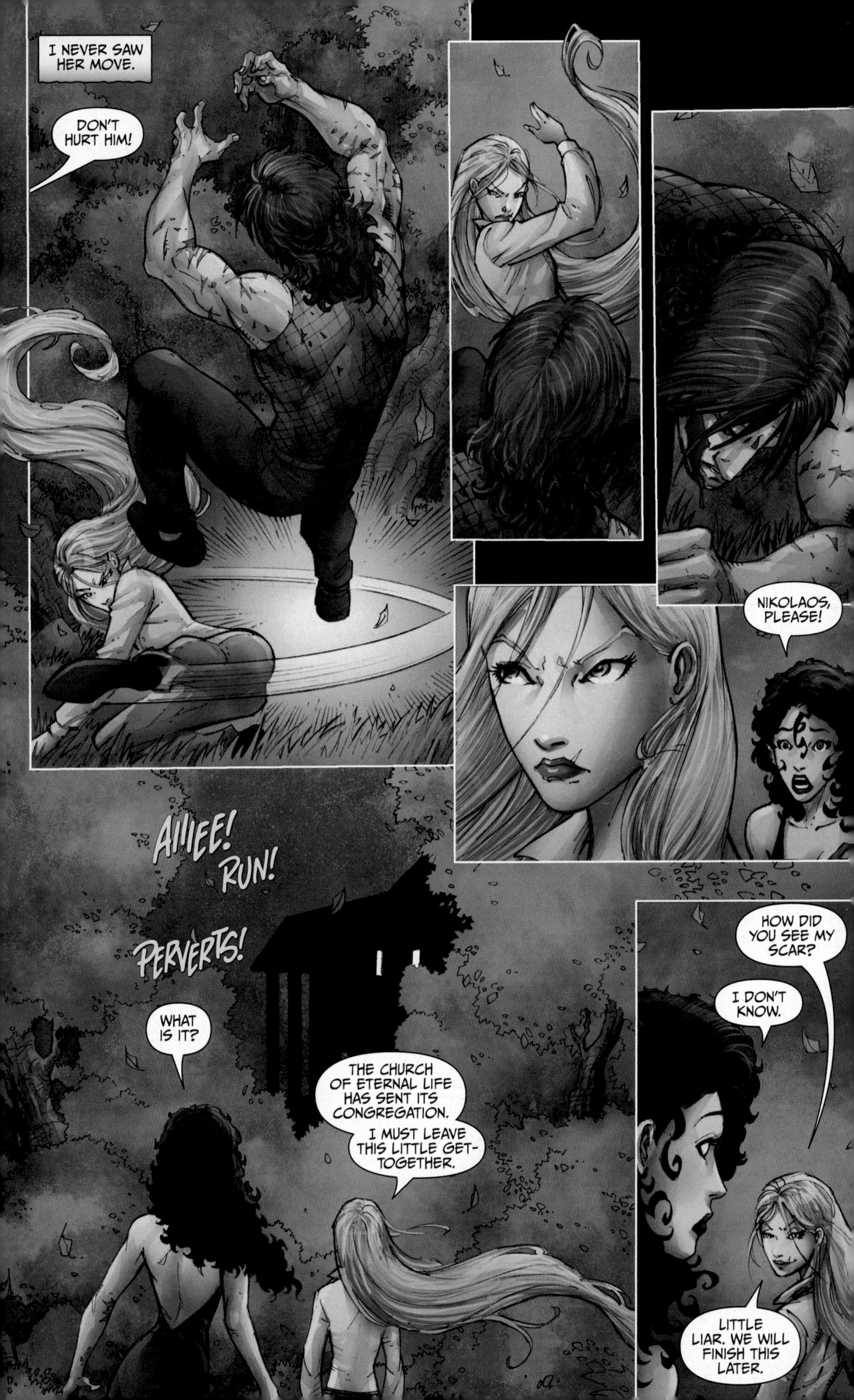
I NEVER SAW HER MOVE.
DON'T HURT HIM!
NIKOLAOS, PLEASE!
AIIIEE!
RUN!
PERVERTS!
WHAT IS IT?
THE CHURCH OF ETERNAL LIFE HAS SENT ITS CONGREGATION.
I MUST LEAVE THIS LITTLE GET-TOGETHER.
HOW DID YOU SEE MY SCAR?
I DON'T KNOW.
LITTLE LIAR. WE WILL FINISH THIS LATER.

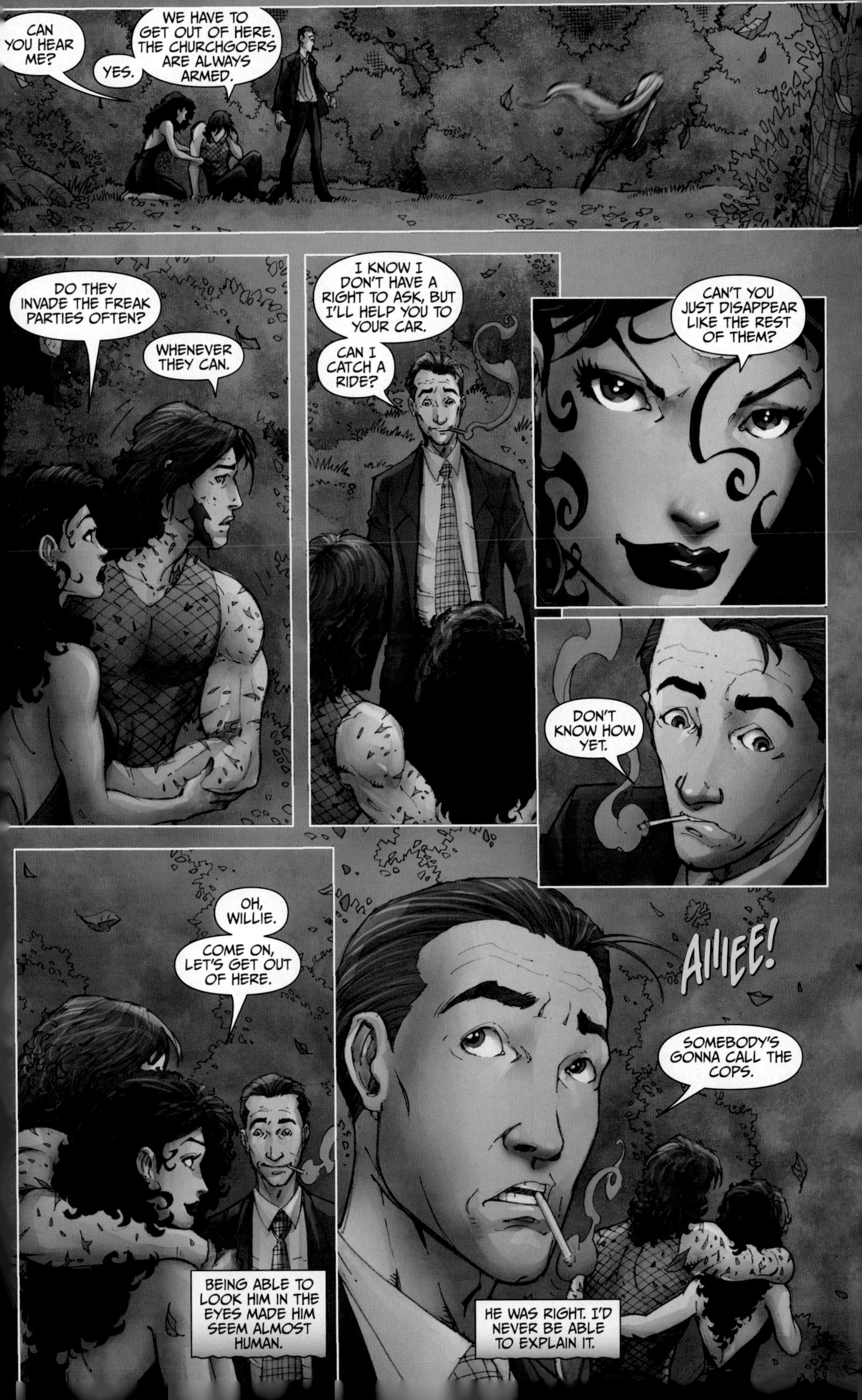
CAN YOU HEAR ME?
YES.
WE HAVE TO GET OUT OF HERE. THE CHURCHGOERS ARE ALWAYS ARMED.
DO THEY INVADE THE FREAK PARTIES OFTEN?
WHENEVER THEY CAN.
I KNOW I DON'T HAVE A RIGHT TO ASK, BUT I'LL HELP YOU TO YOUR CAR.
CAN I CATCH A RIDE?
CAN'T YOU JUST DISAPPEAR LIKE THE REST OF THEM?
DON'T KNOW HOW YET.
OH, WILLIE.
COME ON, LET'S GET OUT OF HERE.
BEING ABLE TO LOOK HIM IN THE EYES MADE HIM SEEM ALMOST HUMAN.
AIIEE!
SOMEBODY'S GONNA CALL THE COPS.
HE WAS RIGHT. I'D NEVER BE ABLE TO EXPLAIN IT.

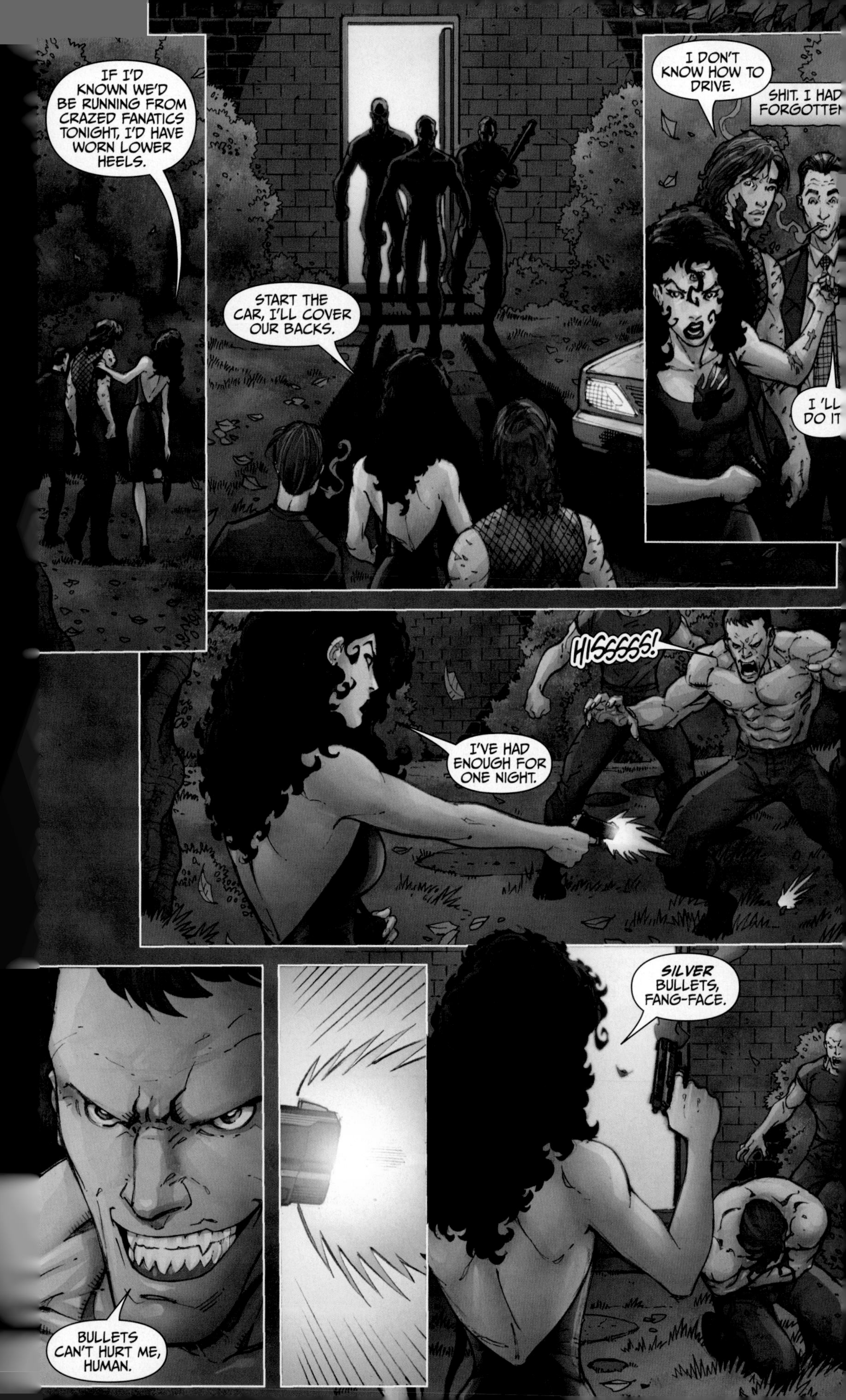
IF I'D KNOWN WE'D BE RUNNING FROM CRAZED FANATICS TONIGHT, I'D HAVE WORN LOWER HEELS.
START THE CAR, I'LL COVER OUR BACKS.
I DON'T KNOW HOW TO DRIVE.
SHIT. I HAD FORGOTTEN
I'LL DO IT
HISSSSS!
I'VE HAD ENOUGH FOR ONE NIGHT.
BULLETS CAN'T HURT ME, HUMAN.
SILVER BULLETS, FANG-FACE.

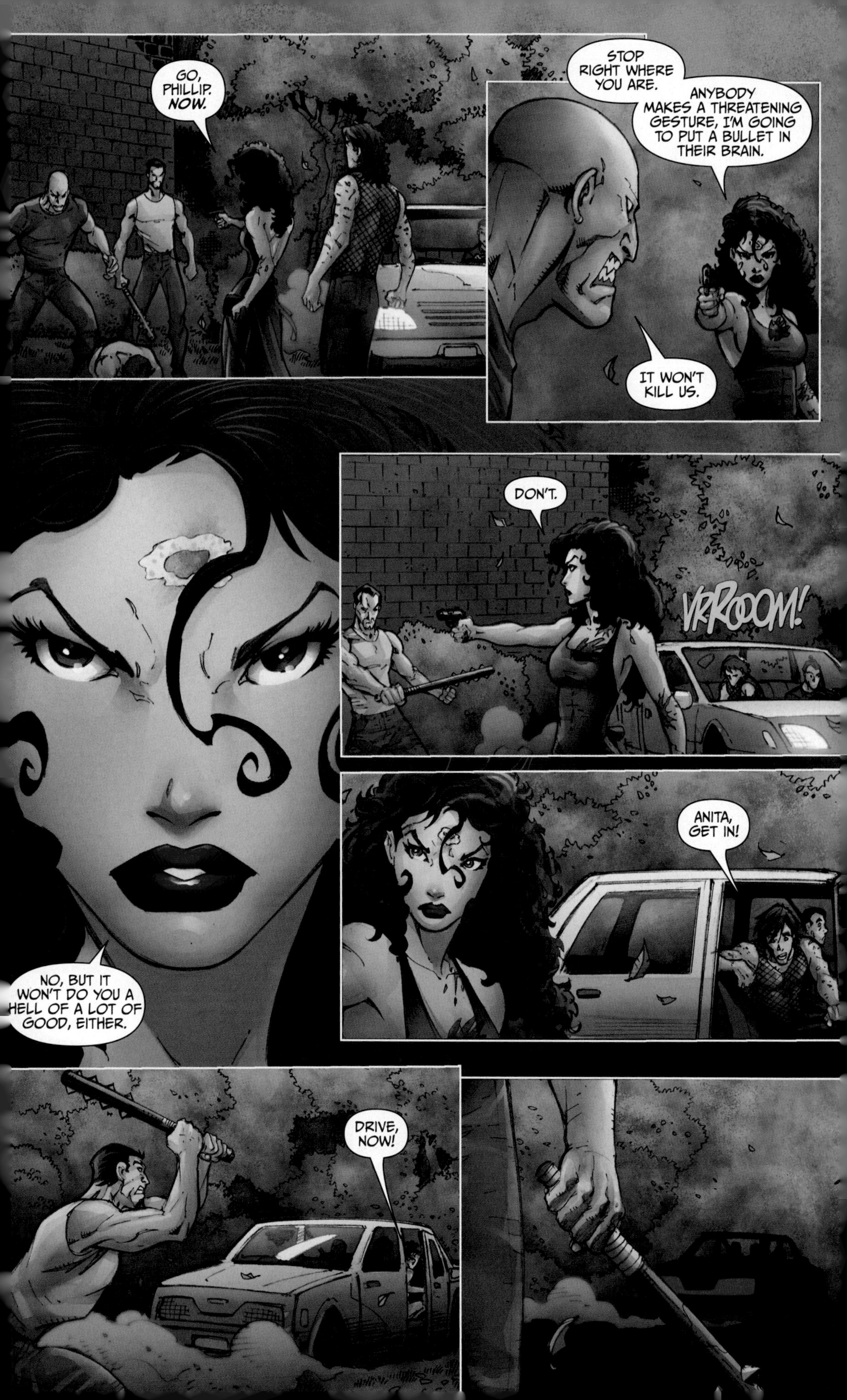

GO, PHILLIP. NOW.
STOP RIGHT WHERE YOU ARE.
ANYBODY MAKES A THREATENING GESTURE, I'M GOING TO PUT A BULLET IN THEIR BRAIN.
IT WON'T KILL US.
NO, BUT IT WON'T DO YOU A HELL OF A LOT OF GOOD, EITHER.
DON'T.
VRROOM!
ANITA, GET IN!
DRIVE, NOW!

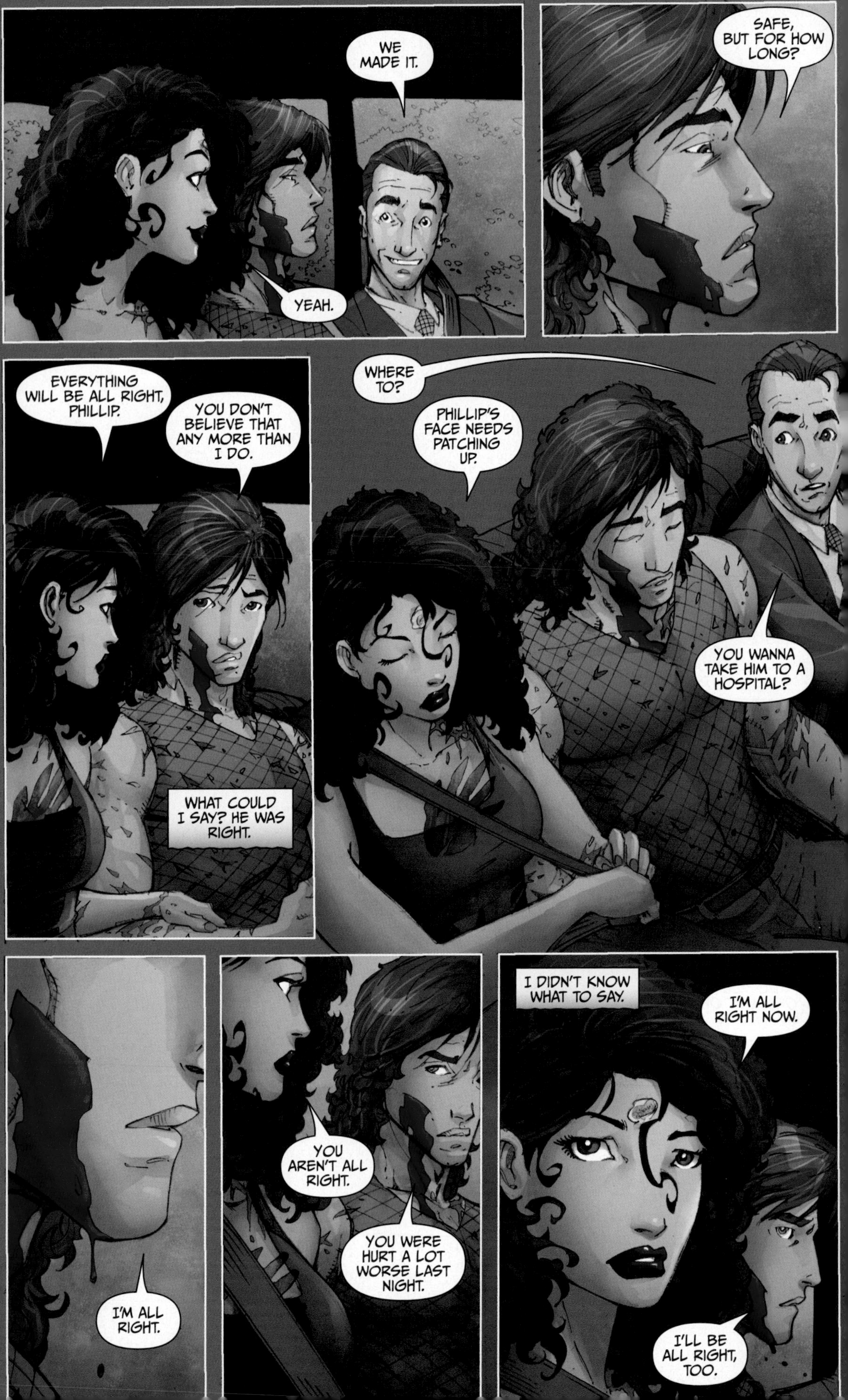
WE MADE IT.
YEAH.
SAFE, BUT FOR HOW LONG?
EVERYTHING WILL BE ALL RIGHT, PHILLIP.
YOU DON'T BELIEVE THAT ANY MORE THAN I DO.
WHAT COULD I SAY? HE WAS RIGHT.
WHERE TO?
PHILLIP'S FACE NEEDS PATCHING UP.
YOU WANNA TAKE HIM TO A HOSPITAL?
I'M ALL RIGHT.
YOU AREN'T ALL RIGHT.
YOU WERE HURT A LOT WORSE LAST NIGHT.
I DIDN'T KNOW WHAT TO SAY.
I'M ALL RIGHT NOW.
I'LL BE ALL RIGHT, TOO.

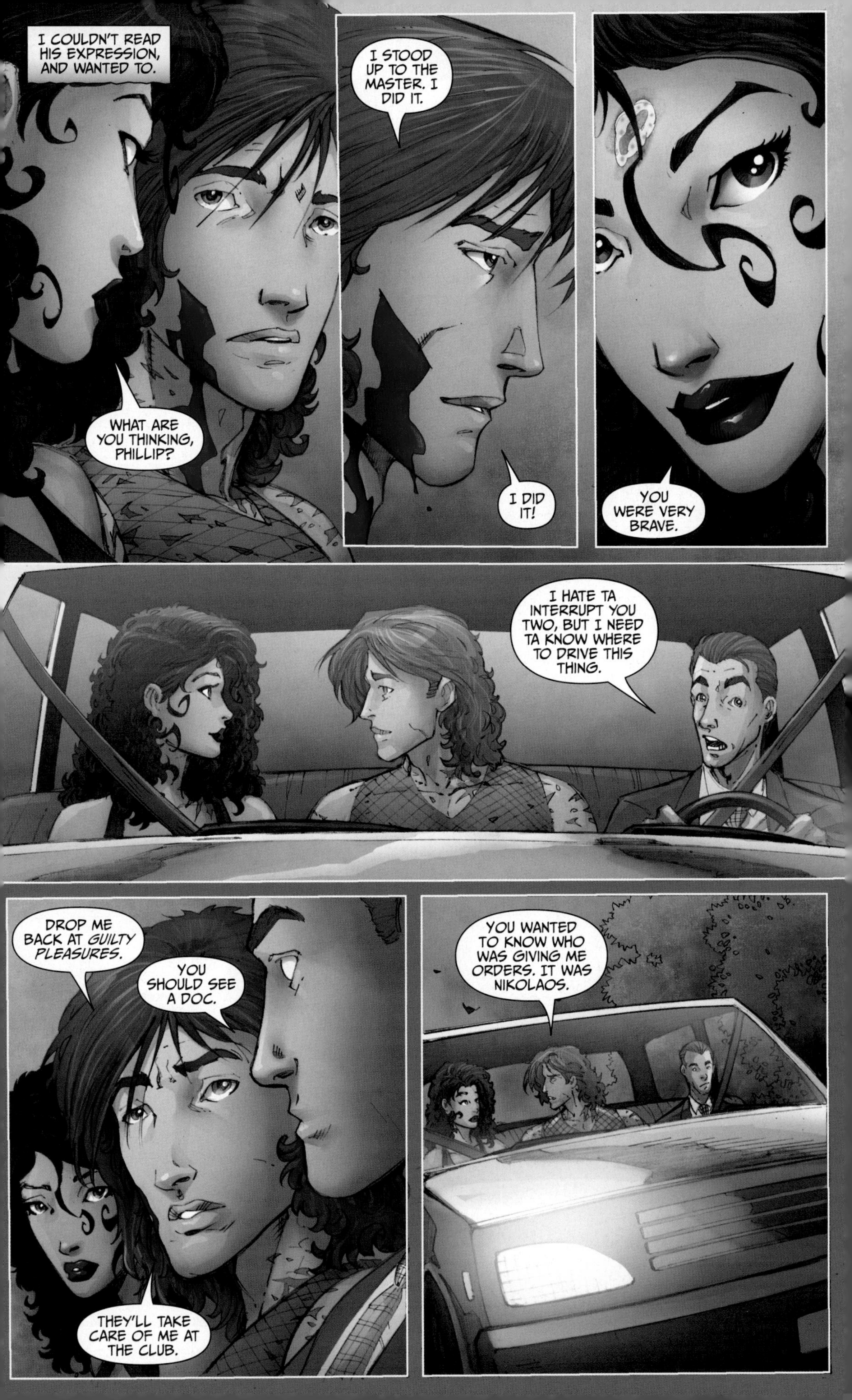
I COULDN'T READ HIS EXPRESSION, AND WANTED TO.
WHAT ARE YOU THINKING, PHILLIP?
I STOOD UP TO THE MASTER. I DID IT.
I DID IT!
YOU WERE VERY BRAVE.
I HATE TA INTERRUPT YOU TWO, BUT I NEED TA KNOW WHERE TO DRIVE THIS THING.
DROP ME BACK AT *GUILTY PLEASURES.*
YOU SHOULD SEE A DOC.
THEY'LL TAKE CARE OF ME AT THE CLUB.
YOU WANTED TO KNOW WHO WAS GIVING ME ORDERS. IT WAS NIKOLAOS.

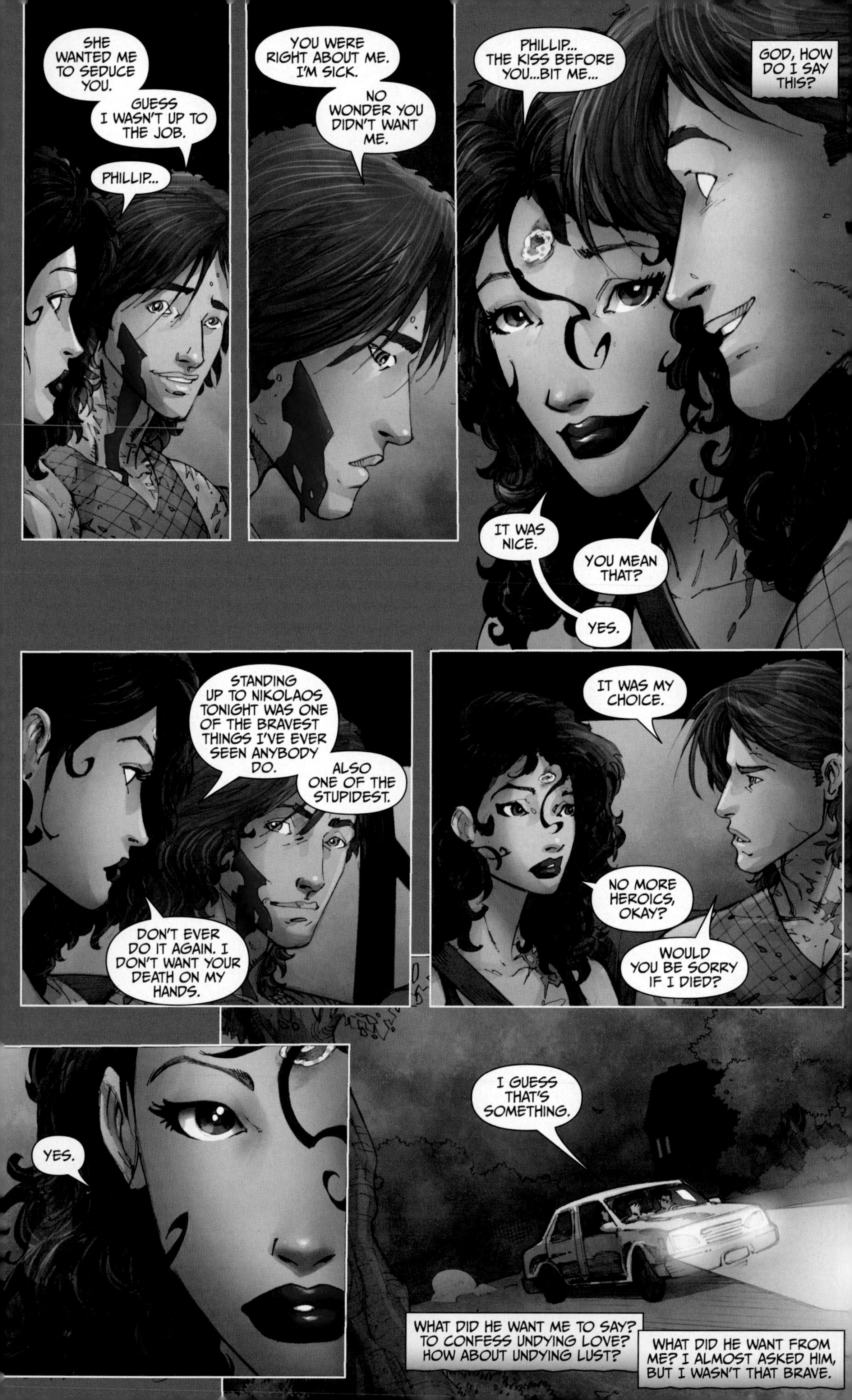
SHE WANTED ME TO SEDUCE YOU.
GUESS I WASN'T UP TO THE JOB.
PHILLIP...
YOU WERE RIGHT ABOUT ME. I'M SICK.
NO WONDER YOU DIDN'T WANT ME.
PHILLIP... THE KISS BEFORE YOU...BIT ME...
GOD, HOW DO I SAY THIS?
IT WAS NICE.
YOU MEAN THAT?
YES.
STANDING UP TO NIKOLAOS TONIGHT WAS ONE OF THE BRAVEST THINGS I'VE EVER SEEN ANYBODY DO.
ALSO ONE OF THE STUPIDEST.
DON'T EVER DO IT AGAIN. I DON'T WANT YOUR DEATH ON MY HANDS.
IT WAS MY CHOICE.
NO MORE HEROICS, OKAY?
WOULD YOU BE SORRY IF I DIED?
YES.
I GUESS THAT'S SOMETHING.
WHAT DID HE WANT ME TO SAY? TO CONFESS UNDYING LOVE? HOW ABOUT UNDYING LUST?
WHAT DID HE WANT FROM ME? I ALMOST ASKED HIM, BUT I WASN'T THAT BRAVE.

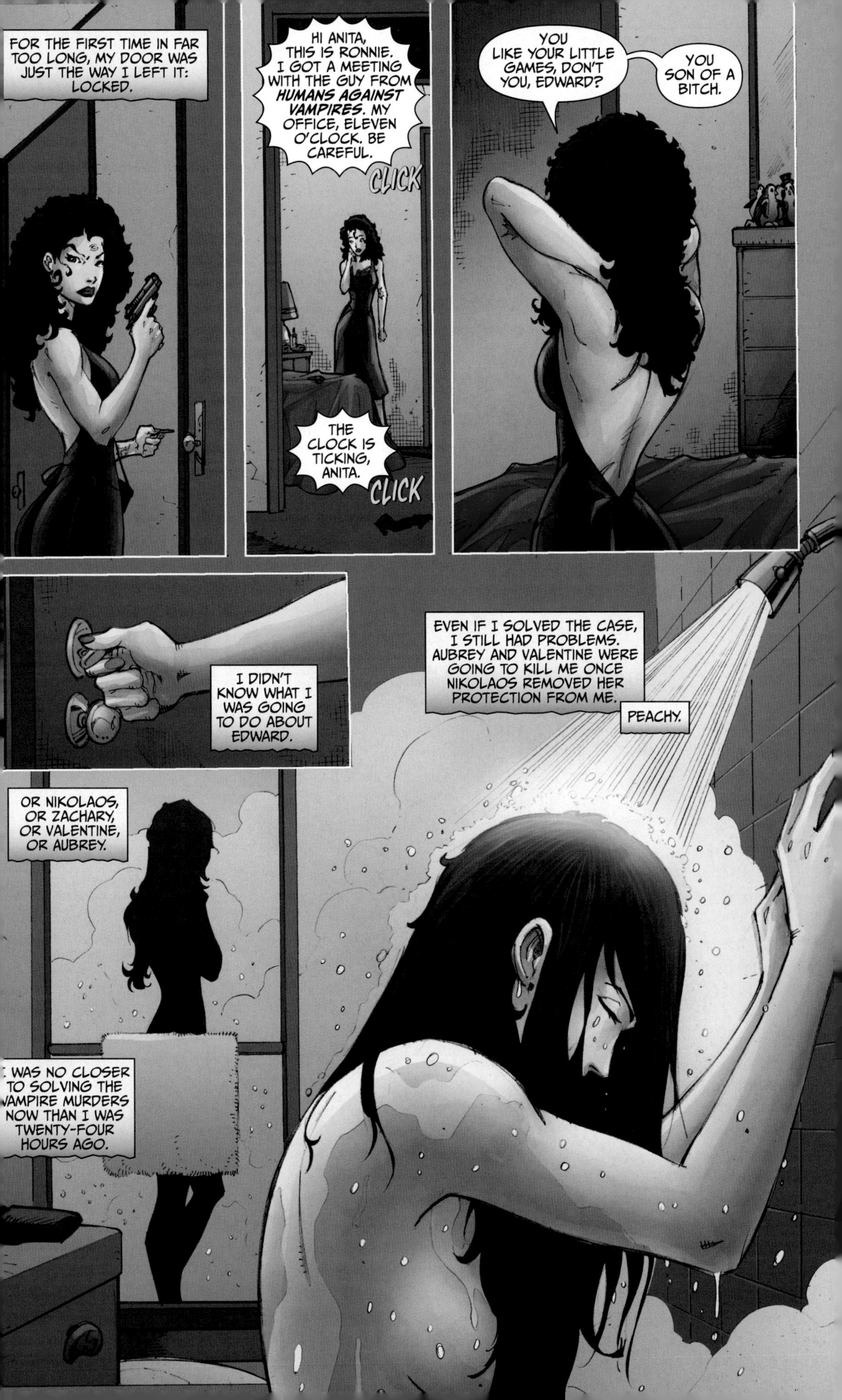

FOR THE FIRST TIME IN FAR TOO LONG, MY DOOR WAS JUST THE WAY I LEFT IT: LOCKED.
HI ANITA, THIS IS RONNIE. I GOT A MEETING WITH THE GUY FROM HUMANS AGAINST VAMPIRES. MY OFFICE, ELEVEN O'CLOCK. BE CAREFUL.
CLICK
THE CLOCK IS TICKING, ANITA.
CLICK
YOU LIKE YOUR LITTLE GAMES, DON'T YOU, EDWARD?
YOU SON OF A BITCH.
I DIDN'T KNOW WHAT I WAS GOING TO DO ABOUT EDWARD.
EVEN IF I SOLVED THE CASE, I STILL HAD PROBLEMS. AUBREY AND VALENTINE WERE GOING TO KILL ME ONCE NIKOLAOS REMOVED HER PROTECTION FROM ME.
PEACHY.
OR NIKOLAOS, OR ZACHARY, OR VALENTINE, OR AUBREY.
I WAS NO CLOSER TO SOLVING THE VAMPIRE MURDERS NOW THAN I WAS TWENTY-FOUR HOURS AGO.

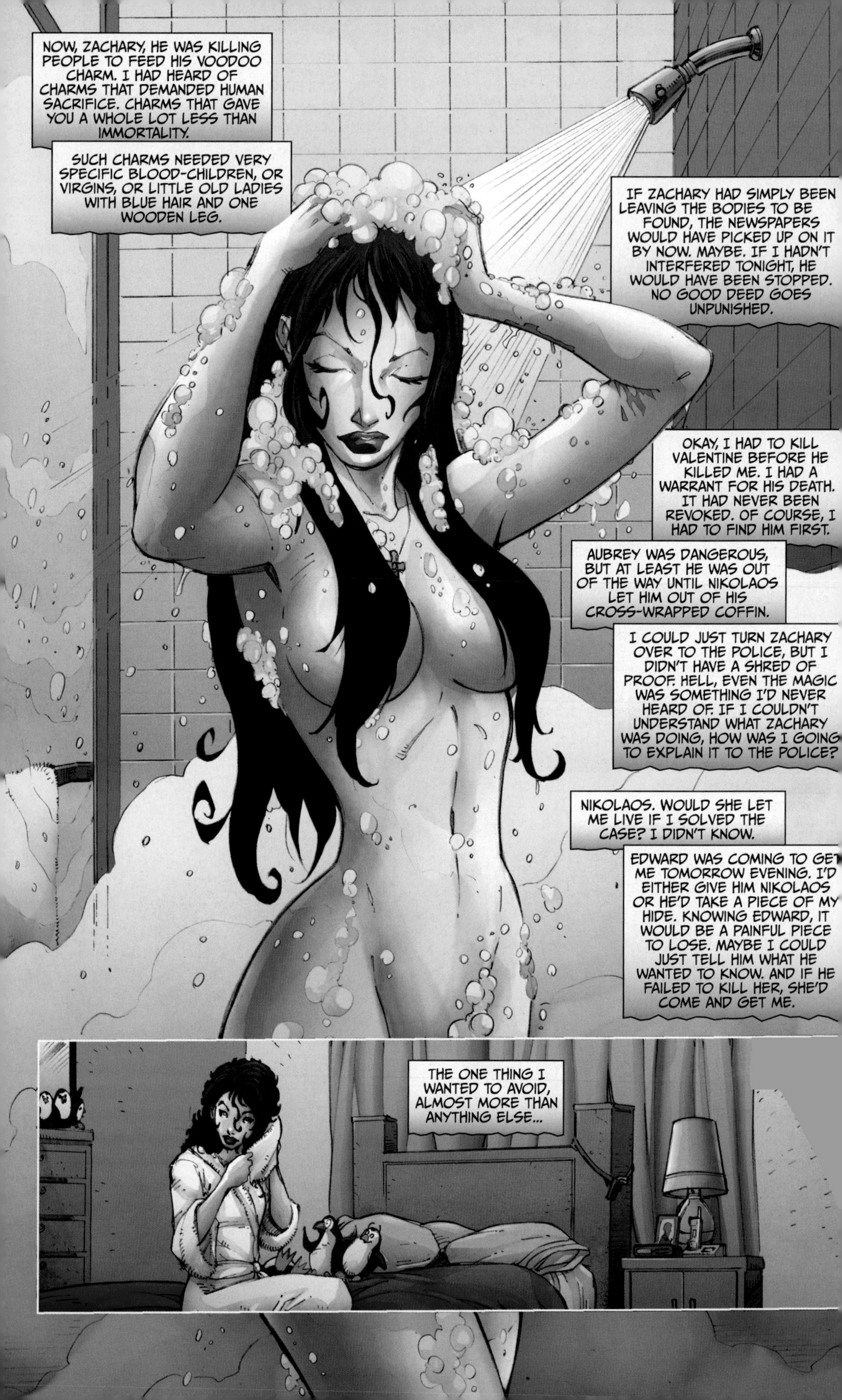
NOW, ZACHARY, HE WAS KILLING PEOPLE TO FEED HIS VOODOO CHARM. I HAD HEARD OF CHARMS THAT DEMANDED HUMAN SACRIFICE. CHARMS THAT GAVE YOU A WHOLE LOT LESS THAN IMMORTALITY.
SUCH CHARMS NEEDED VERY SPECIFIC BLOOD-CHILDREN, OR VIRGINS, OR LITTLE OLD LADIES WITH BLUE HAIR AND ONE WOODEN LEG.
IF ZACHARY HAD SIMPLY BEEN LEAVING THE BODIES TO BE FOUND, THE NEWSPAPERS WOULD HAVE PICKED UP ON IT BY NOW. MAYBE. IF I HADN'T INTERFERED TONIGHT, HE WOULD HAVE BEEN STOPPED. NO GOOD DEED GOES UNPUNISHED.
OKAY, I HAD TO KILL VALENTINE BEFORE HE KILLED ME. I HAD A WARRANT FOR HIS DEATH. IT HAD NEVER BEEN REVOKED. OF COURSE, I HAD TO FIND HIM FIRST.
AUBREY WAS DANGEROUS, BUT AT LEAST HE WAS OUT OF THE WAY UNTIL NIKOLAOS LET HIM OUT OF HIS CROSS-WRAPPED COFFIN.
I COULD JUST TURN ZACHARY OVER TO THE POLICE, BUT I DIDN'T HAVE A SHRED OF PROOF. HELL, EVEN THE MAGIC WAS SOMETHING I'D NEVER HEARD OF. IF I COULDN'T UNDERSTAND WHAT ZACHARY WAS DOING, HOW WAS I GOING TO EXPLAIN IT TO THE POLICE?
NIKOLAOS. WOULD SHE LET ME LIVE IF I SOLVED THE CASE? I DIDN'T KNOW.
EDWARD WAS COMING TO GET ME TOMORROW EVENING. I'D EITHER GIVE HIM NIKOLAOS OR HE'D TAKE A PIECE OF MY HIDE. KNOWING EDWARD, IT WOULD BE A PAINFUL PIECE TO LOSE. MAYBE I COULD JUST TELL HIM WHAT HE WANTED TO KNOW. AND IF HE FAILED TO KILL HER, SHE'D COME AND GET ME.
THE ONE THING I WANTED TO AVOID, ALMOST MORE THAN ANYTHING ELSE...

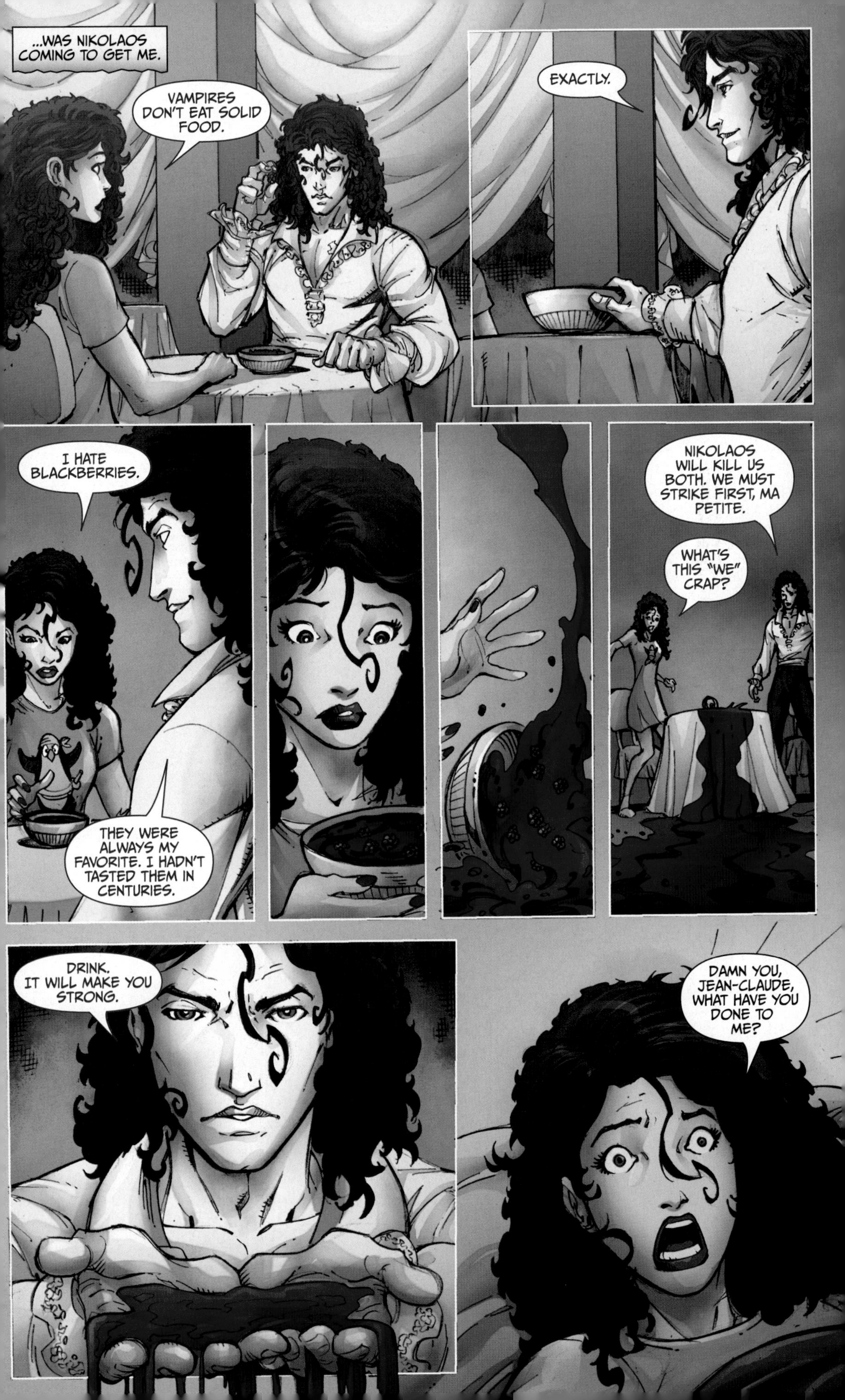
...WAS NIKOLAOS COMING TO GET ME.
VAMPIRES DON'T EAT SOLID FOOD.
EXACTLY.
I HATE BLACKBERRIES.
THEY WERE ALWAYS MY FAVORITE. I HADN'T TASTED THEM IN CENTURIES.
NIKOLAOS WILL KILL US BOTH. WE MUST STRIKE FIRST, MA PETITE.
WHAT'S THIS "WE" CRAP?
DRINK. IT WILL MAKE YOU STRONG.
DAMN YOU, JEAN-CLAUDE, WHAT HAVE YOU DONE TO ME?

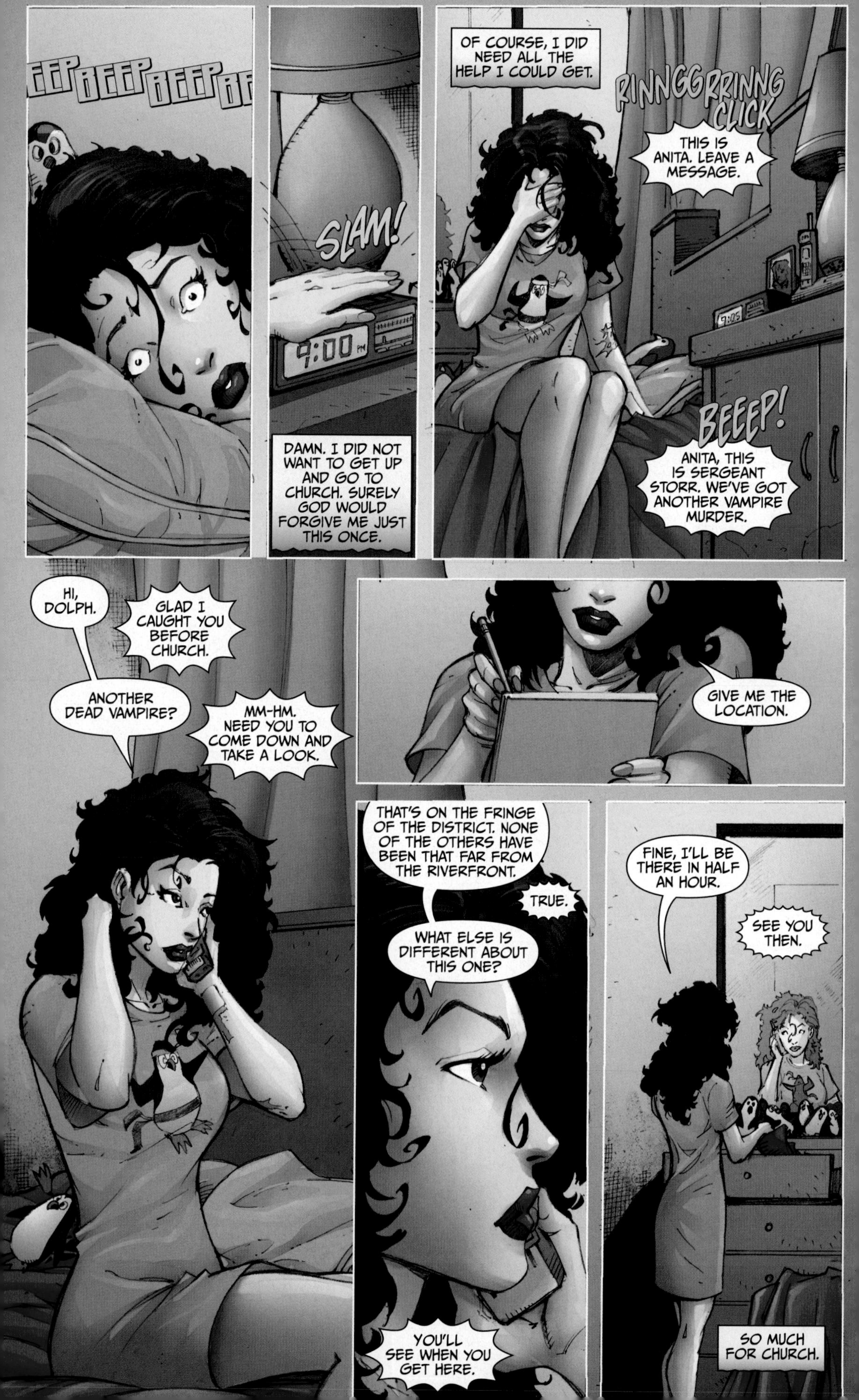
BEEP BEEP BEEP BEEP
SLAM!
DAMN. I DID NOT WANT TO GET UP AND GO TO CHURCH. SURELY GOD WOULD FORGIVE ME JUST THIS ONCE.
OF COURSE, I DID NEED ALL THE HELP I COULD GET.
RINNGGRRINNG CLICK
THIS IS ANITA. LEAVE A MESSAGE.
BEEEP!
ANITA, THIS IS SERGEANT STORR. WE'VE GOT ANOTHER VAMPIRE MURDER.
HI, DOLPH.
GLAD I CAUGHT YOU BEFORE CHURCH.
ANOTHER DEAD VAMPIRE?
MM-HM. NEED YOU TO COME DOWN AND TAKE A LOOK.
GIVE ME THE LOCATION.
THAT'S ON THE FRINGE OF THE DISTRICT. NONE OF THE OTHERS HAVE BEEN THAT FAR FROM THE RIVERFRONT.
TRUE.
WHAT ELSE IS DIFFERENT ABOUT THIS ONE?
YOU'LL SEE WHEN YOU GET HERE.
FINE, I'LL BE THERE IN HALF AN HOUR.
SEE YOU THEN.
SO MUCH FOR CHURCH.

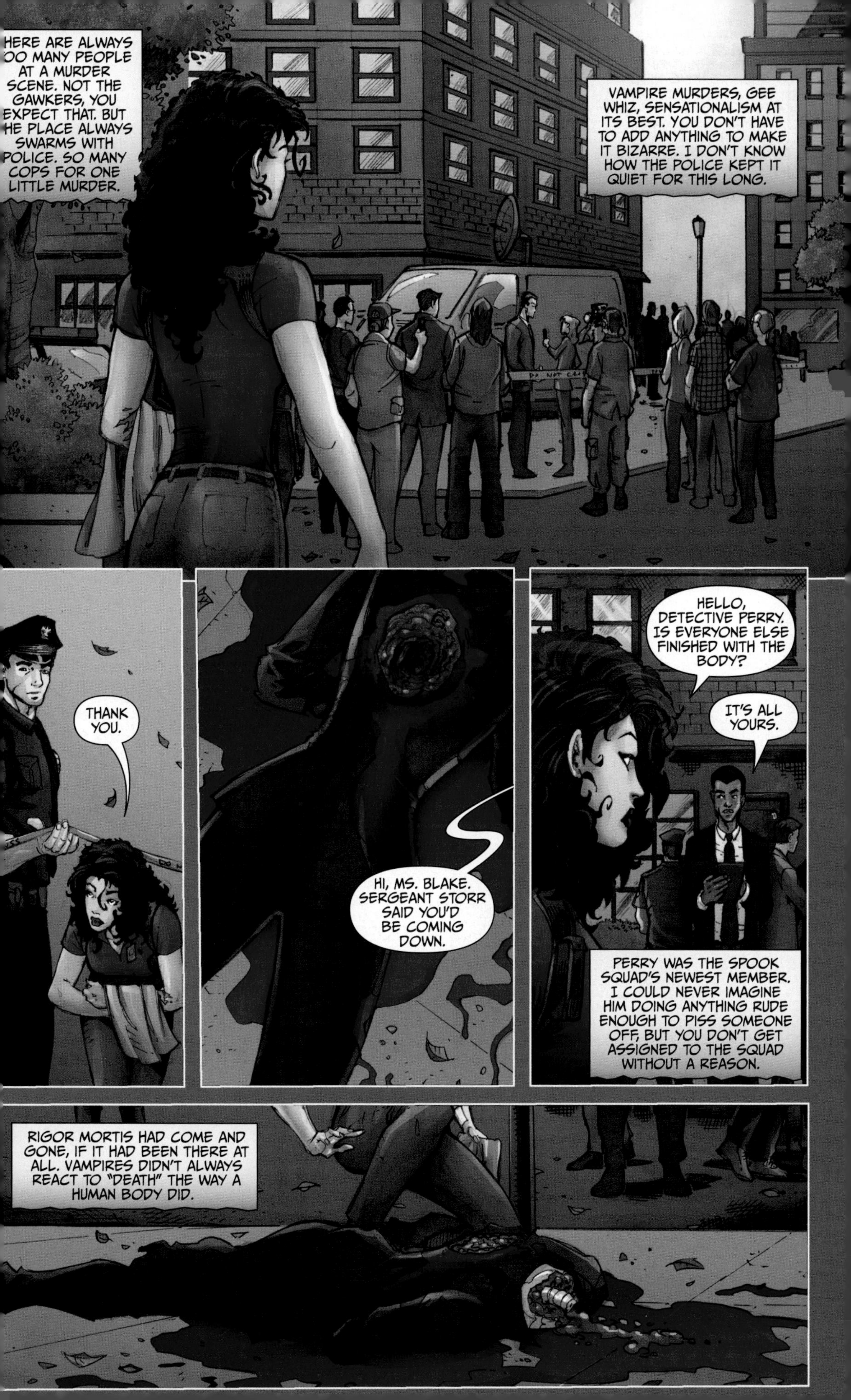
HERE ARE ALWAYS OO MANY PEOPLE AT A MURDER SCENE. NOT THE GAWKERS, YOU EXPECT THAT. BUT HE PLACE ALWAYS SWARMS WITH POLICE. SO MANY COPS FOR ONE LITTLE MURDER.
VAMPIRE MURDERS, GEE WHIZ, SENSATIONALISM AT ITS BEST. YOU DON'T HAVE TO ADD ANYTHING TO MAKE IT BIZARRE. I DON'T KNOW HOW THE POLICE KEPT IT QUIET FOR THIS LONG.
THANK YOU.
HI, MS. BLAKE. SERGEANT STORR SAID YOU'D BE COMING DOWN.
HELLO, DETECTIVE PERRY. IS EVERYONE ELSE FINISHED WITH THE BODY?
IT'S ALL YOURS.
PERRY WAS THE SPOOK SQUAD'S NEWEST MEMBER. I COULD NEVER IMAGINE HIM DOING ANYTHING RUDE ENOUGH TO PISS SOMEONE OFF, BUT YOU DON'T GET ASSIGNED TO THE SQUAD WITHOUT A REASON.
RIGOR MORTIS HAD COME AND GONE, IF IT HAD BEEN THERE AT ALL. VAMPIRES DIDN'T ALWAYS REACT TO "DEATH" THE WAY A HUMAN BODY DID.

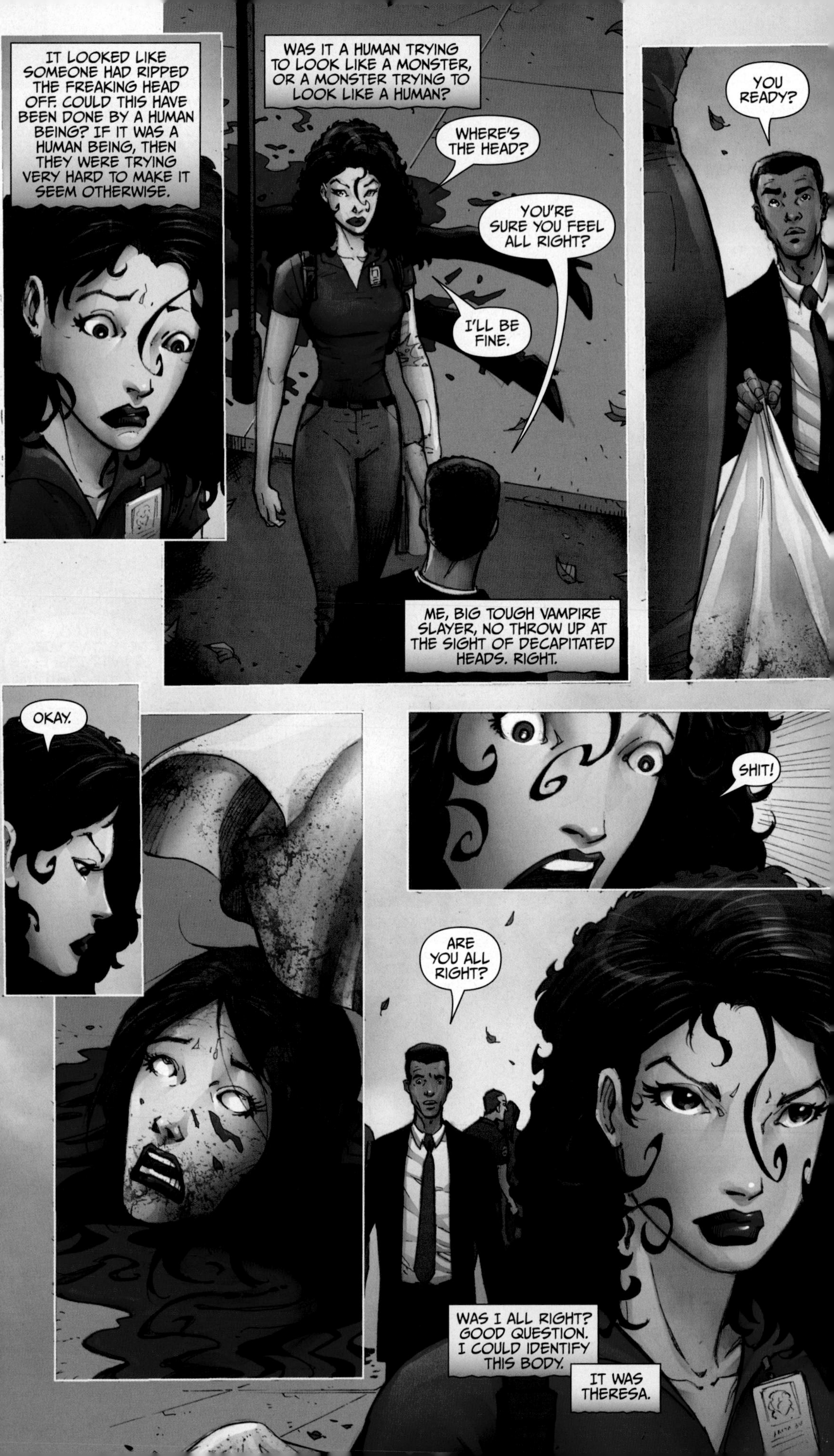
IT LOOKED LIKE SOMEONE HAD RIPPED THE FREAKING HEAD OFF. COULD THIS HAVE BEEN DONE BY A HUMAN BEING? IF IT WAS A HUMAN BEING, THEN THEY WERE TRYING VERY HARD TO MAKE IT SEEM OTHERWISE.
WAS IT A HUMAN TRYING TO LOOK LIKE A MONSTER, OR A MONSTER TRYING TO LOOK LIKE A HUMAN?
WHERE'S THE HEAD?
YOU'RE SURE YOU FEEL ALL RIGHT?
I'LL BE FINE.
ME, BIG TOUGH VAMPIRE SLAYER, NO THROW UP AT THE SIGHT OF DECAPITATED HEADS. RIGHT.
YOU READY?
OKAY.
SHIT!
ARE YOU ALL RIGHT?
WAS I ALL RIGHT? GOOD QUESTION. I COULD IDENTIFY THIS BODY.
IT WAS THERESA.

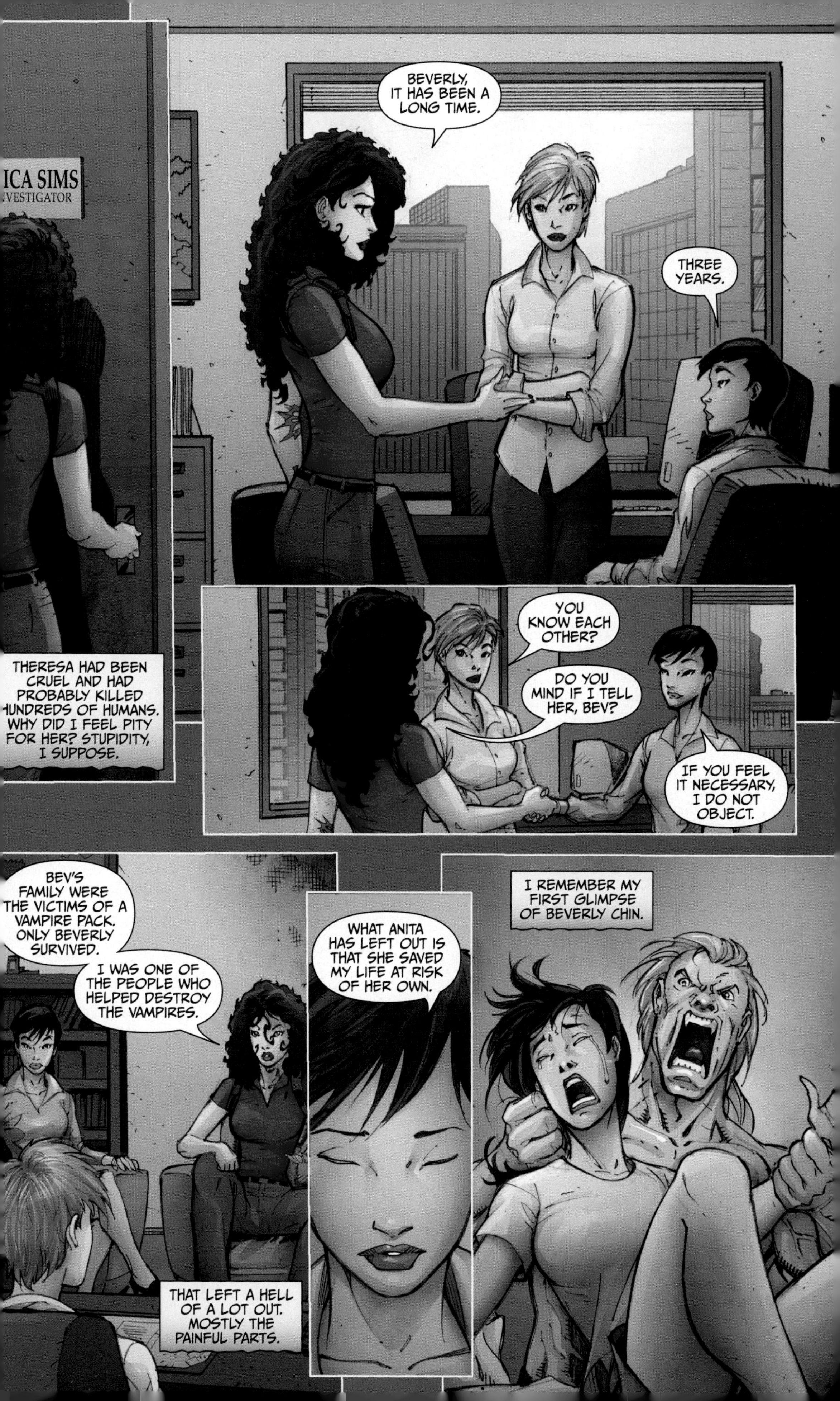
ICA SIMS
VESTIGATOR
BEVERLY, IT HAS BEEN A LONG TIME.
THREE YEARS.
THERESA HAD BEEN CRUEL AND HAD PROBABLY KILLED HUNDREDS OF HUMANS. WHY DID I FEEL PITY FOR HER? STUPIDITY, I SUPPOSE.
YOU KNOW EACH OTHER?
DO YOU MIND IF I TELL HER, BEV?
IF YOU FEEL IT NECESSARY, I DO NOT OBJECT.
BEV'S FAMILY WERE THE VICTIMS OF A VAMPIRE PACK. ONLY BEVERLY SURVIVED.
I WAS ONE OF THE PEOPLE WHO HELPED DESTROY THE VAMPIRES.
THAT LEFT A HELL OF A LOT OUT. MOSTLY THE PAINFUL PARTS.
WHAT ANITA HAS LEFT OUT IS THAT SHE SAVED MY LIFE AT RISK OF HER OWN.
I REMEMBER MY FIRST GLIMPSE OF BEVERLY CHIN.

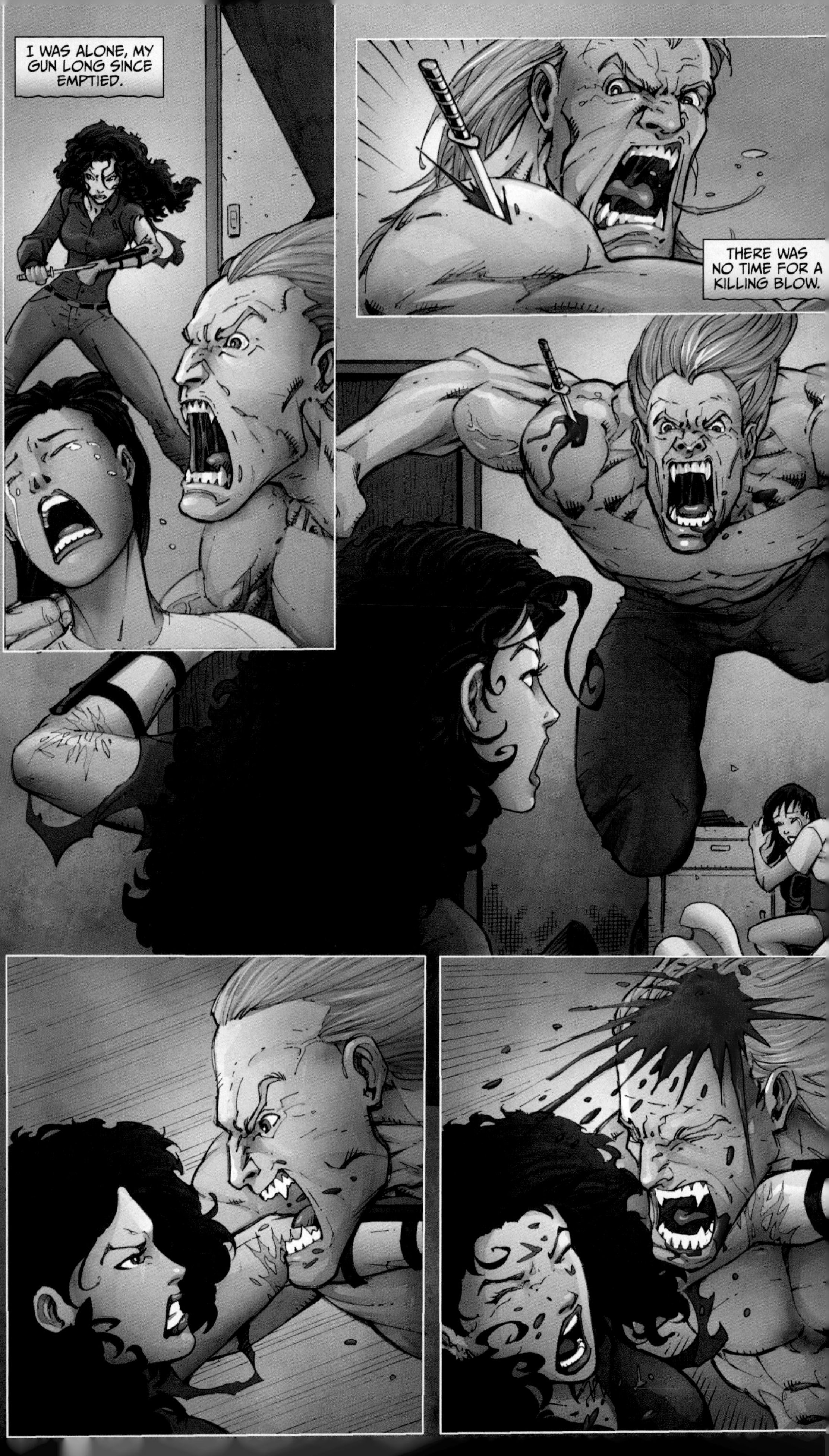
I WAS ALONE, MY GUN LONG SINCE EMPTIED.
THERE WAS NO TIME FOR A KILLING BLOW.

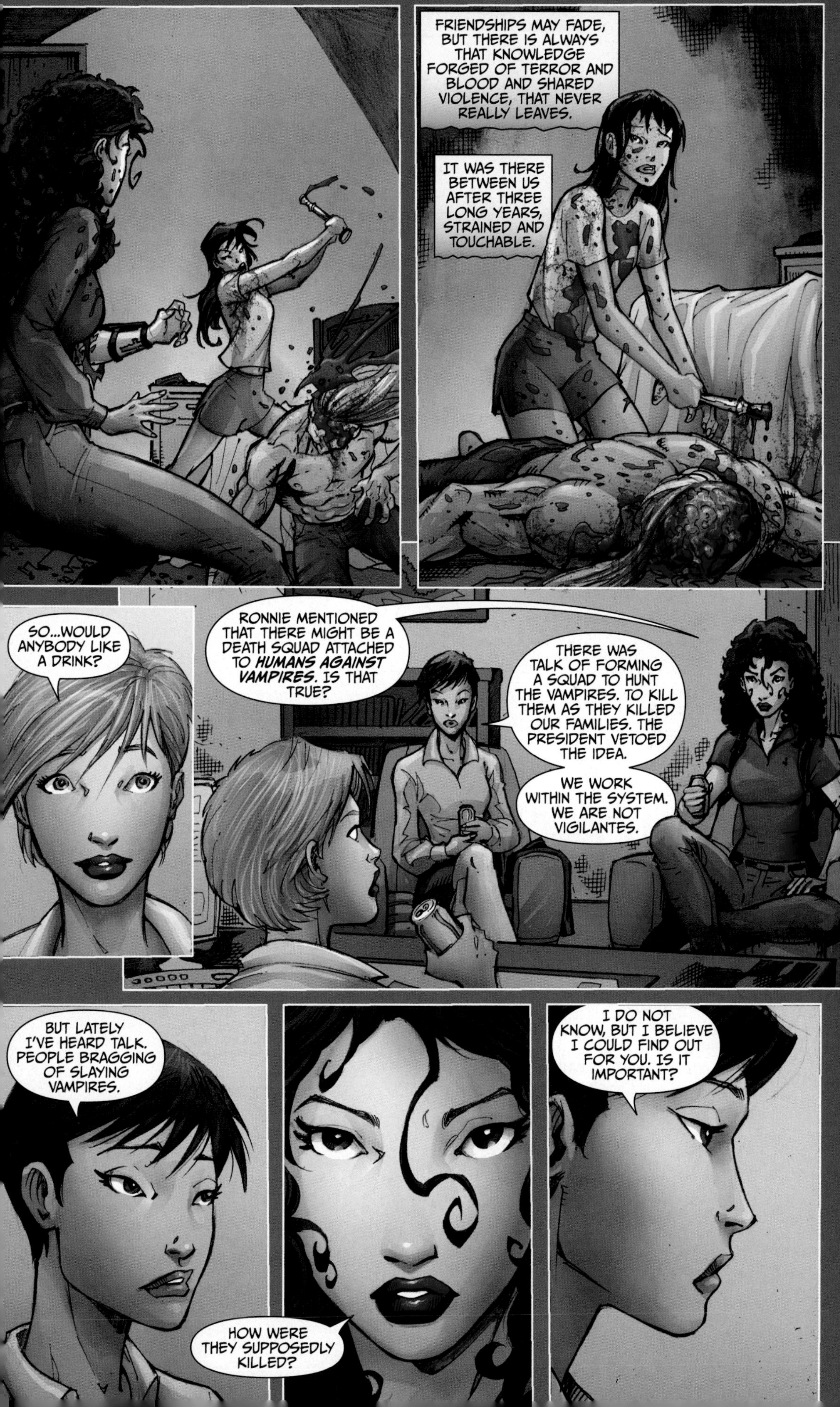

FRIENDSHIPS MAY FADE, BUT THERE IS ALWAYS THAT KNOWLEDGE FORGED OF TERROR AND BLOOD AND SHARED VIOLENCE, THAT NEVER REALLY LEAVES.
IT WAS THERE BETWEEN US AFTER THREE LONG YEARS, STRAINED AND TOUCHABLE.
SO...WOULD ANYBODY LIKE A DRINK?
RONNIE MENTIONED THAT THERE MIGHT BE A DEATH SQUAD ATTACHED TO HUMANS AGAINST VAMPIRES. IS THAT TRUE?
THERE WAS TALK OF FORMING A SQUAD TO HUNT THE VAMPIRES. TO KILL THEM AS THEY KILLED OUR FAMILIES. THE PRESIDENT VETOED THE IDEA.
WE WORK WITHIN THE SYSTEM. WE ARE NOT VIGILANTES.
BUT LATELY I'VE HEARD TALK. PEOPLE BRAGGING OF SLAYING VAMPIRES.
HOW WERE THEY SUPPOSEDLY KILLED?
I DO NOT KNOW, BUT I BELIEVE I COULD FIND OUT FOR YOU. IS IT IMPORTANT?

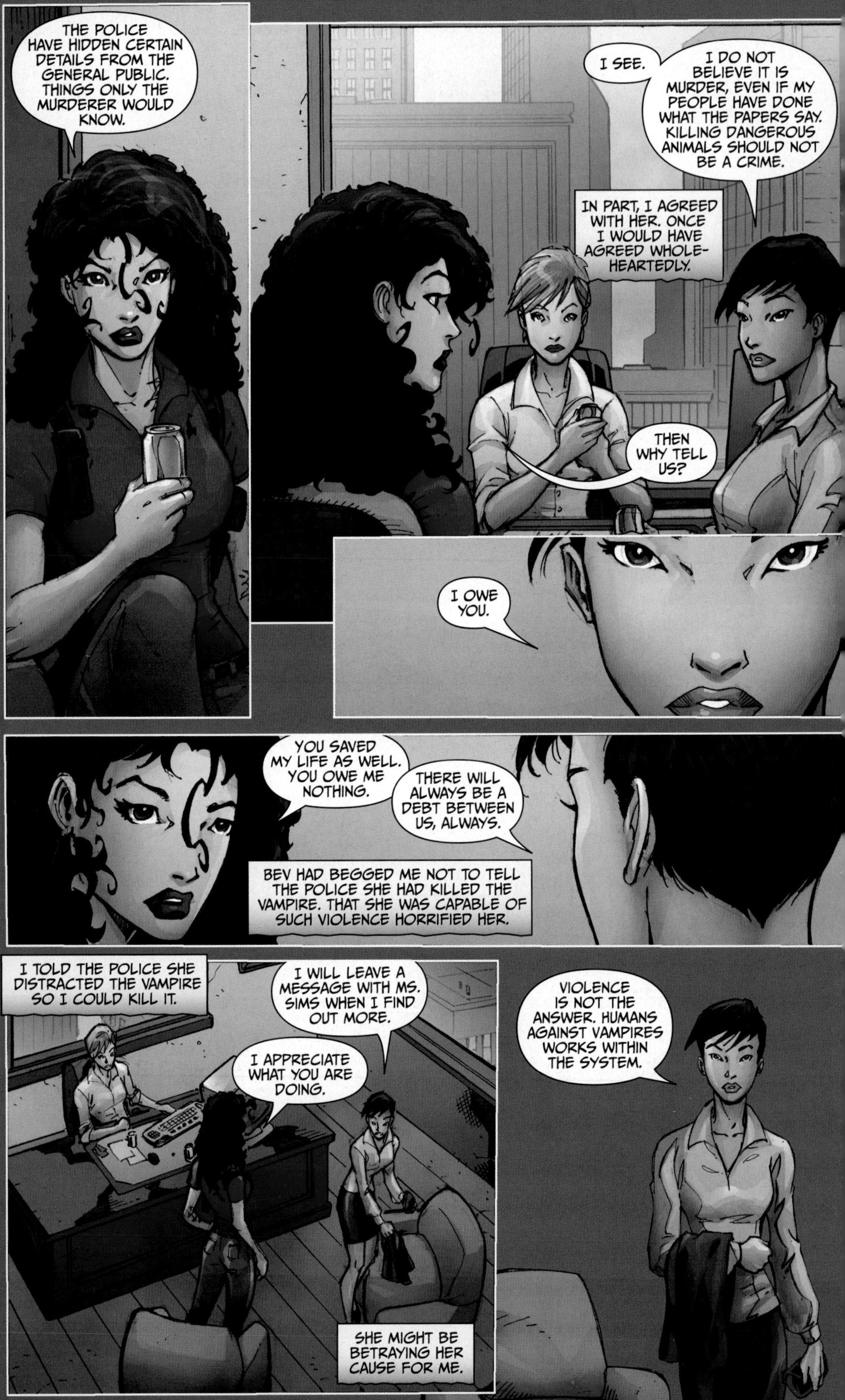
THE POLICE HAVE HIDDEN CERTAIN DETAILS FROM THE GENERAL PUBLIC. THINGS ONLY THE MURDERER WOULD KNOW.
I SEE.
I DO NOT BELIEVE IT IS MURDER, EVEN IF MY PEOPLE HAVE DONE WHAT THE PAPERS SAY. KILLING DANGEROUS ANIMALS SHOULD NOT BE A CRIME.
IN PART, I AGREED WITH HER. ONCE I WOULD HAVE AGREED WHOLE-HEARTEDLY.
THEN WHY TELL US?
I OWE YOU.
YOU SAVED MY LIFE AS WELL. YOU OWE ME NOTHING.
THERE WILL ALWAYS BE A DEBT BETWEEN US, ALWAYS.
BEV HAD BEGGED ME NOT TO TELL THE POLICE SHE HAD KILLED THE VAMPIRE. THAT SHE WAS CAPABLE OF SUCH VIOLENCE HORRIFIED HER.
I TOLD THE POLICE SHE DISTRACTED THE VAMPIRE SO I COULD KILL IT.
I WILL LEAVE A MESSAGE WITH MS. SIMS WHEN I FIND OUT MORE.
I APPRECIATE WHAT YOU ARE DOING.
SHE MIGHT BE BETRAYING HER CAUSE FOR ME.
VIOLENCE IS NOT THE ANSWER. HUMANS AGAINST VAMPIRES WORKS WITHIN THE SYSTEM.

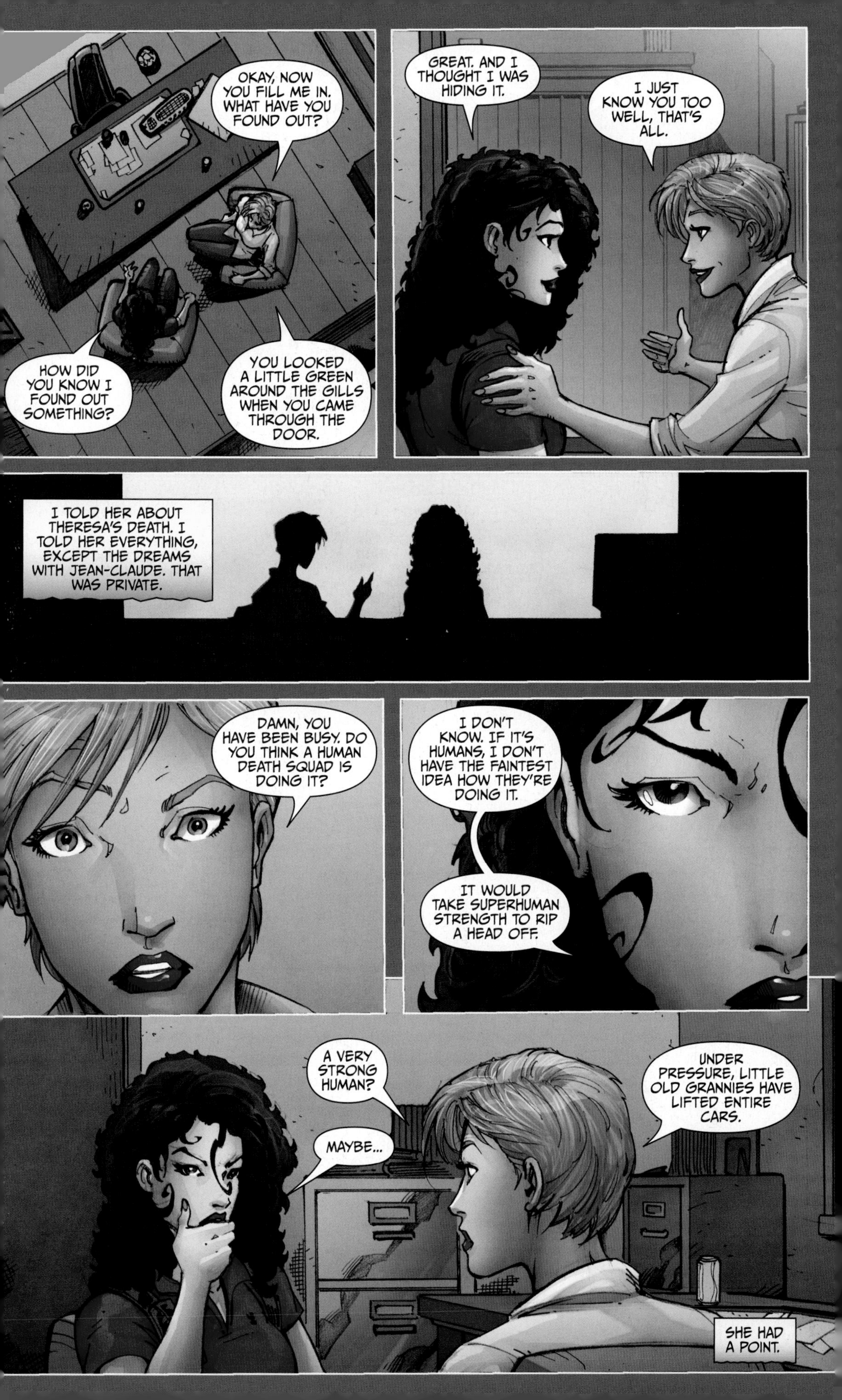
OKAY, NOW YOU FILL ME IN. WHAT HAVE YOU FOUND OUT?
HOW DID YOU KNOW I FOUND OUT SOMETHING?
YOU LOOKED A LITTLE GREEN AROUND THE GILLS WHEN YOU CAME THROUGH THE DOOR.
GREAT. AND I THOUGHT I WAS HIDING IT.
I JUST KNOW YOU TOO WELL, THAT'S ALL.
I TOLD HER ABOUT THERESA'S DEATH. I TOLD HER EVERYTHING, EXCEPT THE DREAMS WITH JEAN-CLAUDE. THAT WAS PRIVATE.
DAMN, YOU HAVE BEEN BUSY. DO YOU THINK A HUMAN DEATH SQUAD IS DOING IT?
I DON'T KNOW. IF IT'S HUMANS, I DON'T HAVE THE FAINTEST IDEA HOW THEY'RE DOING IT.
IT WOULD TAKE SUPERHUMAN STRENGTH TO RIP A HEAD OFF.
A VERY STRONG HUMAN?
MAYBE...
UNDER PRESSURE, LITTLE OLD GRANNIES HAVE LIFTED ENTIRE CARS.
SHE HAD A POINT.

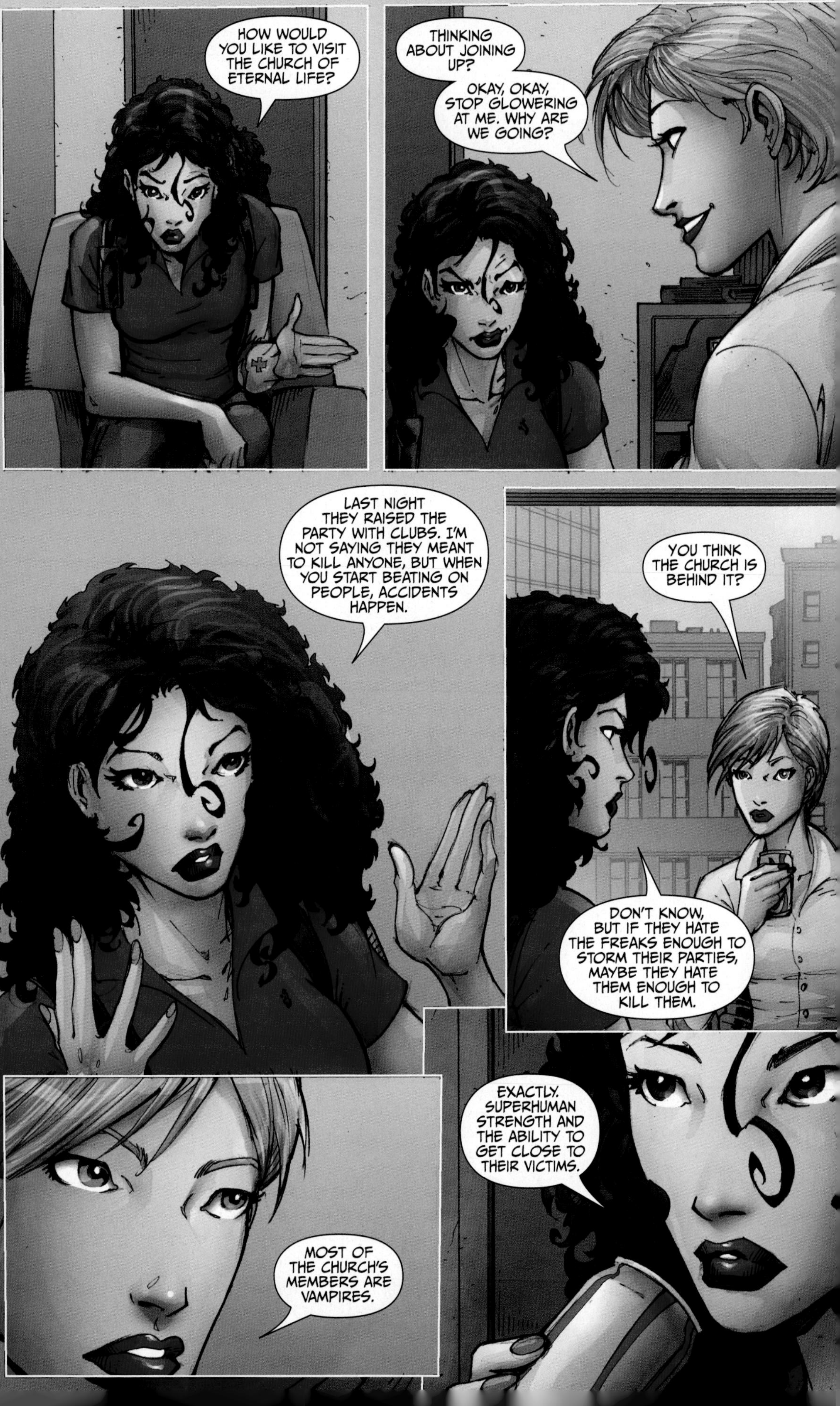
HOW WOULD YOU LIKE TO VISIT THE CHURCH OF ETERNAL LIFE?
THINKING ABOUT JOINING UP?
OKAY, OKAY, STOP GLOWERING AT ME. WHY ARE WE GOING?
LAST NIGHT THEY RAISED THE PARTY WITH CLUBS. I'M NOT SAYING THEY MEANT TO KILL ANYONE, BUT WHEN YOU START BEATING ON PEOPLE, ACCIDENTS HAPPEN.
YOU THINK THE CHURCH IS BEHIND IT?
DON'T KNOW, BUT IF THEY HATE THE FREAKS ENOUGH TO STORM THEIR PARTIES, MAYBE THEY HATE THEM ENOUGH TO KILL THEM.
MOST OF THE CHURCH'S MEMBERS ARE VAMPIRES.
EXACTLY. SUPERHUMAN STRENGTH AND THE ABILITY TO GET CLOSE TO THEIR VICTIMS.

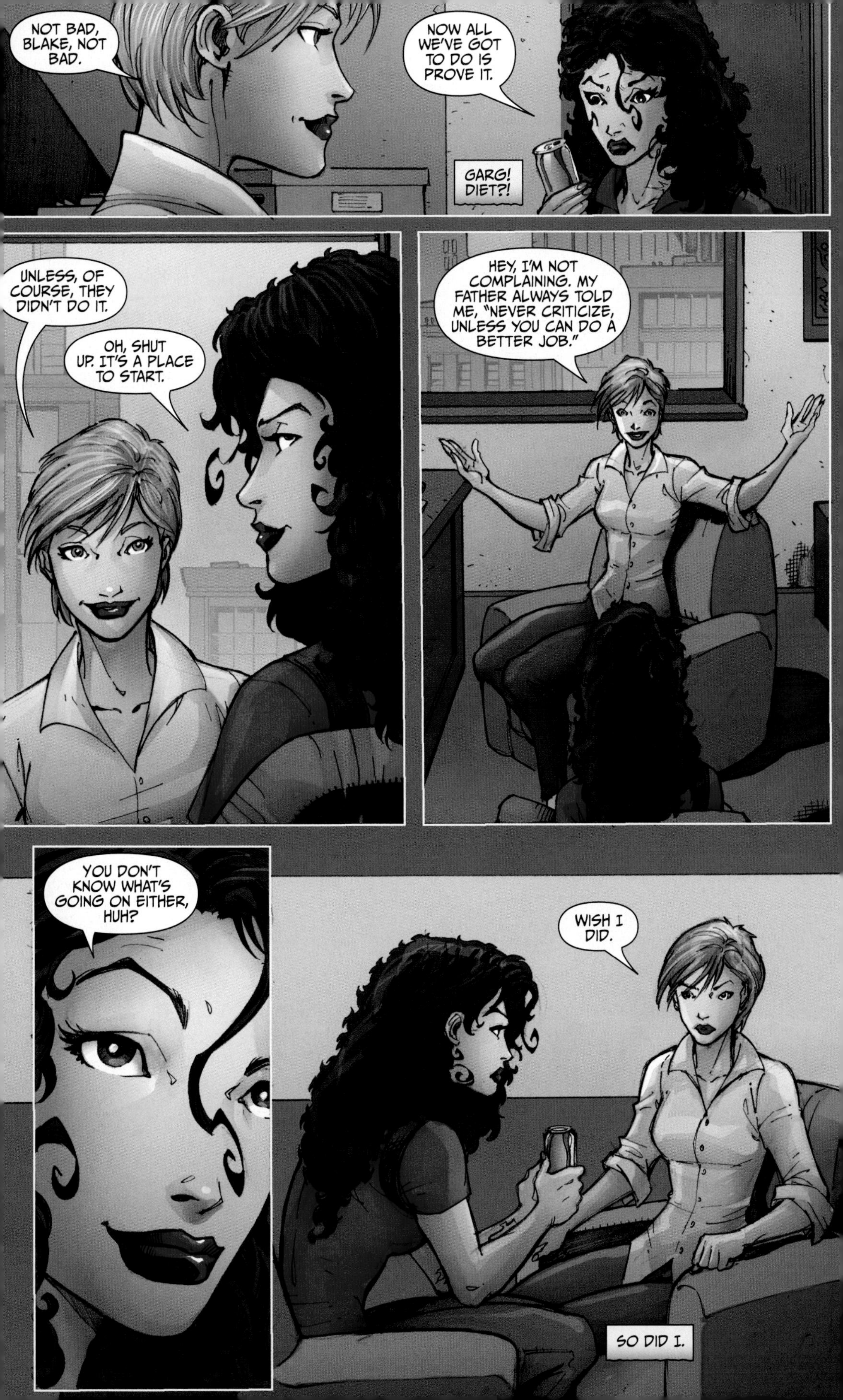

NOT BAD, BLAKE, NOT BAD.
NOW ALL WE'VE GOT TO DO IS PROVE IT.
GARG! DIET?!
UNLESS, OF COURSE, THEY DIDN'T DO IT.
OH, SHUT UP. IT'S A PLACE TO START.
HEY, I'M NOT COMPLAINING. MY FATHER ALWAYS TOLD ME, "NEVER CRITICIZE, UNLESS YOU CAN DO A BETTER JOB."
YOU DON'T KNOW WHAT'S GOING ON EITHER, HUH?
WISH I DID.
SO DID I.

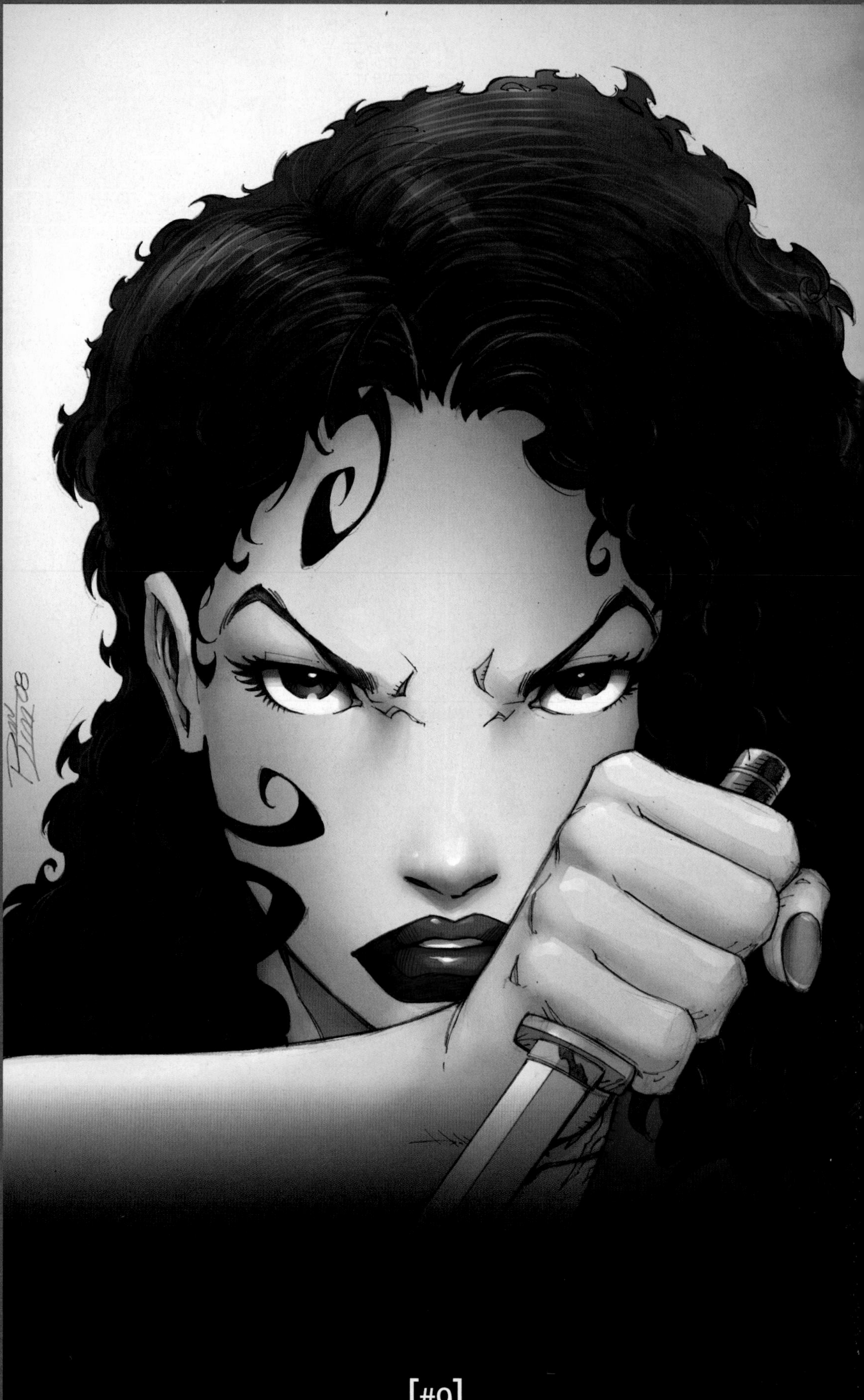

[#9]

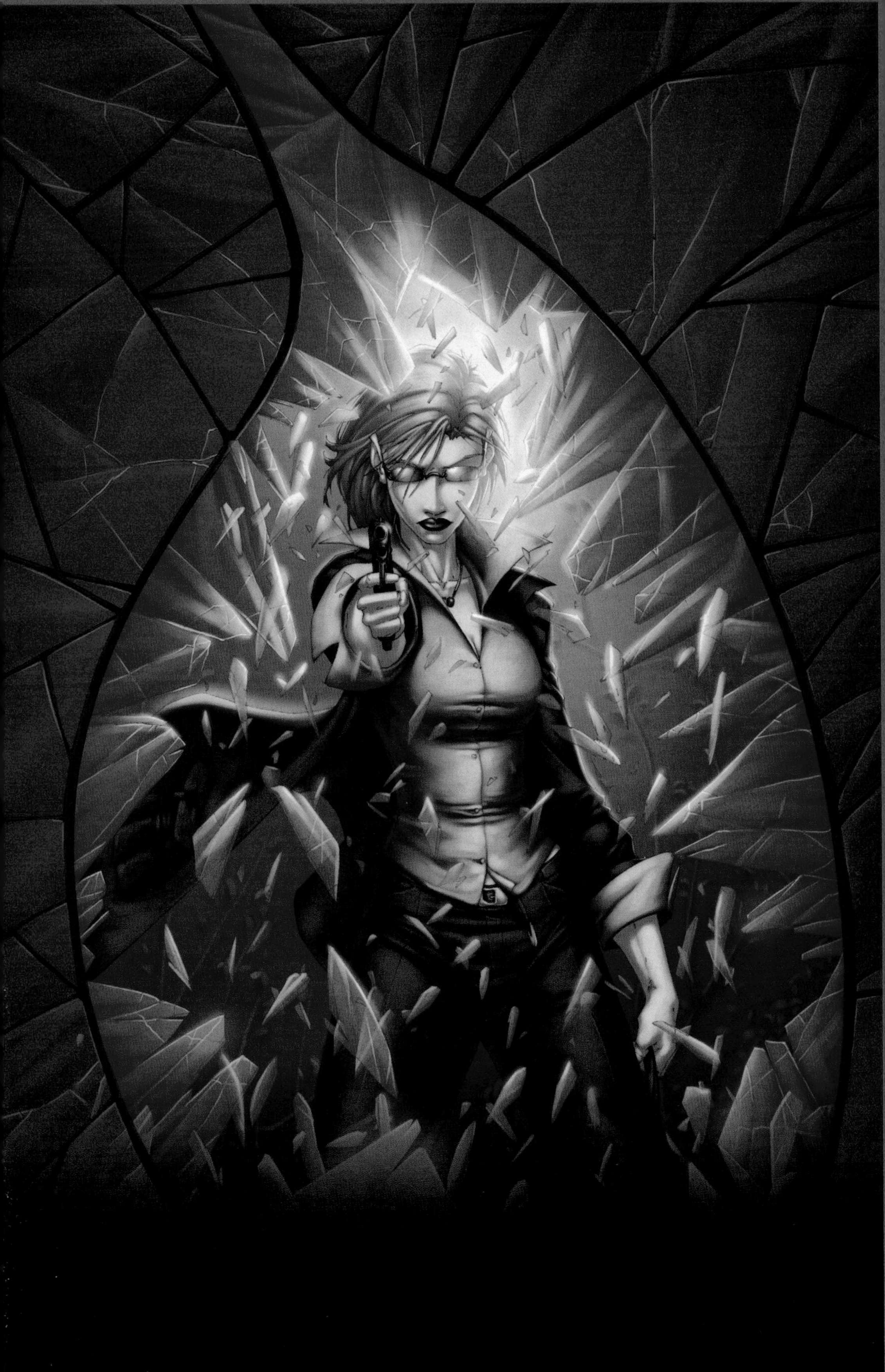

[#9 variant]

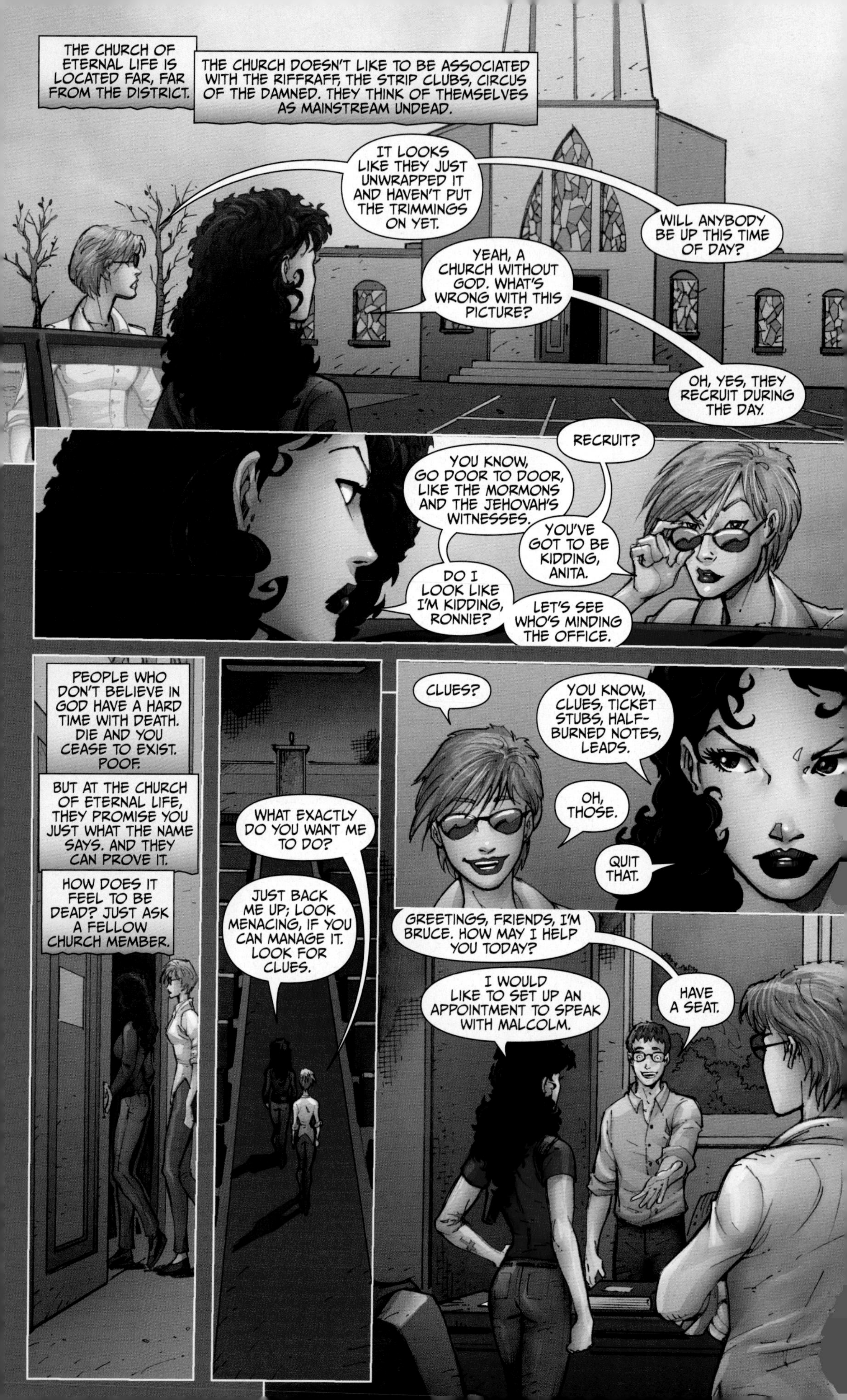
THE CHURCH OF ETERNAL LIFE IS LOCATED FAR, FAR FROM THE DISTRICT.
THE CHURCH DOESN'T LIKE TO BE ASSOCIATED WITH THE RIFFRAFF, THE STRIP CLUBS, CIRCUS OF THE DAMNED. THEY THINK OF THEMSELVES AS MAINSTREAM UNDEAD.
IT LOOKS LIKE THEY JUST UNWRAPPED IT AND HAVEN'T PUT THE TRIMMINGS ON YET.
WILL ANYBODY BE UP THIS TIME OF DAY?
YEAH, A CHURCH WITHOUT GOD. WHAT'S WRONG WITH THIS PICTURE?
OH, YES, THEY RECRUIT DURING THE DAY.
RECRUIT?
YOU KNOW, GO DOOR TO DOOR, LIKE THE MORMONS AND THE JEHOVAH'S WITNESSES.
YOU'VE GOT TO BE KIDDING, ANITA.
DO I LOOK LIKE I'M KIDDING, RONNIE?
LET'S SEE WHO'S MINDING THE OFFICE.
PEOPLE WHO DON'T BELIEVE IN GOD HAVE A HARD TIME WITH DEATH. DIE AND YOU CEASE TO EXIST. POOF.
BUT AT THE CHURCH OF ETERNAL LIFE, THEY PROMISE YOU JUST WHAT THE NAME SAYS. AND THEY CAN PROVE IT.
HOW DOES IT FEEL TO BE DEAD? JUST ASK A FELLOW CHURCH MEMBER.
WHAT EXACTLY DO YOU WANT ME TO DO?
JUST BACK ME UP; LOOK MENACING, IF YOU CAN MANAGE IT. LOOK FOR CLUES.
CLUES?
YOU KNOW, CLUES, TICKET STUBS, HALF-BURNED NOTES, LEADS.
OH, THOSE.
QUIT THAT.
GREETINGS, FRIENDS, I'M BRUCE. HOW MAY I HELP YOU TODAY?
I WOULD LIKE TO SET UP AN APPOINTMENT TO SPEAK WITH MALCOLM.
HAVE A SEAT.

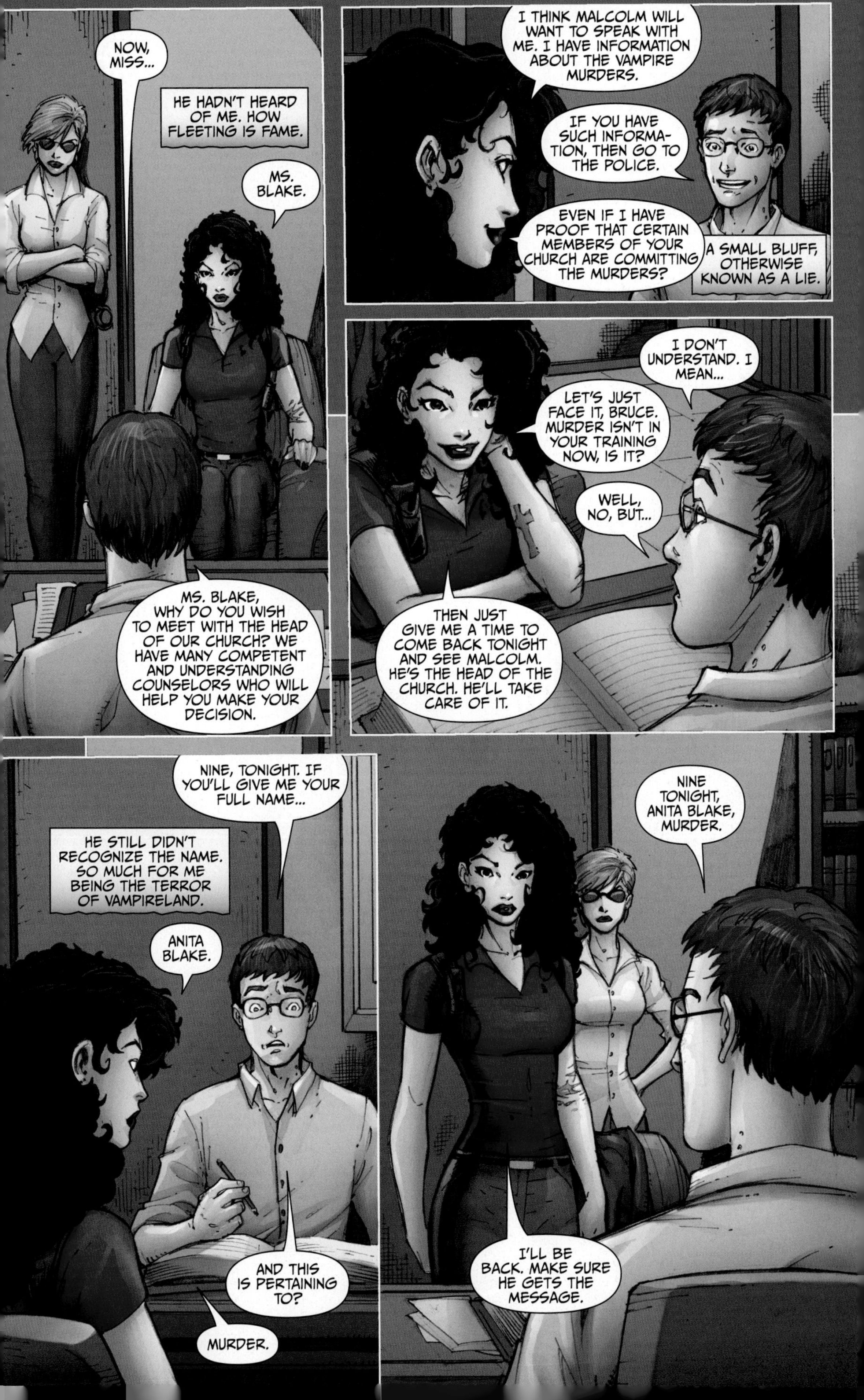
NOW, MISS...
HE HADN'T HEARD OF ME. HOW FLEETING IS FAME.
MS. BLAKE.
MS. BLAKE, WHY DO YOU WISH TO MEET WITH THE HEAD OF OUR CHURCH? WE HAVE MANY COMPETENT AND UNDERSTANDING COUNSELORS WHO WILL HELP YOU MAKE YOUR DECISION.
I THINK MALCOLM WILL WANT TO SPEAK WITH ME. I HAVE INFORMATION ABOUT THE VAMPIRE MURDERS.
IF YOU HAVE SUCH INFORMATION, THEN GO TO THE POLICE.
EVEN IF I HAVE PROOF THAT CERTAIN MEMBERS OF YOUR CHURCH ARE COMMITTING THE MURDERS?
A SMALL BLUFF, OTHERWISE KNOWN AS A LIE.
I DON'T UNDERSTAND. I MEAN...
LET'S JUST FACE IT, BRUCE. MURDER ISN'T IN YOUR TRAINING NOW, IS IT?
WELL, NO, BUT...
THEN JUST GIVE ME A TIME TO COME BACK TONIGHT AND SEE MALCOLM. HE'S THE HEAD OF THE CHURCH. HE'LL TAKE CARE OF IT.
NINE, TONIGHT. IF YOU'LL GIVE ME YOUR FULL NAME...
HE STILL DIDN'T RECOGNIZE THE NAME. SO MUCH FOR ME BEING THE TERROR OF VAMPIRELAND.
ANITA BLAKE.
AND THIS IS PERTAINING TO?
MURDER.
NINE TONIGHT, ANITA BLAKE, MURDER.
I'LL BE BACK. MAKE SURE HE GETS THE MESSAGE.

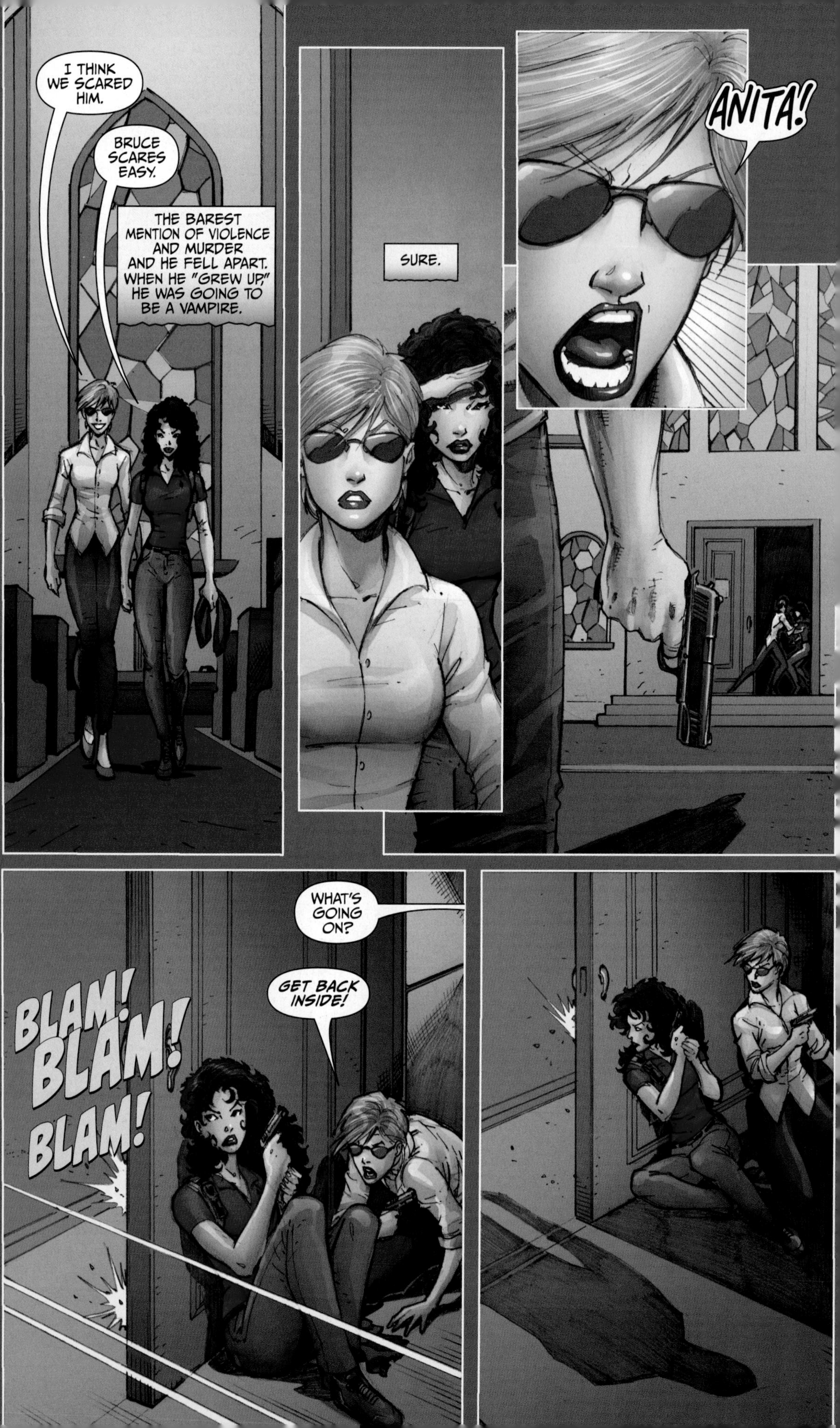
I THINK WE SCARED HIM.
BRUCE SCARES EASY.
THE BAREST MENTION OF VIOLENCE AND MURDER AND HE FELL APART. WHEN HE "GREW UP," HE WAS GOING TO BE A VAMPIRE.
SURE.
ANITA!
BLAM! BLAM! BLAM!
WHAT'S GOING ON?
GET BACK INSIDE!

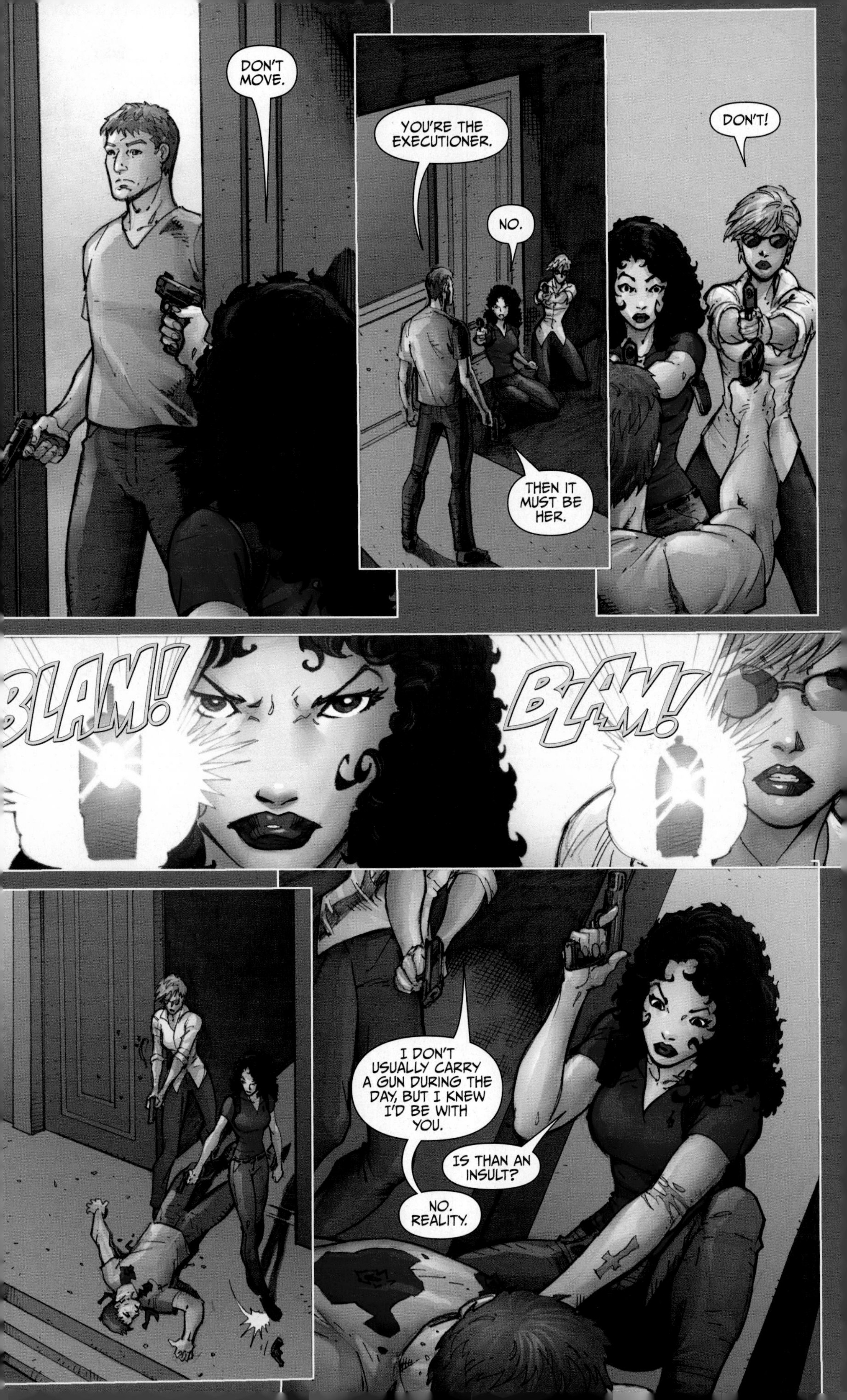
DON'T MOVE.
YOU'RE THE EXECUTIONER.
NO.
THEN IT MUST BE HER.
DON'T!
BLAM!
BLAM!
I DON'T USUALLY CARRY A GUN DURING THE DAY, BUT I KNEW I'D BE WITH YOU.
IS THAN AN INSULT?
NO. REALITY.

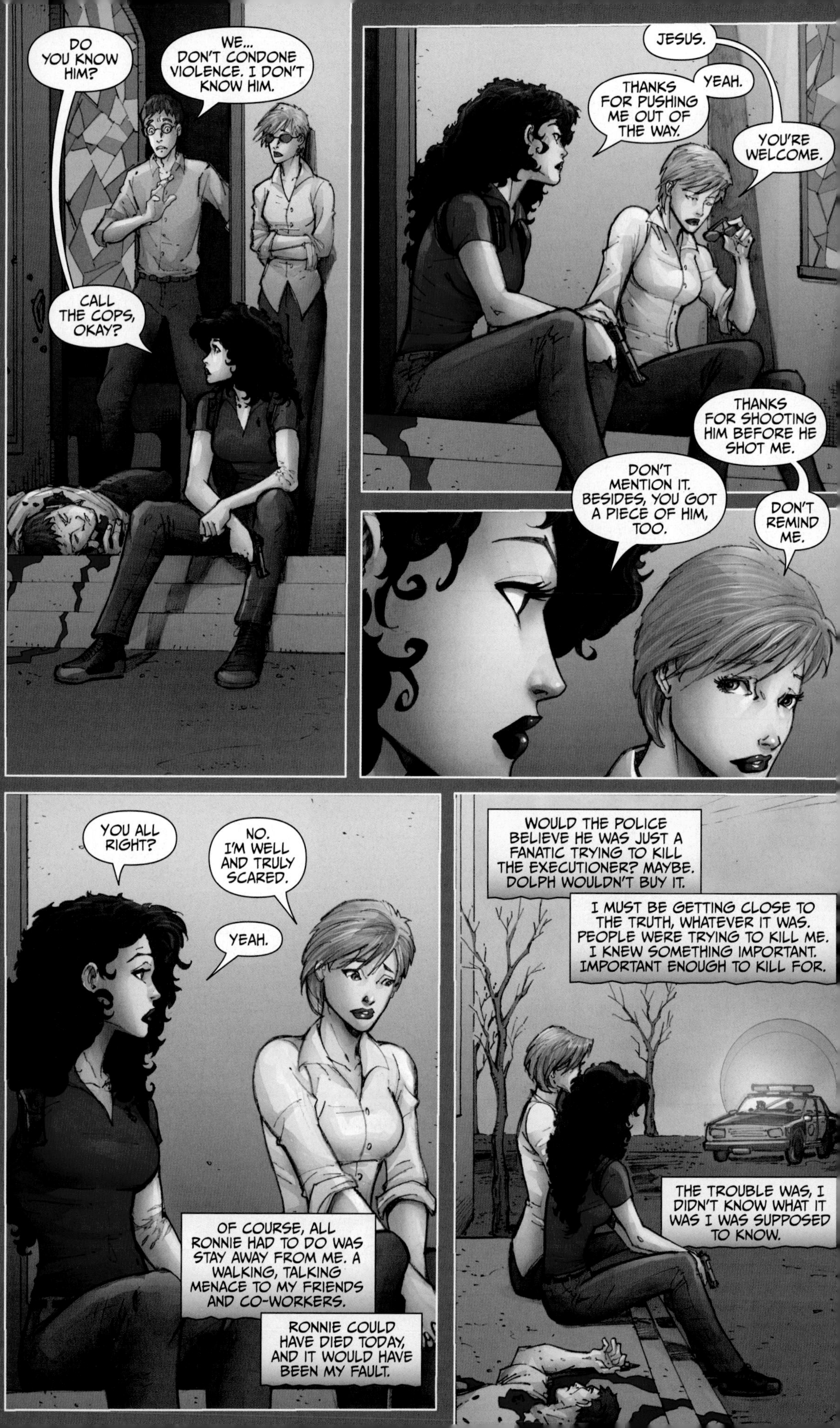
DO YOU KNOW HIM?
WE... DON'T CONDONE VIOLENCE. I DON'T KNOW HIM.
CALL THE COPS, OKAY?
JESUS.
THANKS FOR PUSHING ME OUT OF THE WAY.
YEAH.
YOU'RE WELCOME.
THANKS FOR SHOOTING HIM BEFORE HE SHOT ME.
DON'T MENTION IT. BESIDES, YOU GOT A PIECE OF HIM, TOO.
DON'T REMIND ME.
YOU ALL RIGHT?
NO. I'M WELL AND TRULY SCARED.
YEAH.
OF COURSE, ALL RONNIE HAD TO DO WAS STAY AWAY FROM ME. A WALKING, TALKING MENACE TO MY FRIENDS AND CO-WORKERS.
RONNIE COULD HAVE DIED TODAY, AND IT WOULD HAVE BEEN MY FAULT.
WOULD THE POLICE BELIEVE HE WAS JUST A FANATIC TRYING TO KILL THE EXECUTIONER? MAYBE. DOLPH WOULDN'T BUY IT.
I MUST BE GETTING CLOSE TO THE TRUTH, WHATEVER IT WAS. PEOPLE WERE TRYING TO KILL ME. I KNEW SOMETHING IMPORTANT. IMPORTANT ENOUGH TO KILL FOR.
THE TROUBLE WAS, I DIDN'T KNOW WHAT IT WAS I WAS SUPPOSED TO KNOW.

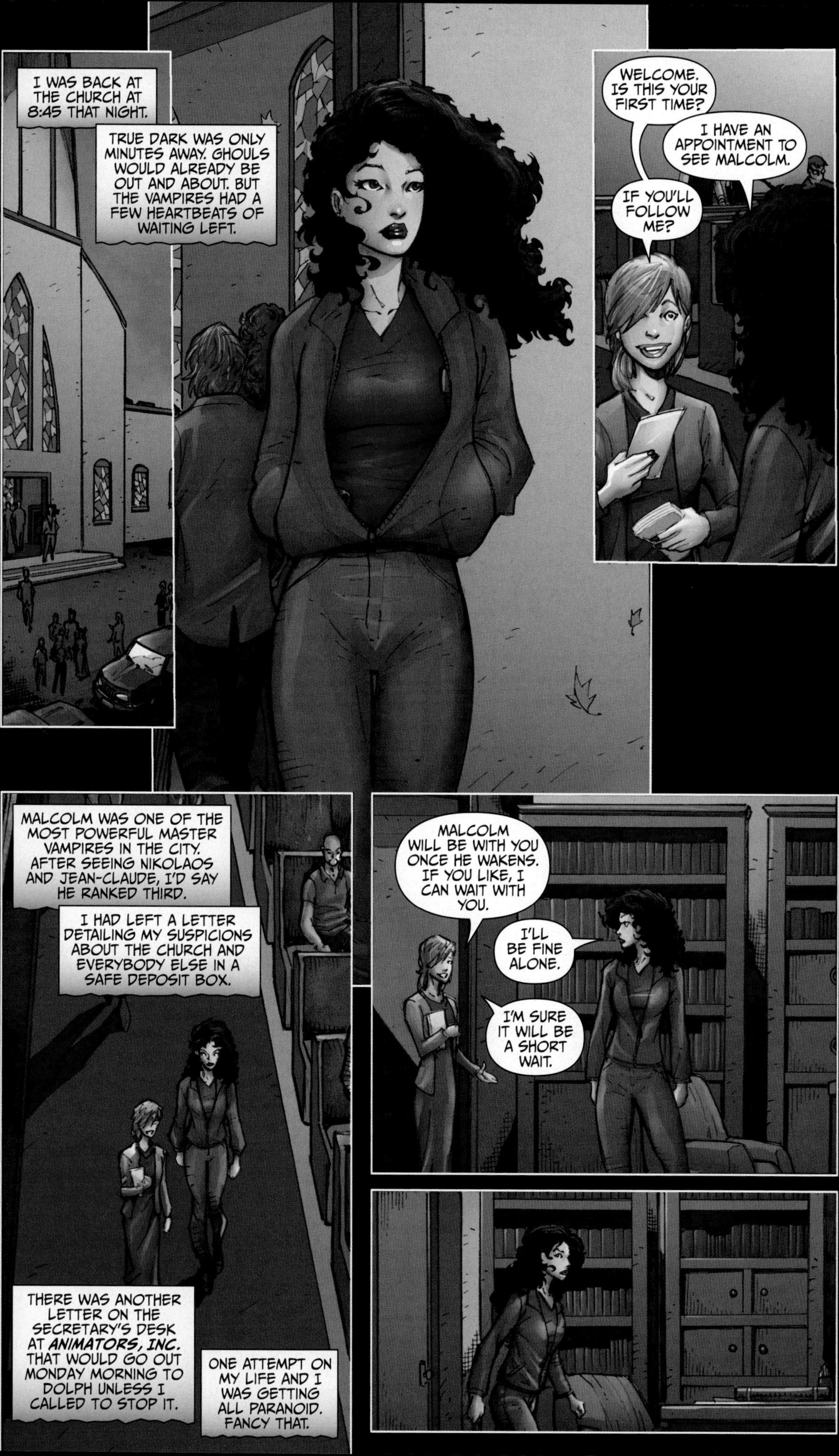
I WAS BACK AT THE CHURCH AT 8:45 THAT NIGHT.
TRUE DARK WAS ONLY MINUTES AWAY. GHOULS WOULD ALREADY BE OUT AND ABOUT. BUT THE VAMPIRES HAD A FEW HEARTBEATS OF WAITING LEFT.
WELCOME. IS THIS YOUR FIRST TIME?
I HAVE AN APPOINTMENT TO SEE MALCOLM.
IF YOU'LL FOLLOW ME?
MALCOLM WAS ONE OF THE MOST POWERFUL MASTER VAMPIRES IN THE CITY. AFTER SEEING NIKOLAOS AND JEAN-CLAUDE, I'D SAY HE RANKED THIRD.
I HAD LEFT A LETTER DETAILING MY SUSPICIONS ABOUT THE CHURCH AND EVERYBODY ELSE IN A SAFE DEPOSIT BOX.
THERE WAS ANOTHER LETTER ON THE SECRETARY'S DESK AT ANIMATORS, INC. THAT WOULD GO OUT MONDAY MORNING TO DOLPH UNLESS I CALLED TO STOP IT.
ONE ATTEMPT ON MY LIFE AND I WAS GETTING ALL PARANOID. FANCY THAT.
MALCOLM WILL BE WITH YOU ONCE HE WAKENS. IF YOU LIKE, I CAN WAIT WITH YOU.
I'LL BE FINE ALONE.
I'M SURE IT WILL BE A SHORT WAIT.

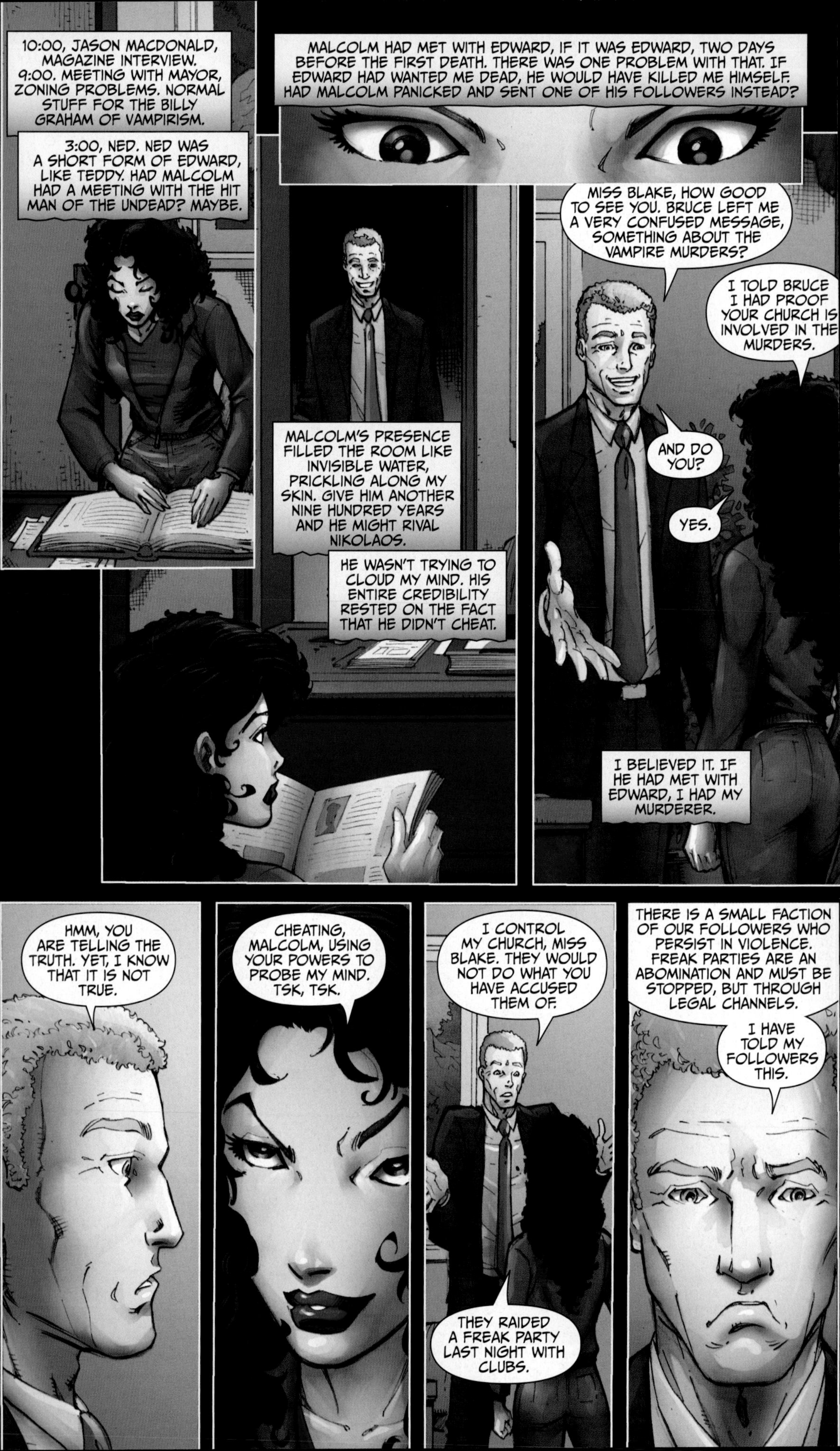

10:00, JASON MACDONALD, MAGAZINE INTERVIEW. 9:00. MEETING WITH MAYOR, ZONING PROBLEMS. NORMAL STUFF FOR THE BILLY GRAHAM OF VAMPIRISM.
3:00, NED. NED WAS A SHORT FORM OF EDWARD, LIKE TEDDY. HAD MALCOLM HAD A MEETING WITH THE HIT MAN OF THE UNDEAD? MAYBE.
MALCOLM HAD MET WITH EDWARD, IF IT WAS EDWARD, TWO DAYS BEFORE THE FIRST DEATH. THERE WAS ONE PROBLEM WITH THAT. IF EDWARD HAD WANTED ME DEAD, HE WOULD HAVE KILLED ME HIMSELF. HAD MALCOLM PANICKED AND SENT ONE OF HIS FOLLOWERS INSTEAD?
MALCOLM'S PRESENCE FILLED THE ROOM LIKE INVISIBLE WATER, PRICKLING ALONG MY SKIN. GIVE HIM ANOTHER NINE HUNDRED YEARS AND HE MIGHT RIVAL NIKOLAOS.
HE WASN'T TRYING TO CLOUD MY MIND. HIS ENTIRE CREDIBILITY RESTED ON THE FACT THAT HE DIDN'T CHEAT.
MISS BLAKE, HOW GOOD TO SEE YOU. BRUCE LEFT ME A VERY CONFUSED MESSAGE, SOMETHING ABOUT THE VAMPIRE MURDERS?
I TOLD BRUCE I HAD PROOF YOUR CHURCH IS INVOLVED IN THE MURDERS.
AND DO YOU?
YES.
I BELIEVED IT. IF HE HAD MET WITH EDWARD, I HAD MY MURDERER.
HMM, YOU ARE TELLING THE TRUTH. YET, I KNOW THAT IT IS NOT TRUE.
CHEATING, MALCOLM, USING YOUR POWERS TO PROBE MY MIND. TSK, TSK.
I CONTROL MY CHURCH, MISS BLAKE. THEY WOULD NOT DO WHAT YOU HAVE ACCUSED THEM OF.
THEY RAIDED A FREAK PARTY LAST NIGHT WITH CLUBS.
THERE IS A SMALL FACTION OF OUR FOLLOWERS WHO PERSIST IN VIOLENCE. FREAK PARTIES ARE AN ABOMINATION AND MUST BE STOPPED, BUT THROUGH LEGAL CHANNELS.
I HAVE TOLD MY FOLLOWERS THIS.

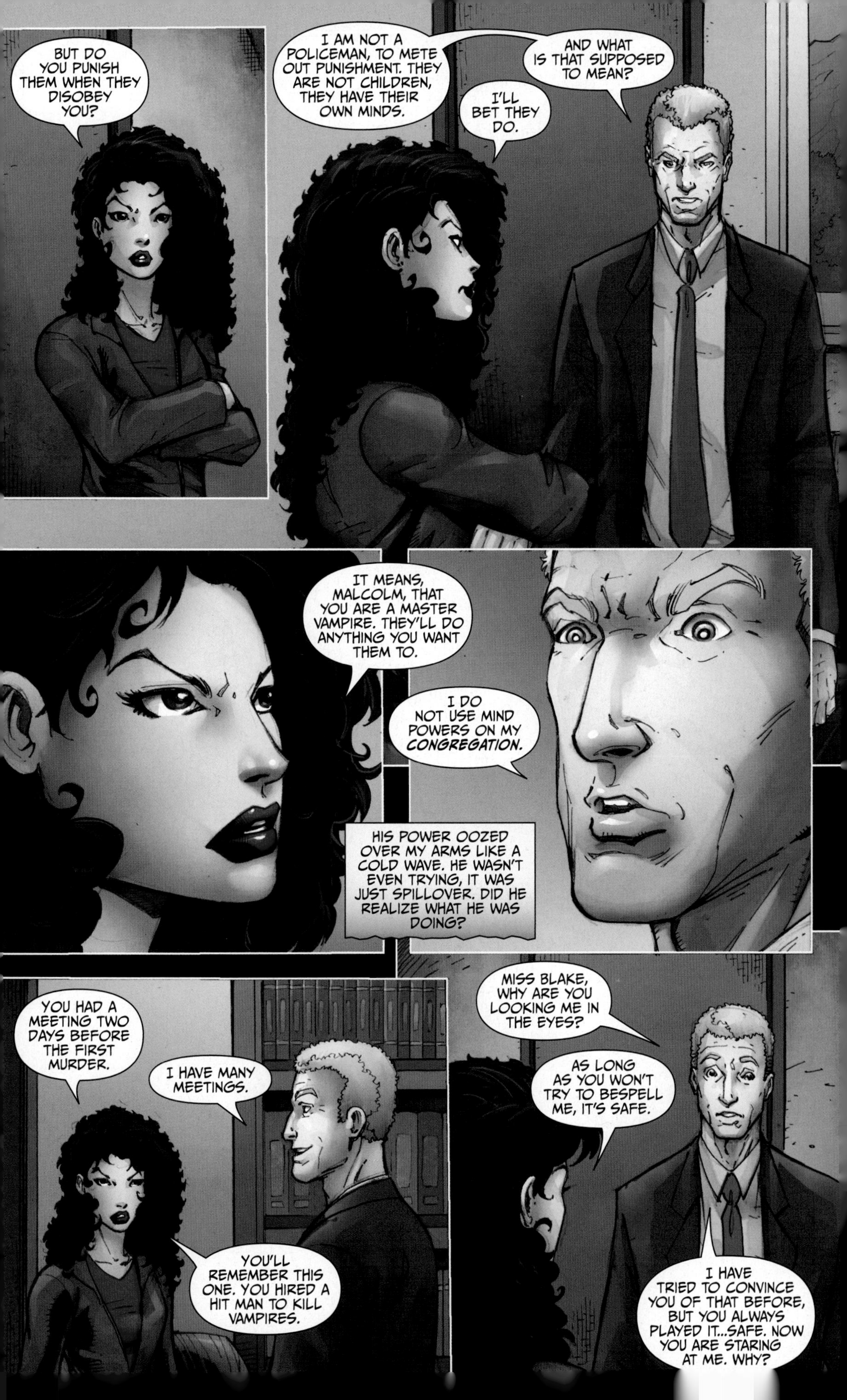
BUT DO YOU PUNISH THEM WHEN THEY DISOBEY YOU?
I AM NOT A POLICEMAN, TO METE OUT PUNISHMENT. THEY ARE NOT CHILDREN, THEY HAVE THEIR OWN MINDS.
I'LL BET THEY DO.
AND WHAT IS THAT SUPPOSED TO MEAN?
IT MEANS, MALCOLM, THAT YOU ARE A MASTER VAMPIRE. THEY'LL DO ANYTHING YOU WANT THEM TO.
I DO NOT USE MIND POWERS ON MY *CONGREGATION.*
HIS POWER OOZED OVER MY ARMS LIKE A COLD WAVE. HE WASN'T EVEN TRYING, IT WAS JUST SPILLOVER. DID HE REALIZE WHAT HE WAS DOING?
YOU HAD A MEETING TWO DAYS BEFORE THE FIRST MURDER.
I HAVE MANY MEETINGS.
YOU'LL REMEMBER THIS ONE. YOU HIRED A HIT MAN TO KILL VAMPIRES.
MISS BLAKE, WHY ARE YOU LOOKING ME IN THE EYES?
AS LONG AS YOU WON'T TRY TO BESPELL ME, IT'S SAFE.
I HAVE TRIED TO CONVINCE YOU OF THAT BEFORE, BUT YOU ALWAYS PLAYED IT...SAFE. NOW YOU ARE STARING AT ME. WHY?

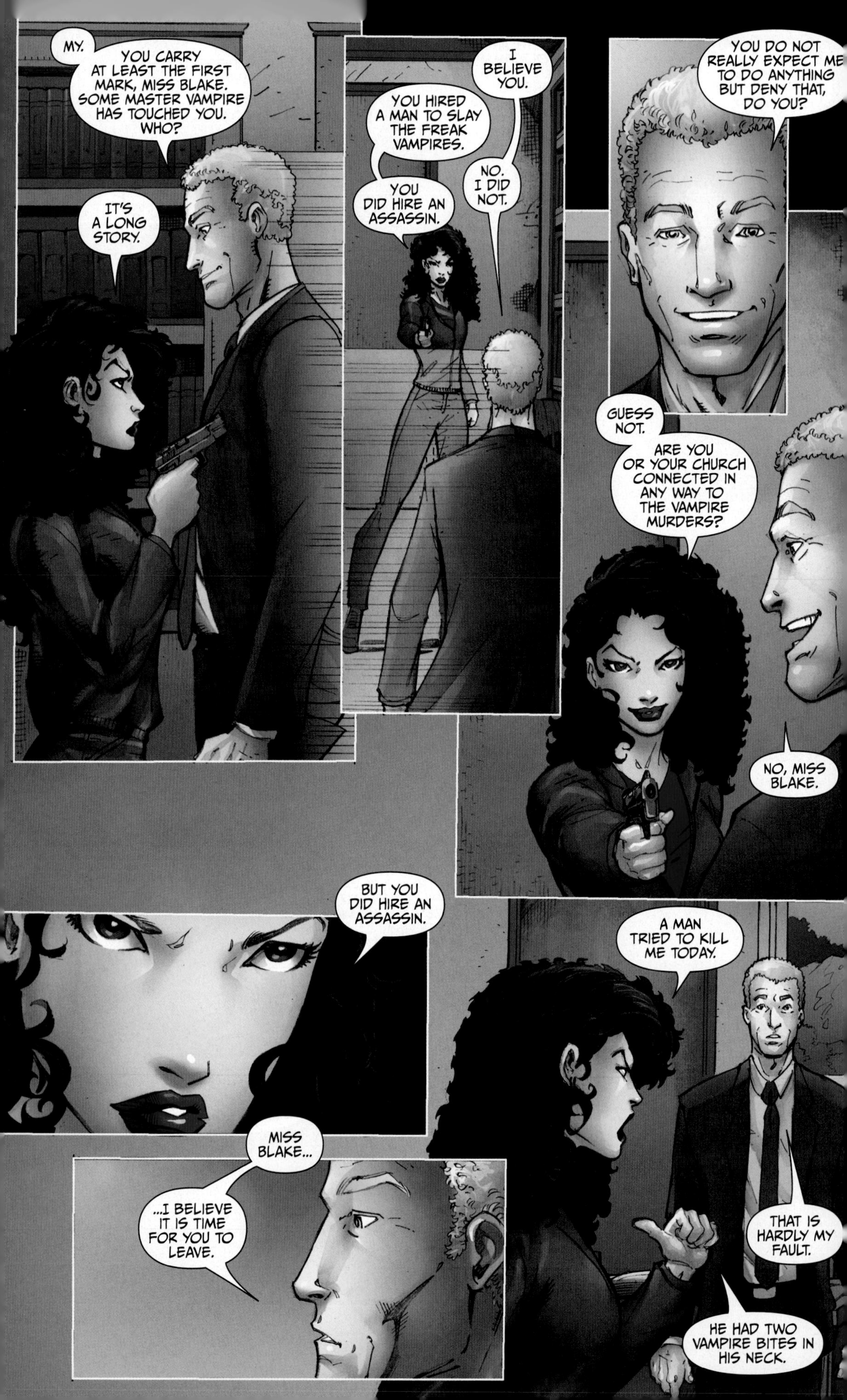
MY.
YOU CARRY AT LEAST THE FIRST MARK, MISS BLAKE. SOME MASTER VAMPIRE HAS TOUCHED YOU. WHO?
IT'S A LONG STORY.
YOU HIRED A MAN TO SLAY THE FREAK VAMPIRES.
YOU DID HIRE AN ASSASSIN.
I BELIEVE YOU.
NO. I DID NOT.
YOU DO NOT REALLY EXPECT ME TO DO ANYTHING BUT DENY THAT, DO YOU?
GUESS NOT.
ARE YOU OR YOUR CHURCH CONNECTED IN ANY WAY TO THE VAMPIRE MURDERS?
NO, MISS BLAKE.
BUT YOU DID HIRE AN ASSASSIN.
A MAN TRIED TO KILL ME TODAY.
THAT IS HARDLY MY FAULT.
HE HAD TWO VAMPIRE BITES IN HIS NECK.
MISS BLAKE...
...I BELIEVE IT IS TIME FOR YOU TO LEAVE.

HE WAS WAITING FOR ME OUTSIDE YOUR CHURCH. I WAS FORCED TO KILL HIM ON YOUR STEPS.

I WILL LOOK INTO IT, MISS BLAKE. IF HE WAS A MEMBER OF OUR CHURCH, WE OWE YOU AN EXTREME APOLOGY.

WHAT COULD I SAY TO THAT? THANK YOU?

I KNOW YOU HIRED A HIT MAN, MALCOLM. I THINK YOU ARE BEHIND THE VAMPIRE MURDERS. YOUR HANDS MAY NOT HAVE SPILLED THE BLOOD, BUT IT WAS DONE WITH YOUR APPROVAL.

PLEASE GO NOW, MISS BLAKE.

SURE I'LL GO, BUT I WON'T GO AWAY.

DO YOU KNOW WHAT IT MEANS TO BE MARKED BY A MASTER VAMPIRE?

NO.

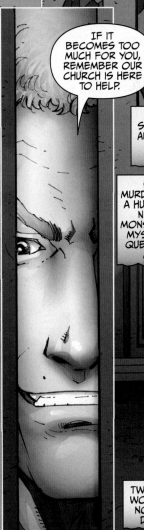

IF IT BECOMES TOO MUCH FOR YOU, REMEMBER OUR CHURCH IS HERE TO HELP.

WHAT IS THAT SUPPOSED TO MEAN? ANOTHER QUESTION I DIDN'T HAVE THE ANSWER TO.

EDWARD WAS MY MURDERER. COULD I TURN A HUMAN BEING OVER TO NIKOLAOS AND THE MONSTERS, EVEN TO SAVE MYSELF? YET ANOTHER QUESTION I DIDN'T HAVE AN ANSWER FOR.

TWO DAYS AGO I WOULD HAVE SAID NO. NOW I JUST DIDN'T KNOW.

I DIDN'T WANT TO GO BACK TO MY APARTMENT. EDWARD WOULD BE COMING TONIGHT. IF I DIDN'T TELL HIM WHERE NIKOLAOS SLEPT IN DAYLIGHT, HE'D FORCE THE INFORMATION FROM ME. COMPLICATED.

AND NOW I THOUGHT HE WAS MY MURDERER. VERY COMPLICATED.

THE ONLY THING I COULD DO WAS AVOID HIM. THAT WOULDN'T WORK FOREVER, BUT MAYBE I'D HAVE A BRAINSTORM AND FIGURE IT ALL OUT.

ALL RIGHT, THERE WASN'T MUCH CHANCE OF THAT, BUT ONE COULD ALWAYS HOPE.

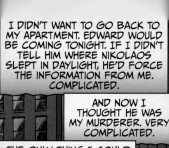

MAYBE RONNIE WOULD HAVE A MESSAGE FOR ME. SOMETHING HELPFUL.

MAYBE I COULD AVOID EDWARD ALL NIGHT IF I SLEPT IN A HOTEL. IF I'D HAD ANY SOLID PROOF AT ALL, I'D HAVE CALLED THE POLICE.

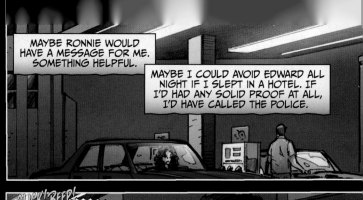

CLICK! BEEP!

ANITA, IT'S WILLIE! THEY'VE GOT PHILLIP! THEY'RE HURTIN' HIM BAD! YOU GOTTA COME--

CLICK! BEEP!

THIS IS NIKOLAOS. YOU'VE HEARD WILLIE'S MESSAGE. COME AND GET IT, ANIMATOR. I DON'T REALLY HAVE TO THREATEN YOUR PRETTY LOVER, DO I?

CLICK! ANITA, TELL ME WHERE YOU ARE. I CAN HELP YOU.

GOD HELP ME, THEN.

WHAM!

I'M THE CLOSEST THING YOU'VE GOT TO AN ALLY.

DAMMIT!

WHAT ARE YOU LOOKING AT?!

PHILLIP WAS BEING HURT BECAUSE OF ME. JUST LIKE CATHERINE AND RONNIE. NO MORE. NO FREAKING MORE.

I WAS GOING TO GET PHILLIP, SAVE HIM ANY WAY I COULD. THEN I WAS TURNING THE WHOLE BLASTED THING OVER TO THE POLICE. I WAS BAILING OUT BEFORE MORE PEOPLE GOT HURT.

I WAS GOING BACK DOWN THOSE STAIRS INTO THE MASTER'S LAIR, AT NIGHT. THE ANGER WAS FADING IN A WASH OF COLD, SKIN-SHIVERING FEAR. I WOULD NOT GO IN THERE AFRAID.

I HELD ONTO MY ANGER WITH EVERYTHING I HAD.

THIS WAS THE CLOSEST I'D COME TO HATE IN A LONG TIME. MOST HATRED IS BASED ON FEAR, ONE WAY OR ANOTHER.

I WRAPPED MYSELF IN ANGER WITH A DASH OF HATE... AND AT THE BOTTOM OF IT ALL WAS AN ICY CENTER OF PURE TERROR.

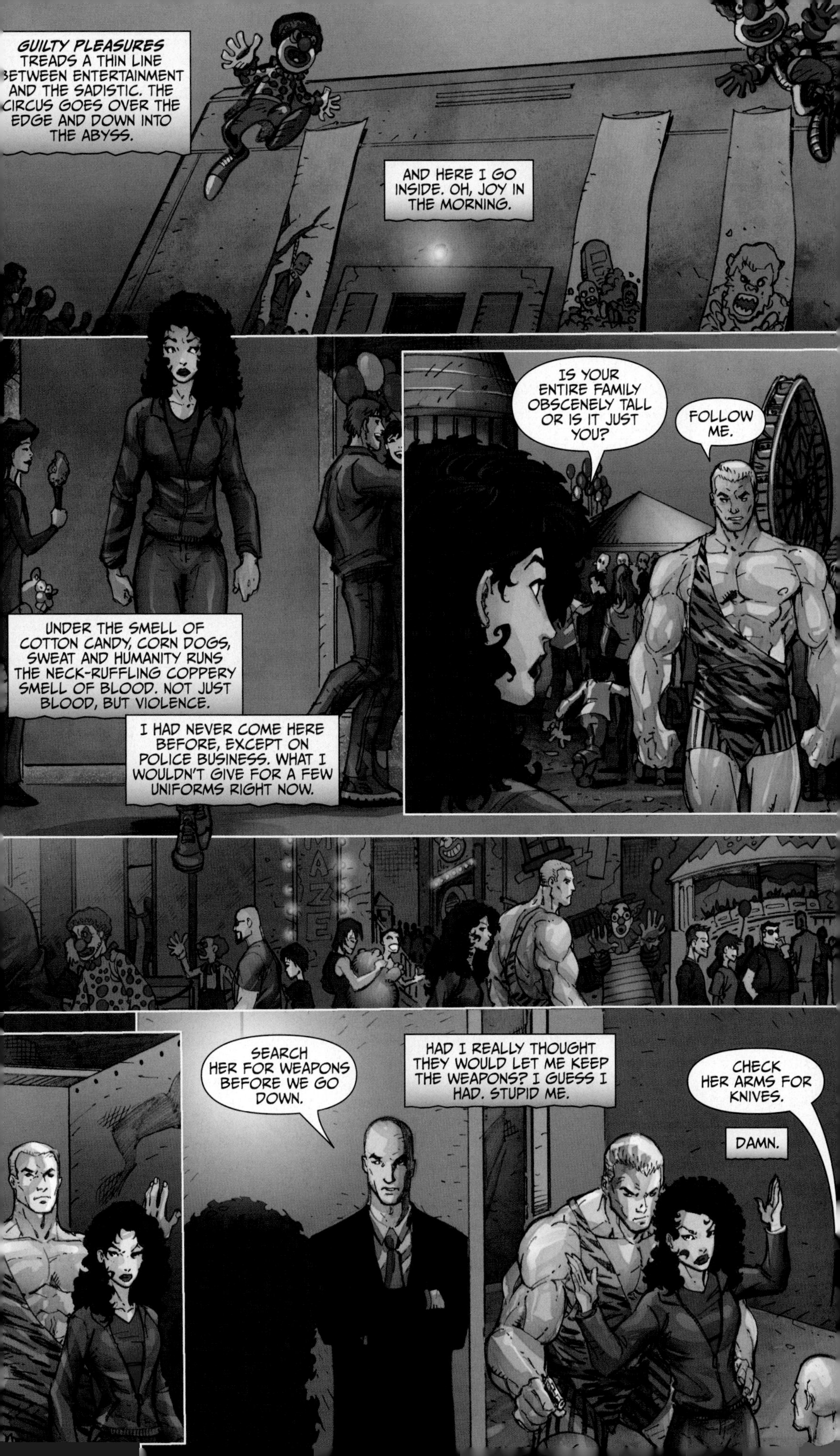
GUILTY PLEASURES TREADS A THIN LINE BETWEEN ENTERTAINMENT AND THE SADISTIC. THE CIRCUS GOES OVER THE EDGE AND DOWN INTO THE ABYSS.
AND HERE I GO INSIDE. OH, JOY IN THE MORNING.
UNDER THE SMELL OF COTTON CANDY, CORN DOGS, SWEAT AND HUMANITY RUNS THE NECK-RUFFLING COPPERY SMELL OF BLOOD. NOT JUST BLOOD, BUT VIOLENCE.
I HAD NEVER COME HERE BEFORE, EXCEPT ON POLICE BUSINESS. WHAT I WOULDN'T GIVE FOR A FEW UNIFORMS RIGHT NOW.
IS YOUR ENTIRE FAMILY OBSCENELY TALL OR IS IT JUST YOU?
FOLLOW ME.
SEARCH HER FOR WEAPONS BEFORE WE GO DOWN.
HAD I REALLY THOUGHT THEY WOULD LET ME KEEP THE WEAPONS? I GUESS I HAD. STUPID ME.
CHECK HER ARMS FOR KNIVES.
DAMN.

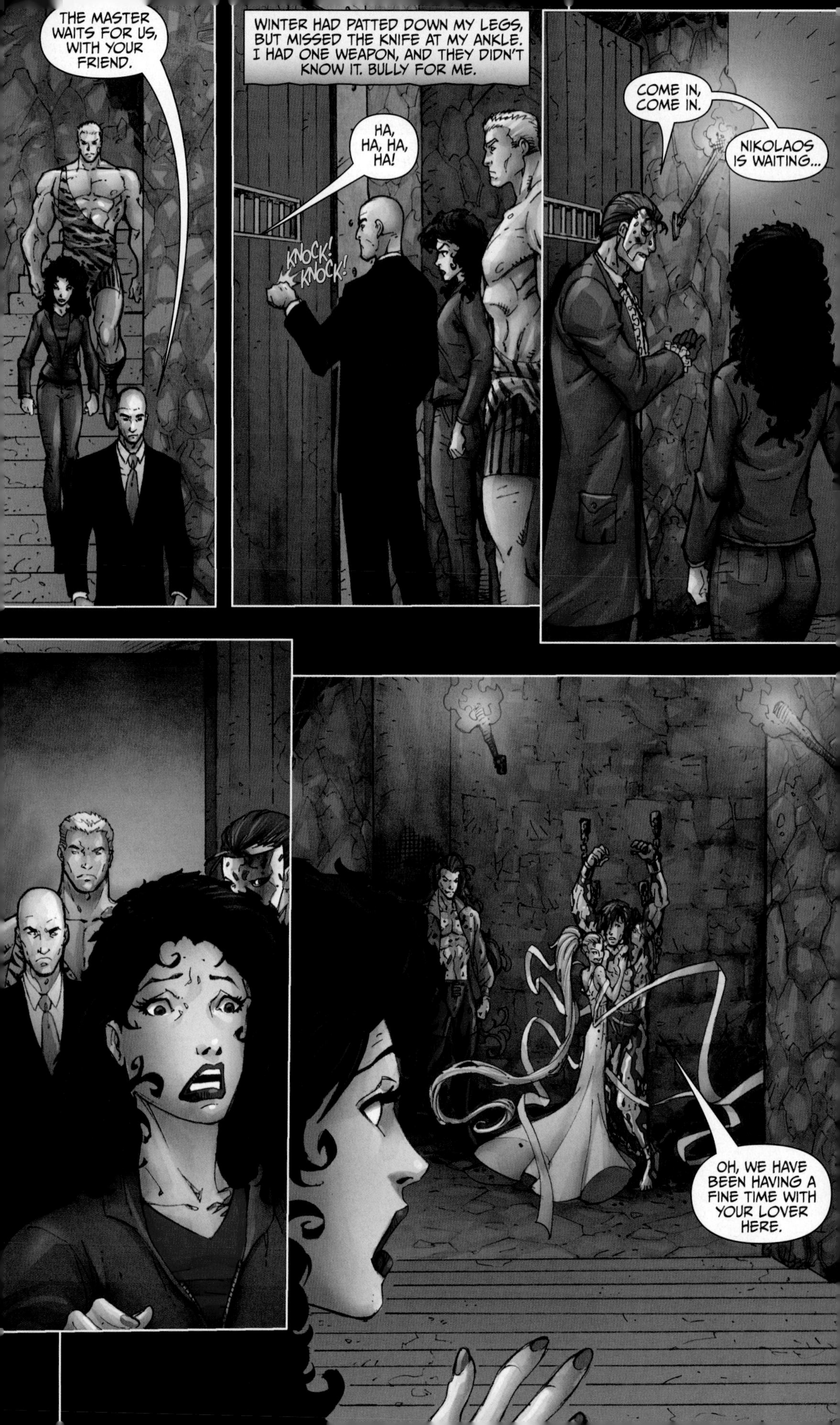
THE MASTER WAITS FOR US, WITH YOUR FRIEND.
WINTER HAD PATTED DOWN MY LEGS, BUT MISSED THE KNIFE AT MY ANKLE. I HAD ONE WEAPON, AND THEY DIDN'T KNOW IT. BULLY FOR ME.
HA, HA, HA, HA!
KNOCK! KNOCK!
COME IN, COME IN.
NIKOLAOS IS WAITING...
OH, WE HAVE BEEN HAVING A FINE TIME WITH YOUR LOVER HERE.

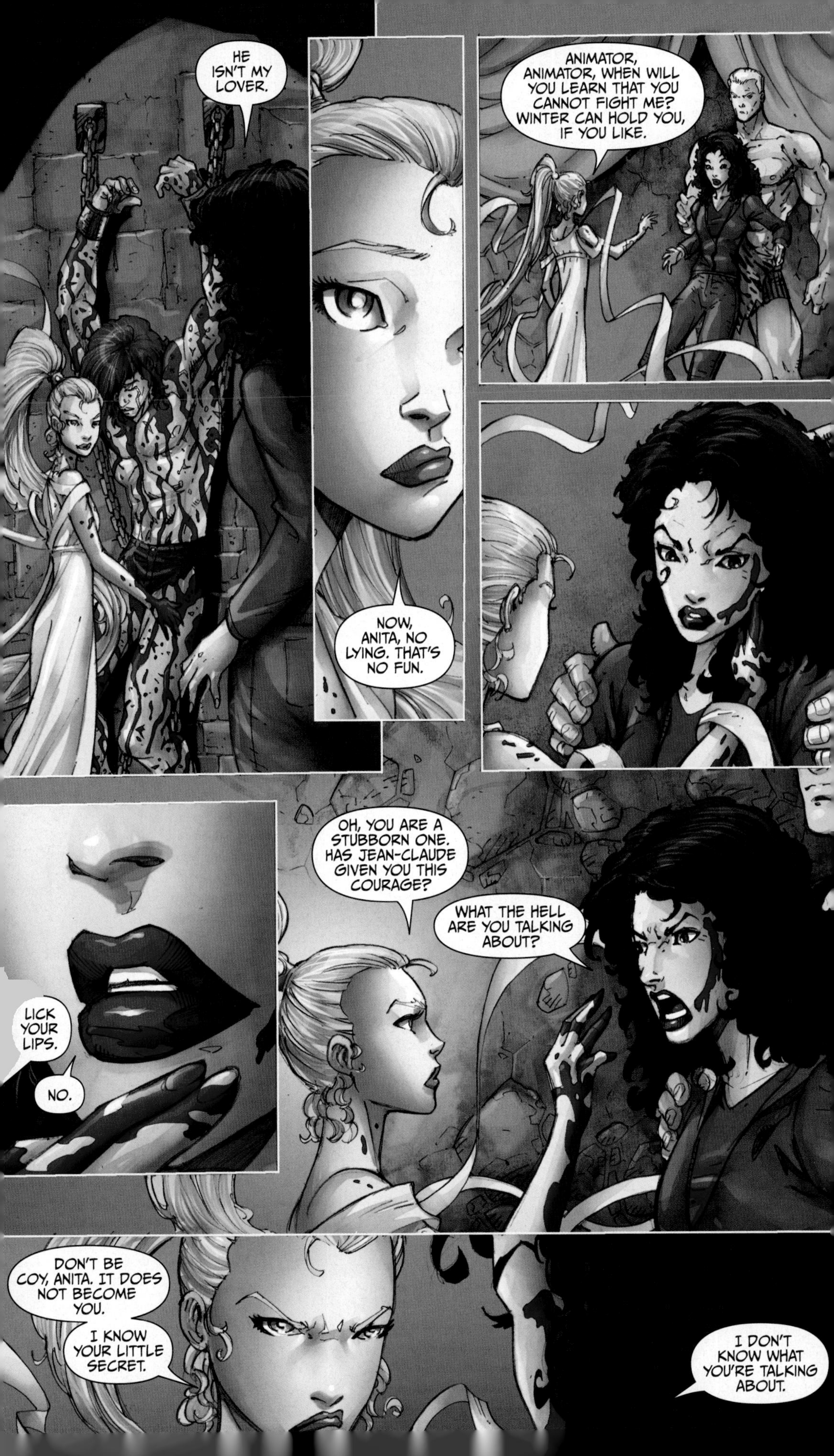
HE ISN'T MY LOVER.
NOW, ANITA, NO LYING. THAT'S NO FUN.
ANIMATOR, ANIMATOR, WHEN WILL YOU LEARN THAT YOU CANNOT FIGHT ME? WINTER CAN HOLD YOU, IF YOU LIKE.
LICK YOUR LIPS.
NO.
OH, YOU ARE A STUBBORN ONE. HAS JEAN-CLAUDE GIVEN YOU THIS COURAGE?
WHAT THE HELL ARE YOU TALKING ABOUT?
DON'T BE COY, ANITA. IT DOES NOT BECOME YOU.
I KNOW YOUR LITTLE SECRET.
I DON'T KNOW WHAT YOU'RE TALKING ABOUT.

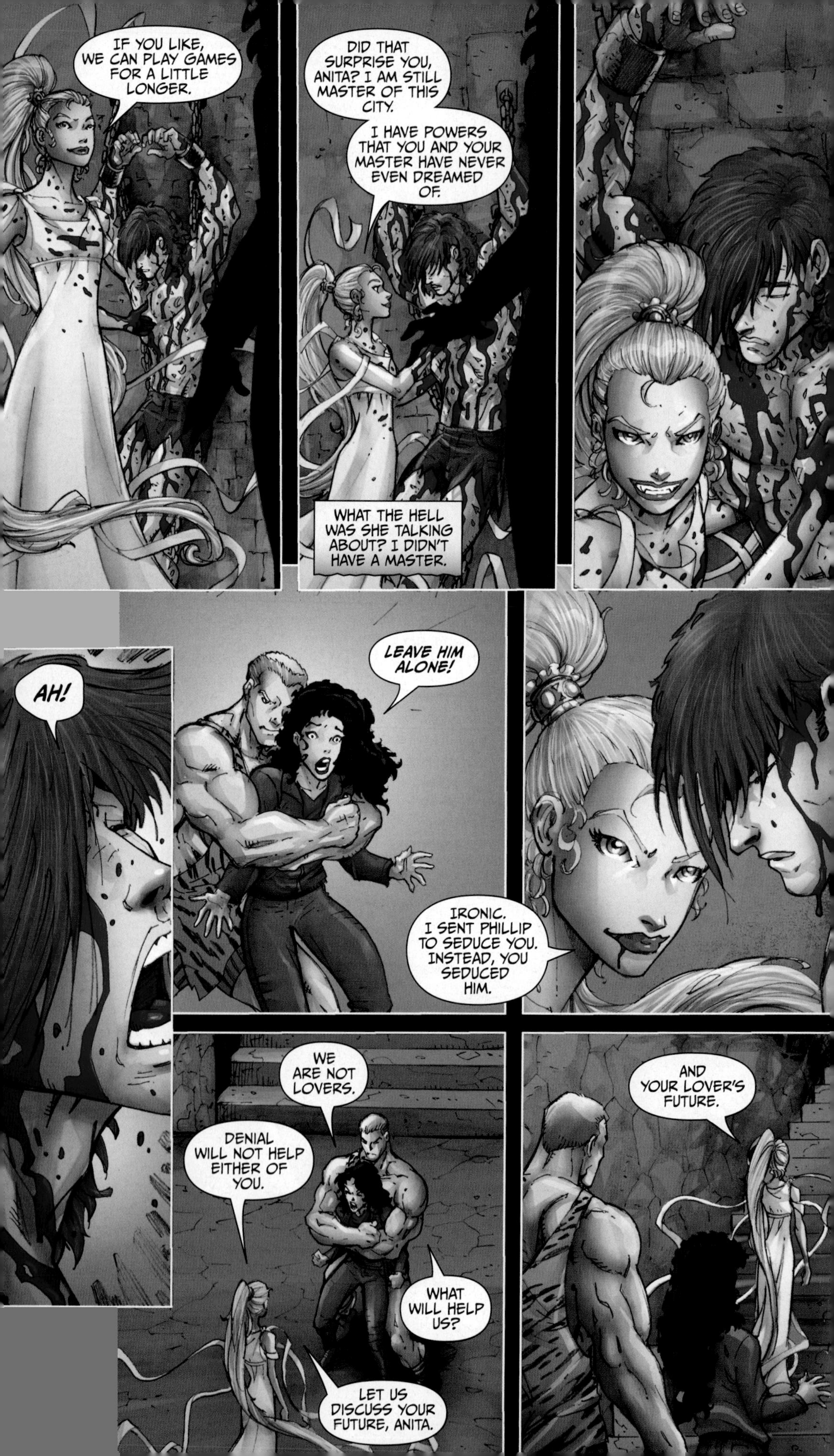
IF YOU LIKE, WE CAN PLAY GAMES FOR A LITTLE LONGER.
DID THAT SURPRISE YOU, ANITA? I AM STILL MASTER OF THIS CITY.
I HAVE POWERS THAT YOU AND YOUR MASTER HAVE NEVER EVEN DREAMED OF.
WHAT THE HELL WAS SHE TALKING ABOUT? I DIDN'T HAVE A MASTER.
AH!
LEAVE HIM ALONE!
IRONIC. I SENT PHILLIP TO SEDUCE YOU. INSTEAD, YOU SEDUCED HIM.
WE ARE NOT LOVERS.
DENIAL WILL NOT HELP EITHER OF YOU.
WHAT WILL HELP US?
LET US DISCUSS YOUR FUTURE, ANITA.
AND YOUR LOVER'S FUTURE.

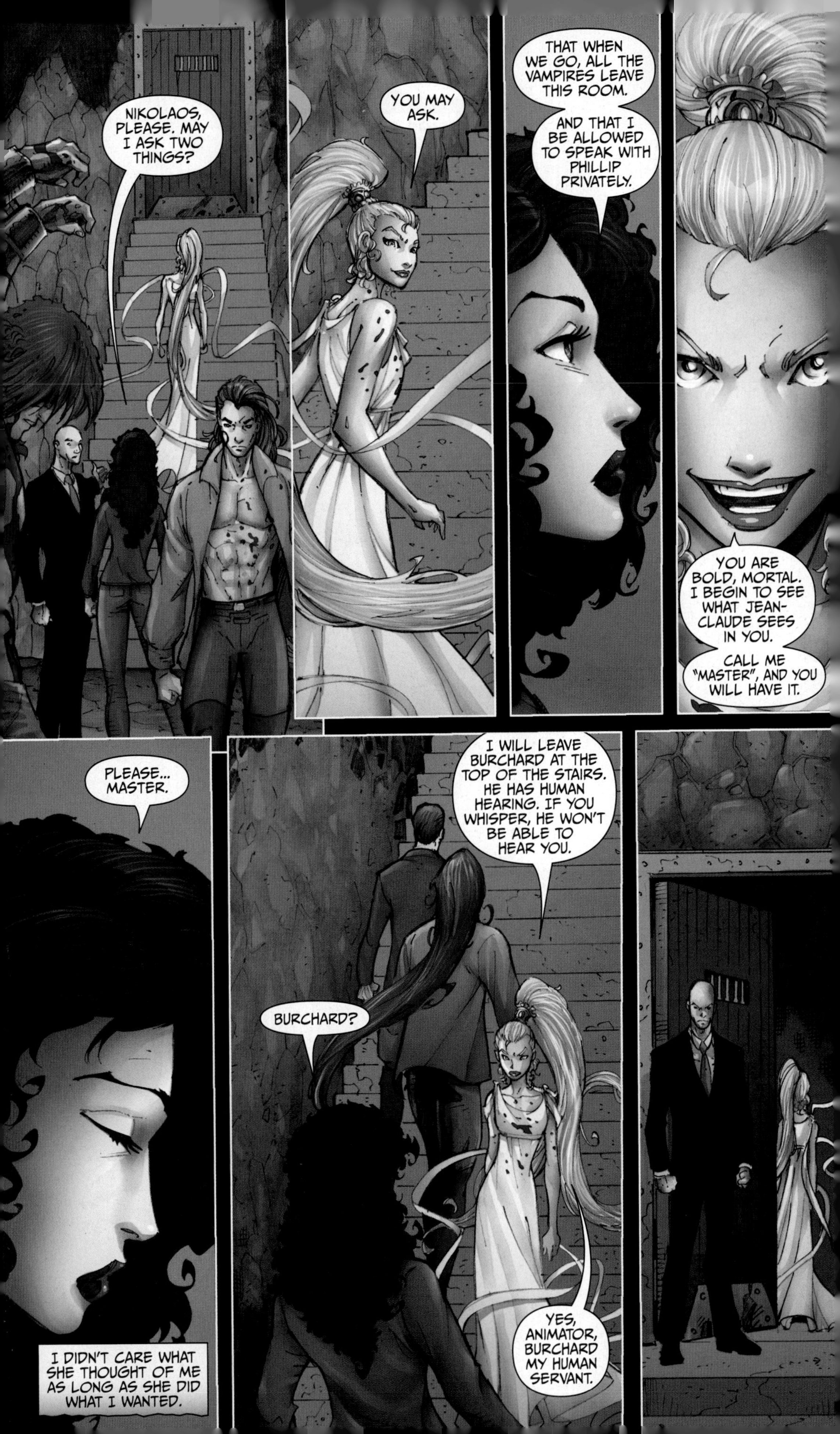
NIKOLAOS, PLEASE. MAY I ASK TWO THINGS?
YOU MAY ASK.
THAT WHEN WE GO, ALL THE VAMPIRES LEAVE THIS ROOM.
AND THAT I BE ALLOWED TO SPEAK WITH PHILLIP PRIVATELY.
YOU ARE BOLD, MORTAL. I BEGIN TO SEE WHAT JEAN-CLAUDE SEES IN YOU.
CALL ME "MASTER", AND YOU WILL HAVE IT.
PLEASE... MASTER.
I DIDN'T CARE WHAT SHE THOUGHT OF ME AS LONG AS SHE DID WHAT I WANTED.
I WILL LEAVE BURCHARD AT THE TOP OF THE STAIRS. HE HAS HUMAN HEARING. IF YOU WHISPER, HE WON'T BE ABLE TO HEAR YOU.
BURCHARD?
YES, ANIMATOR, BURCHARD MY HUMAN SERVANT.

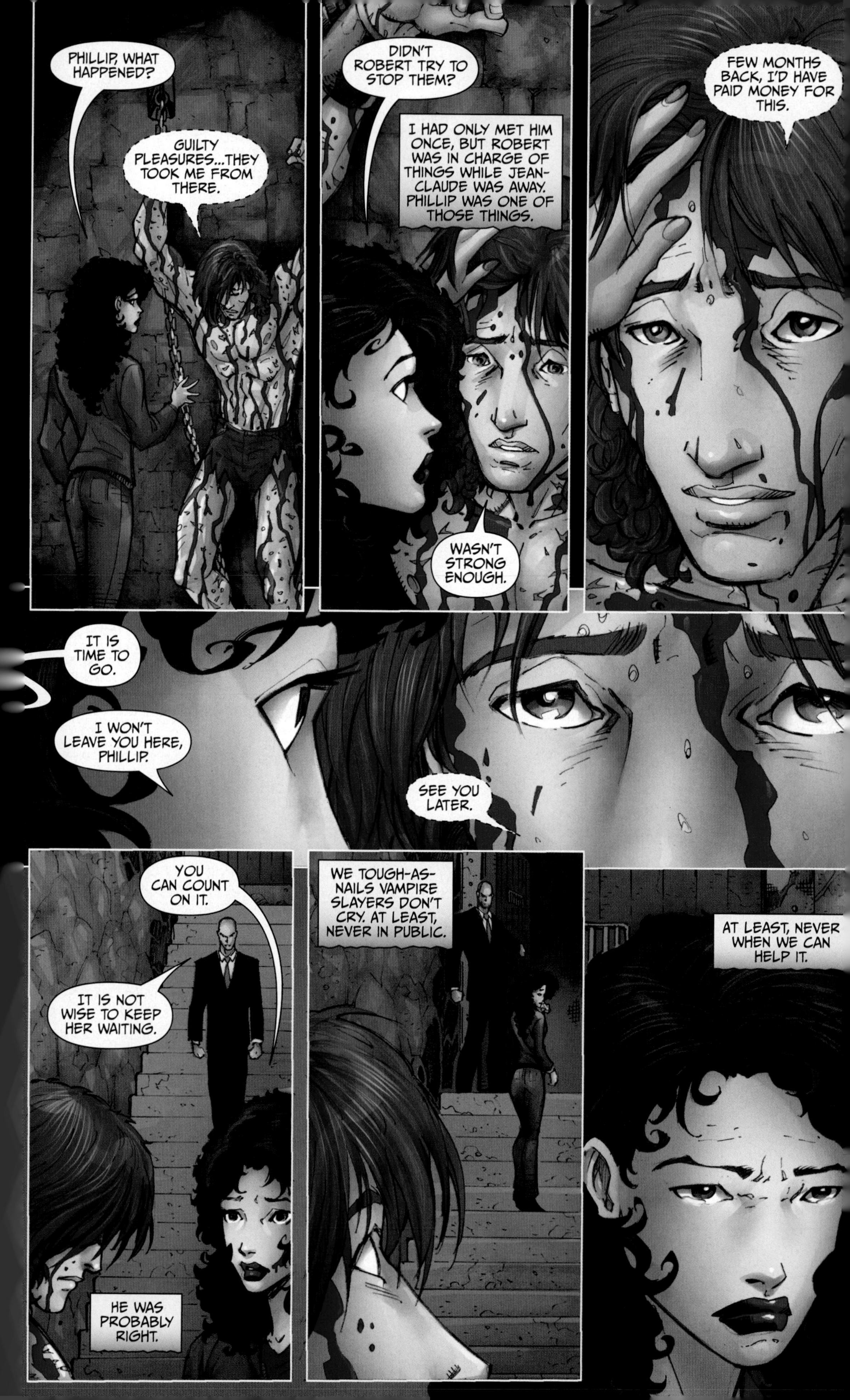
PHILLIP, WHAT HAPPENED?
GUILTY PLEASURES...THEY TOOK ME FROM THERE.
DIDN'T ROBERT TRY TO STOP THEM?
I HAD ONLY MET HIM ONCE, BUT ROBERT WAS IN CHARGE OF THINGS WHILE JEAN-CLAUDE WAS AWAY. PHILLIP WAS ONE OF THOSE THINGS.
WASN'T STRONG ENOUGH.
FEW MONTHS BACK, I'D HAVE PAID MONEY FOR THIS.
IT IS TIME TO GO.
I WON'T LEAVE YOU HERE, PHILLIP.
SEE YOU LATER.
YOU CAN COUNT ON IT.
IT IS NOT WISE TO KEEP HER WAITING.
HE WAS PROBABLY RIGHT.
WE TOUGH-AS-NAILS VAMPIRE SLAYERS DON'T CRY. AT LEAST, NEVER IN PUBLIC.
AT LEAST, NEVER WHEN WE CAN HELP IT.

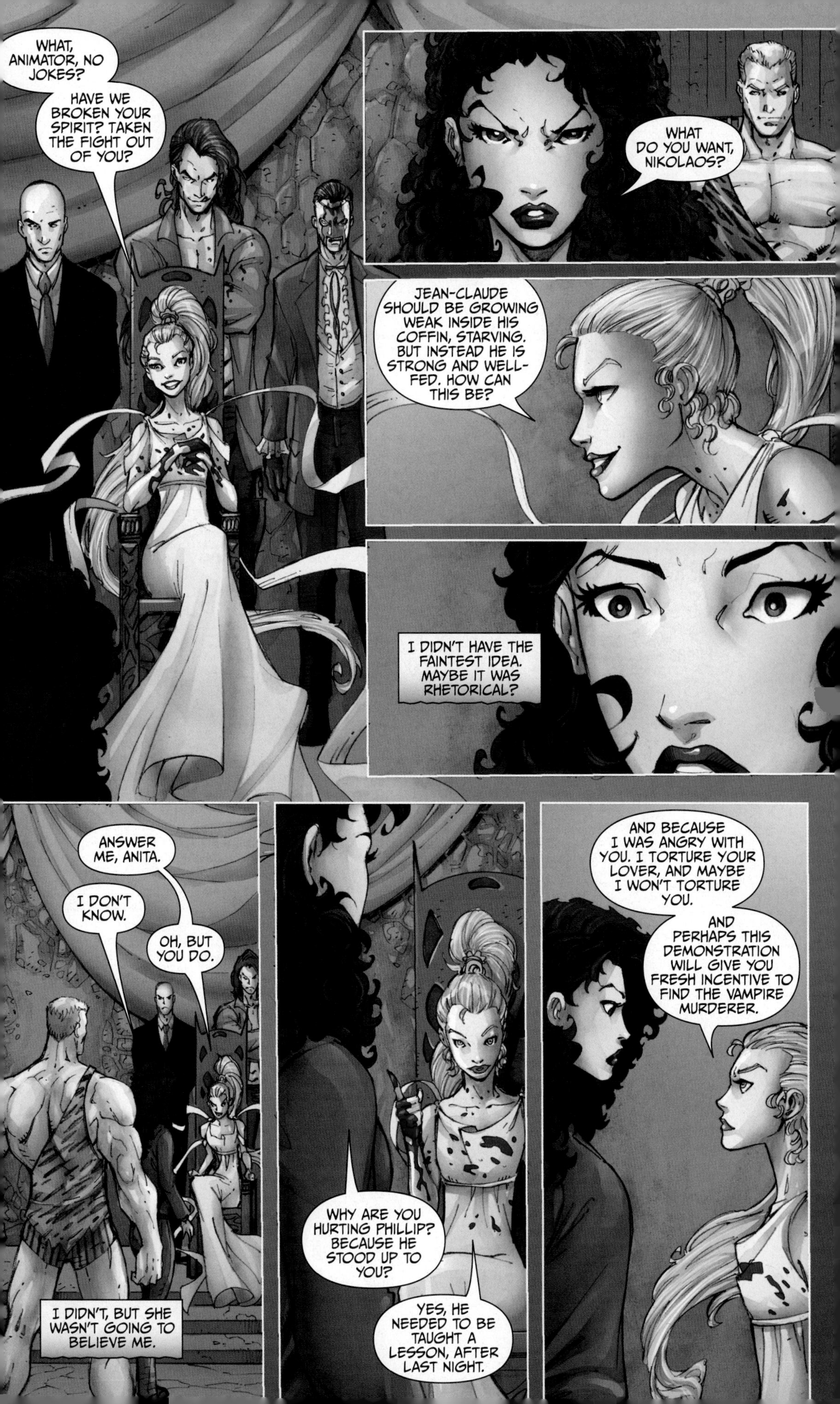
WHAT, ANIMATOR, NO JOKES?
HAVE WE BROKEN YOUR SPIRIT? TAKEN THE FIGHT OUT OF YOU?
WHAT DO YOU WANT, NIKOLAOS?
JEAN-CLAUDE SHOULD BE GROWING WEAK INSIDE HIS COFFIN, STARVING. BUT INSTEAD HE IS STRONG AND WELL-FED. HOW CAN THIS BE?
I DIDN'T HAVE THE FAINTEST IDEA. MAYBE IT WAS RHETORICAL?
ANSWER ME, ANITA.
I DON'T KNOW.
OH, BUT YOU DO.
I DIDN'T, BUT SHE WASN'T GOING TO BELIEVE ME.
WHY ARE YOU HURTING PHILLIP? BECAUSE HE STOOD UP TO YOU?
YES, HE NEEDED TO BE TAUGHT A LESSON, AFTER LAST NIGHT.
AND BECAUSE I WAS ANGRY WITH YOU. I TORTURE YOUR LOVER, AND MAYBE I WON'T TORTURE YOU.
AND PERHAPS THIS DEMONSTRATION WILL GIVE YOU FRESH INCENTIVE TO FIND THE VAMPIRE MURDERER.

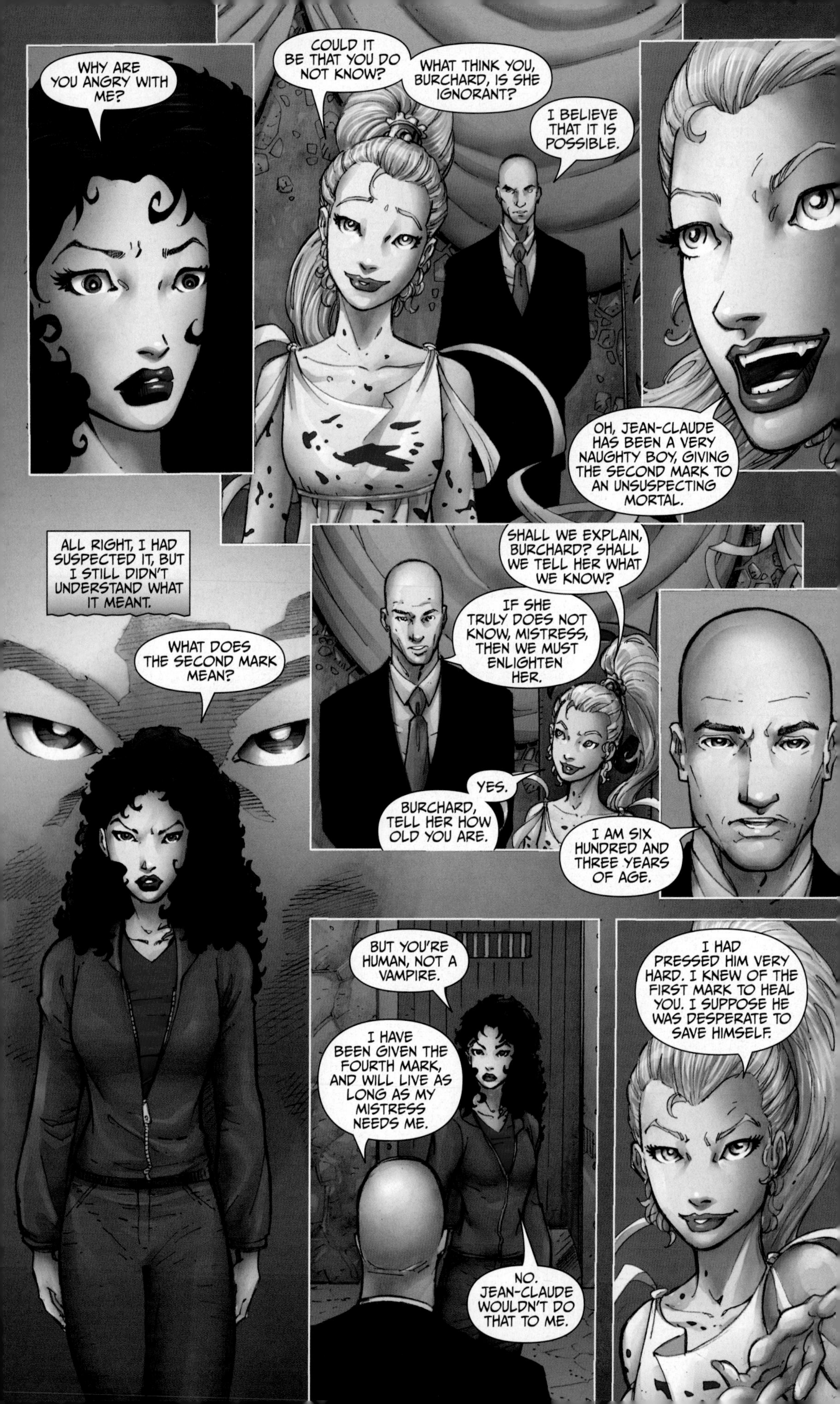

WHY ARE YOU ANGRY WITH ME?
COULD IT BE THAT YOU DO NOT KNOW?
WHAT THINK YOU, BURCHARD, IS SHE IGNORANT?
I BELIEVE THAT IT IS POSSIBLE.
OH, JEAN-CLAUDE HAS BEEN A VERY NAUGHTY BOY, GIVING THE SECOND MARK TO AN UNSUSPECTING MORTAL.
ALL RIGHT, I HAD SUSPECTED IT, BUT I STILL DIDN'T UNDERSTAND WHAT IT MEANT.
WHAT DOES THE SECOND MARK MEAN?
SHALL WE EXPLAIN, BURCHARD? SHALL WE TELL HER WHAT WE KNOW?
IF SHE TRULY DOES NOT KNOW, MISTRESS, THEN WE MUST ENLIGHTEN HER.
YES.
BURCHARD, TELL HER HOW OLD YOU ARE.
I AM SIX HUNDRED AND THREE YEARS OF AGE.
BUT YOU'RE HUMAN, NOT A VAMPIRE.
I HAVE BEEN GIVEN THE FOURTH MARK, AND WILL LIVE AS LONG AS MY MISTRESS NEEDS ME.
NO. JEAN-CLAUDE WOULDN'T DO THAT TO ME.
I HAD PRESSED HIM VERY HARD. I KNEW OF THE FIRST MARK TO HEAL YOU. I SUPPOSE HE WAS DESPERATE TO SAVE HIMSELF.

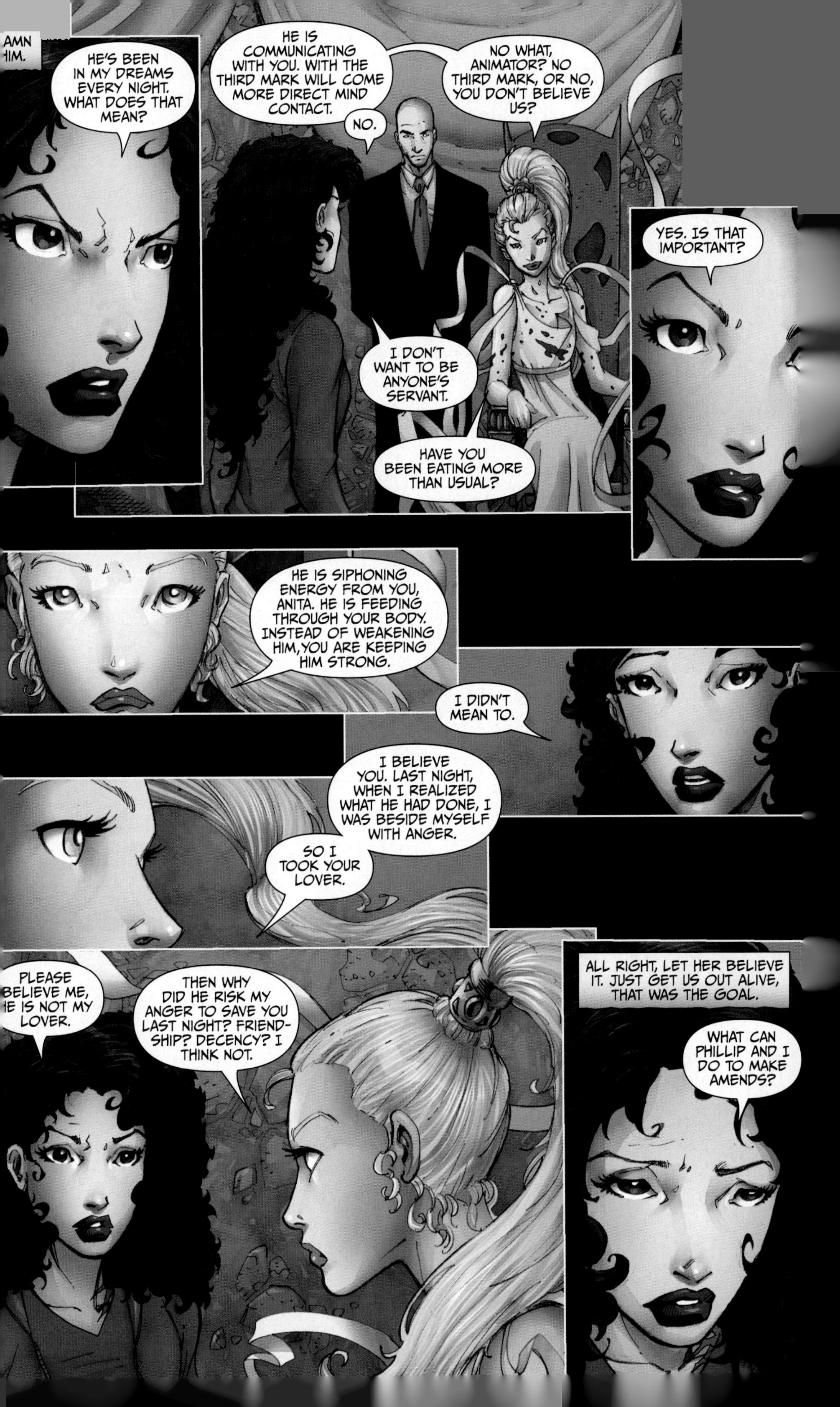

AMN
HIM.
HE'S BEEN IN MY DREAMS EVERY NIGHT. WHAT DOES THAT MEAN?
HE IS COMMUNICATING WITH YOU. WITH THE THIRD MARK WILL COME MORE DIRECT MIND CONTACT.
NO.
NO WHAT, ANIMATOR? NO THIRD MARK, OR NO, YOU DON'T BELIEVE US?
I DON'T WANT TO BE ANYONE'S SERVANT.
HAVE YOU BEEN EATING MORE THAN USUAL?
YES. IS THAT IMPORTANT?
HE IS SIPHONING ENERGY FROM YOU, ANITA. HE IS FEEDING THROUGH YOUR BODY. INSTEAD OF WEAKENING HIM,YOU ARE KEEPING HIM STRONG.
I DIDN'T MEAN TO.
I BELIEVE YOU. LAST NIGHT, WHEN I REALIZED WHAT HE HAD DONE, I WAS BESIDE MYSELF WITH ANGER.
SO I TOOK YOUR LOVER.
PLEASE BELIEVE ME, IE IS NOT MY LOVER.
THEN WHY DID HE RISK MY ANGER TO SAVE YOU LAST NIGHT? FRIEND-SHIP? DECENCY? I THINK NOT.
ALL RIGHT, LET HER BELIEVE IT. JUST GET US OUT ALIVE, THAT WAS THE GOAL.
WHAT CAN PHILLIP AND I DO TO MAKE AMENDS?

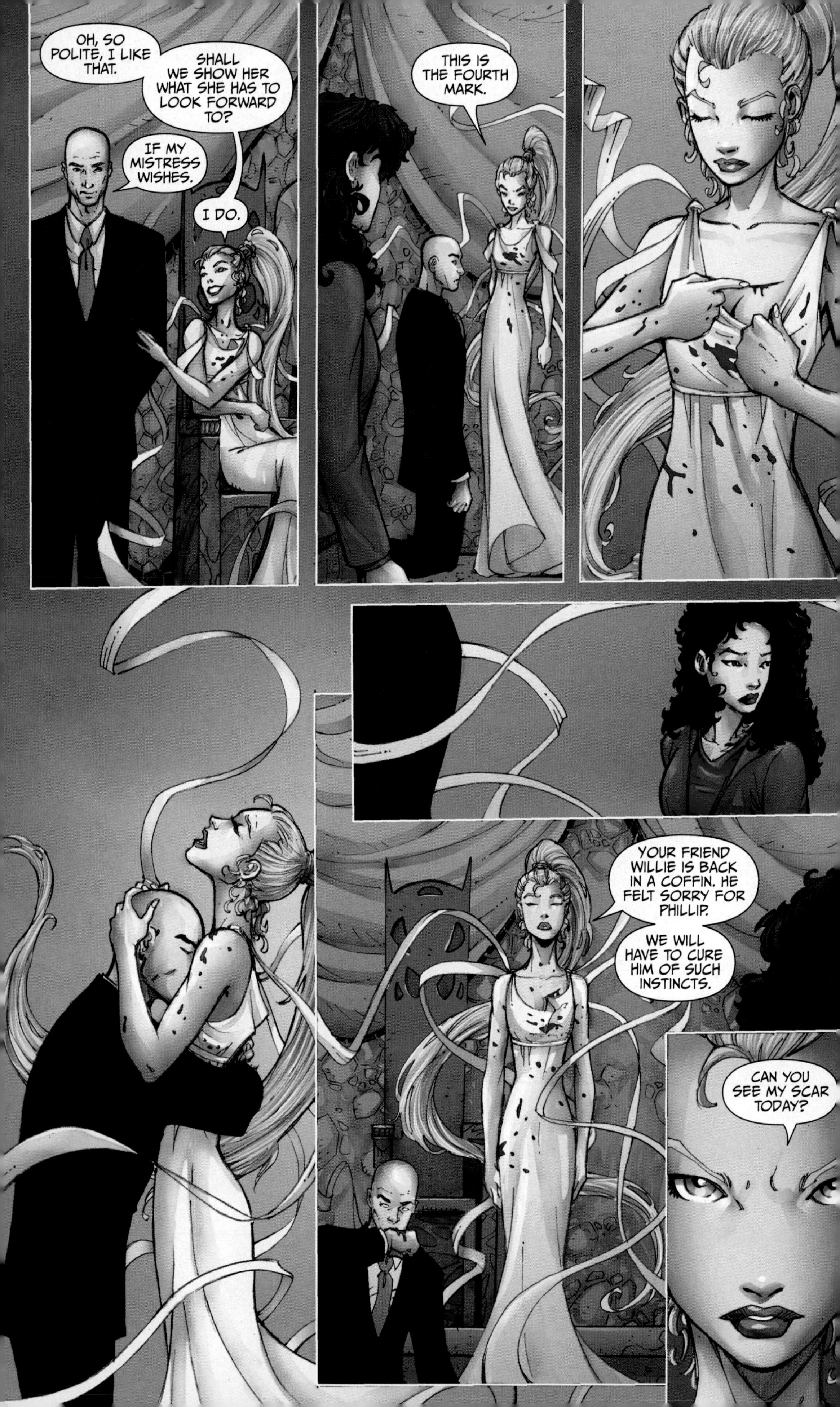
OH, SO POLITE, I LIKE THAT.
SHALL WE SHOW HER WHAT SHE HAS TO LOOK FORWARD TO?
IF MY MISTRESS WISHES.
I DO.
THIS IS THE FOURTH MARK.
YOUR FRIEND WILLIE IS BACK IN A COFFIN. HE FELT SORRY FOR PHILLIP.
WE WILL HAVE TO CURE HIM OF SUCH INSTINCTS.
CAN YOU SEE MY SCAR TODAY?

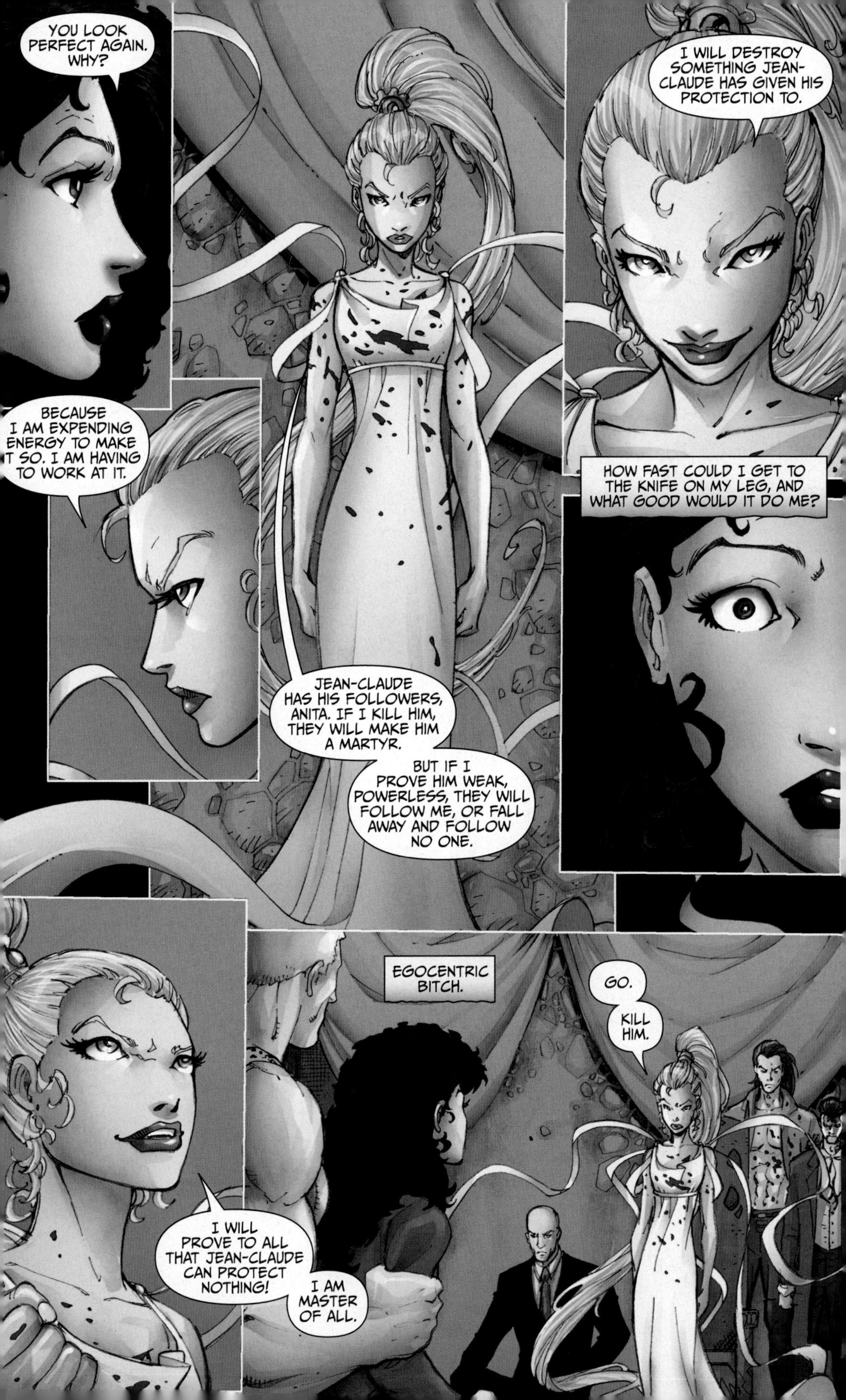
YOU LOOK PERFECT AGAIN. WHY?
BECAUSE I AM EXPENDING ENERGY TO MAKE IT SO. I AM HAVING TO WORK AT IT.
JEAN-CLAUDE HAS HIS FOLLOWERS, ANITA. IF I KILL HIM, THEY WILL MAKE HIM A MARTYR.
BUT IF I PROVE HIM WEAK, POWERLESS, THEY WILL FOLLOW ME, OR FALL AWAY AND FOLLOW NO ONE.
I WILL DESTROY SOMETHING JEAN-CLAUDE HAS GIVEN HIS PROTECTION TO.
HOW FAST COULD I GET TO THE KNIFE ON MY LEG, AND WHAT GOOD WOULD IT DO ME?
I WILL PROVE TO ALL THAT JEAN-CLAUDE CAN PROTECT NOTHING!
I AM MASTER OF ALL.
EGOCENTRIC BITCH.
GO.
KILL HIM.

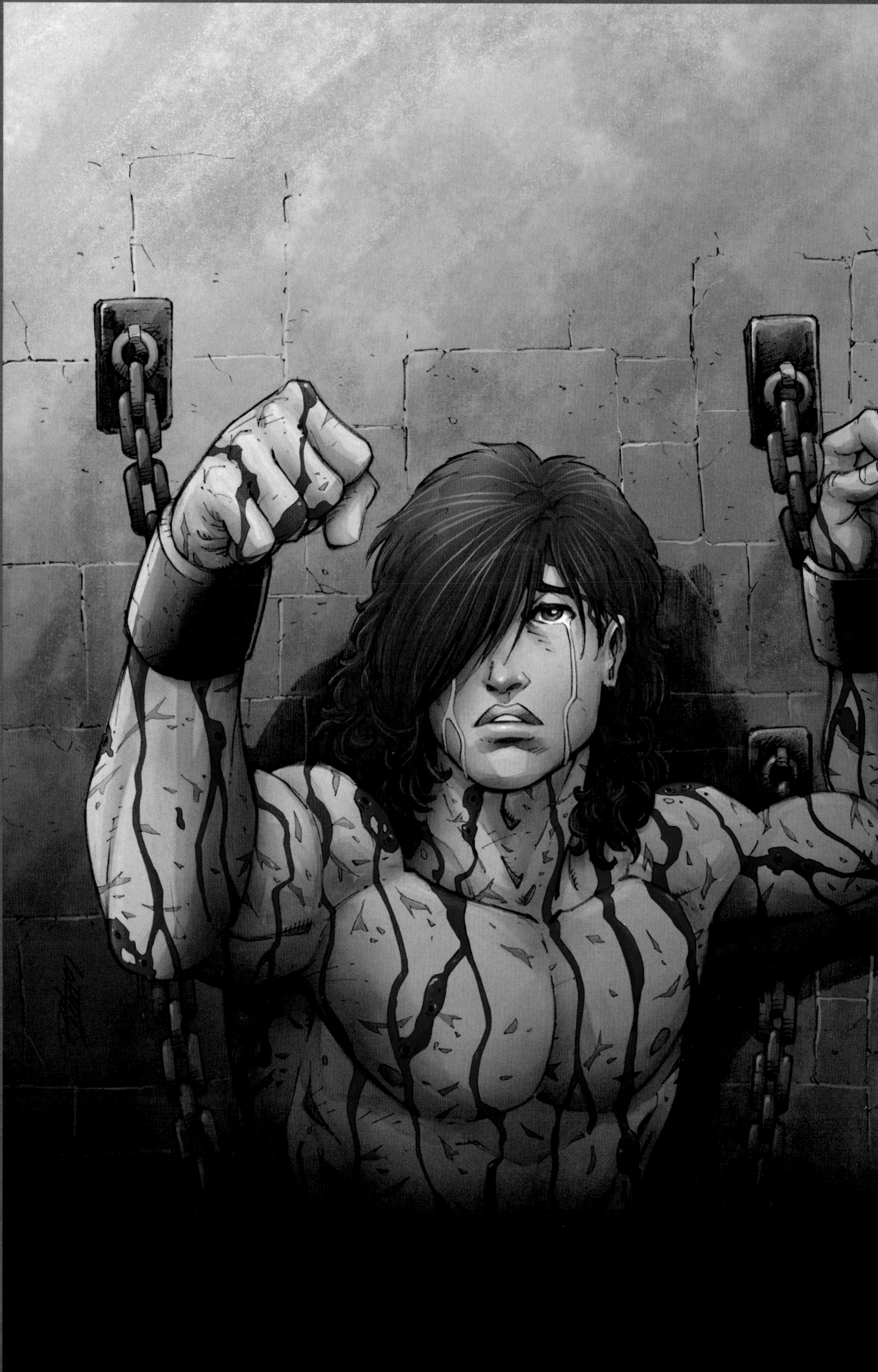

[#10]

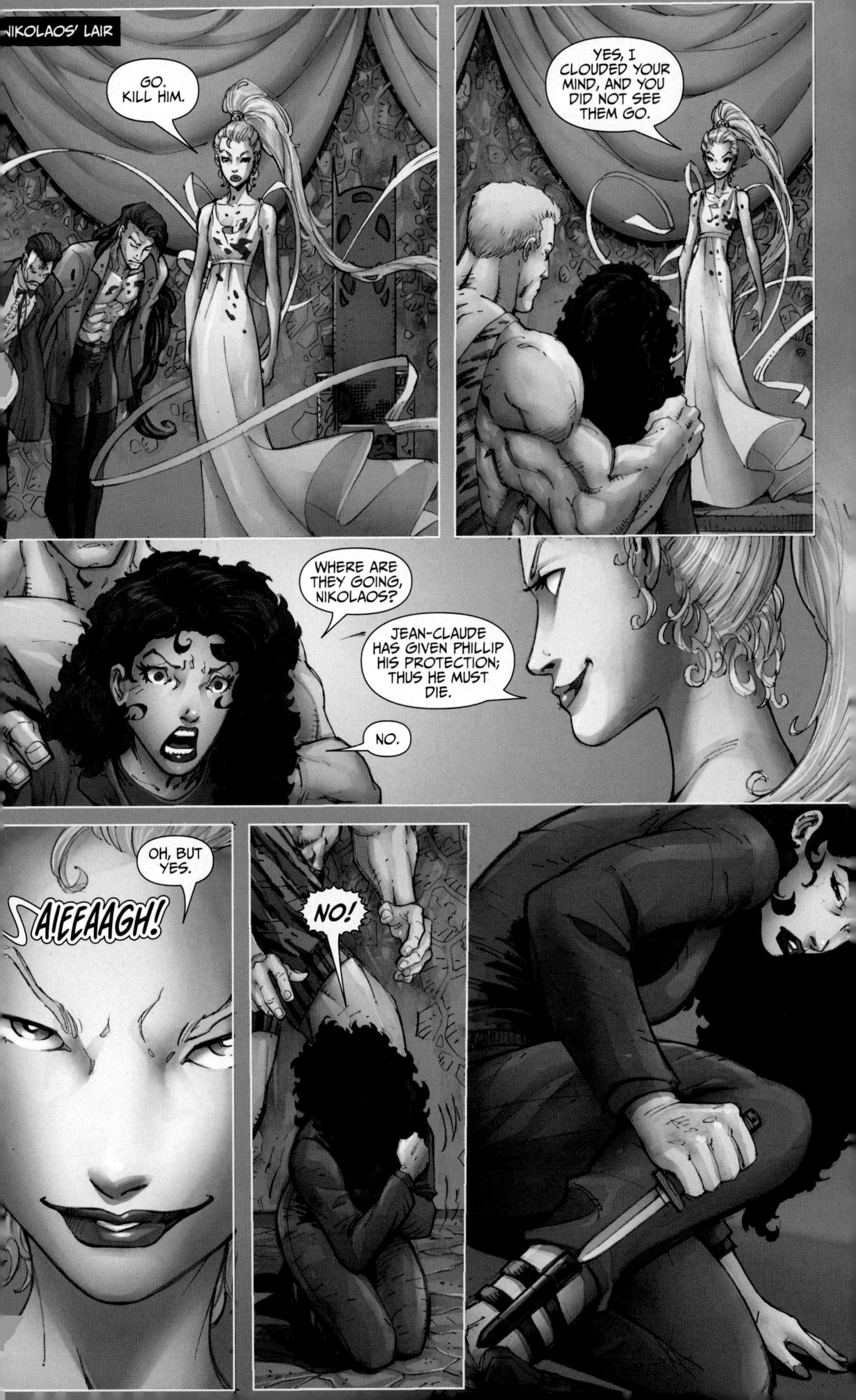
NIKOLAOS' LAIR
GO. KILL HIM.
YES, I CLOUDED YOUR MIND, AND YOU DID NOT SEE THEM GO.
WHERE ARE THEY GOING, NIKOLAOS?
JEAN-CLAUDE HAS GIVEN PHILLIP HIS PROTECTION; THUS HE MUST DIE.
NO.
OH, BUT YES.
AIEEAAGH!
NO!

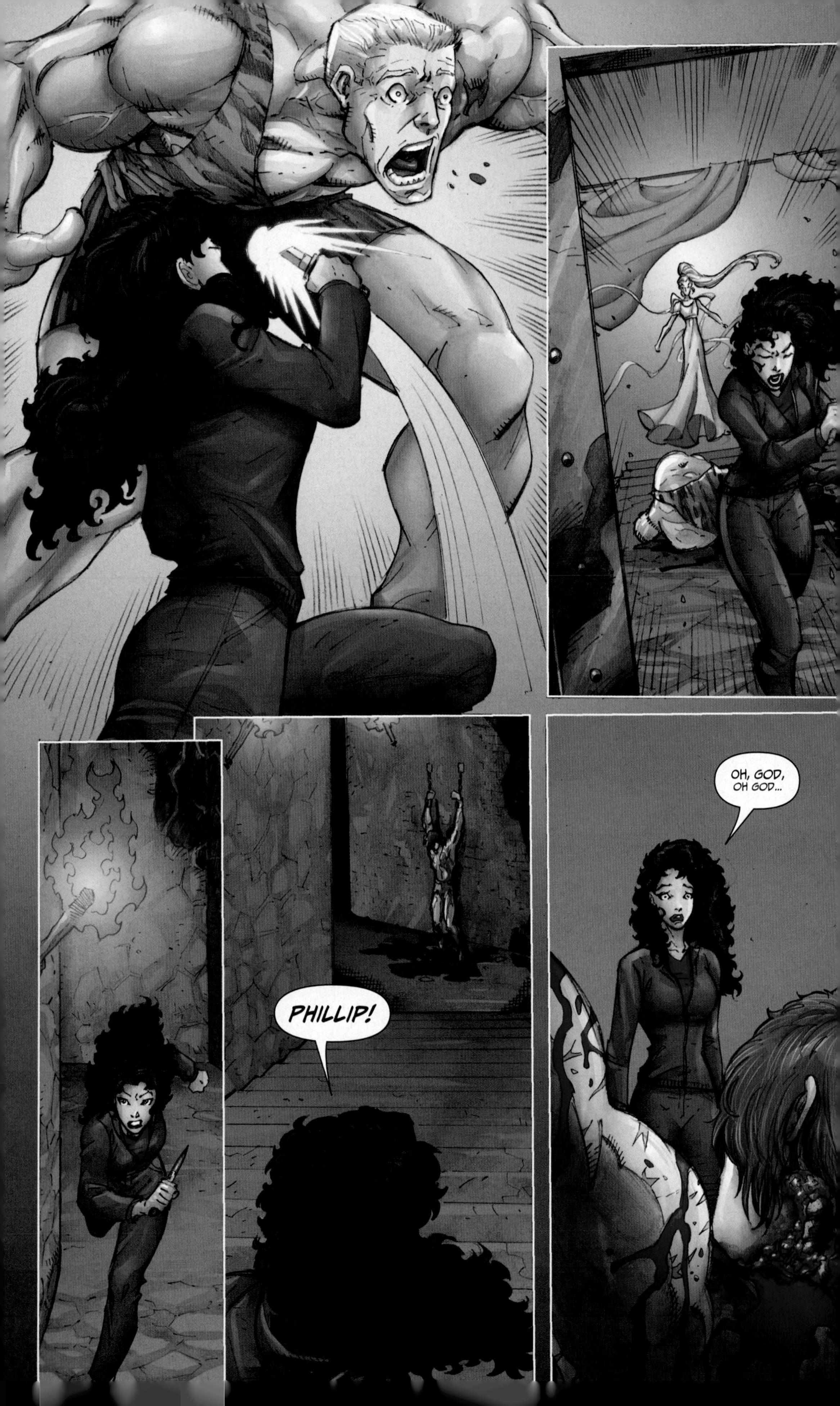
PHILLIP!
OH, GOD,
OH GOD...

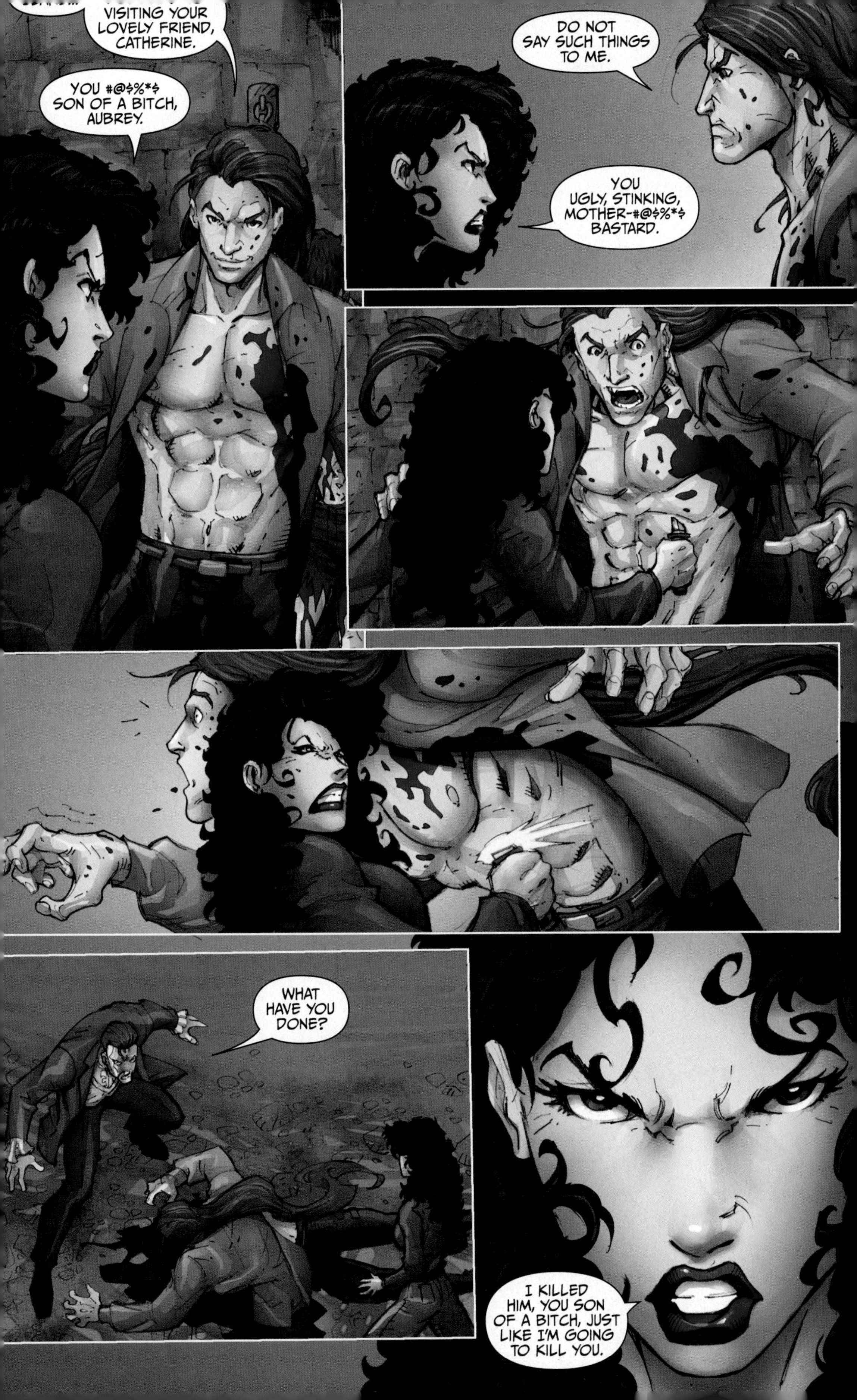
VISITING YOUR LOVELY FRIEND, CATHERINE.
YOU #@$%*$ SON OF A BITCH, AUBREY.
DO NOT SAY SUCH THINGS TO ME.
YOU UGLY, STINKING, MOTHER-#@$%*$ BASTARD.
WHAT HAVE YOU DONE?
I KILLED HIM, YOU SON OF A BITCH, JUST LIKE I'M GOING TO KILL YOU.

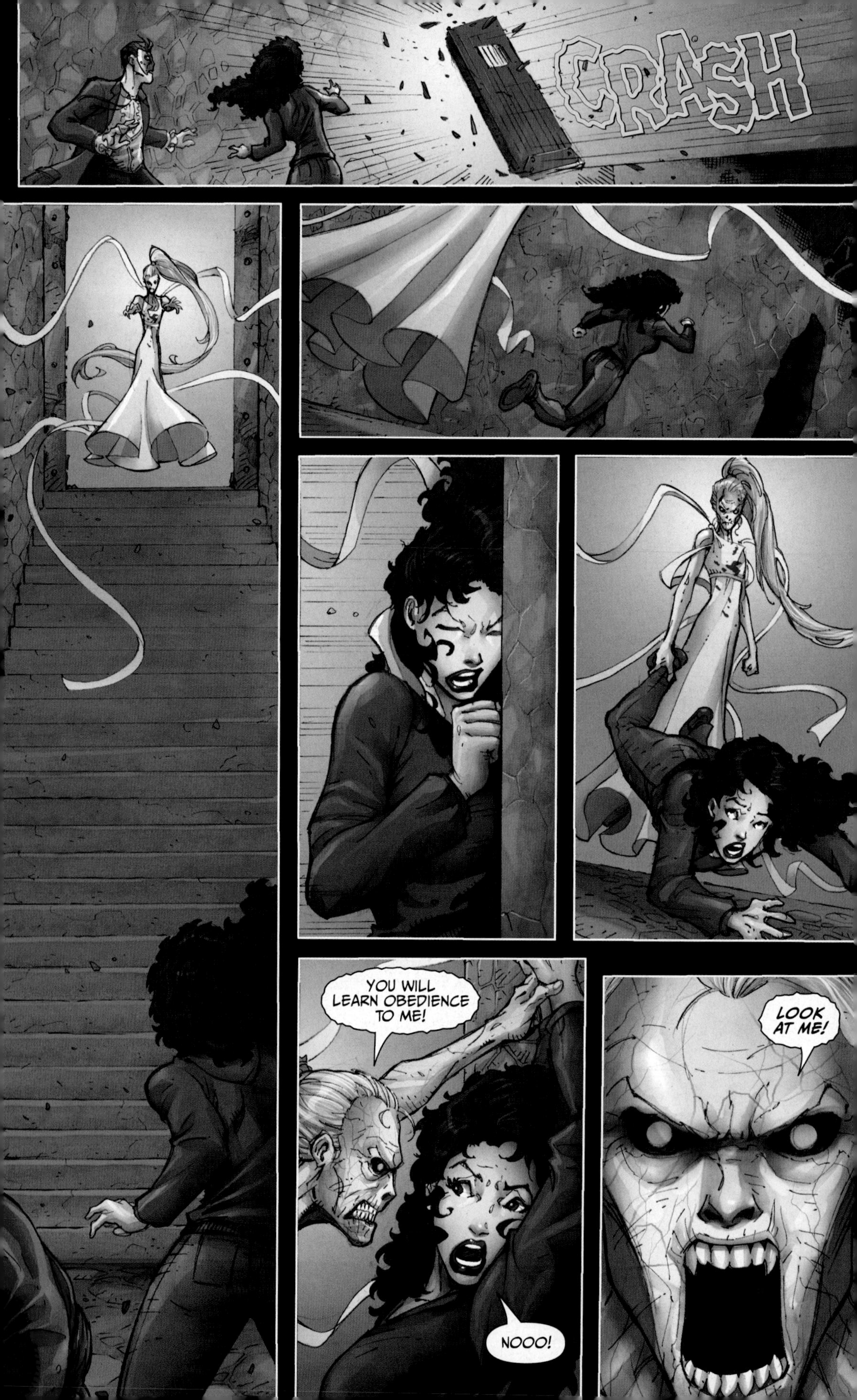
CRASH
YOU WILL LEARN OBEDIENCE TO ME!
NOOO!
LOOK AT ME!

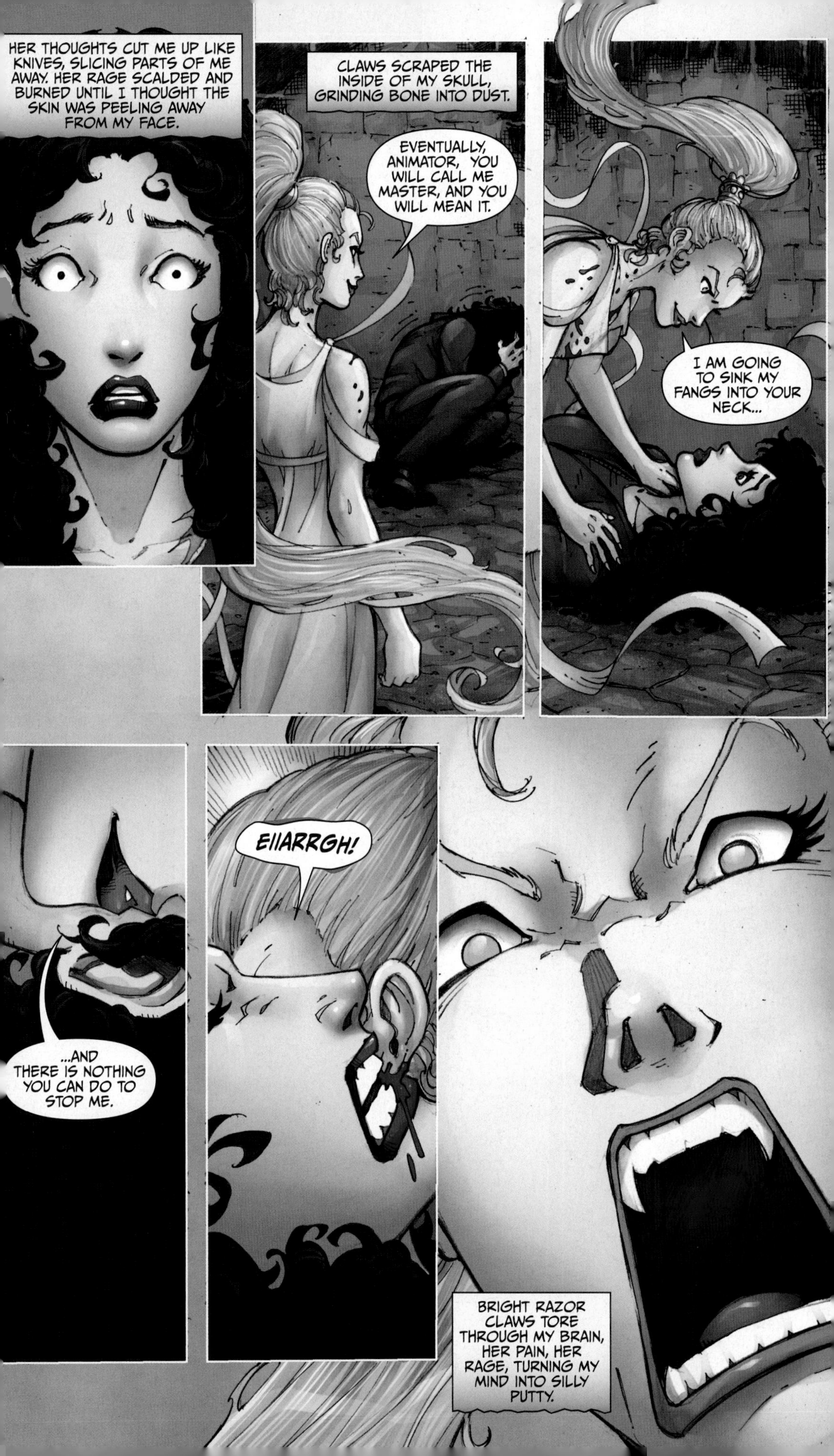
HER THOUGHTS CUT ME UP LIKE KNIVES, SLICING PARTS OF ME AWAY. HER RAGE SCALDED AND BURNED UNTIL I THOUGHT THE SKIN WAS PEELING AWAY FROM MY FACE.
CLAWS SCRAPED THE INSIDE OF MY SKULL, GRINDING BONE INTO DUST.
EVENTUALLY, ANIMATOR, YOU WILL CALL ME MASTER, AND YOU WILL MEAN IT.
I AM GOING TO SINK MY FANGS INTO YOUR NECK...
...AND THERE IS NOTHING YOU CAN DO TO STOP ME.
EIIARRGH!
BRIGHT RAZOR CLAWS TORE THROUGH MY BRAIN, HER PAIN, HER RAGE, TURNING MY MIND INTO SILLY PUTTY.

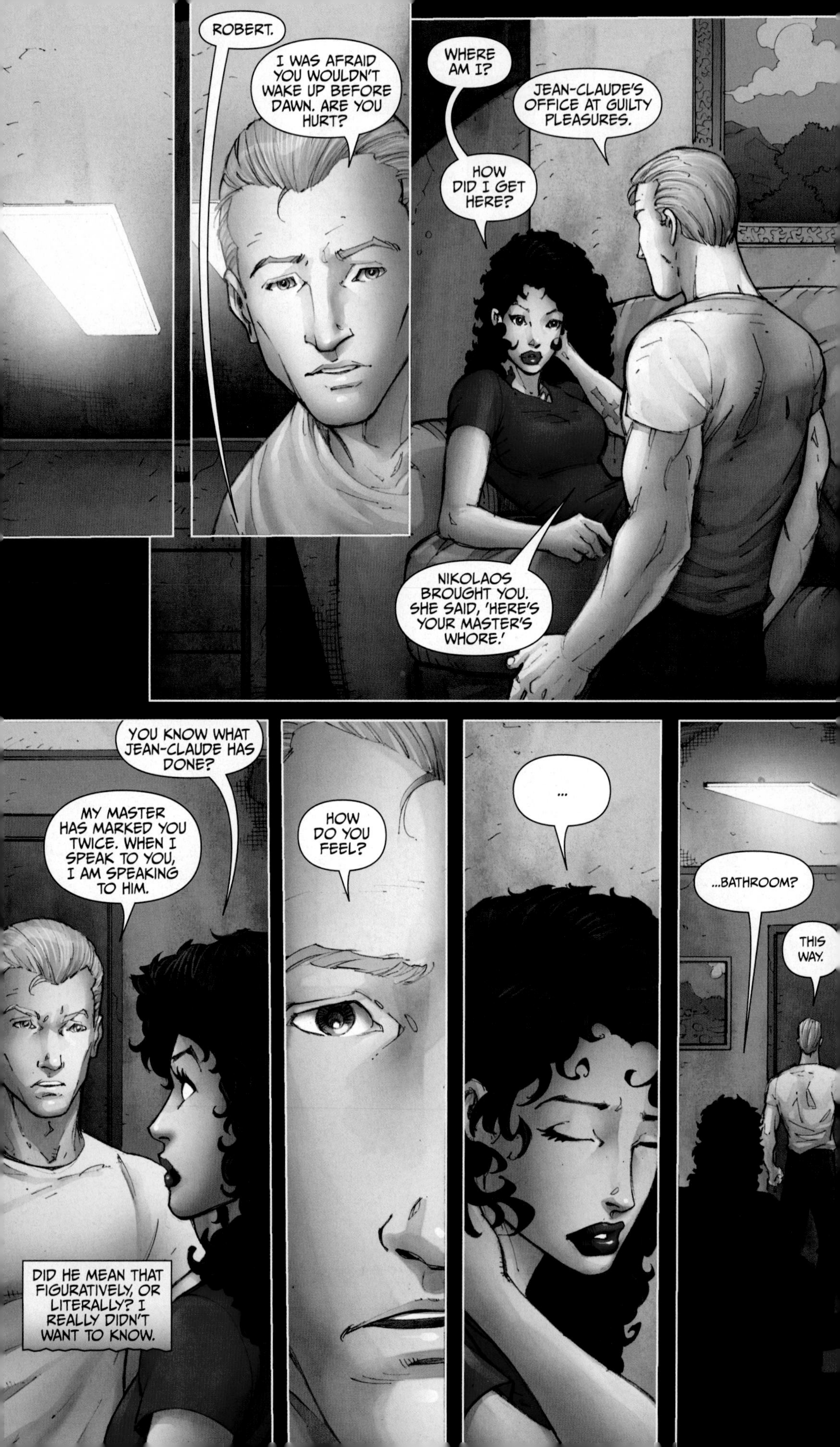
ROBERT.
I WAS AFRAID YOU WOULDN'T WAKE UP BEFORE DAWN. ARE YOU HURT?
WHERE AM I?
JEAN-CLAUDE'S OFFICE AT GUILTY PLEASURES.
HOW DID I GET HERE?
NIKOLAOS BROUGHT YOU. SHE SAID, 'HERE'S YOUR MASTER'S WHORE.'
YOU KNOW WHAT JEAN-CLAUDE HAS DONE?
MY MASTER HAS MARKED YOU TWICE. WHEN I SPEAK TO YOU, I AM SPEAKING TO HIM.
DID HE MEAN THAT FIGURATIVELY, OR LITERALLY? I REALLY DIDN'T WANT TO KNOW.
HOW DO YOU FEEL?
...
...BATHROOM?
THIS WAY.

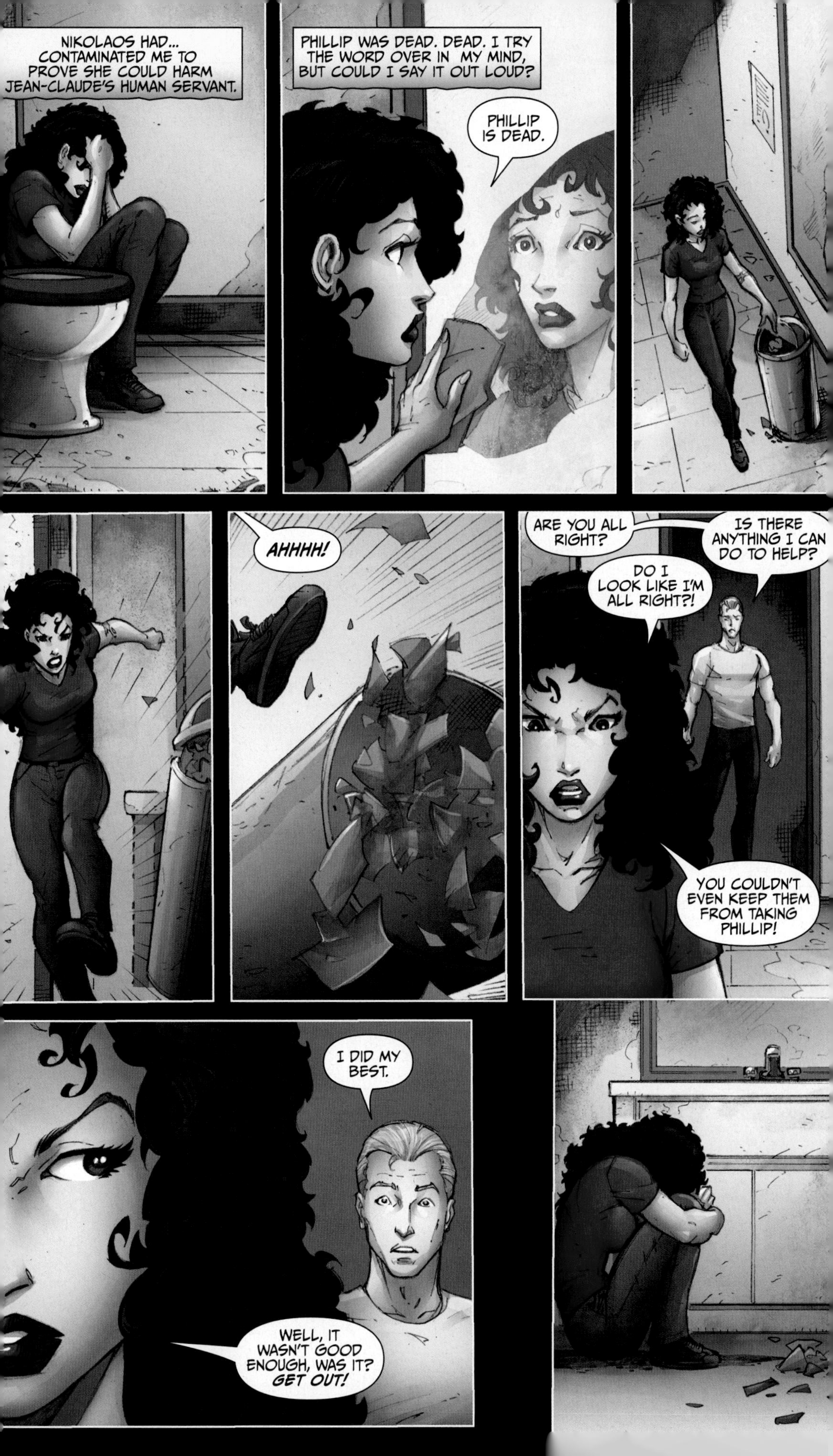
NIKOLAOS HAD... CONTAMINATED ME TO PROVE SHE COULD HARM JEAN-CLAUDE'S HUMAN SERVANT.
PHILLIP WAS DEAD. DEAD. I TRY THE WORD OVER IN MY MIND, BUT COULD I SAY IT OUT LOUD?
PHILLIP IS DEAD.
AHHHH!
ARE YOU ALL RIGHT?
IS THERE ANYTHING I CAN DO TO HELP?
DO I LOOK LIKE I'M ALL RIGHT?!
YOU COULDN'T EVEN KEEP THEM FROM TAKING PHILLIP!
I DID MY BEST.
WELL, IT WASN'T GOOD ENOUGH, WAS IT? GET OUT!

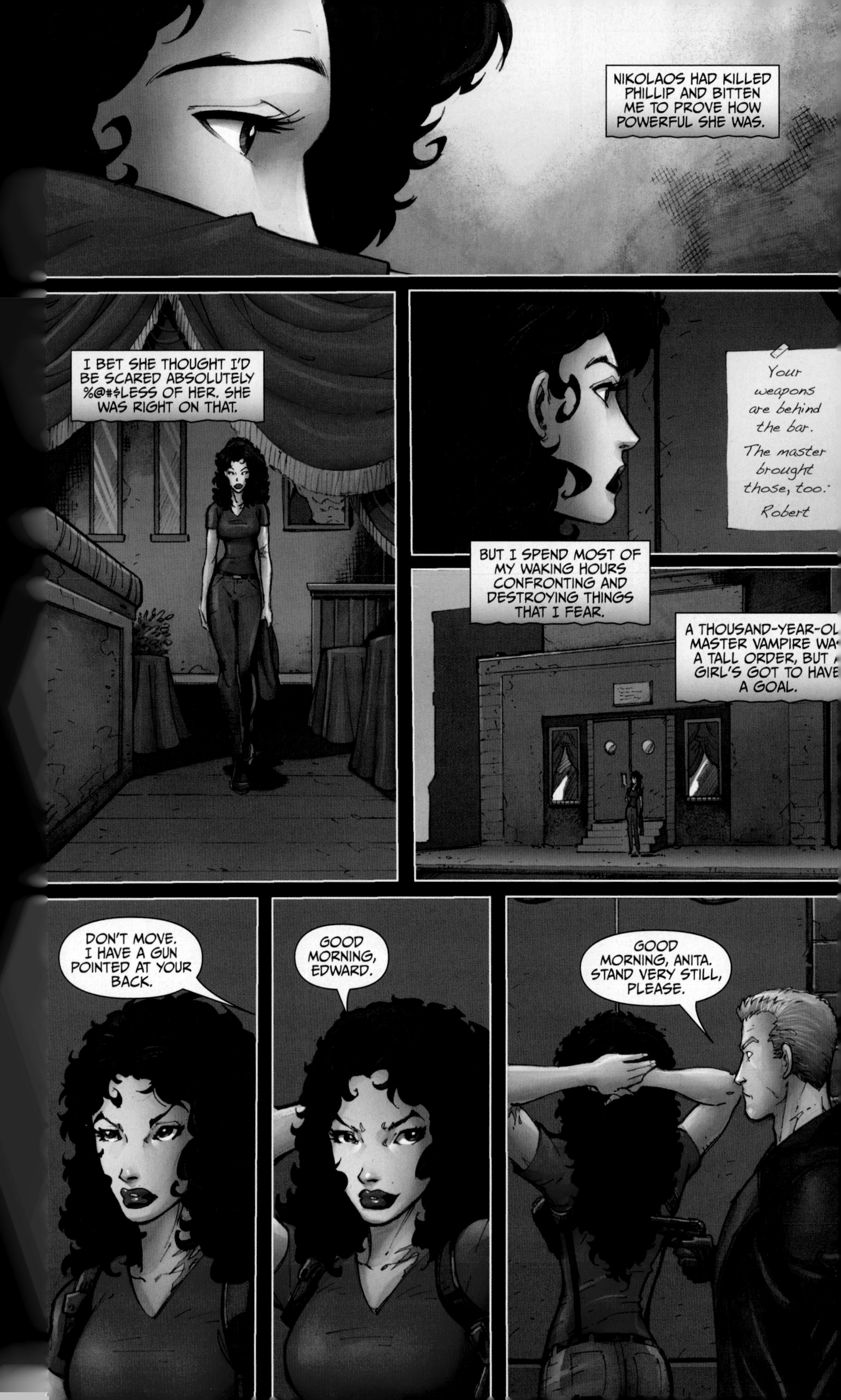
NIKOLAOS HAD KILLED PHILLIP AND BITTEN ME TO PROVE HOW POWERFUL SHE WAS.
I BET SHE THOUGHT I'D BE SCARED ABSOLUTELY %@#$LESS OF HER. SHE WAS RIGHT ON THAT.
Your weapons are behind the bar.
The master brought those, too.
Robert
BUT I SPEND MOST OF MY WAKING HOURS CONFRONTING AND DESTROYING THINGS THAT I FEAR.
A THOUSAND-YEAR-OL MASTER VAMPIRE WA A TALL ORDER, BUT GIRL'S GOT TO HAVE A GOAL.
DON'T MOVE. I HAVE A GUN POINTED AT YOUR BACK.
GOOD MORNING, EDWARD.
GOOD MORNING, ANITA. STAND VERY STILL, PLEASE.

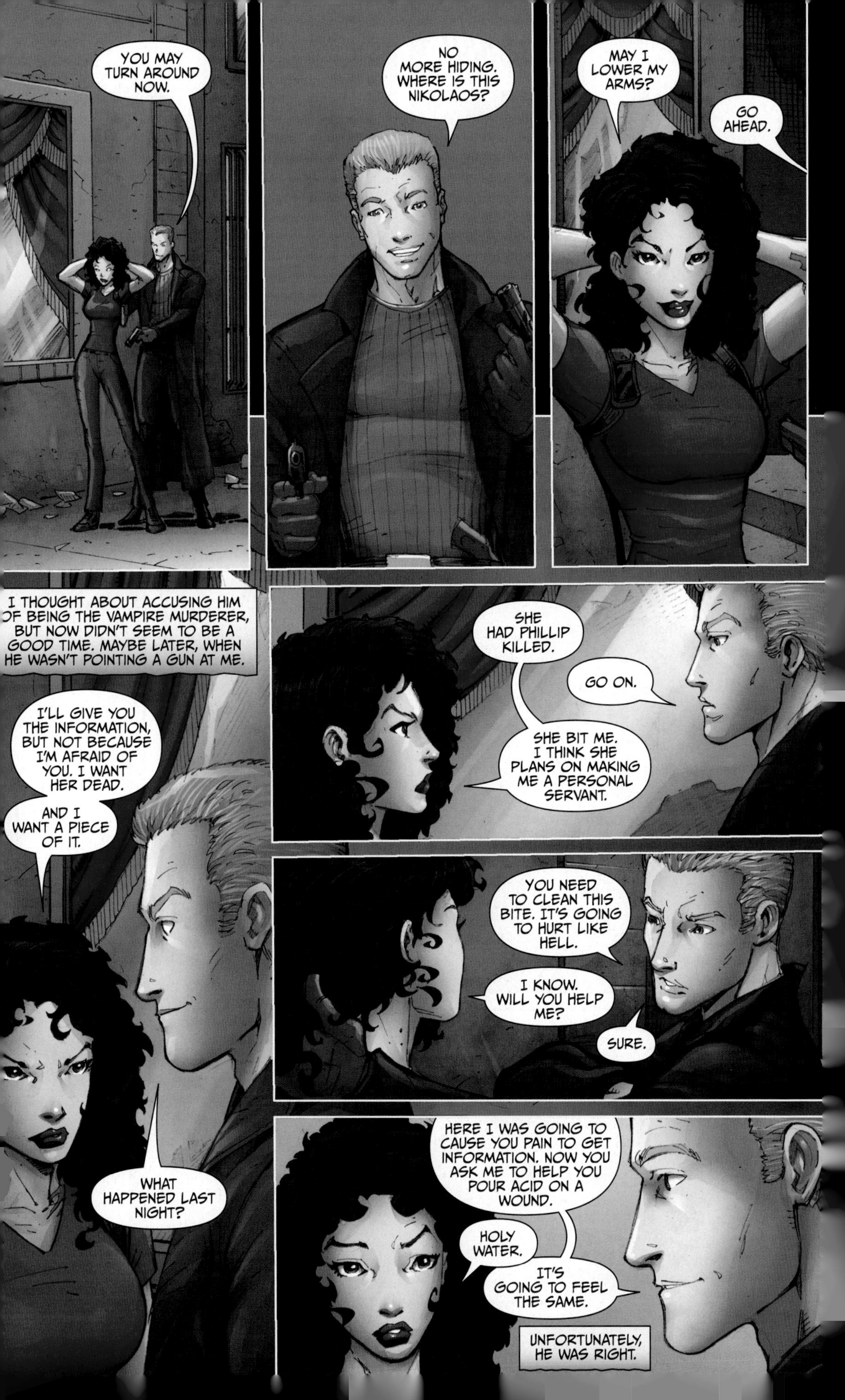
YOU MAY TURN AROUND NOW.
NO MORE HIDING. WHERE IS THIS NIKOLAOS?
MAY I LOWER MY ARMS?
GO AHEAD.
I THOUGHT ABOUT ACCUSING HIM OF BEING THE VAMPIRE MURDERER, BUT NOW DIDN'T SEEM TO BE A GOOD TIME. MAYBE LATER, WHEN HE WASN'T POINTING A GUN AT ME.
I'LL GIVE YOU THE INFORMATION, BUT NOT BECAUSE I'M AFRAID OF YOU. I WANT HER DEAD.
AND I WANT A PIECE OF IT.
WHAT HAPPENED LAST NIGHT?
SHE HAD PHILLIP KILLED.
GO ON.
SHE BIT ME. I THINK SHE PLANS ON MAKING ME A PERSONAL SERVANT.
YOU NEED TO CLEAN THIS BITE. IT'S GOING TO HURT LIKE HELL.
I KNOW. WILL YOU HELP ME?
SURE.
HERE I WAS GOING TO CAUSE YOU PAIN TO GET INFORMATION. NOW YOU ASK ME TO HELP YOU POUR ACID ON A WOUND.
HOLY WATER.
IT'S GOING TO FEEL THE SAME.
UNFORTUNATELY, HE WAS RIGHT.

AAAHHH!

YOU SON OF A BITCH!

HOW DO YOU FEEL?

LIKE SOMEONE'S BEEN SHOVING A RED HOT KNIFE AGAINST MY THROAT.

DO YOU WANT TO STOP AND REST?

NO. I WANT IT CLEAN, EDWARD. ALL THE WAY.

IT IS CUSTOMARY TO DO THIS OVER A MATTER OF DAYS, YOU KNOW.

I DON'T HAVE A FEW DAYS. I NEED THIS WOUND CLEANED BEFORE NIGHTFALL.

BECAUSE NIKOLAOS WILL HAVE A HOLD ON YOU UNLESS THE WOUND IS PURIFIED.

YES.

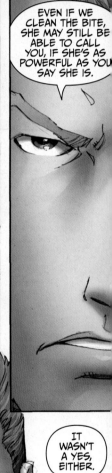

EVEN IF WE CLEAN THE BITE, SHE MAY STILL BE ABLE TO CALL YOU, IF SHE'S AS POWERFUL AS YOU SAY SHE IS.

YOU THINK NIKOLAOS CAN TURN ME AGAINST YOU, EVEN IF WE CLEAN THE BITE?

WE VAMPIRE SLAYERS TAKE OUR CHANCES.

THAT WASN'T A NO.

IT WASN'T A YES, EITHER.

OH GOODY, EDWARD DIDN'T KNOW EITHER.

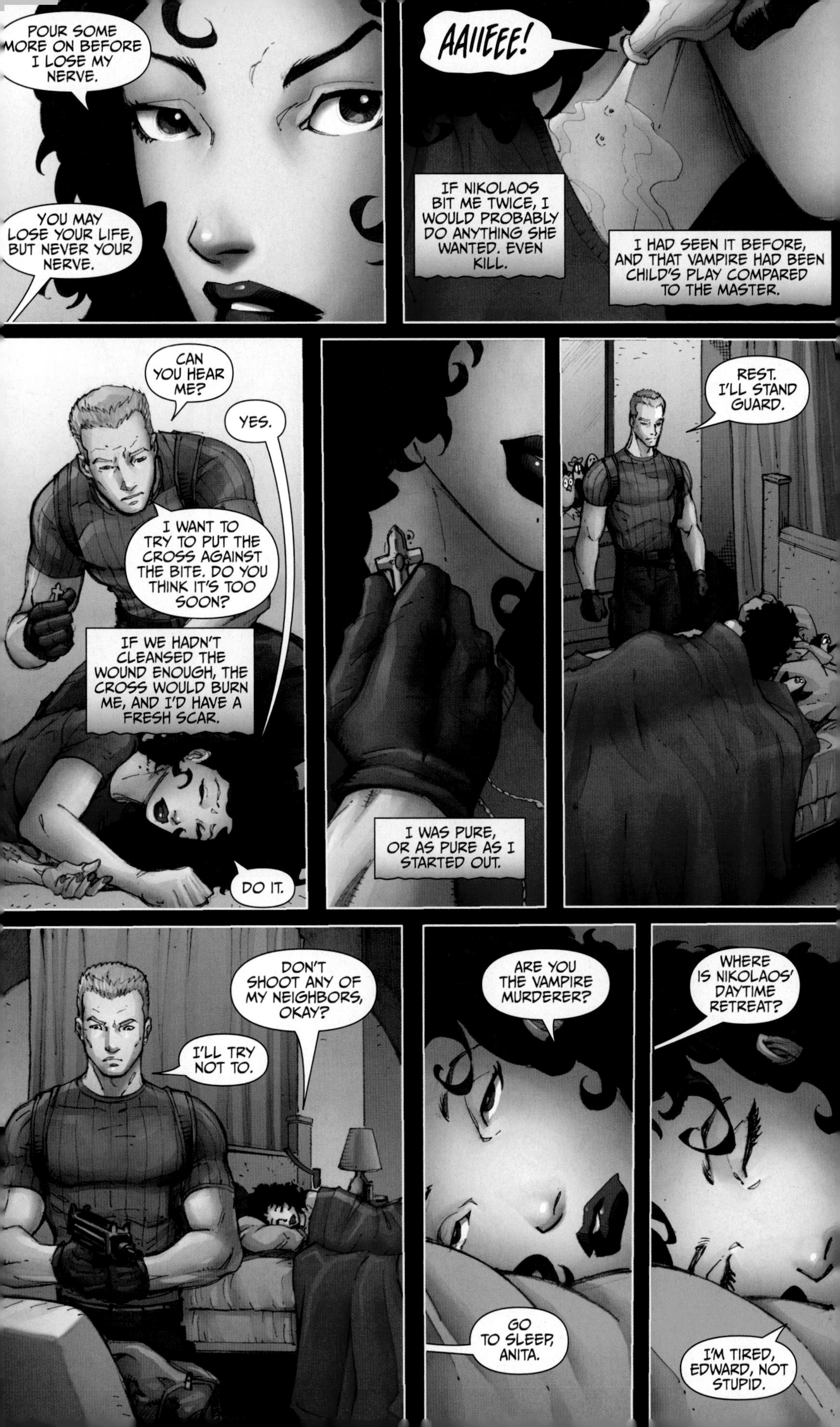
POUR SOME MORE ON BEFORE I LOSE MY NERVE.
YOU MAY LOSE YOUR LIFE, BUT NEVER YOUR NERVE.
AAIIEEE!
IF NIKOLAOS BIT ME TWICE, I WOULD PROBABLY DO ANYTHING SHE WANTED. EVEN KILL.
I HAD SEEN IT BEFORE, AND THAT VAMPIRE HAD BEEN CHILD'S PLAY COMPARED TO THE MASTER.
CAN YOU HEAR ME?
YES.
I WANT TO TRY TO PUT THE CROSS AGAINST THE BITE. DO YOU THINK IT'S TOO SOON?
IF WE HADN'T CLEANSED THE WOUND ENOUGH, THE CROSS WOULD BURN ME, AND I'D HAVE A FRESH SCAR.
DO IT.
I WAS PURE, OR AS PURE AS I STARTED OUT.
REST. I'LL STAND GUARD.
DON'T SHOOT ANY OF MY NEIGHBORS, OKAY?
I'LL TRY NOT TO.
ARE YOU THE VAMPIRE MURDERER?
GO TO SLEEP, ANITA.
WHERE IS NIKOLAOS' DAYTIME RETREAT?
I'M TIRED, EDWARD, NOT STUPID.

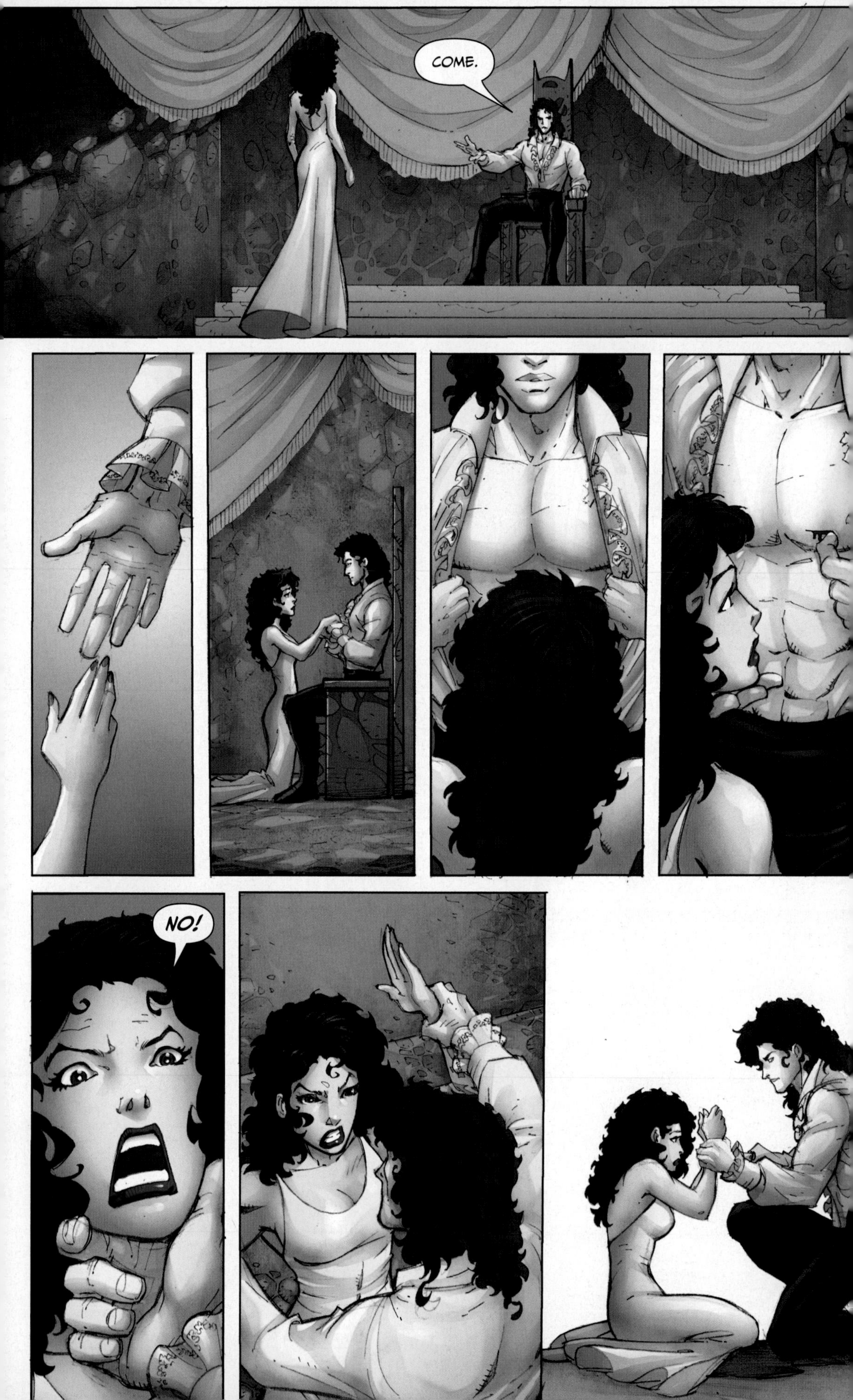
COME.
NO!

AH, HAHAHAH!

JEAN-CLAUDE, PLEASE, DON'T DO THIS!

BLOOD OF MY BLOOD, FLESH OF MY FLESH, TWO MINDS WITH BUT ONE BODY, TWO SOULS WEDDED AS ONE.

JEAN-CLAUDE, NO! GOD HELP ME!

SCRATCH THE SURFACE, AND WE ARE ALL MUCH ALIKE, ANIMATOR.

ANITA, ANITA, IT'S EDWARD. LOOK AT ME!

ARE YOU ALL RIGHT?

I HAD A NIGHTMARE.

NO #%@$.

WHAT TIME IS IT?

YOU'VE GOT ABOUT FOUR HOURS UNTIL DUSK.

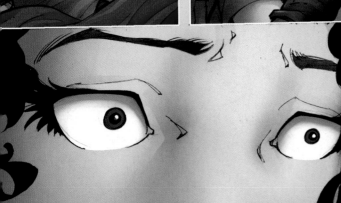

HAD THE DREAM BEEN JEAN-CLAUDE'S, OR NIKOLAOS'? IF IT WAS NIKOLAOS, DID SHE ALREADY CONTROL ME? NO ANSWERS.

NO ANSWERS TO ANYTHING.

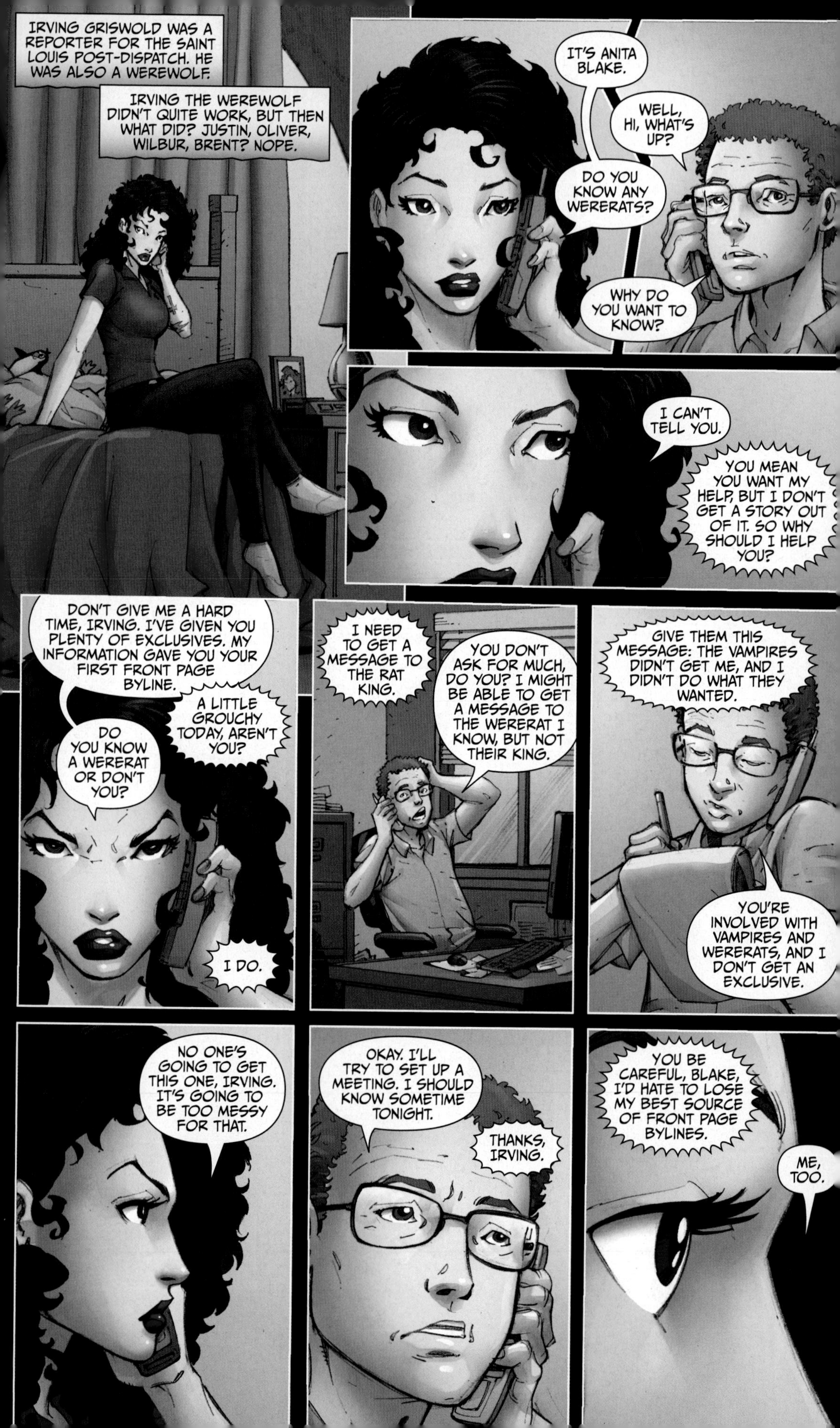
IRVING GRISWOLD WAS A REPORTER FOR THE SAINT LOUIS POST-DISPATCH. HE WAS ALSO A WEREWOLF.
IRVING THE WEREWOLF DIDN'T QUITE WORK, BUT THEN WHAT DID? JUSTIN, OLIVER, WILBUR, BRENT? NOPE.
IT'S ANITA BLAKE.
WELL, HI, WHAT'S UP?
DO YOU KNOW ANY WERERATS?
WHY DO YOU WANT TO KNOW?
I CAN'T TELL YOU.
YOU MEAN YOU WANT MY HELP, BUT I DON'T GET A STORY OUT OF IT. SO WHY SHOULD I HELP YOU?
DON'T GIVE ME A HARD TIME, IRVING. I'VE GIVEN YOU PLENTY OF EXCLUSIVES. MY INFORMATION GAVE YOU YOUR FIRST FRONT PAGE BYLINE.
A LITTLE GROUCHY TODAY, AREN'T YOU?
DO YOU KNOW A WERERAT OR DON'T YOU?
I DO.
I NEED TO GET A MESSAGE TO THE RAT KING.
YOU DON'T ASK FOR MUCH, DO YOU? I MIGHT BE ABLE TO GET A MESSAGE TO THE WERERAT I KNOW, BUT NOT THEIR KING.
GIVE THEM THIS MESSAGE: THE VAMPIRES DIDN'T GET ME, AND I DIDN'T DO WHAT THEY WANTED.
YOU'RE INVOLVED WITH VAMPIRES AND WERERATS, AND I DON'T GET AN EXCLUSIVE.
NO ONE'S GOING TO GET THIS ONE, IRVING. IT'S GOING TO BE TOO MESSY FOR THAT.
OKAY. I'LL TRY TO SET UP A MEETING. I SHOULD KNOW SOMETIME TONIGHT.
THANKS, IRVING.
YOU BE CAREFUL, BLAKE, I'D HATE TO LOSE MY BEST SOURCE OF FRONT PAGE BYLINES.
ME, TOO.

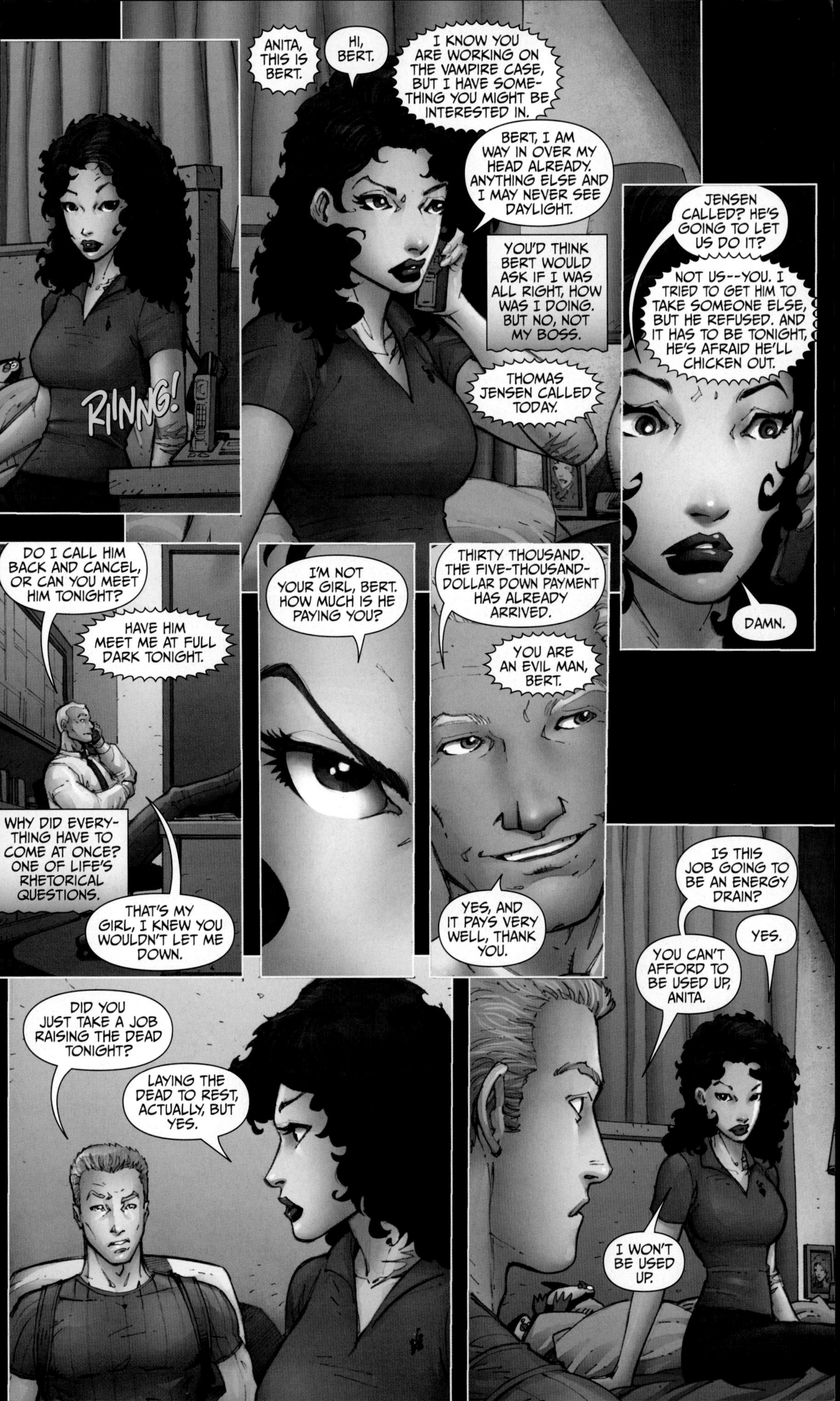
RIINNG!
ANITA, THIS IS BERT.
HI, BERT.
I KNOW YOU ARE WORKING ON THE VAMPIRE CASE, BUT I HAVE SOMETHING YOU MIGHT BE INTERESTED IN.
BERT, I AM WAY IN OVER MY HEAD ALREADY. ANYTHING ELSE AND I MAY NEVER SEE DAYLIGHT.
YOU'D THINK BERT WOULD ASK IF I WAS ALL RIGHT, HOW WAS I DOING. BUT NO, NOT MY BOSS.
THOMAS JENSEN CALLED TODAY.
JENSEN CALLED? HE'S GOING TO LET US DO IT?
NOT US--YOU. I TRIED TO GET HIM TO TAKE SOMEONE ELSE, BUT HE REFUSED. AND IT HAS TO BE TONIGHT, HE'S AFRAID HE'LL CHICKEN OUT.
DAMN.
DO I CALL HIM BACK AND CANCEL, OR CAN YOU MEET HIM TONIGHT?
HAVE HIM MEET ME AT FULL DARK TONIGHT.
WHY DID EVERYTHING HAVE TO COME AT ONCE? ONE OF LIFE'S RHETORICAL QUESTIONS.
THAT'S MY GIRL, I KNEW YOU WOULDN'T LET ME DOWN.
I'M NOT YOUR GIRL, BERT. HOW MUCH IS HE PAYING YOU?
THIRTY THOUSAND. THE FIVE-THOUSAND-DOLLAR DOWN PAYMENT HAS ALREADY ARRIVED.
YOU ARE AN EVIL MAN, BERT.
YES, AND IT PAYS VERY WELL, THANK YOU.
DID YOU JUST TAKE A JOB RAISING THE DEAD TONIGHT?
LAYING THE DEAD TO REST, ACTUALLY, BUT YES.
IS THIS JOB GOING TO BE AN ENERGY DRAIN?
YES.
YOU CAN'T AFFORD TO BE USED UP, ANITA.
I WON'T BE USED UP.

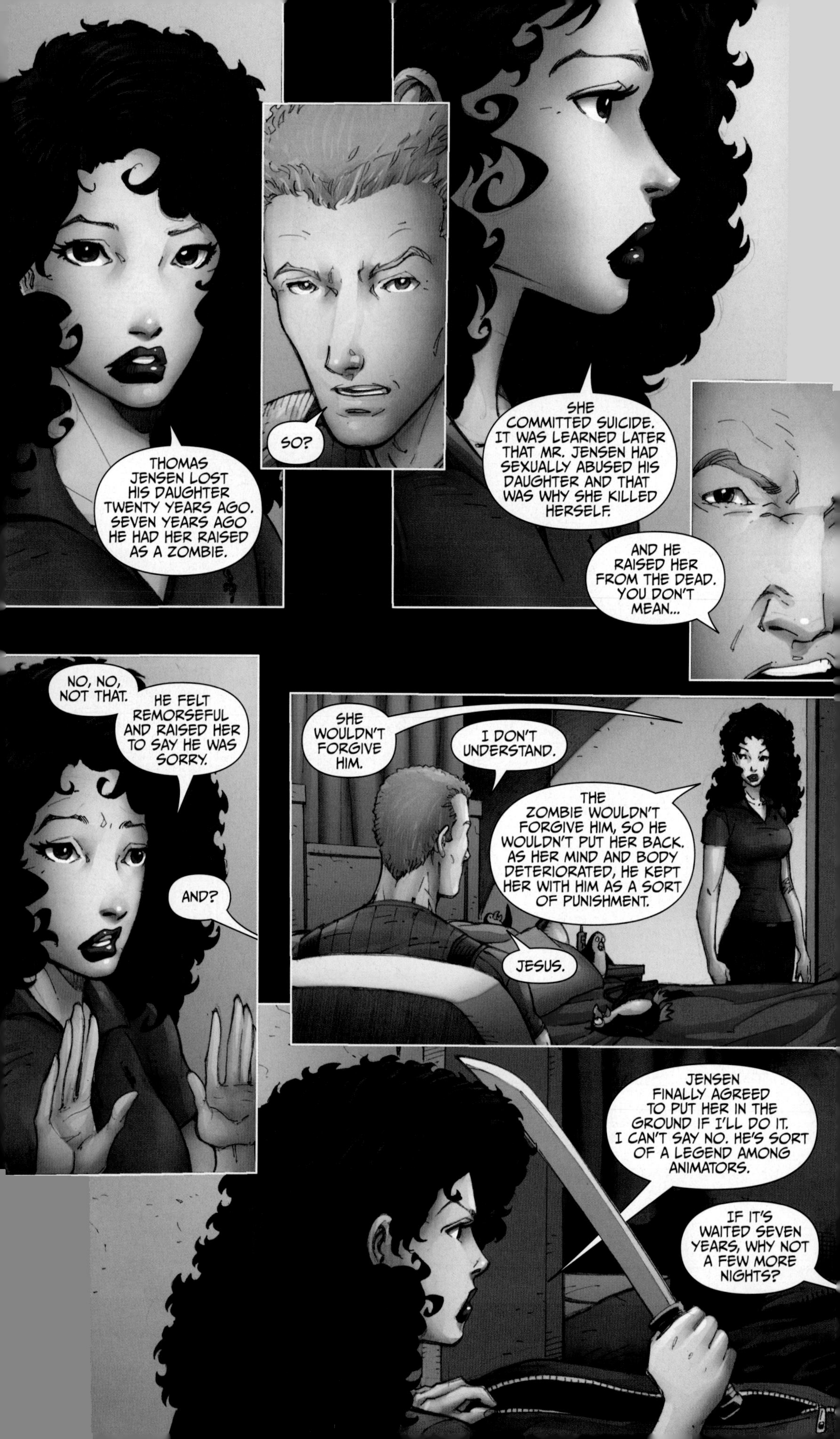
THOMAS JENSEN LOST HIS DAUGHTER TWENTY YEARS AGO. SEVEN YEARS AGO HE HAD HER RAISED AS A ZOMBIE.
SO?
SHE COMMITTED SUICIDE. IT WAS LEARNED LATER THAT MR. JENSEN HAD SEXUALLY ABUSED HIS DAUGHTER AND THAT WAS WHY SHE KILLED HERSELF.
AND HE RAISED HER FROM THE DEAD. YOU DON'T MEAN...
NO, NO, NOT THAT.
HE FELT REMORSEFUL AND RAISED HER TO SAY HE WAS SORRY.
AND?
SHE WOULDN'T FORGIVE HIM.
I DON'T UNDERSTAND.
THE ZOMBIE WOULDN'T FORGIVE HIM, SO HE WOULDN'T PUT HER BACK. AS HER MIND AND BODY DETERIORATED, HE KEPT HER WITH HIM AS A SORT OF PUNISHMENT.
JESUS.
JENSEN FINALLY AGREED TO PUT HER IN THE GROUND IF I'LL DO IT. I CAN'T SAY NO. HE'S SORT OF A LEGEND AMONG ANIMATORS.
IF IT'S WAITED SEVEN YEARS, WHY NOT A FEW MORE NIGHTS?

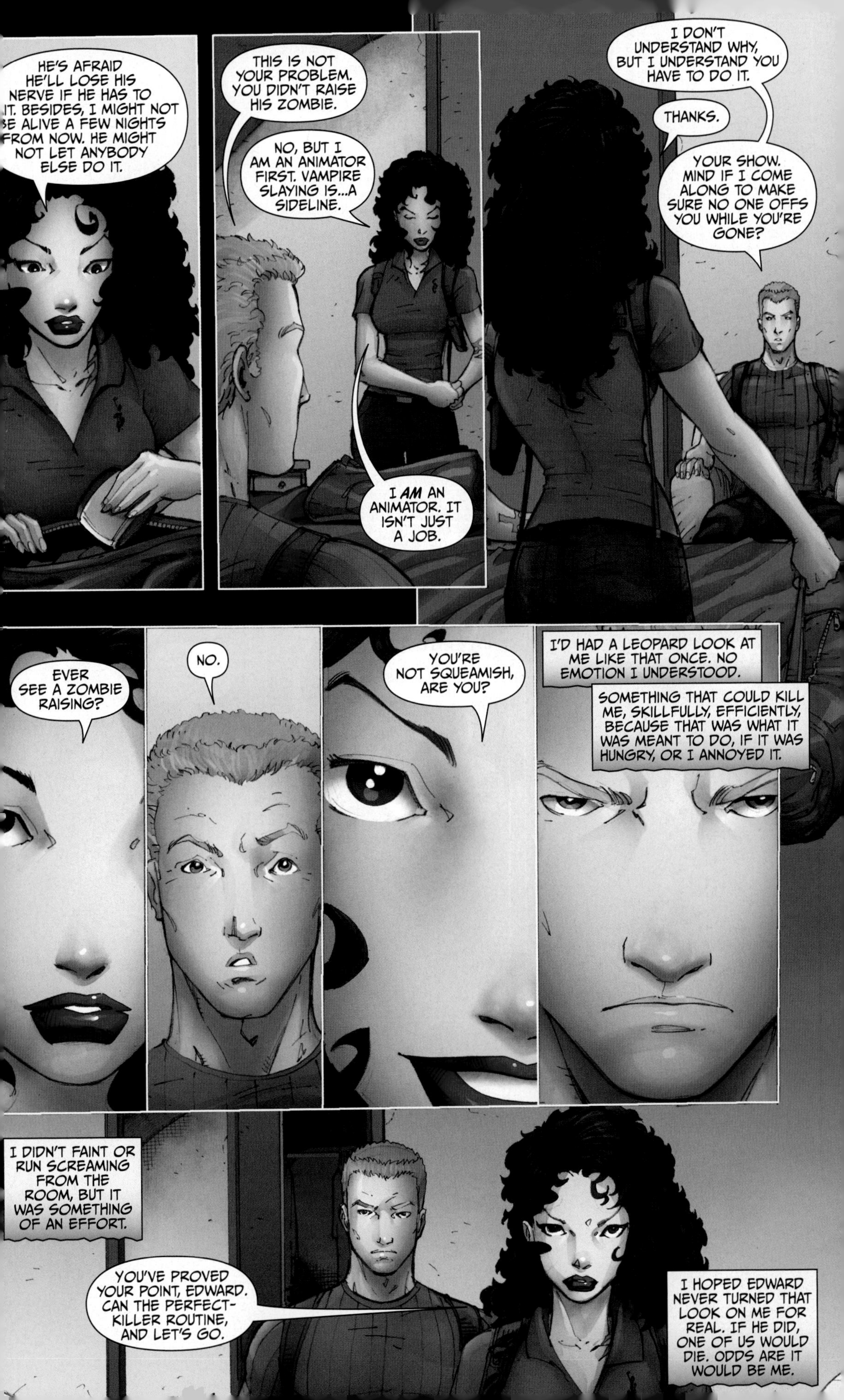
HE'S AFRAID HE'LL LOSE HIS NERVE IF HE HAS TO IT. BESIDES, I MIGHT NOT BE ALIVE A FEW NIGHTS FROM NOW. HE MIGHT NOT LET ANYBODY ELSE DO IT.
THIS IS NOT YOUR PROBLEM. YOU DIDN'T RAISE HIS ZOMBIE.
NO, BUT I AM AN ANIMATOR FIRST. VAMPIRE SLAYING IS...A SIDELINE.
I AM AN ANIMATOR. IT ISN'T JUST A JOB.
I DON'T UNDERSTAND WHY, BUT I UNDERSTAND YOU HAVE TO DO IT.
THANKS.
YOUR SHOW. MIND IF I COME ALONG TO MAKE SURE NO ONE OFFS YOU WHILE YOU'RE GONE?
EVER SEE A ZOMBIE RAISING?
NO.
YOU'RE NOT SQUEAMISH, ARE YOU?
I'D HAD A LEOPARD LOOK AT ME LIKE THAT ONCE. NO EMOTION I UNDERSTOOD.
SOMETHING THAT COULD KILL ME, SKILLFULLY, EFFICIENTLY, BECAUSE THAT WAS WHAT IT WAS MEANT TO DO, IF IT WAS HUNGRY, OR I ANNOYED IT.
I DIDN'T FAINT OR RUN SCREAMING FROM THE ROOM, BUT IT WAS SOMETHING OF AN EFFORT.
YOU'VE PROVED YOUR POINT, EDWARD. CAN THE PERFECT-KILLER ROUTINE, AND LET'S GO.
I HOPED EDWARD NEVER TURNED THAT LOOK ON ME FOR REAL. IF HE DID, ONE OF US WOULD DIE. ODDS ARE IT WOULD BE ME.

BELOVED DAUGHTER SADLY MISS

THE SAME MAN WHO HAD HAD THE ANGEL CARVED, WHO SADLY MISSED HER, HAD BEEN MOLESTING HER. SHE HAD KILLED HERSELF TO ESCAPE HIM, AND HE HAD BROUGHT HER BACK.

THAT WAS WHY I WAS OUT HERE IN THE DARK, WAITING FOR THE JENSENS: NOT HIM, BUT HER. EVEN THOUGH I KNEW HER MIND WAS GONE BY NOW, I WANTED IRIS JENSEN IN THE GROUND AND AT PEACE.

WHER IS HE

I DON'T KNOW.

IT HAD BEEN ALMOST AN HOUR SINCE FULL DARK. HAD JENSEN CHICKENED OUT?

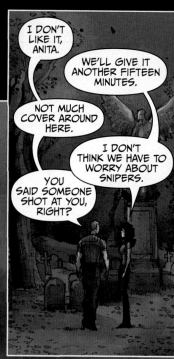

I DON'T LIKE IT, ANITA.

WE'LL GIVE IT ANOTHER FIFTEEN MINUTES.

NOT MUCH COVER AROUND HERE.

I DON'T THINK WE HAVE TO WORRY ABOUT SNIPERS.

YOU SAID SOMEONE SHOT AT YOU, RIGHT?

WHAT'S THAT?

THE MAINTENANCE SHED. YOU THINK THE GRASS CUTS ITSELF?

NEVER THOUGHT ABOUT IT.

SCREEK SCREEK

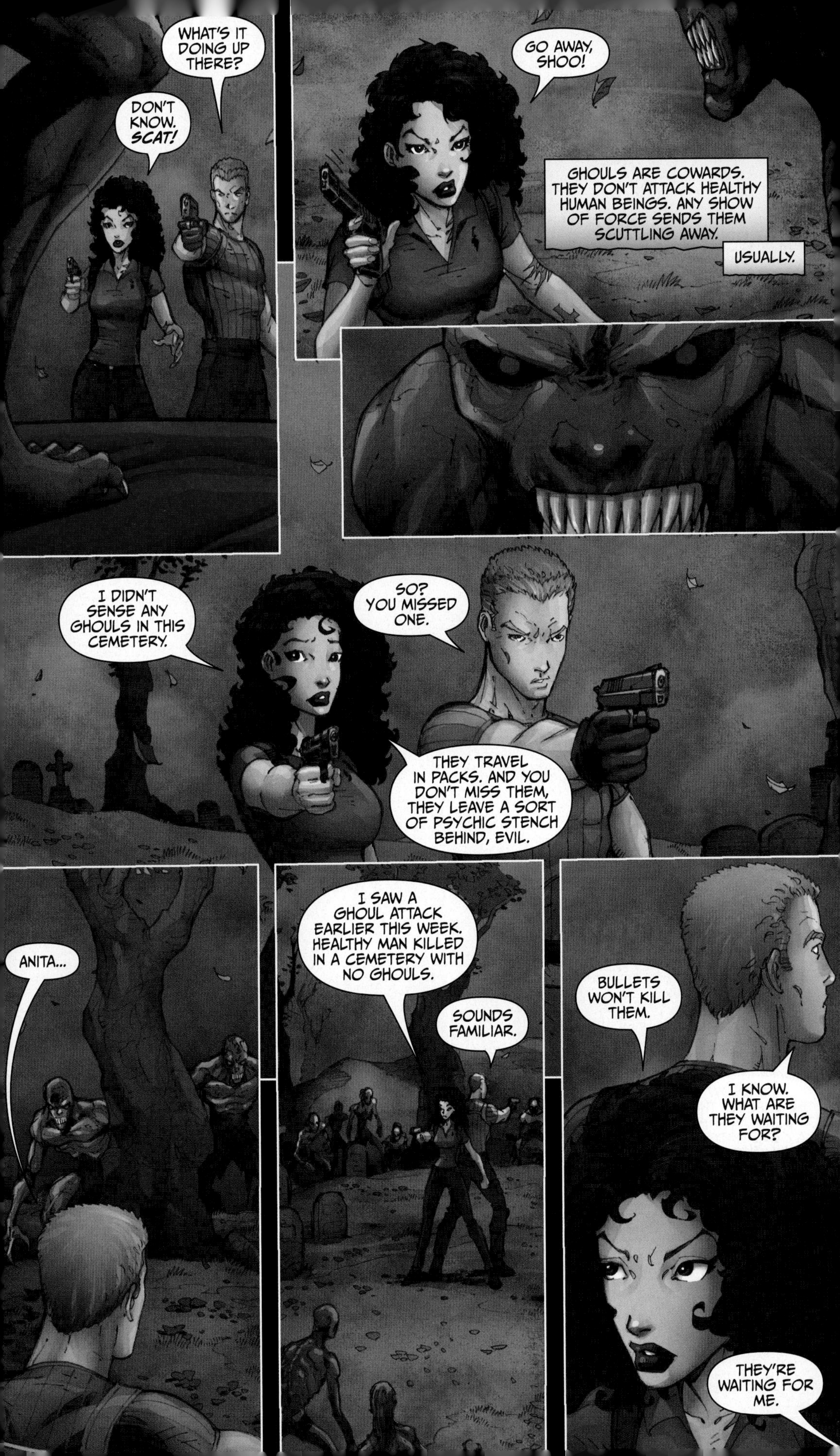
WHAT'S IT DOING UP THERE?
DON'T KNOW. SCAT!
GO AWAY, SHOO!
GHOULS ARE COWARDS. THEY DON'T ATTACK HEALTHY HUMAN BEINGS. ANY SHOW OF FORCE SENDS THEM SCUTTLING AWAY.
USUALLY.
I DIDN'T SENSE ANY GHOULS IN THIS CEMETERY.
SO? YOU MISSED ONE.
THEY TRAVEL IN PACKS. AND YOU DON'T MISS THEM, THEY LEAVE A SORT OF PSYCHIC STENCH BEHIND, EVIL.
ANITA...
I SAW A GHOUL ATTACK EARLIER THIS WEEK. HEALTHY MAN KILLED IN A CEMETERY WITH NO GHOULS.
SOUNDS FAMILIAR.
BULLETS WON'T KILL THEM.
I KNOW. WHAT ARE THEY WAITING FOR?
THEY'RE WAITING FOR ME.

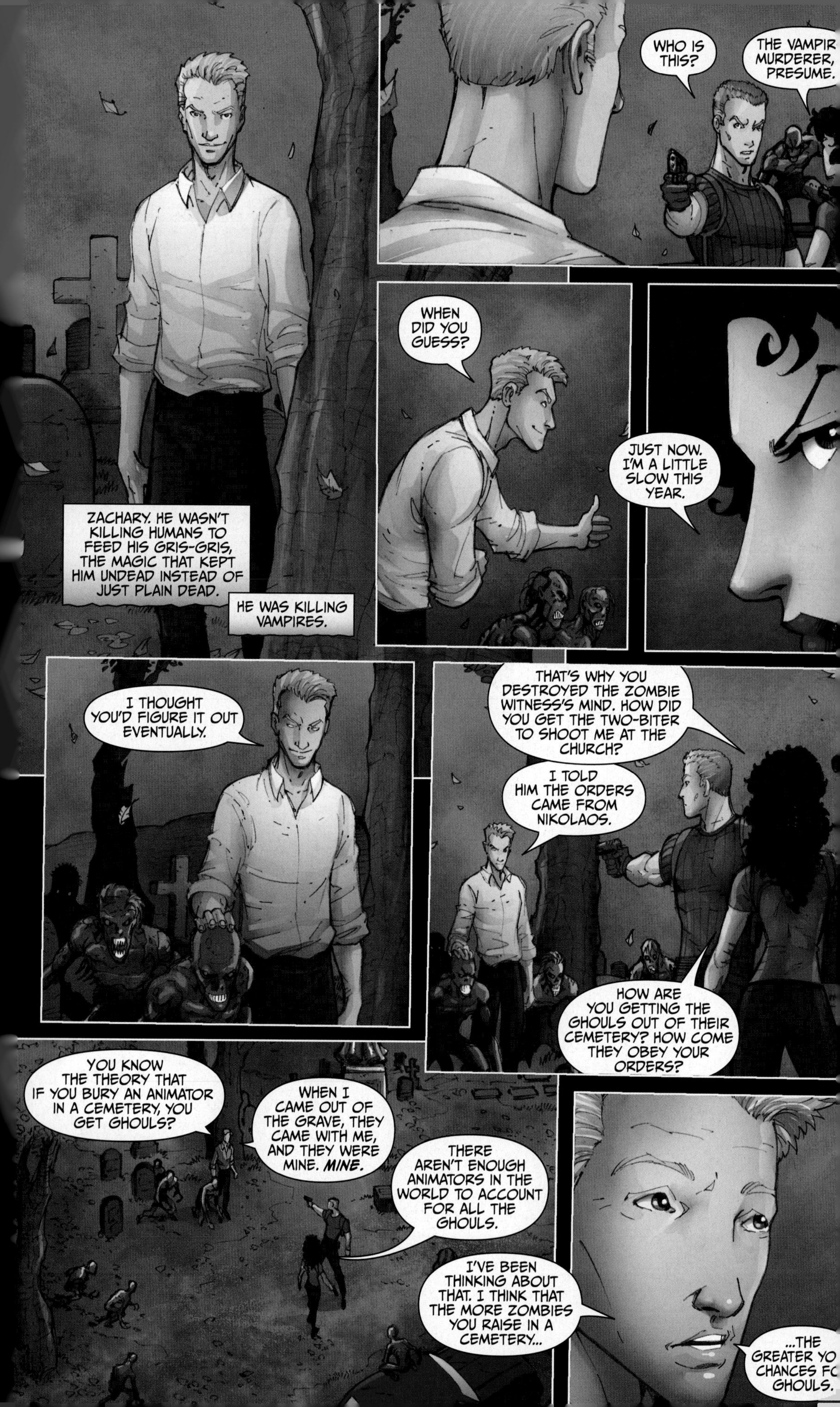
WHO IS THIS?
THE VAMPIR MURDERER, PRESUME.
ZACHARY. HE WASN'T KILLING HUMANS TO FEED HIS GRIS-GRIS, THE MAGIC THAT KEPT HIM UNDEAD INSTEAD OF JUST PLAIN DEAD.
HE WAS KILLING VAMPIRES.
WHEN DID YOU GUESS?
JUST NOW. I'M A LITTLE SLOW THIS YEAR.
I THOUGHT YOU'D FIGURE IT OUT EVENTUALLY.
THAT'S WHY YOU DESTROYED THE ZOMBIE WITNESS'S MIND. HOW DID YOU GET THE TWO-BITER TO SHOOT ME AT THE CHURCH?
I TOLD HIM THE ORDERS CAME FROM NIKOLAOS.
HOW ARE YOU GETTING THE GHOULS OUT OF THEIR CEMETERY? HOW COME THEY OBEY YOUR ORDERS?
YOU KNOW THE THEORY THAT IF YOU BURY AN ANIMATOR IN A CEMETERY, YOU GET GHOULS?
WHEN I CAME OUT OF THE GRAVE, THEY CAME WITH ME, AND THEY WERE MINE. MINE.
THERE AREN'T ENOUGH ANIMATORS IN THE WORLD TO ACCOUNT FOR ALL THE GHOULS.
I'VE BEEN THINKING ABOUT THAT. I THINK THAT THE MORE ZOMBIES YOU RAISE IN A CEMETERY...
...THE GREATER YO CHANCES FO GHOULS.

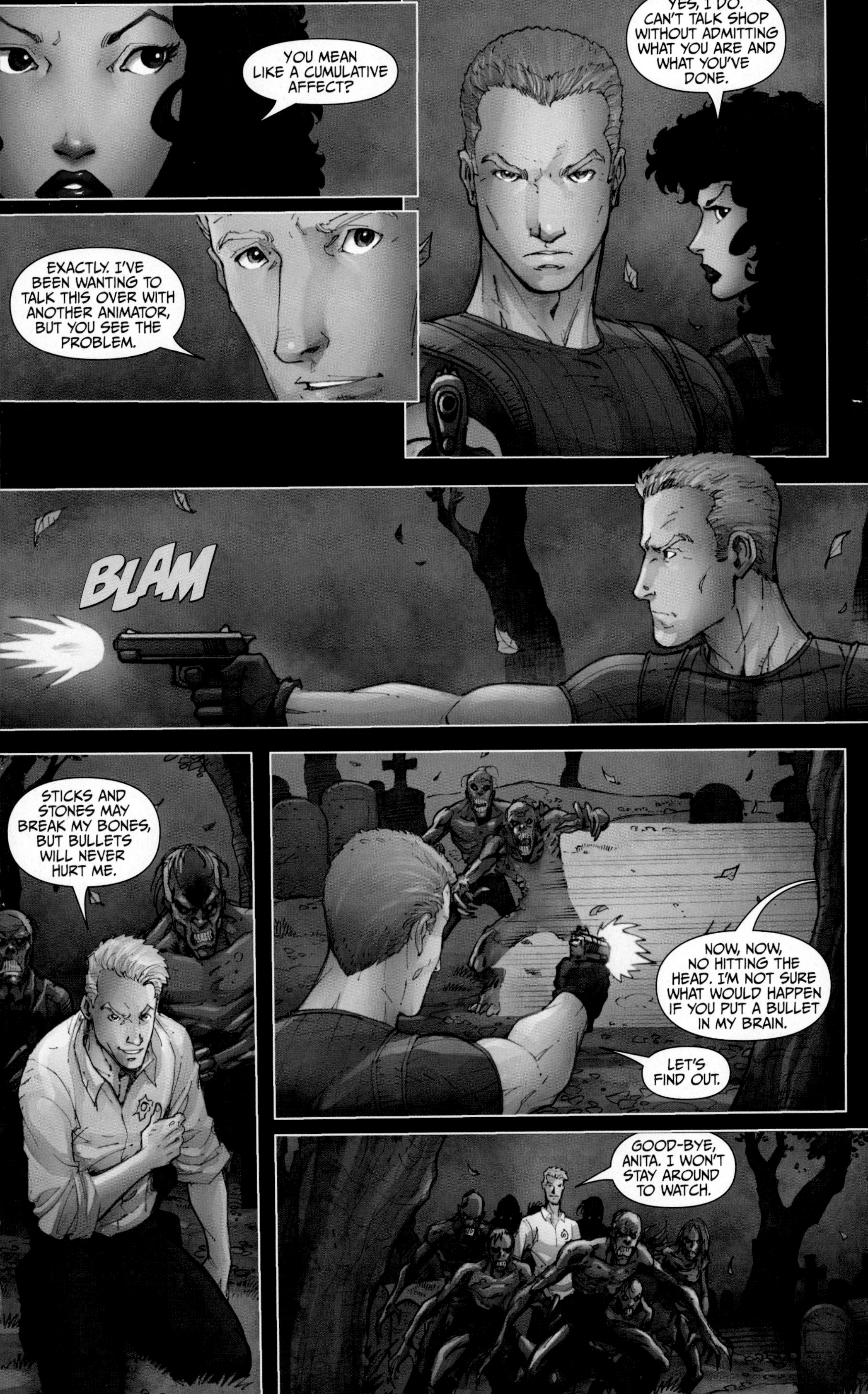
YOU MEAN LIKE A CUMULATIVE AFFECT?
EXACTLY. I'VE BEEN WANTING TO TALK THIS OVER WITH ANOTHER ANIMATOR, BUT YOU SEE THE PROBLEM.
YES, I DO. CAN'T TALK SHOP WITHOUT ADMITTING WHAT YOU ARE AND WHAT YOU'VE DONE.
BLAM
STICKS AND STONES MAY BREAK MY BONES, BUT BULLETS WILL NEVER HURT ME.
NOW, NOW, NO HITTING THE HEAD. I'M NOT SURE WHAT WOULD HAPPEN IF YOU PUT A BULLET IN MY BRAIN.
LET'S FIND OUT.
GOOD-BYE, ANITA. I WON'T STAY AROUND TO WATCH.

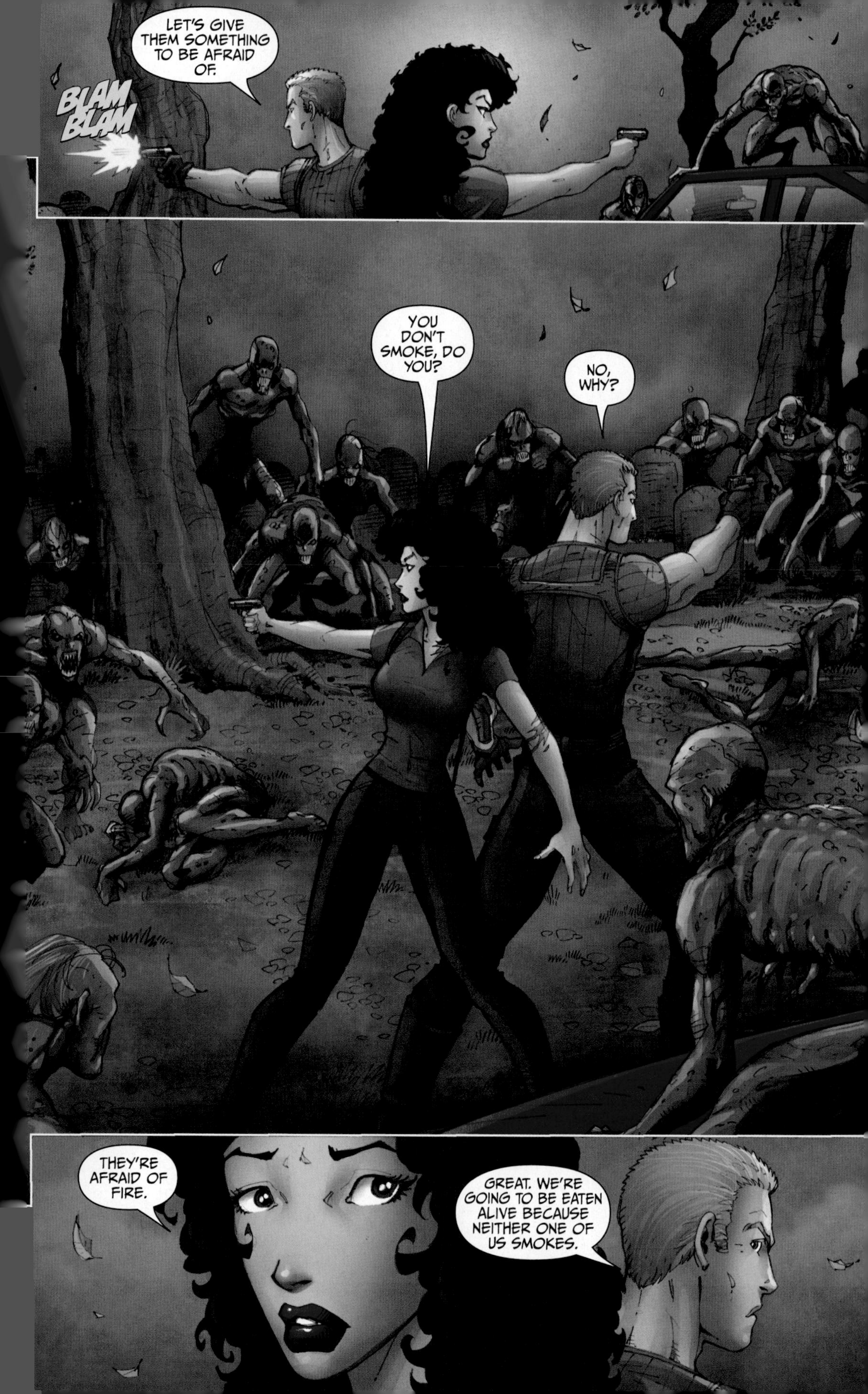
LET'S GIVE THEM SOMETHING TO BE AFRAID OF.
BLAM BLAM
YOU DON'T SMOKE, DO YOU?
NO, WHY?
THEY'RE AFRAID OF FIRE.
GREAT. WE'RE GOING TO BE EATEN ALIVE BECAUSE NEITHER ONE OF US SMOKES.

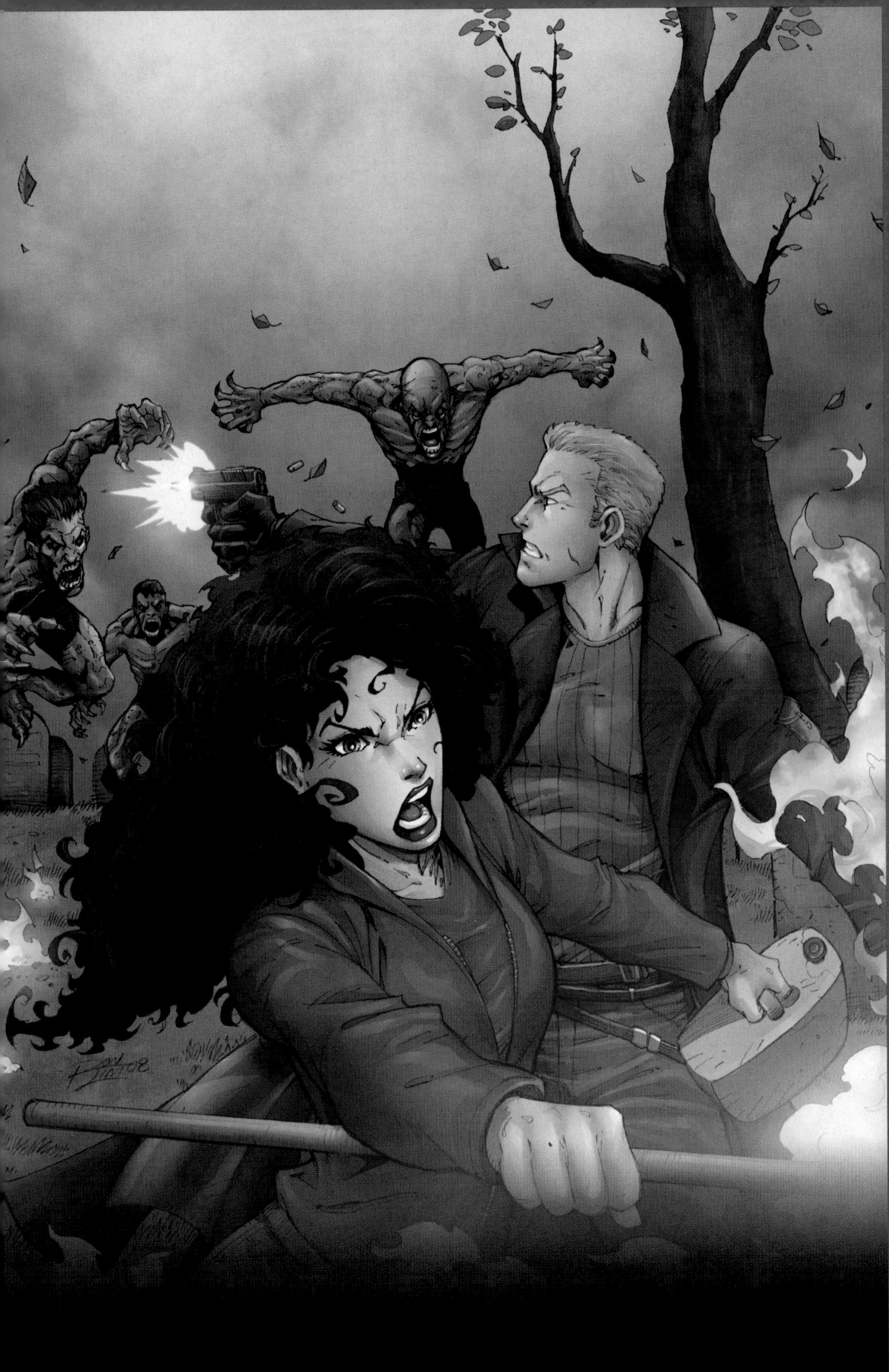

[#11]

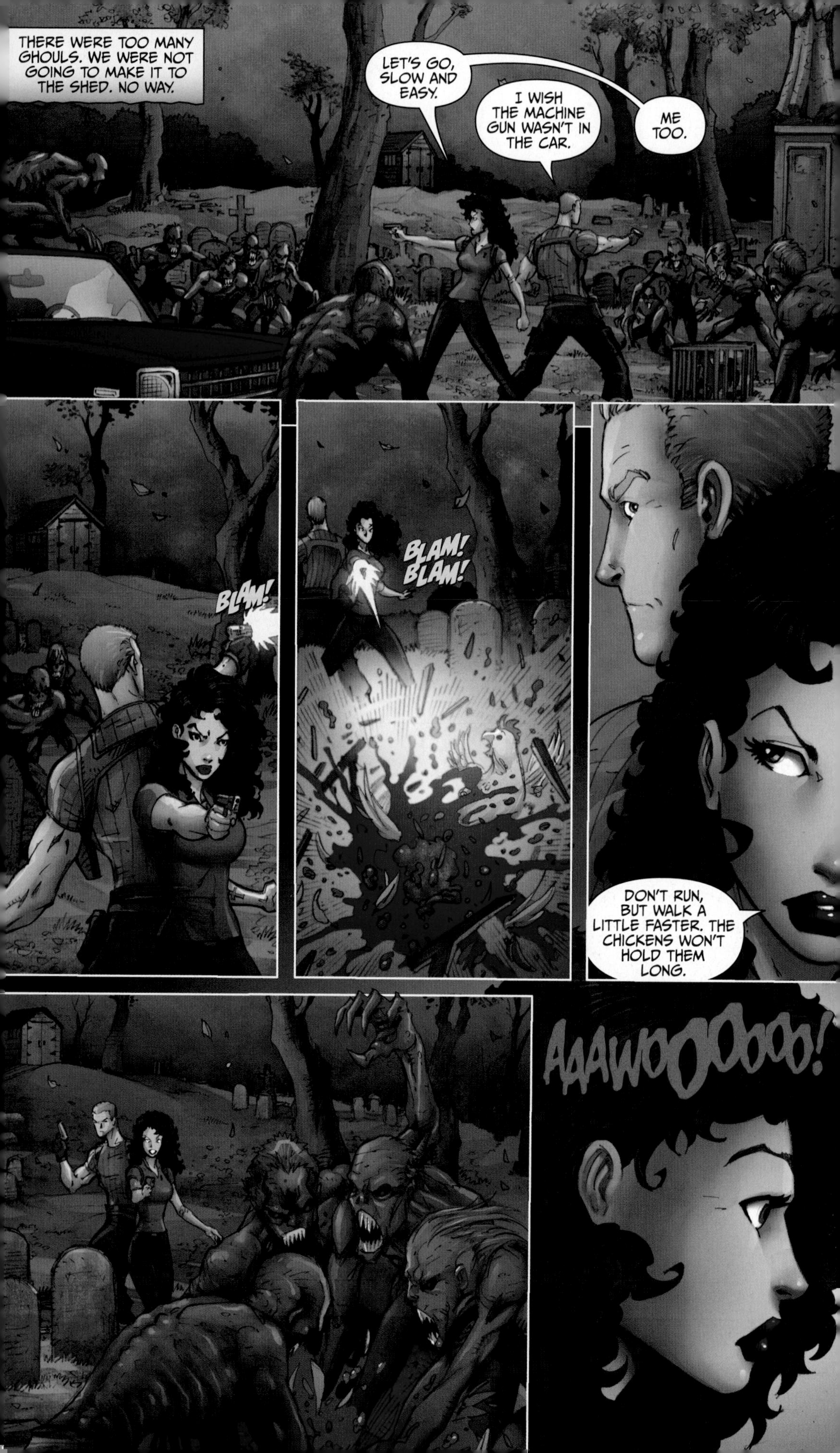

THERE WERE TOO MANY GHOULS. WE WERE NOT GOING TO MAKE IT TO THE SHED. NO WAY.
LET'S GO, SLOW AND EASY.
I WISH THE MACHINE GUN WASN'T IN THE CAR.
ME TOO.
BLAM!
BLAM! BLAM!
DON'T RUN, BUT WALK A LITTLE FASTER. THE CHICKENS WON'T HOLD THEM LONG.
AAAWOOOOOOO!

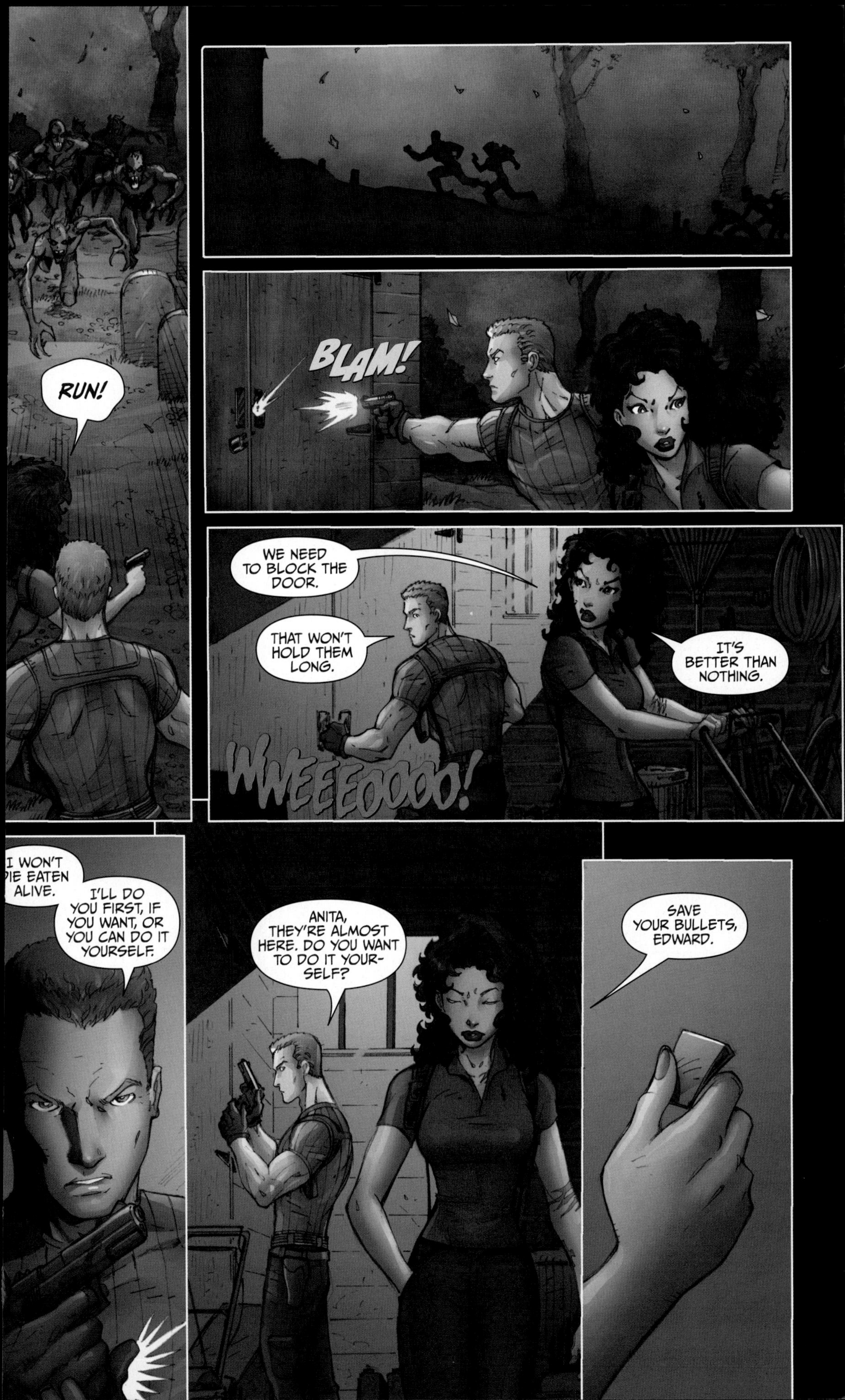
RUN!
BLAM!
WE NEED TO BLOCK THE DOOR.
THAT WON'T HOLD THEM LONG.
IT'S BETTER THAN NOTHING.
WWEEEOOOO!
I WON'T DIE EATEN ALIVE.
I'LL DO YOU FIRST, IF YOU WANT, OR YOU CAN DO IT YOURSELF.
ANITA, THEY'RE ALMOST HERE. DO YOU WANT TO DO IT YOUR-SELF?
SAVE YOUR BULLETS, EDWARD.

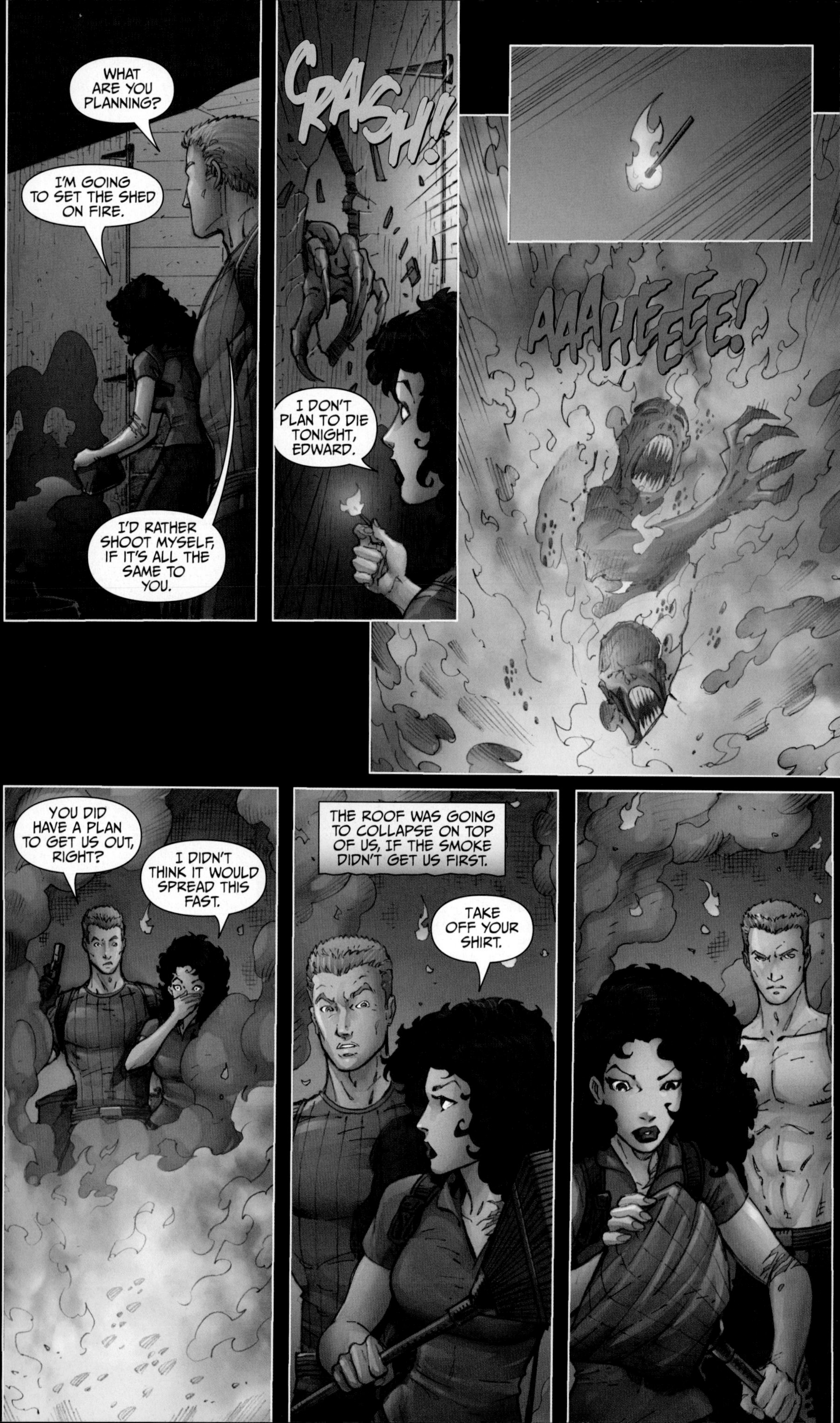
WHAT ARE YOU PLANNING?
I'M GOING TO SET THE SHED ON FIRE.
I'D RATHER SHOOT MYSELF, IF IT'S ALL THE SAME TO YOU.
CRASH!!
I DON'T PLAN TO DIE TONIGHT, EDWARD.
AAAHEEEE!
YOU DID HAVE A PLAN TO GET US OUT, RIGHT?
I DIDN'T THINK IT WOULD SPREAD THIS FAST.
THE ROOF WAS GOING TO COLLAPSE ON TOP OF US, IF THE SMOKE DIDN'T GET US FIRST.
TAKE OFF YOUR SHIRT.

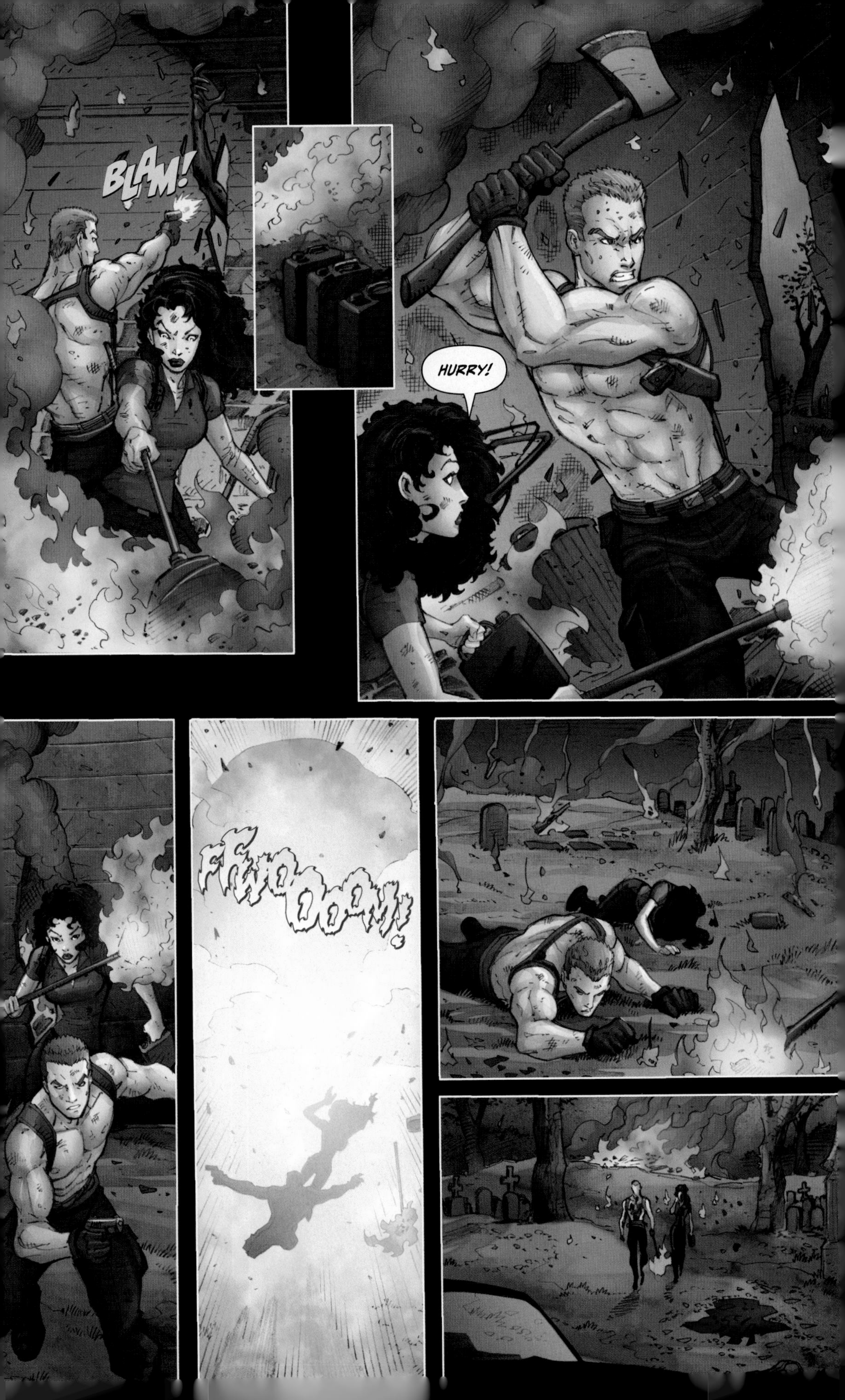
BLAM!
HURRY!
FWOOOM!

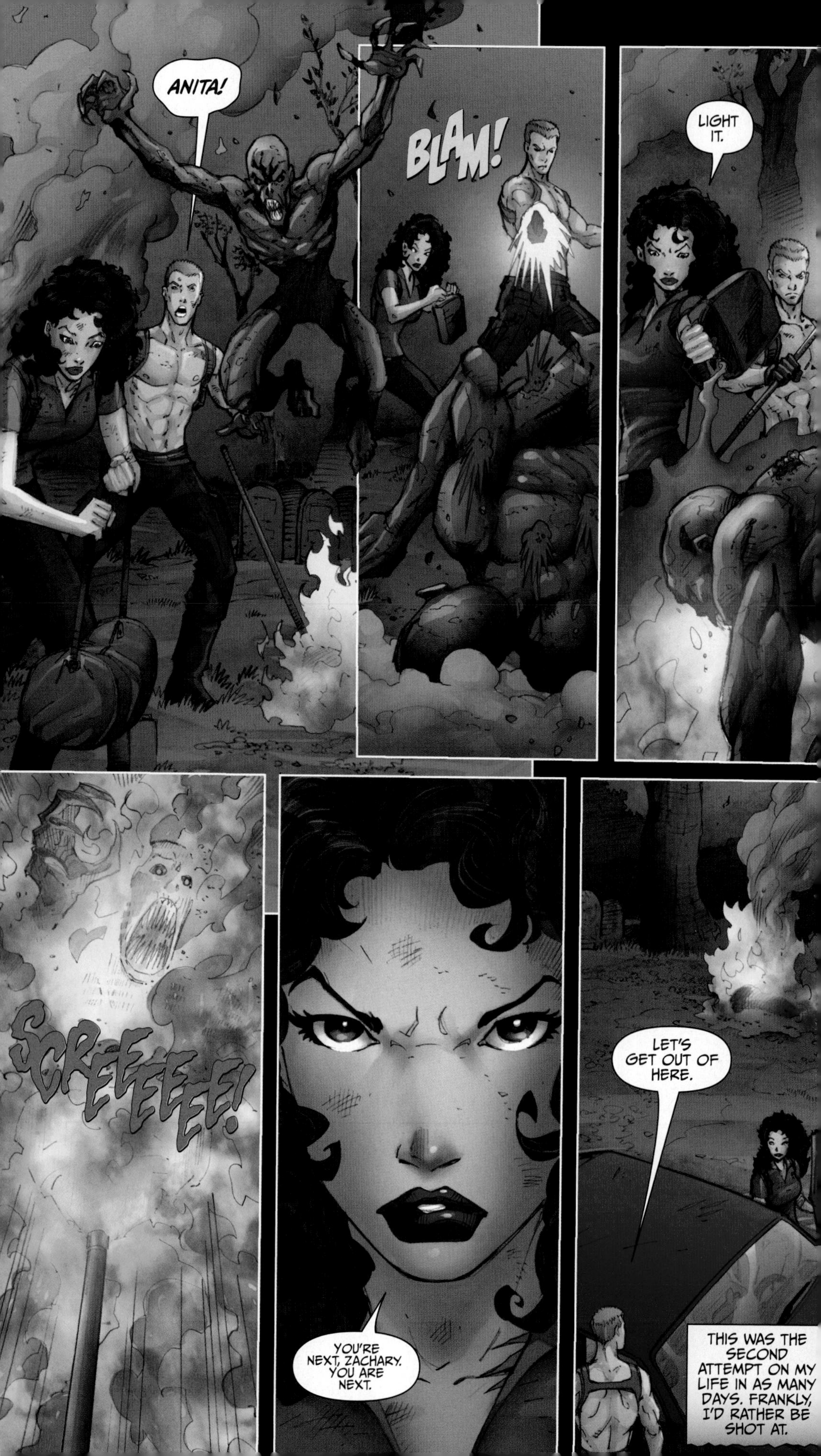
ANITA!
BLAM!
LIGHT IT.
SCREEEEEE!
YOU'RE NEXT, ZACHARY. YOU ARE NEXT.
LET'S GET OUT OF HERE.
THIS WAS THE SECOND ATTEMPT ON MY LIFE IN AS MANY DAYS. FRANKLY, I'D RATHER BE SHOT AT.

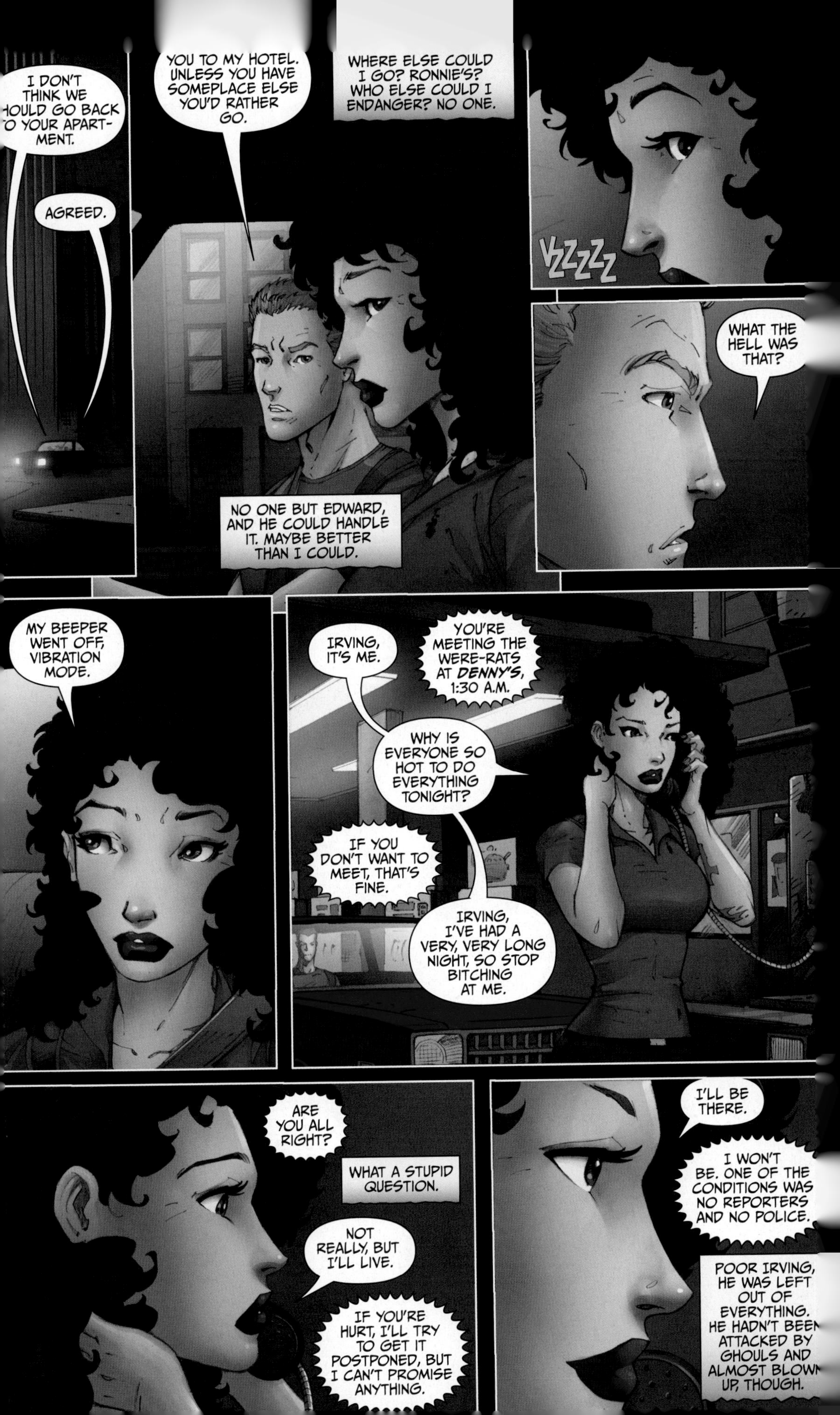

I DON'T THINK WE HOULD GO BACK O YOUR APARTMENT.
AGREED.
YOU TO MY HOTEL. UNLESS YOU HAVE SOMEPLACE ELSE YOU'D RATHER GO.
WHERE ELSE COULD I GO? RONNIE'S? WHO ELSE COULD I ENDANGER? NO ONE.
NO ONE BUT EDWARD, AND HE COULD HANDLE IT. MAYBE BETTER THAN I COULD.
VZZZZZ
WHAT THE HELL WAS THAT?
MY BEEPER WENT OFF, VIBRATION MODE.
IRVING, IT'S ME.
YOU'RE MEETING THE WERE-RATS AT DENNY'S, 1:30 A.M.
WHY IS EVERYONE SO HOT TO DO EVERYTHING TONIGHT?
IF YOU DON'T WANT TO MEET, THAT'S FINE.
IRVING, I'VE HAD A VERY, VERY LONG NIGHT, SO STOP BITCHING AT ME.
ARE YOU ALL RIGHT?
WHAT A STUPID QUESTION.
NOT REALLY, BUT I'LL LIVE.
IF YOU'RE HURT, I'LL TRY TO GET IT POSTPONED, BUT I CAN'T PROMISE ANYTHING.
I'LL BE THERE.
I WON'T BE. ONE OF THE CONDITIONS WAS NO REPORTERS AND NO POLICE.
POOR IRVING, HE WAS LEFT OUT OF EVERYTHING. HE HADN'T BEEN ATTACKED BY GHOULS AND ALMOST BLOWN UP, THOUGH.

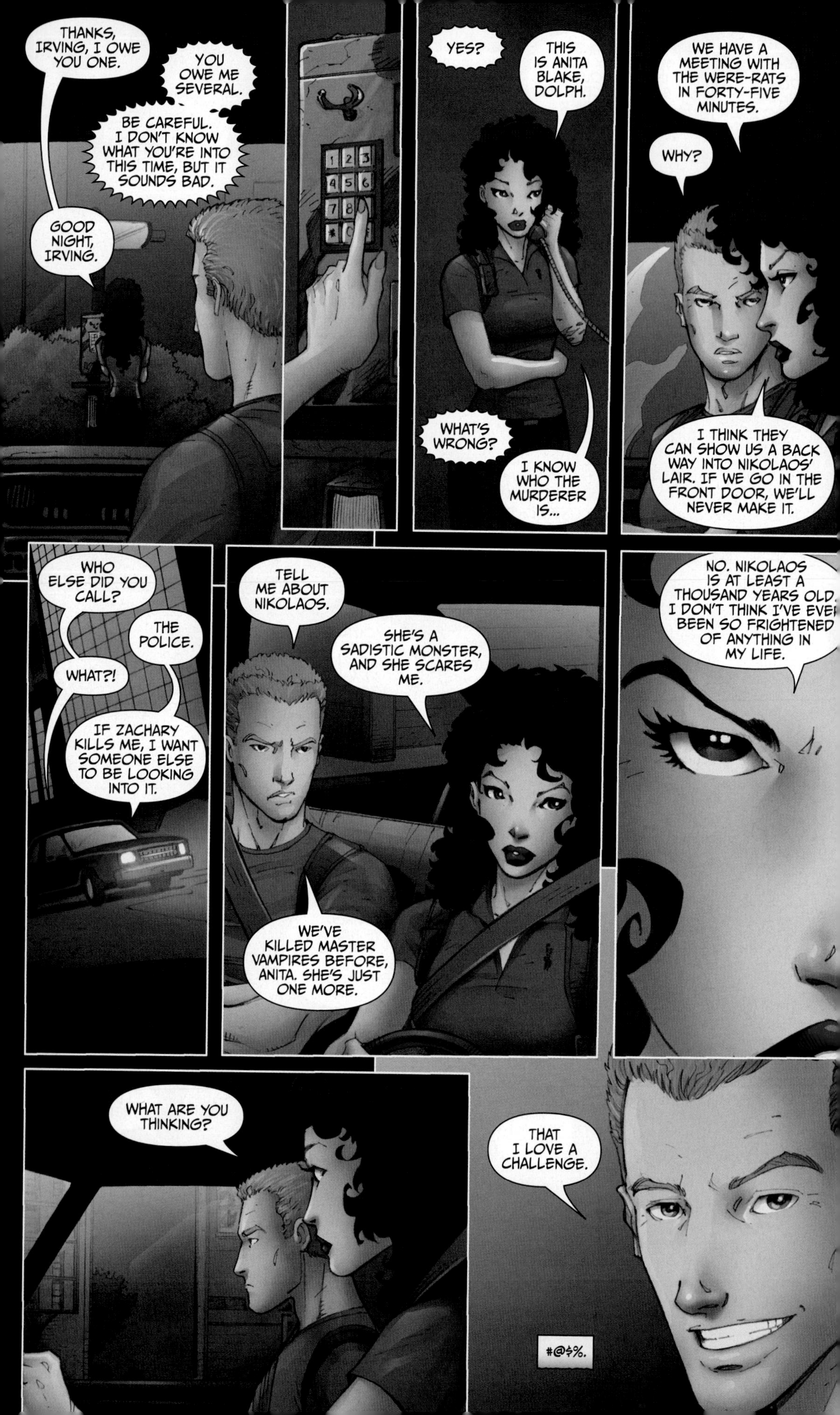
THANKS, IRVING, I OWE YOU ONE.
YOU OWE ME SEVERAL.
BE CAREFUL. I DON'T KNOW WHAT YOU'RE INTO THIS TIME, BUT IT SOUNDS BAD.
GOOD NIGHT, IRVING.
YES?
THIS IS ANITA BLAKE, DOLPH.
WHAT'S WRONG?
I KNOW WHO THE MURDERER IS...
WE HAVE A MEETING WITH THE WERE-RATS IN FORTY-FIVE MINUTES.
WHY?
I THINK THEY CAN SHOW US A BACK WAY INTO NIKOLAOS' LAIR. IF WE GO IN THE FRONT DOOR, WE'LL NEVER MAKE IT.
WHO ELSE DID YOU CALL?
THE POLICE.
WHAT?!
IF ZACHARY KILLS ME, I WANT SOMEONE ELSE TO BE LOOKING INTO IT.
TELL ME ABOUT NIKOLAOS.
SHE'S A SADISTIC MONSTER, AND SHE SCARES ME.
WE'VE KILLED MASTER VAMPIRES BEFORE, ANITA. SHE'S JUST ONE MORE.
NO. NIKOLAOS IS AT LEAST A THOUSAND YEARS OLD. I DON'T THINK I'VE EVER BEEN SO FRIGHTENED OF ANYTHING IN MY LIFE.
WHAT ARE YOU THINKING?
THAT I LOVE A CHALLENGE.
#@$%.

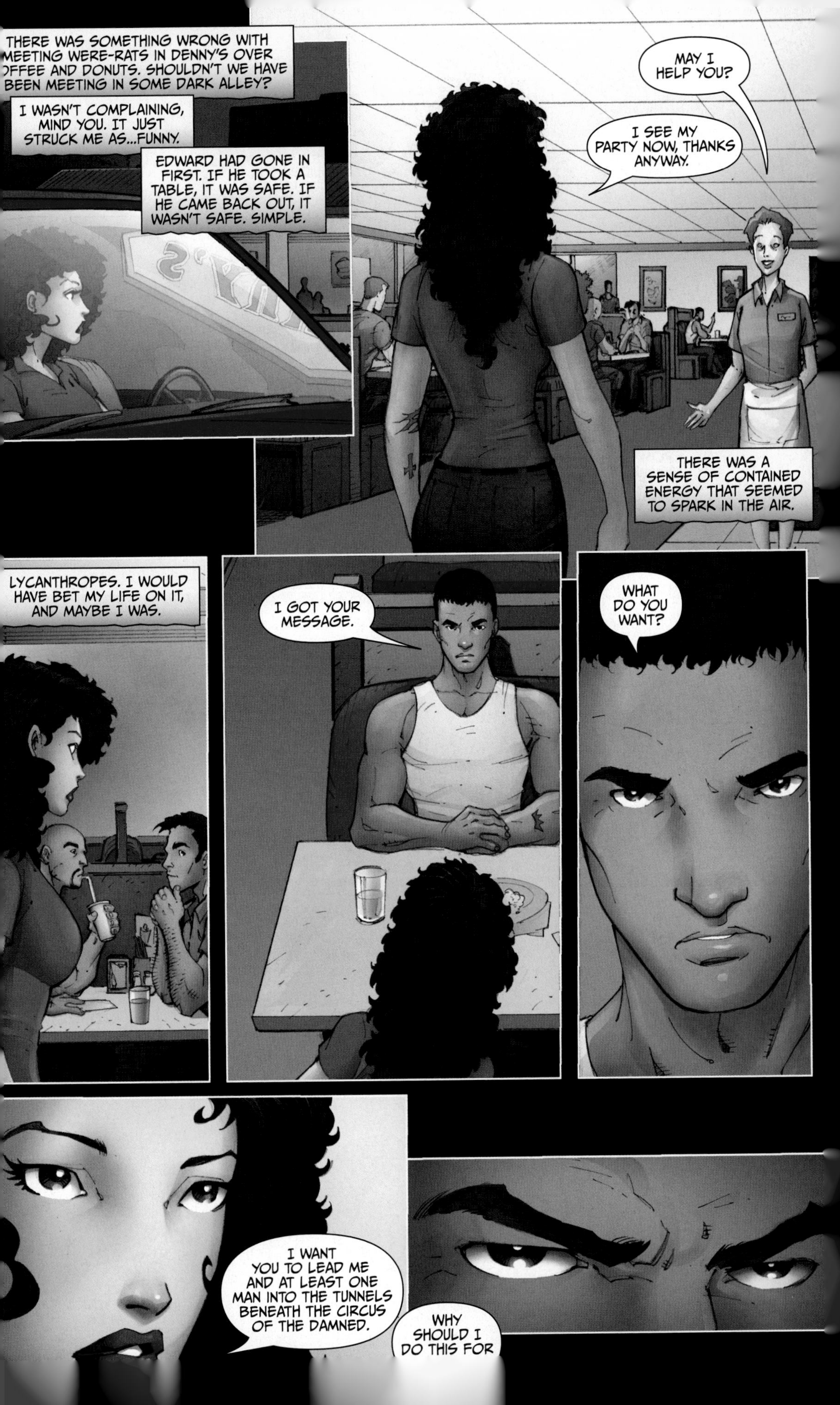
THERE WAS SOMETHING WRONG WITH MEETING WERE-RATS IN DENNY'S OVER OFFEE AND DONUTS. SHOULDN'T WE HAVE BEEN MEETING IN SOME DARK ALLEY?
I WASN'T COMPLAINING, MIND YOU. IT JUST STRUCK ME AS...FUNNY.
EDWARD HAD GONE IN FIRST. IF HE TOOK A TABLE, IT WAS SAFE. IF HE CAME BACK OUT, IT WASN'T SAFE. SIMPLE.
MAY I HELP YOU?
I SEE MY PARTY NOW, THANKS ANYWAY.
THERE WAS A SENSE OF CONTAINED ENERGY THAT SEEMED TO SPARK IN THE AIR.
LYCANTHROPES. I WOULD HAVE BET MY LIFE ON IT, AND MAYBE I WAS.
I GOT YOUR MESSAGE.
WHAT DO YOU WANT?
I WANT YOU TO LEAD ME AND AT LEAST ONE MAN INTO THE TUNNELS BENEATH THE CIRCUS OF THE DAMNED.
WHY SHOULD I DO THIS FOR

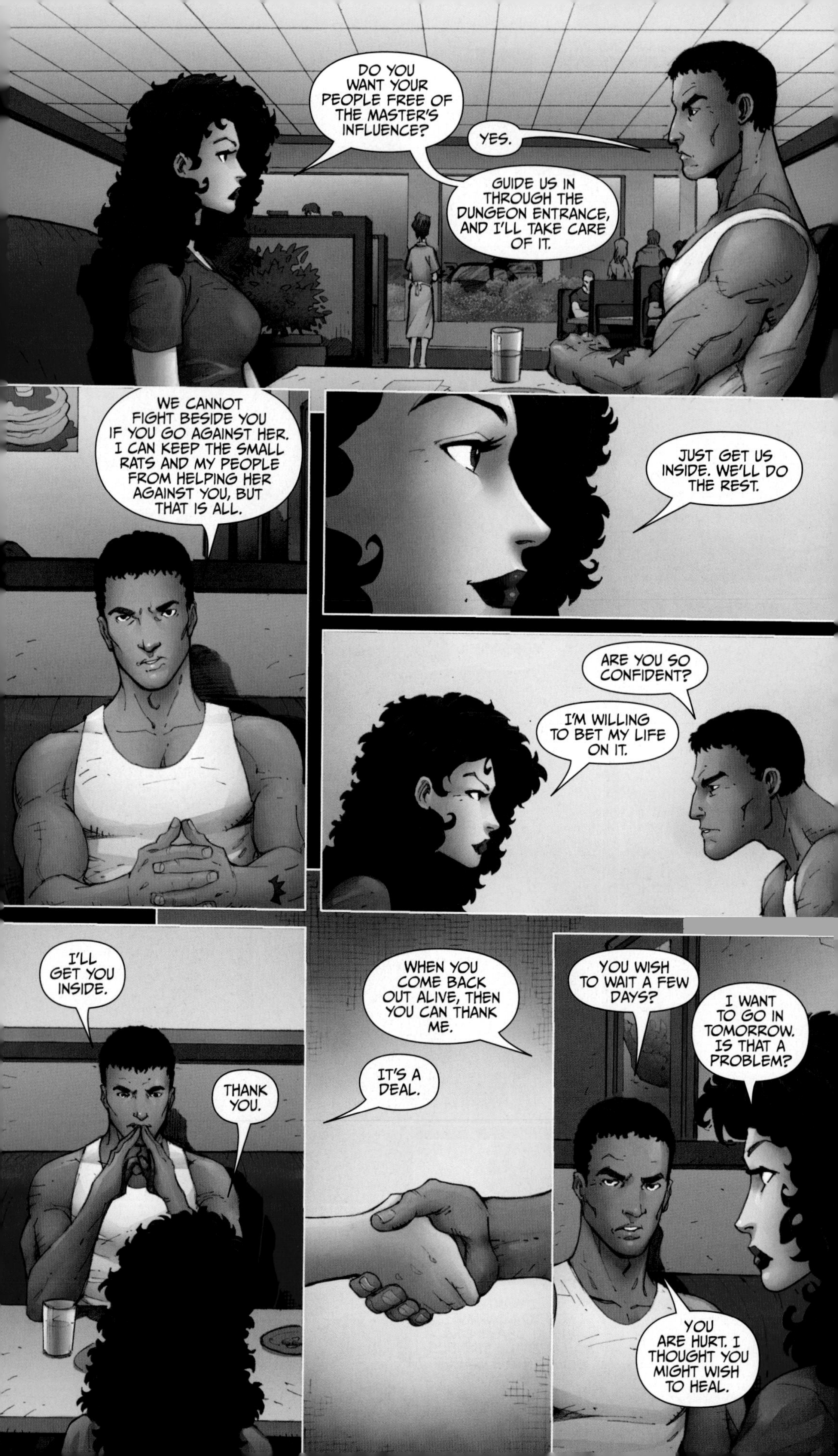
DO YOU WANT YOUR PEOPLE FREE OF THE MASTER'S INFLUENCE?
YES.
GUIDE US IN THROUGH THE DUNGEON ENTRANCE, AND I'LL TAKE CARE OF IT.
WE CANNOT FIGHT BESIDE YOU IF YOU GO AGAINST HER. I CAN KEEP THE SMALL RATS AND MY PEOPLE FROM HELPING HER AGAINST YOU, BUT THAT IS ALL.
JUST GET US INSIDE. WE'LL DO THE REST.
ARE YOU SO CONFIDENT?
I'M WILLING TO BET MY LIFE ON IT.
I'LL GET YOU INSIDE.
THANK YOU.
WHEN YOU COME BACK OUT ALIVE, THEN YOU CAN THANK ME.
IT'S A DEAL.
YOU WISH TO WAIT A FEW DAYS?
I WANT TO GO IN TOMORROW. IS THAT A PROBLEM?
YOU ARE HURT. I THOUGHT YOU MIGHT WISH TO HEAL.

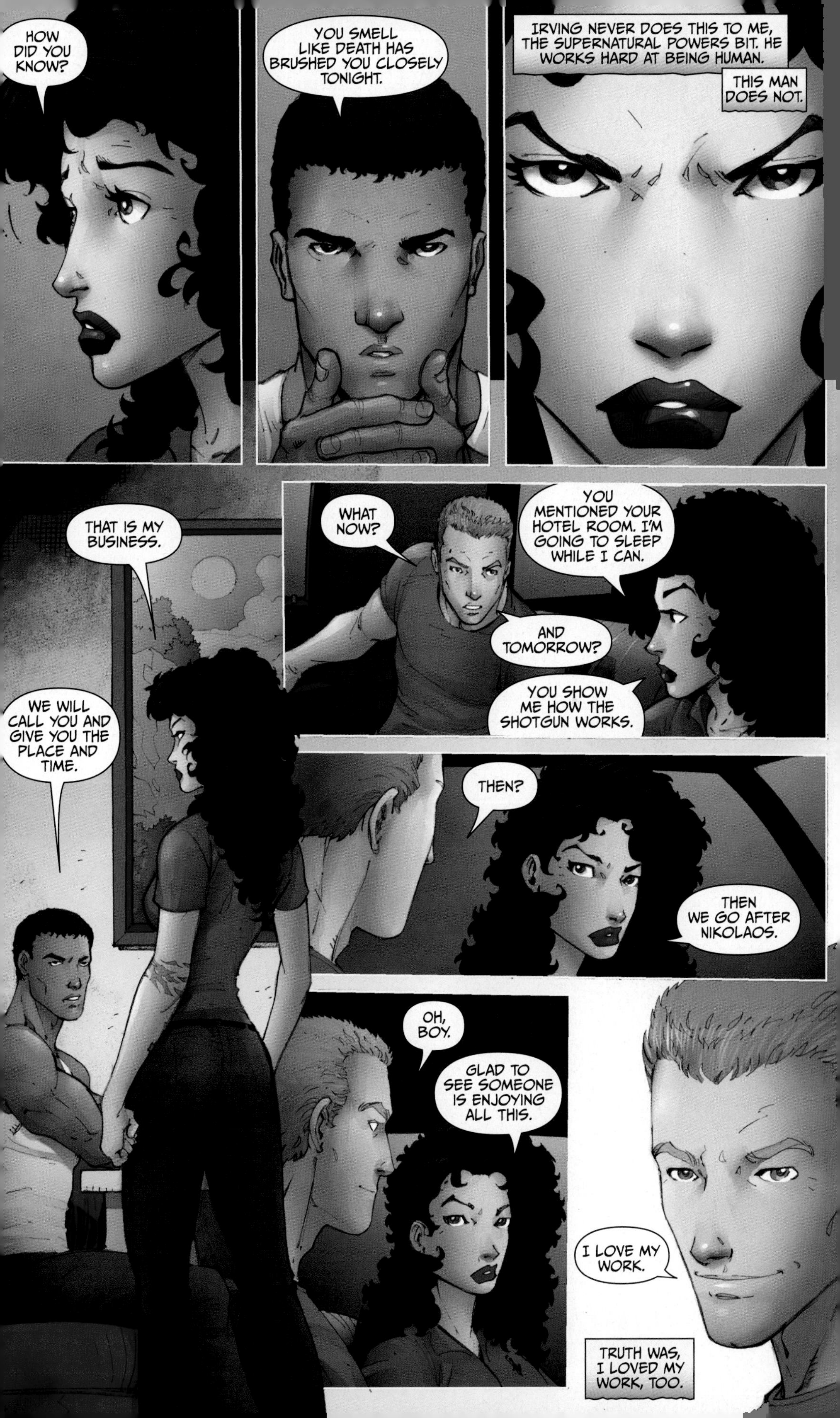
HOW DID YOU KNOW?
YOU SMELL LIKE DEATH HAS BRUSHED YOU CLOSELY TONIGHT.
IRVING NEVER DOES THIS TO ME, THE SUPERNATURAL POWERS BIT. HE WORKS HARD AT BEING HUMAN.
THIS MAN DOES NOT.
THAT IS MY BUSINESS.
WE WILL CALL YOU AND GIVE YOU THE PLACE AND TIME.
WHAT NOW?
YOU MENTIONED YOUR HOTEL ROOM. I'M GOING TO SLEEP WHILE I CAN.
AND TOMORROW?
YOU SHOW ME HOW THE SHOTGUN WORKS.
THEN?
THEN WE GO AFTER NIKOLAOS.
OH, BOY.
GLAD TO SEE SOMEONE IS ENJOYING ALL THIS.
I LOVE MY WORK.
TRUTH WAS, I LOVED MY WORK, TOO.

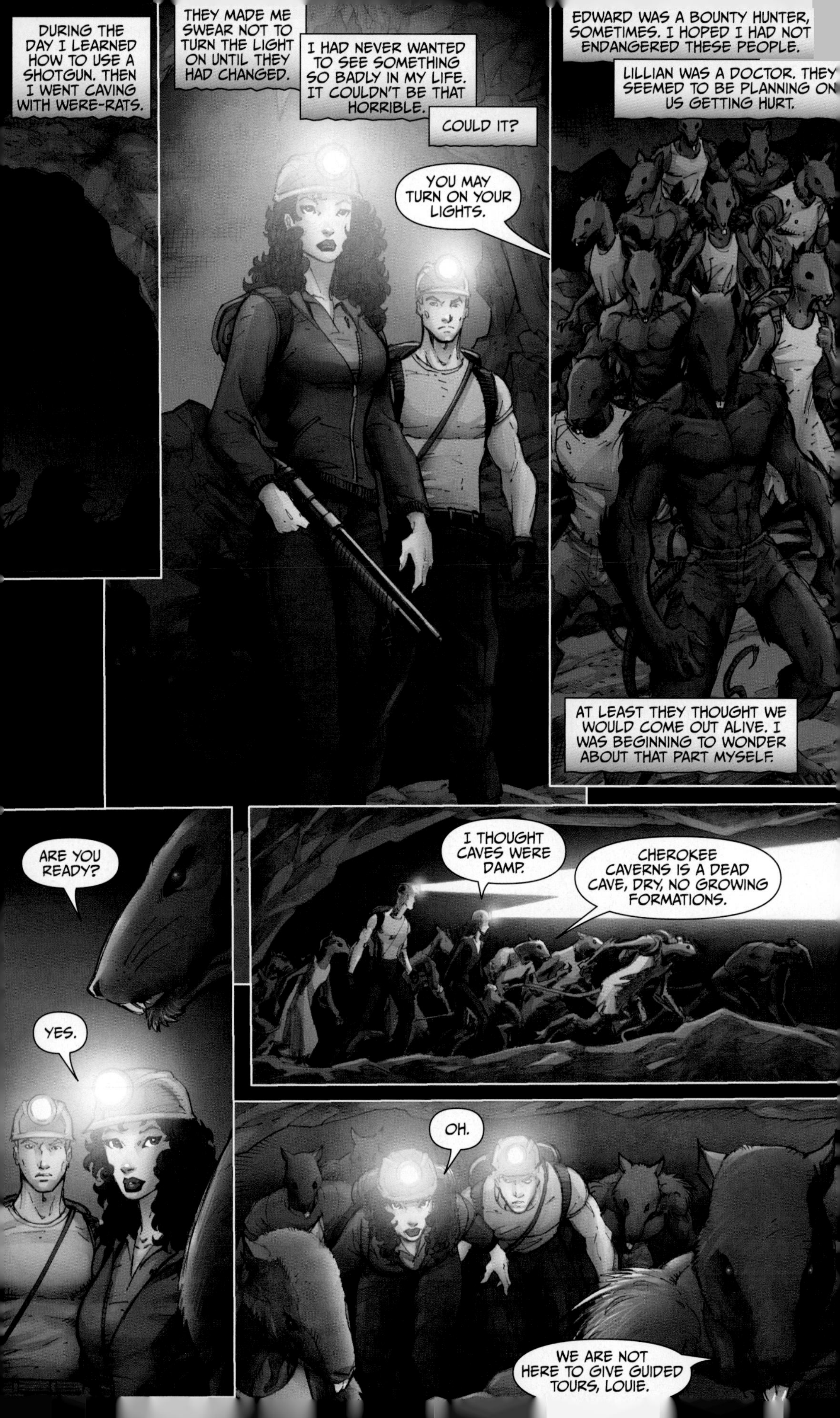
DURING THE DAY I LEARNED HOW TO USE A SHOTGUN. THEN I WENT CAVING WITH WERE-RATS.
THEY MADE ME SWEAR NOT TO TURN THE LIGHT ON UNTIL THEY HAD CHANGED.
I HAD NEVER WANTED TO SEE SOMETHING SO BADLY IN MY LIFE. IT COULDN'T BE THAT HORRIBLE.
COULD IT?
YOU MAY TURN ON YOUR LIGHTS.
EDWARD WAS A BOUNTY HUNTER, SOMETIMES. I HOPED I HAD NOT ENDANGERED THESE PEOPLE.
LILLIAN WAS A DOCTOR. THEY SEEMED TO BE PLANNING ON US GETTING HURT.
AT LEAST THEY THOUGHT WE WOULD COME OUT ALIVE. I WAS BEGINNING TO WONDER ABOUT THAT PART MYSELF.
ARE YOU READY?
YES.
I THOUGHT CAVES WERE DAMP.
CHEROKEE CAVERNS IS A DEAD CAVE, DRY, NO GROWING FORMATIONS.
OH.
WE ARE NOT HERE TO GIVE GUIDED TOURS, LOUIE.

DUNGEON. WE WILL WAIT HERE UNTIL NEAR DARK. IF YOU HAVE NOT COME OUT, WE WILL LEAVE.

AFTER NIKOLAOS IS DEAD, IF WE CAN, WE WILL HELP YOU.

THANK YOU FOR HELPING US.

DELIVERED YOU TO THE DEVIL'S DOOR.

DO NOT THANK ME FOR THAT.

IT WAS DAYLIGHT OUTSIDE. THERE SHOULDN'T BE A VAMPIRE STIRRING, BUT BURCHARD WOULD BE THERE.

AND IF HE SAW US, NIKOLAOS WOULD KNOW. SOMEHOW, SHE'D KNOW.

ANITA, WHAT'S WRONG?

SHE KILLED PHILLIP IN HERE.

KEEP YOUR MIND ON BUSINESS. I DON'T WANT TO DIE BECAUSE YOU'RE DAYDREAMING.

I STARTED TO ET ANGRY AND WALLOWED IT. E WAS RIGHT.

INTO THE DRAGON'S LAIR. I DIDN'T FEEL MUCH LIKE A KNIGHT. I WAS FRESH OUT OF SHINY STEEDS, OR WAS THAT SHINY ARMOR?

WHATEVER. WE WERE THERE. THIS WAS IT. I COULD TASTE MY HEART IN MY THROAT.

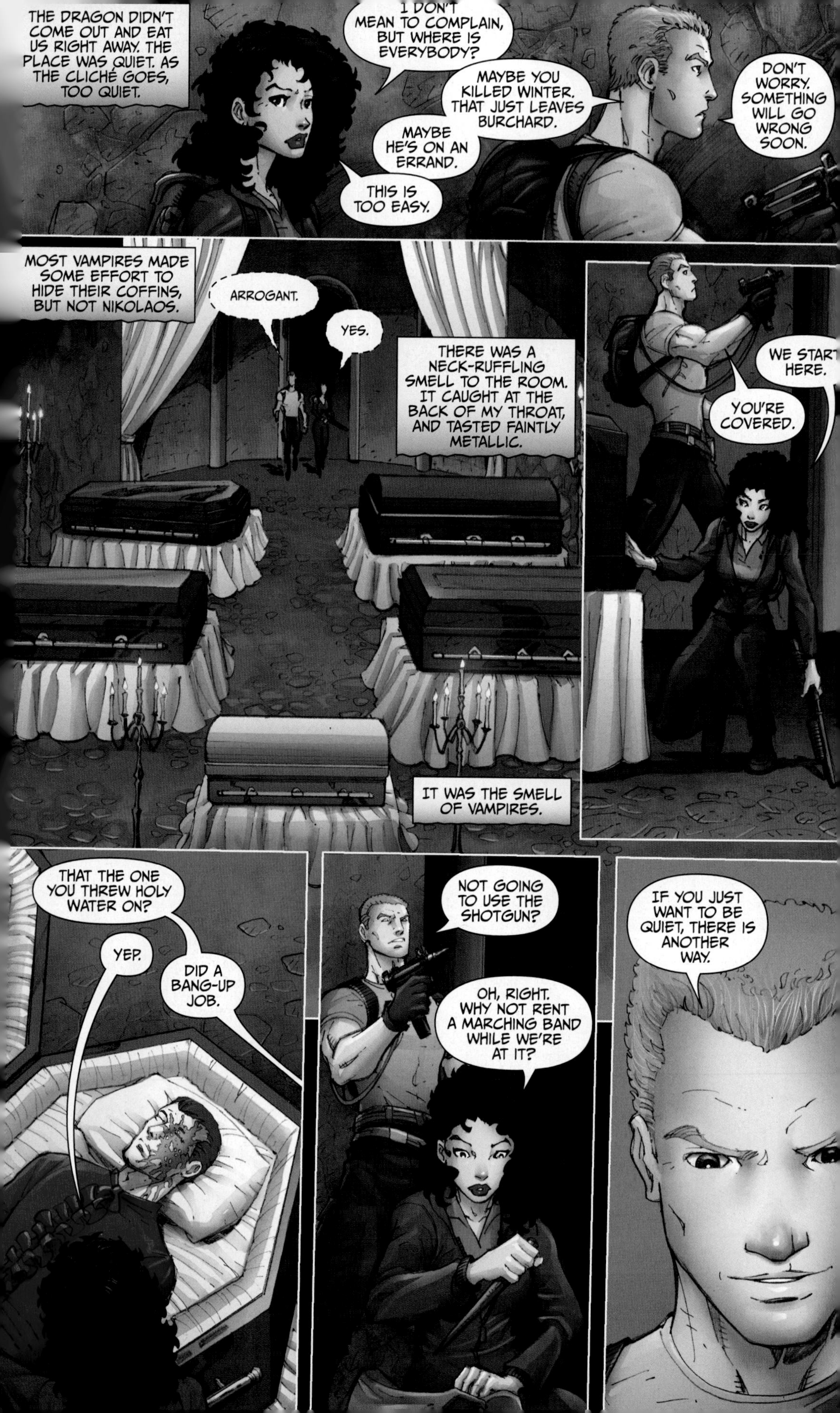
THE DRAGON DIDN'T COME OUT AND EAT US RIGHT AWAY. THE PLACE WAS QUIET. AS THE CLICHÉ GOES, TOO QUIET.
I DON'T MEAN TO COMPLAIN, BUT WHERE IS EVERYBODY?
MAYBE YOU KILLED WINTER. THAT JUST LEAVES BURCHARD.
MAYBE HE'S ON AN ERRAND.
THIS IS TOO EASY.
DON'T WORRY. SOMETHING WILL GO WRONG SOON.
MOST VAMPIRES MADE SOME EFFORT TO HIDE THEIR COFFINS, BUT NOT NIKOLAOS.
ARROGANT.
YES.
THERE WAS A NECK-RUFFLING SMELL TO THE ROOM. IT CAUGHT AT THE BACK OF MY THROAT, AND TASTED FAINTLY METALLIC.
IT WAS THE SMELL OF VAMPIRES.
WE START HERE.
YOU'RE COVERED.
THAT THE ONE YOU THREW HOLY WATER ON?
YEP.
DID A BANG-UP JOB.
NOT GOING TO USE THE SHOTGUN?
OH, RIGHT. WHY NOT RENT A MARCHING BAND WHILE WE'RE AT IT?
IF YOU JUST WANT TO BE QUIET, THERE IS ANOTHER WAY.

I'VE STAKED MOST OF THE VAMPIRES THAT I'VE KILLED. IT IS HARD, MESSY WORK, THOUGH I DON'T THROW UP ANYMORE.

I AM A PROFESSIONAL, AFTER ALL.

SILVER NITRATE.

DOES IT WORK?

IT WORKS.

HOW OLD IS THIS ONE?

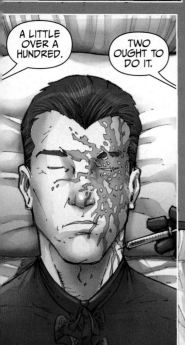

A LITTLE OVER A HUNDRED.

TWO OUGHT TO DO IT.

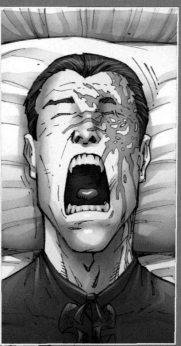

HE DOESN'T LOOK VERY DEAD.

THEY NEVER DO.

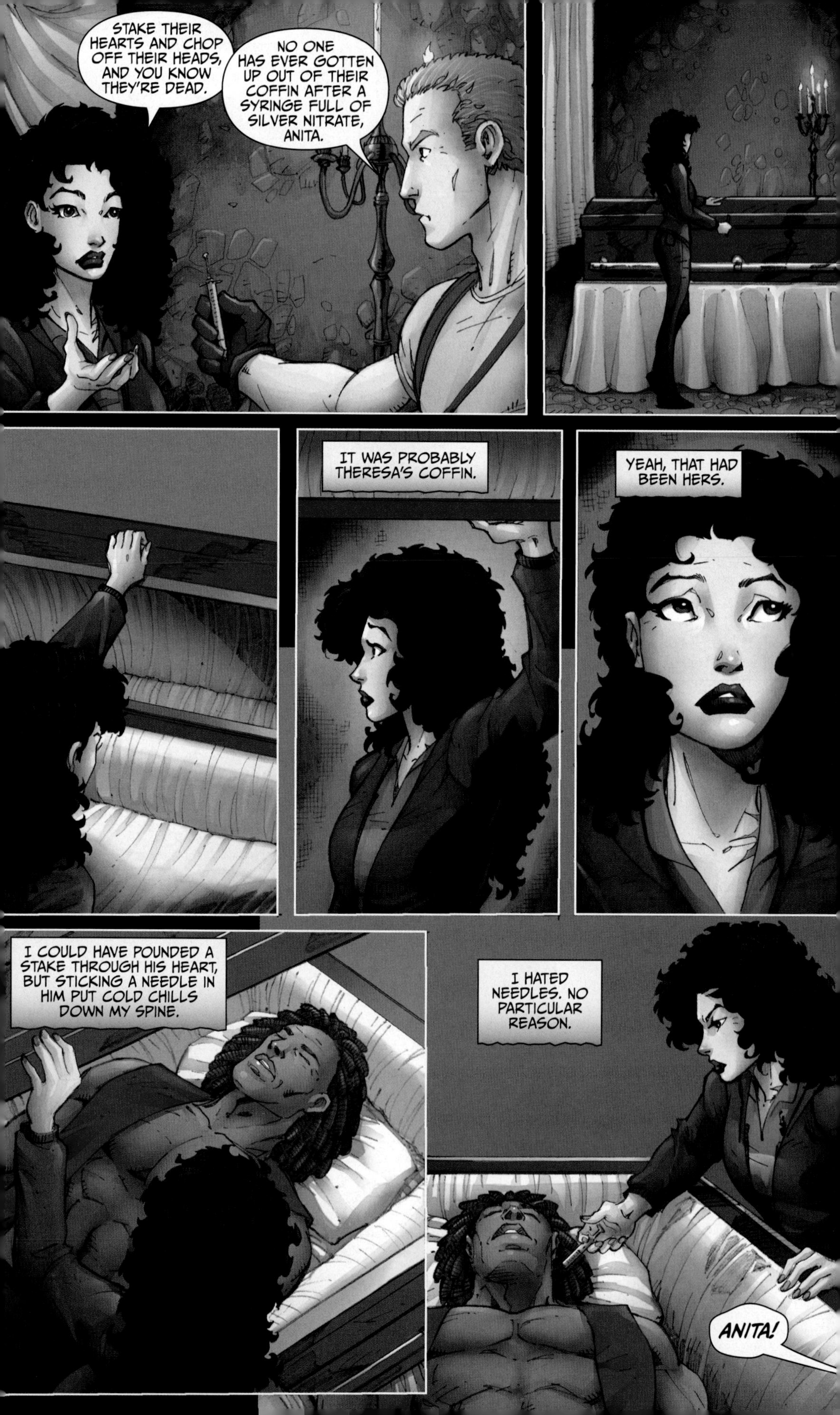
STAKE THEIR HEARTS AND CHOP OFF THEIR HEADS, AND YOU KNOW THEY'RE DEAD.
NO ONE HAS EVER GOTTEN UP OUT OF THEIR COFFIN AFTER A SYRINGE FULL OF SILVER NITRATE, ANITA.
IT WAS PROBABLY THERESA'S COFFIN.
YEAH, THAT HAD BEEN HERS.
I COULD HAVE POUNDED A STAKE THROUGH HIS HEART, BUT STICKING A NEEDLE IN HIM PUT COLD CHILLS DOWN MY SPINE.
I HATED NEEDLES. NO PARTICULAR REASON.
ANITA!

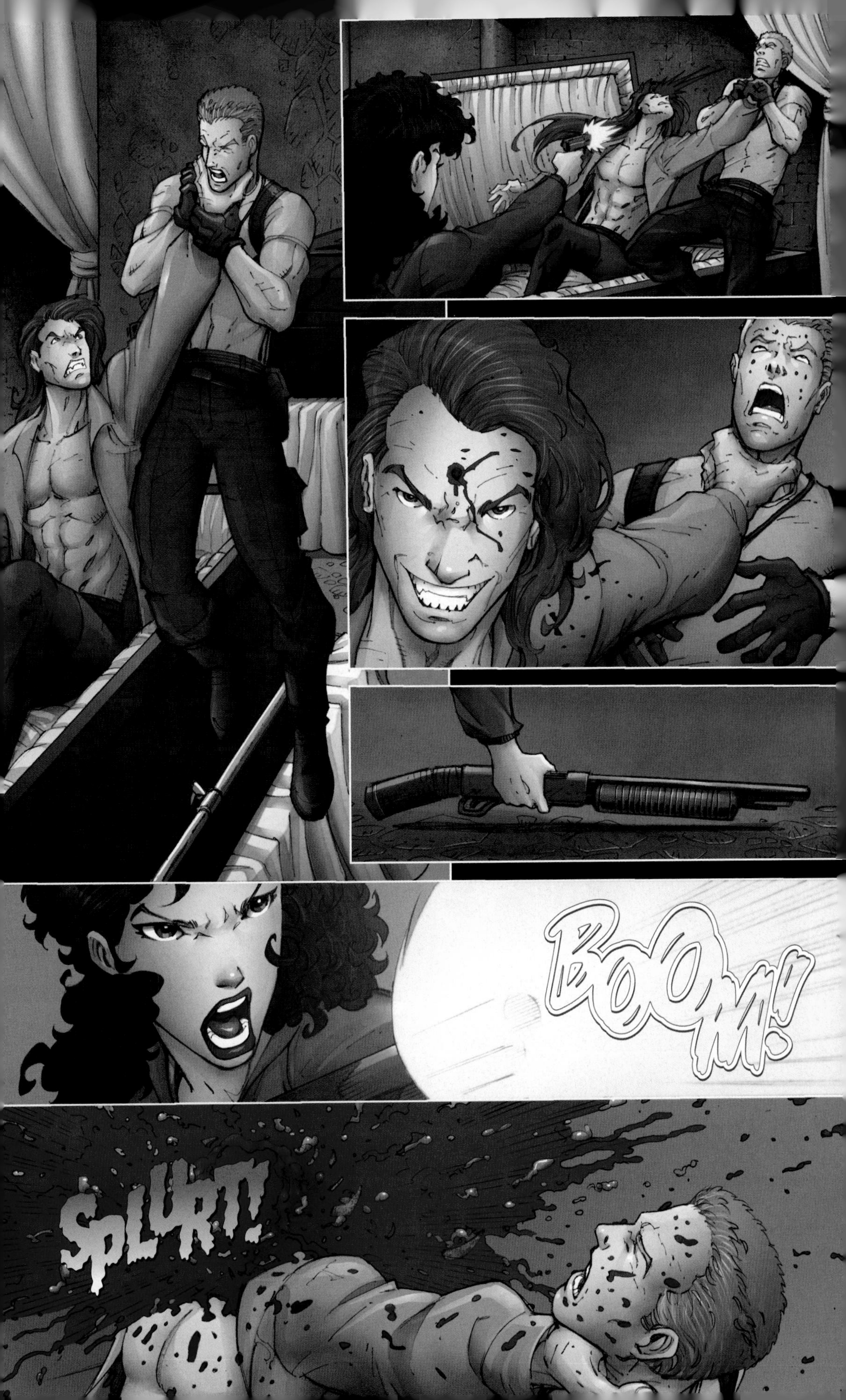
BOOM!
SPLURT!

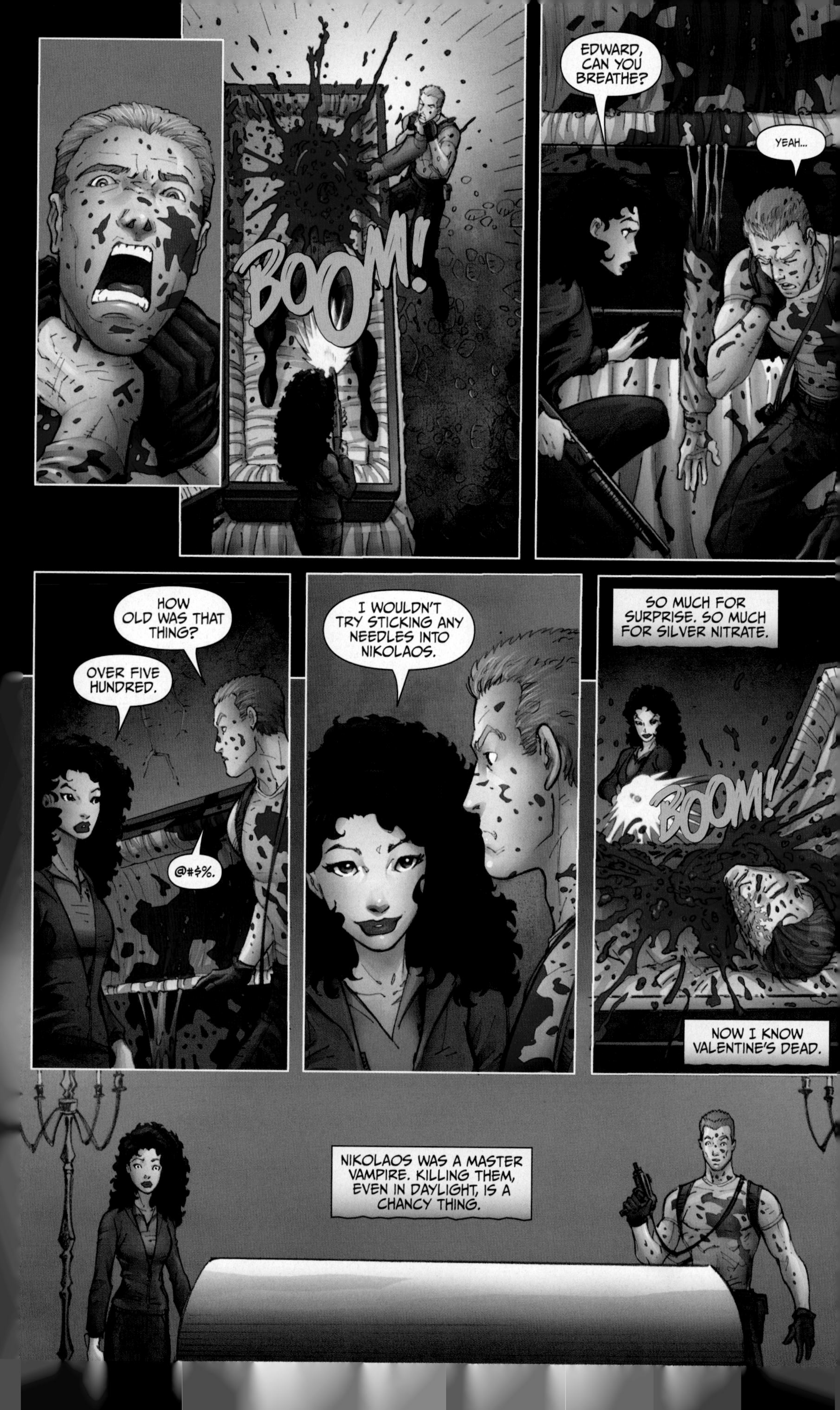

BOOM!
EDWARD, CAN YOU BREATHE?
YEAH...
HOW OLD WAS THAT THING?
OVER FIVE HUNDRED.
@#$%.
I WOULDN'T TRY STICKING ANY NEEDLES INTO NIKOLAOS.
SO MUCH FOR SURPRISE. SO MUCH FOR SILVER NITRATE.
BOOM!
NOW I KNOW VALENTINE'S DEAD.
NIKOLAOS WAS A MASTER VAMPIRE. KILLING THEM, EVEN IN DAYLIGHT, IS A CHANCY THING.

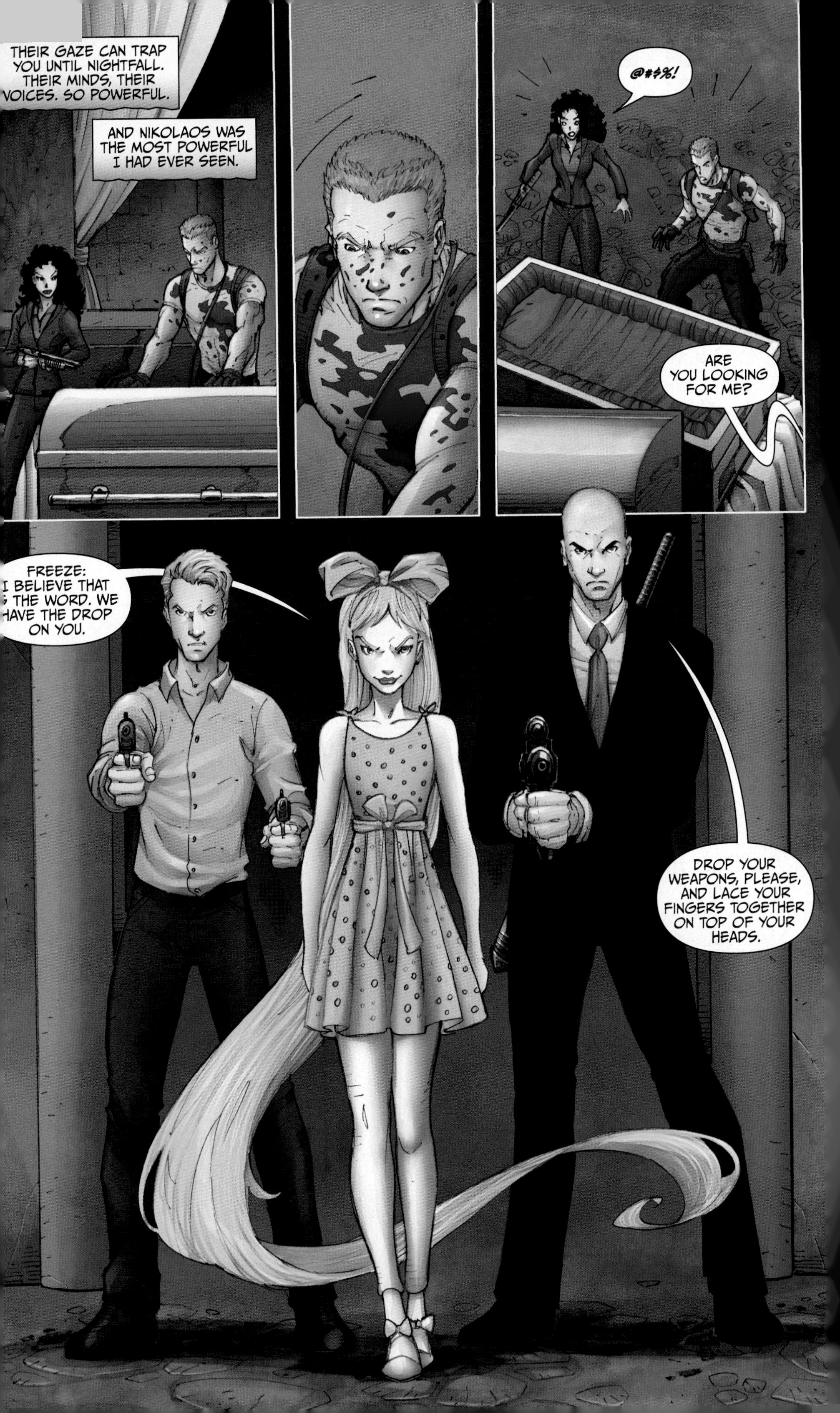
THEIR GAZE CAN TRAP YOU UNTIL NIGHTFALL. THEIR MINDS, THEIR VOICES. SO POWERFUL.
AND NIKOLAOS WAS THE MOST POWERFUL I HAD EVER SEEN.
@#$%!
ARE YOU LOOKING FOR ME?
FREEZE: I BELIEVE THAT THE WORD. WE HAVE THE DROP ON YOU.
DROP YOUR WEAPONS, PLEASE, AND LACE YOUR FINGERS TOGETHER ON TOP OF YOUR HEADS.

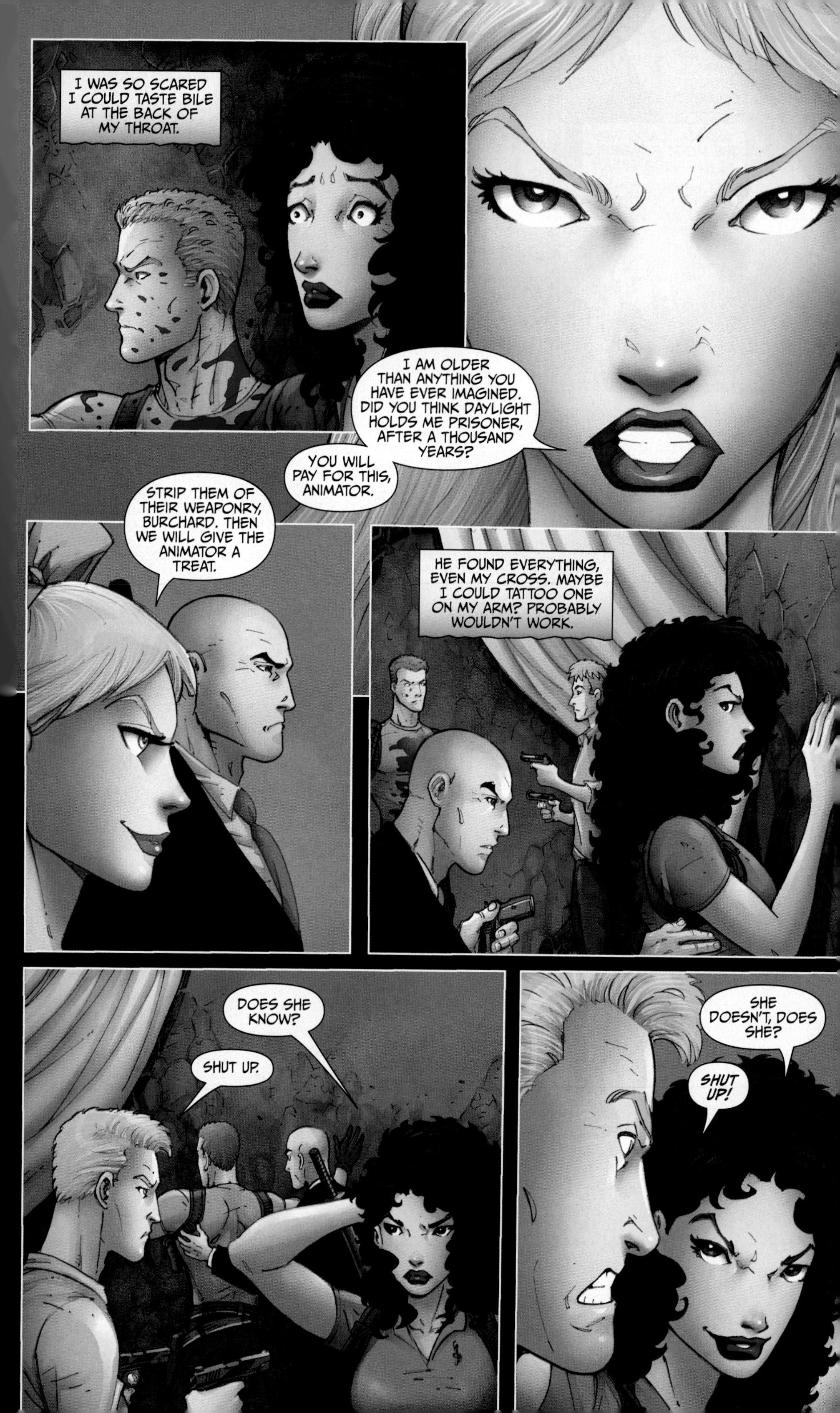
I WAS SO SCARED I COULD TASTE BILE AT THE BACK OF MY THROAT.
I AM OLDER THAN ANYTHING YOU HAVE EVER IMAGINED. DID YOU THINK DAYLIGHT HOLDS ME PRISONER, AFTER A THOUSAND YEARS?
YOU WILL PAY FOR THIS, ANIMATOR.
STRIP THEM OF THEIR WEAPONRY, BURCHARD. THEN WE WILL GIVE THE ANIMATOR A TREAT.
HE FOUND EVERYTHING, EVEN MY CROSS. MAYBE I COULD TATTOO ONE ON MY ARM? PROBABLY WOULDN'T WORK.
DOES SHE KNOW?
SHUT UP.
SHE DOESN'T, DOES SHE?
SHUT UP!

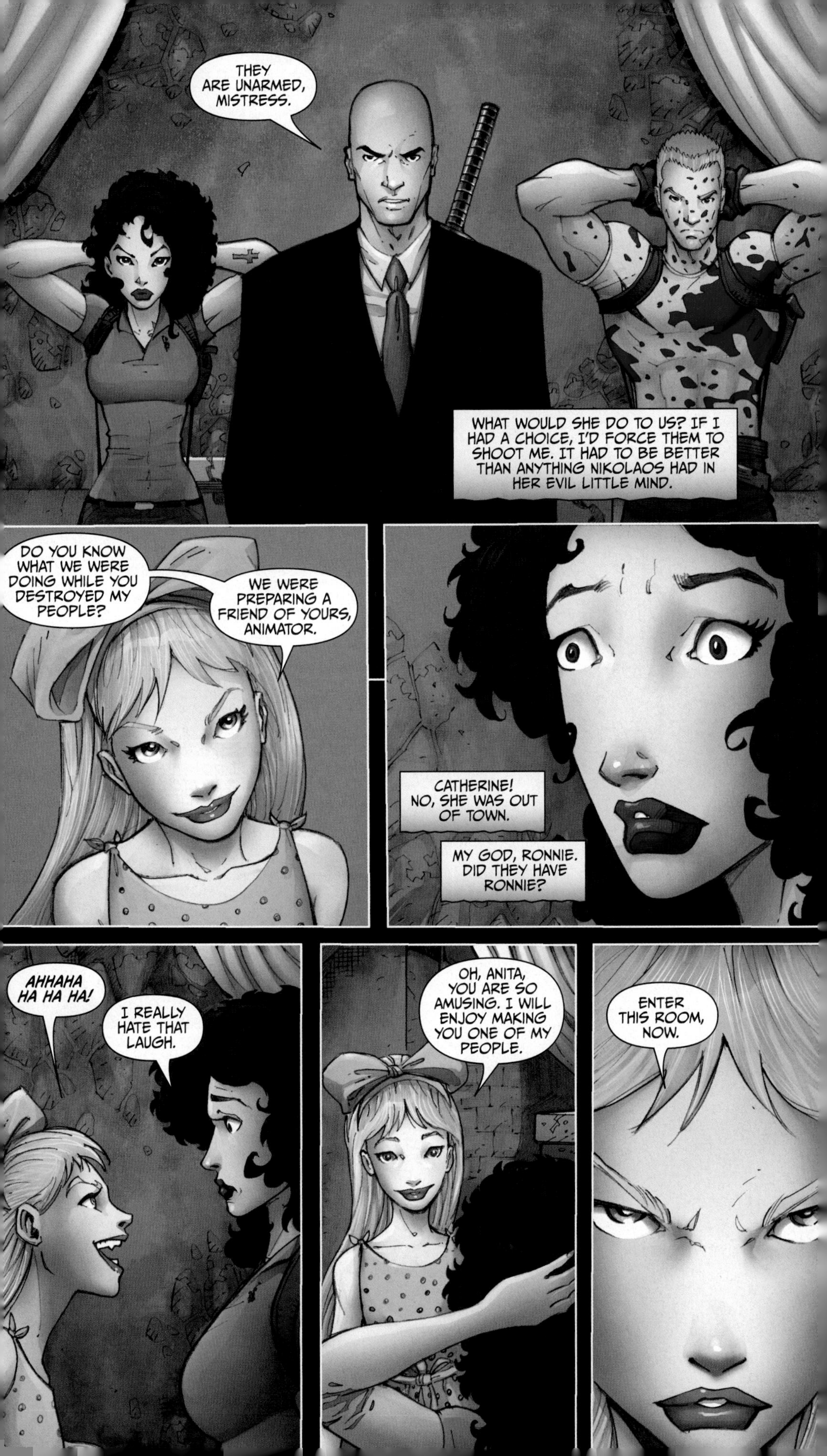
THEY ARE UNARMED, MISTRESS.
WHAT WOULD SHE DO TO US? IF I HAD A CHOICE, I'D FORCE THEM TO SHOOT ME. IT HAD TO BE BETTER THAN ANYTHING NIKOLAOS HAD IN HER EVIL LITTLE MIND.
DO YOU KNOW WHAT WE WERE DOING WHILE YOU DESTROYED MY PEOPLE?
WE WERE PREPARING A FRIEND OF YOURS, ANIMATOR.
CATHERINE! NO, SHE WAS OUT OF TOWN.
MY GOD, RONNIE. DID THEY HAVE RONNIE?
AHHAHA HA HA HA!
I REALLY HATE THAT LAUGH.
OH, ANITA, YOU ARE SO AMUSING. I WILL ENJOY MAKING YOU ONE OF MY PEOPLE.
ENTER THIS ROOM, NOW.

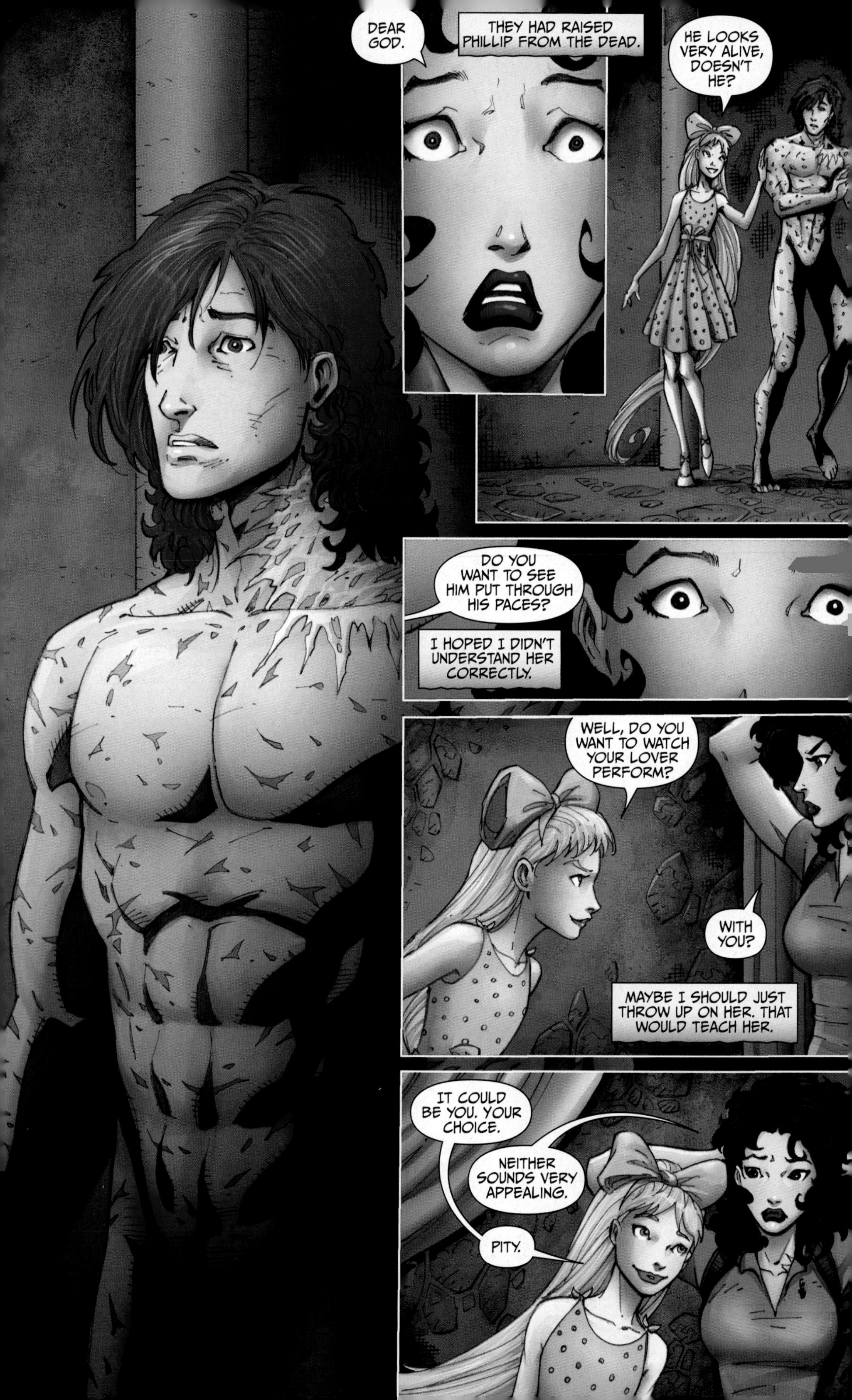

DEAR GOD.
THEY HAD RAISED PHILLIP FROM THE DEAD.
HE LOOKS VERY ALIVE, DOESN'T HE?
DO YOU WANT TO SEE HIM PUT THROUGH HIS PACES?
I HOPED I DIDN'T UNDERSTAND HER CORRECTLY.
WELL, DO YOU WANT TO WATCH YOUR LOVER PERFORM?
WITH YOU?
MAYBE I SHOULD JUST THROW UP ON HER. THAT WOULD TEACH HER.
IT COULD BE YOU. YOUR CHOICE.
NEITHER SOUNDS VERY APPEALING.
PITY.

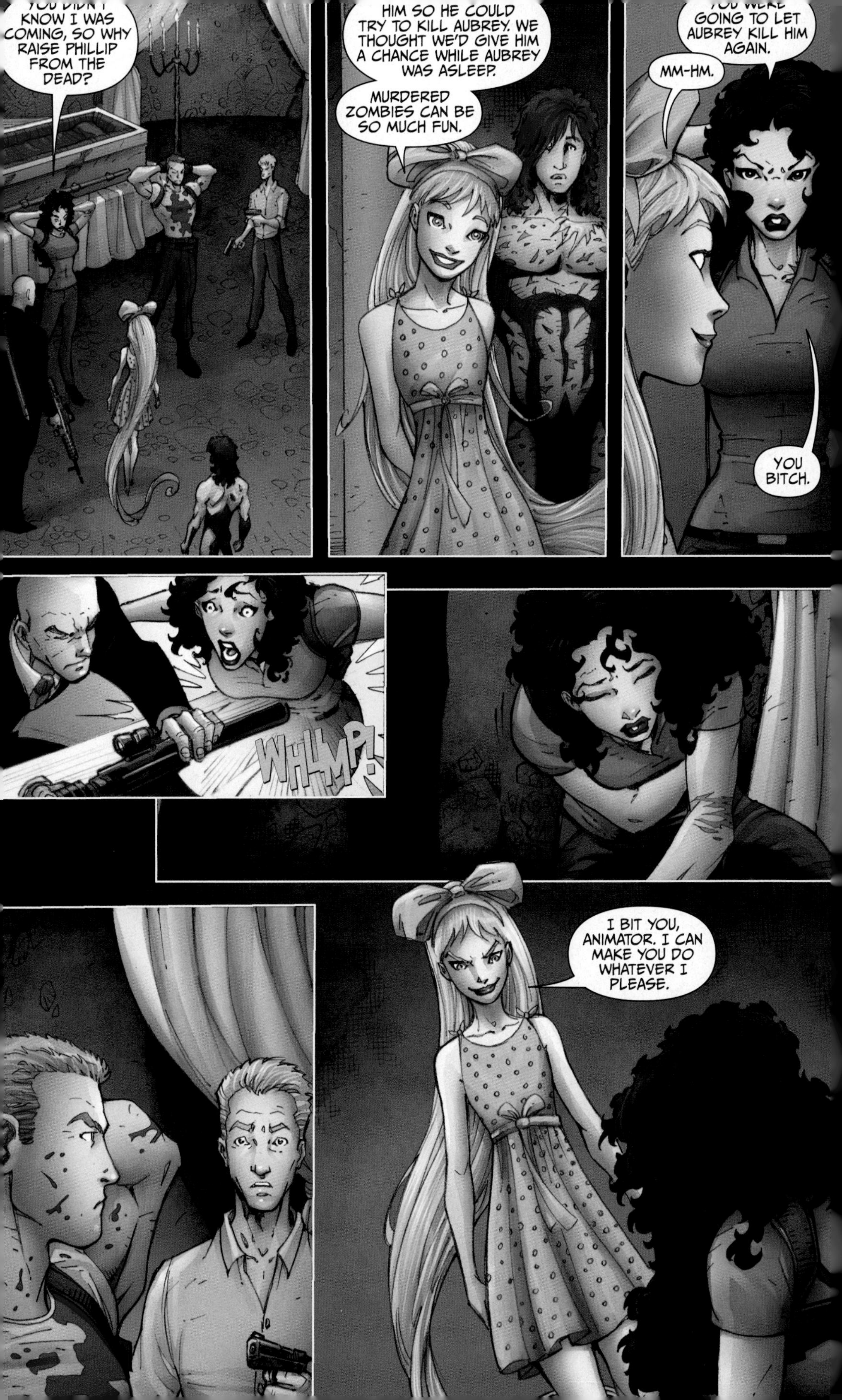
YOU DIDN'T KNOW I WAS COMING, SO WHY RAISE PHILLIP FROM THE DEAD?
HIM SO HE COULD TRY TO KILL AUBREY. WE THOUGHT WE'D GIVE HIM A CHANCE WHILE AUBREY WAS ASLEEP.
MURDERED ZOMBIES CAN BE SO MUCH FUN.
YOU WERE GOING TO LET AUBREY KILL HIM AGAIN.
MM-HM.
YOU BITCH.
WHUMP!
I BIT YOU, ANIMATOR. I CAN MAKE YOU DO WHATEVER I PLEASE.

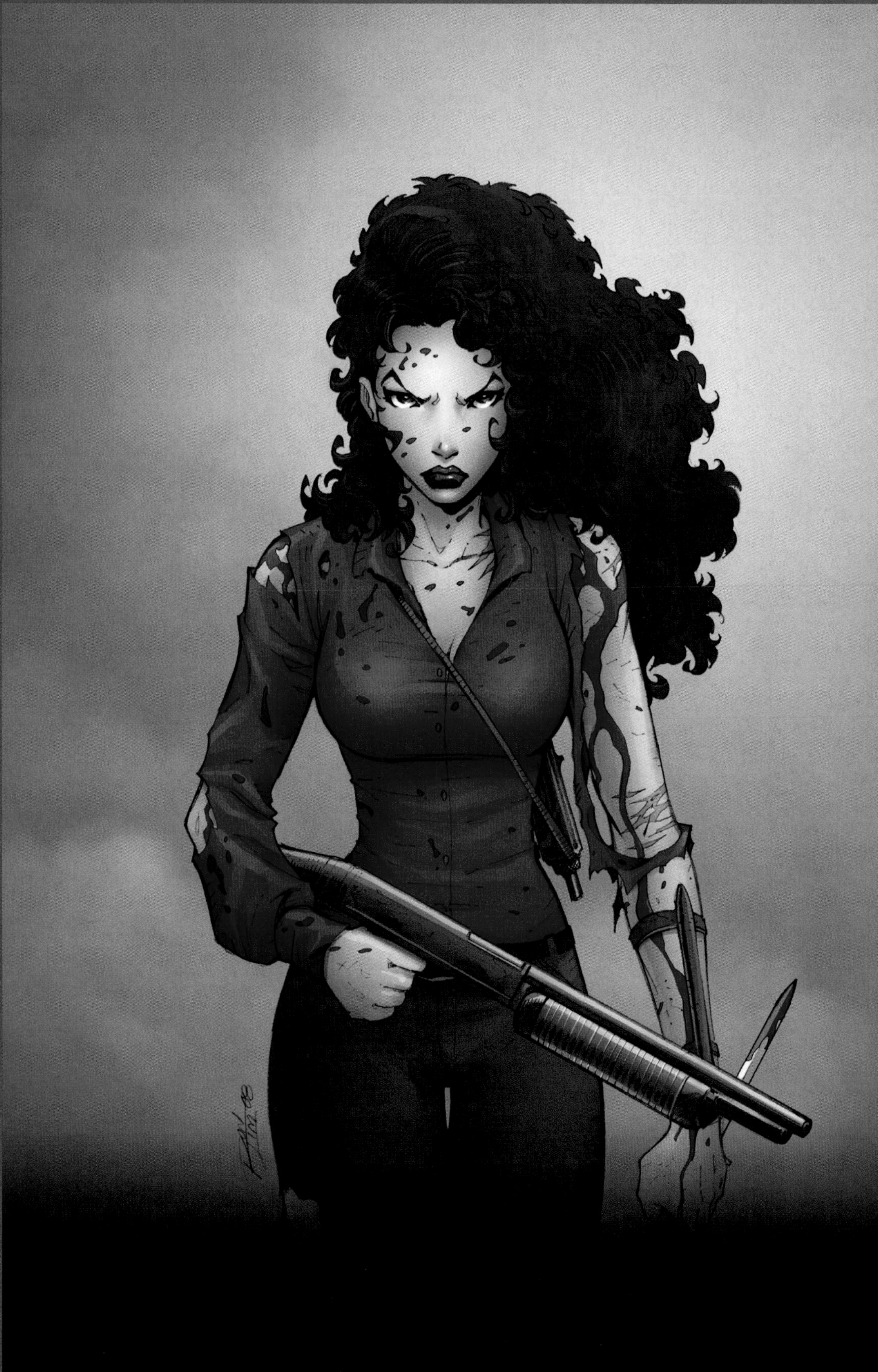

[#12]

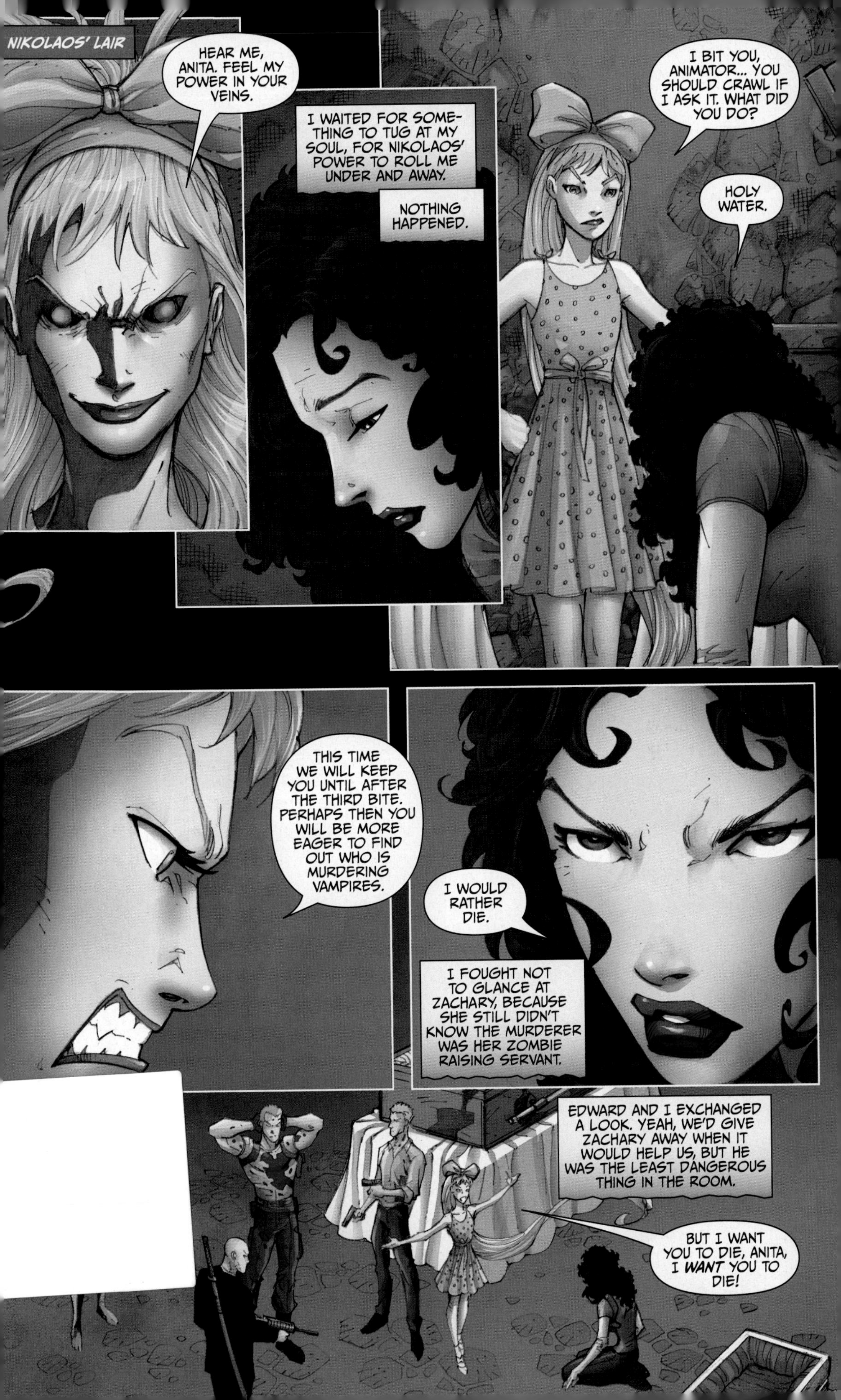

NIKOLAOS' LAIR
HEAR ME, ANITA. FEEL MY POWER IN YOUR VEINS.
I WAITED FOR SOMETHING TO TUG AT MY SOUL, FOR NIKOLAOS' POWER TO ROLL ME UNDER AND AWAY.
NOTHING HAPPENED.
I BIT YOU, ANIMATOR... YOU SHOULD CRAWL IF I ASK IT. WHAT DID YOU DO?
HOLY WATER.
THIS TIME WE WILL KEEP YOU UNTIL AFTER THE THIRD BITE. PERHAPS THEN YOU WILL BE MORE EAGER TO FIND OUT WHO IS MURDERING VAMPIRES.
I WOULD RATHER DIE.
I FOUGHT NOT TO GLANCE AT ZACHARY, BECAUSE SHE STILL DIDN'T KNOW THE MURDERER WAS HER ZOMBIE RAISING SERVANT.
EDWARD AND I EXCHANGED A LOOK. YEAH, WE'D GIVE ZACHARY AWAY WHEN IT WOULD HELP US, BUT HE WAS THE LEAST DANGEROUS THING IN THE ROOM.
BUT I WANT YOU TO DIE, ANITA, I *WANT* YOU TO DIE!

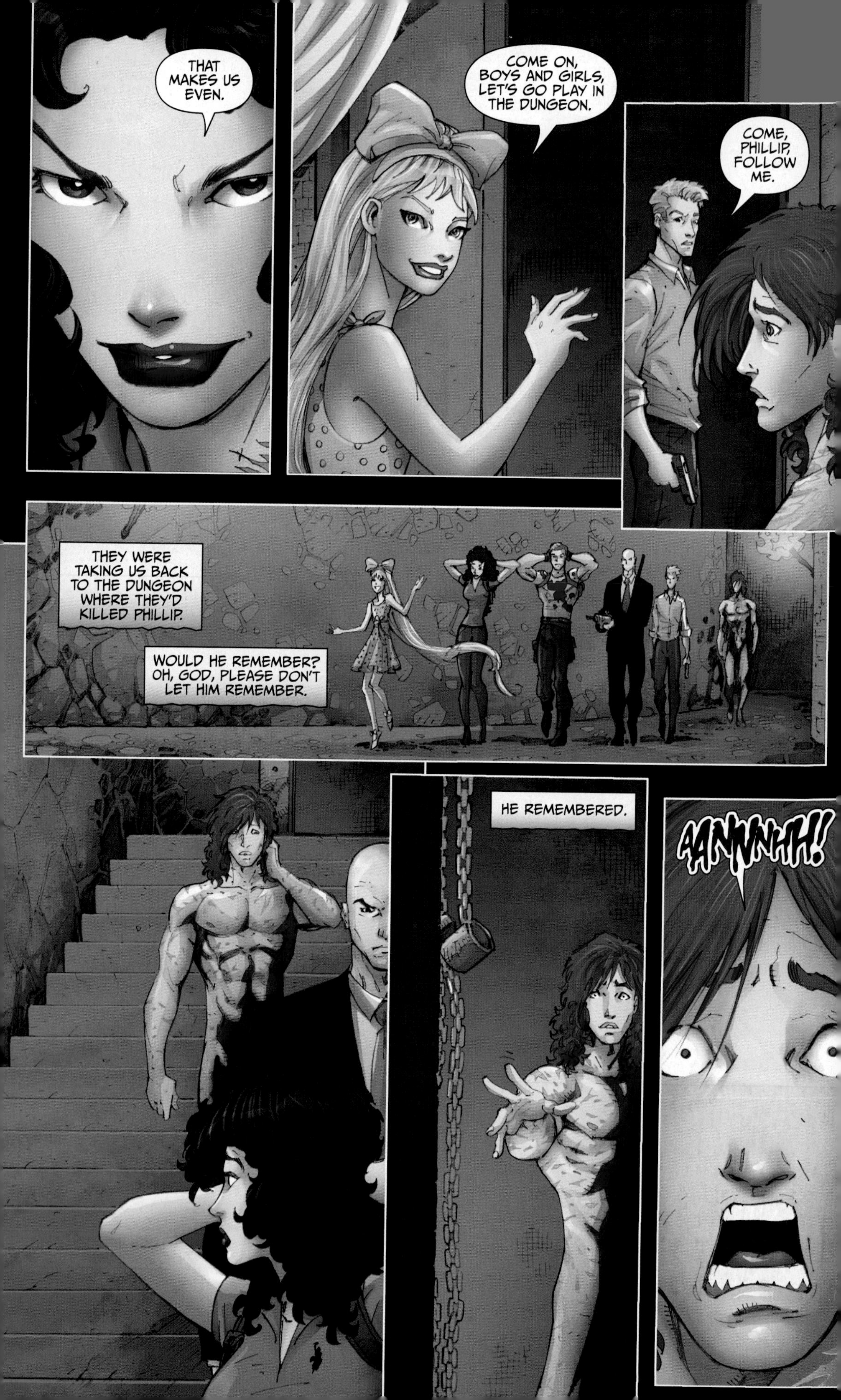
THAT MAKES US EVEN.
COME ON, BOYS AND GIRLS, LET'S GO PLAY IN THE DUNGEON.
COME, PHILLIP, FOLLOW ME.
THEY WERE TAKING US BACK TO THE DUNGEON WHERE THEY'D KILLED PHILLIP.
WOULD HE REMEMBER? OH, GOD, PLEASE DON'T LET HIM REMEMBER.
HE REMEMBERED.
AANNNHH!

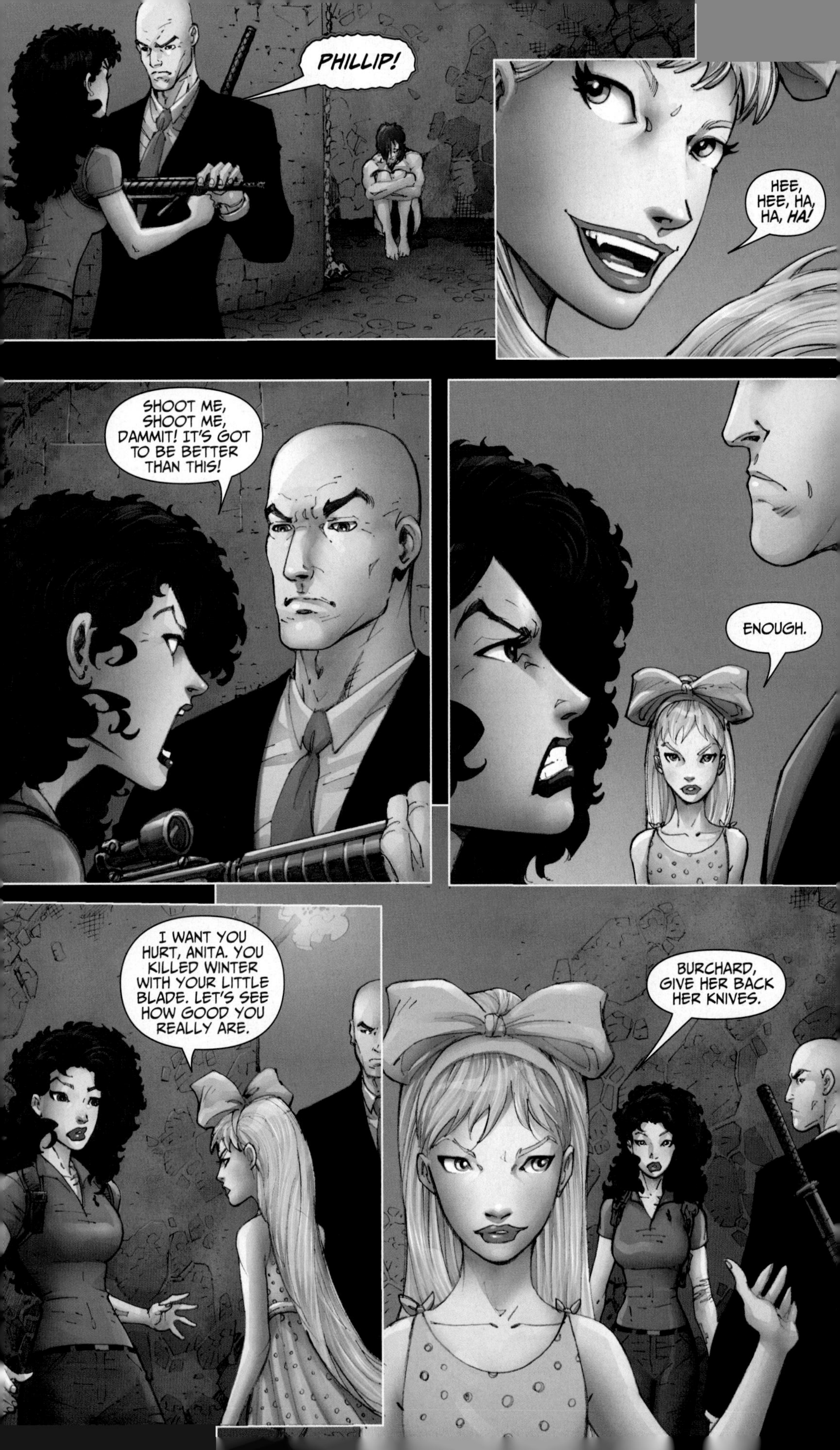
PHILLIP!
HEE, HEE, HA, HA, HA!
SHOOT ME, SHOOT ME, DAMMIT! IT'S GOT TO BE BETTER THAN THIS!
ENOUGH.
I WANT YOU HURT, ANITA. YOU KILLED WINTER WITH YOUR LITTLE BLADE. LET'S SEE HOW GOOD YOU REALLY ARE.
BURCHARD, GIVE HER BACK HER KNIVES.

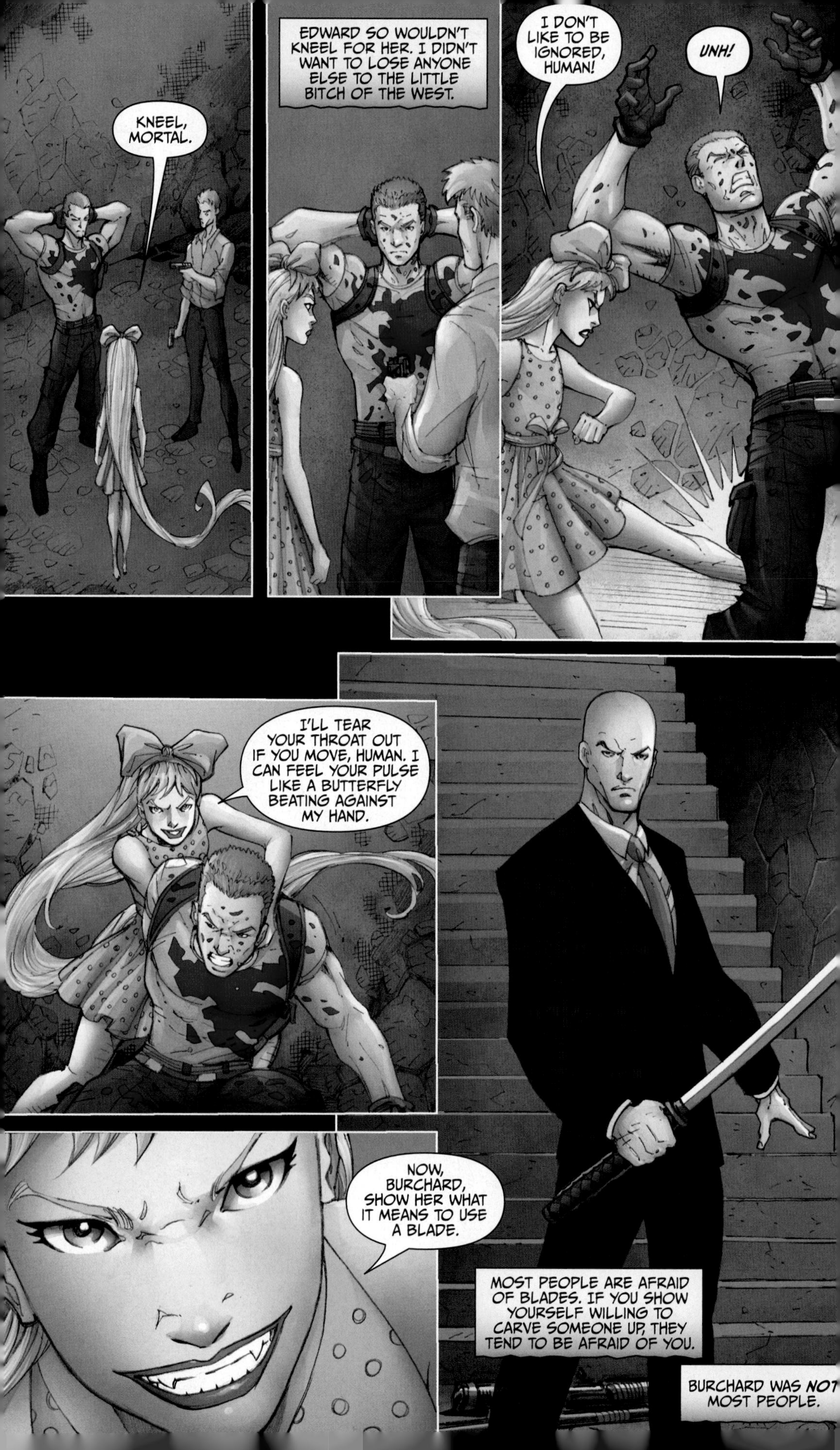
KNEEL, MORTAL.
EDWARD SO WOULDN'T KNEEL FOR HER. I DIDN'T WANT TO LOSE ANYONE ELSE TO THE LITTLE BITCH OF THE WEST.
I DON'T LIKE TO BE IGNORED, HUMAN!
UNH!
I'LL TEAR YOUR THROAT OUT IF YOU MOVE, HUMAN. I CAN FEEL YOUR PULSE LIKE A BUTTERFLY BEATING AGAINST MY HAND.
NOW, BURCHARD, SHOW HER WHAT IT MEANS TO USE A BLADE.
MOST PEOPLE ARE AFRAID OF BLADES. IF YOU SHOW YOURSELF WILLING TO CARVE SOMEONE UP, THEY TEND TO BE AFRAID OF YOU.
BURCHARD WAS NOT MOST PEOPLE.

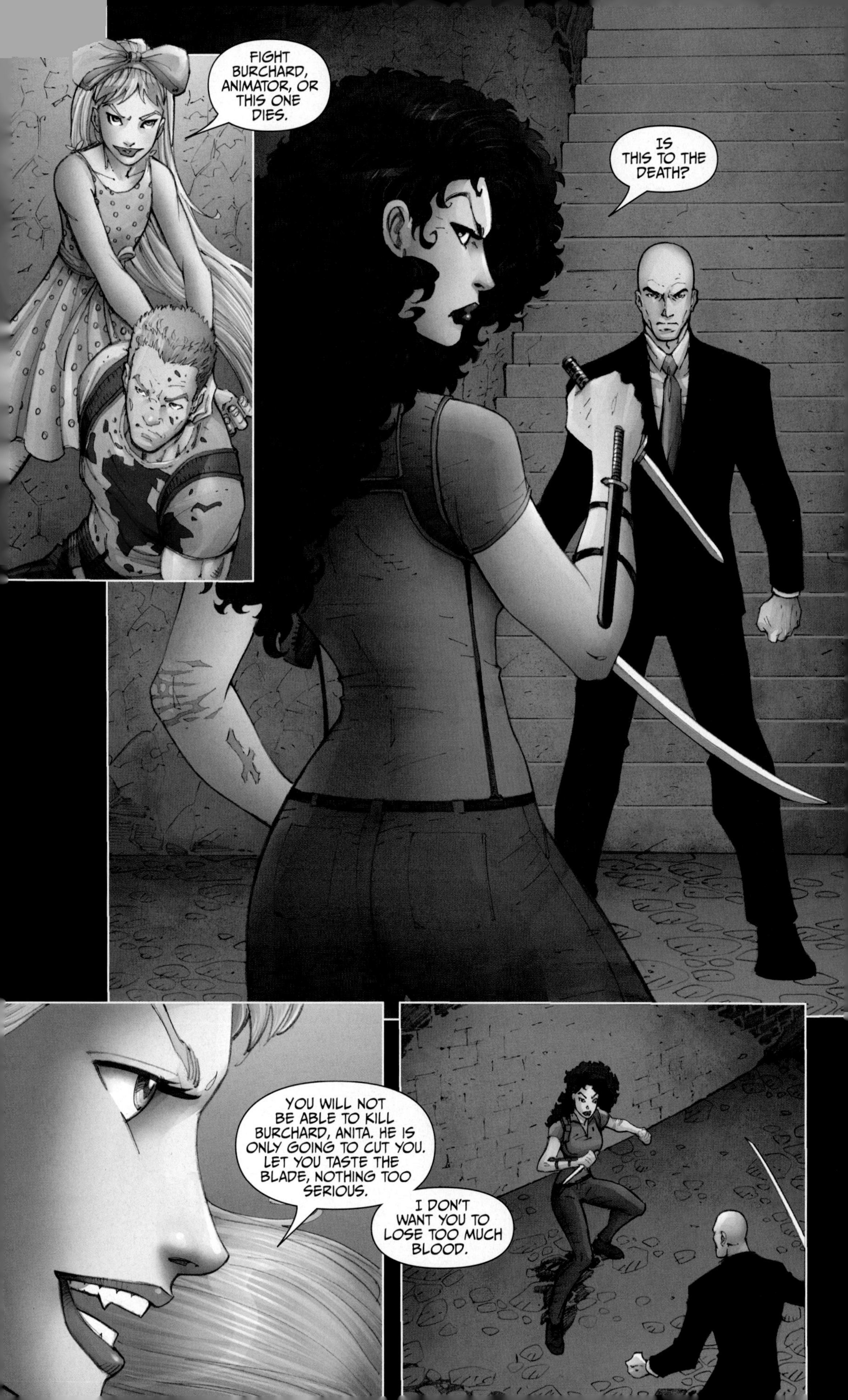
FIGHT BURCHARD, ANIMATOR, OR THIS ONE DIES.
IS THIS TO THE DEATH?
YOU WILL NOT BE ABLE TO KILL BURCHARD, ANITA. HE IS ONLY GOING TO CUT YOU. LET YOU TASTE THE BLADE, NOTHING TOO SERIOUS.
I DON'T WANT YOU TO LOSE TOO MUCH BLOOD.

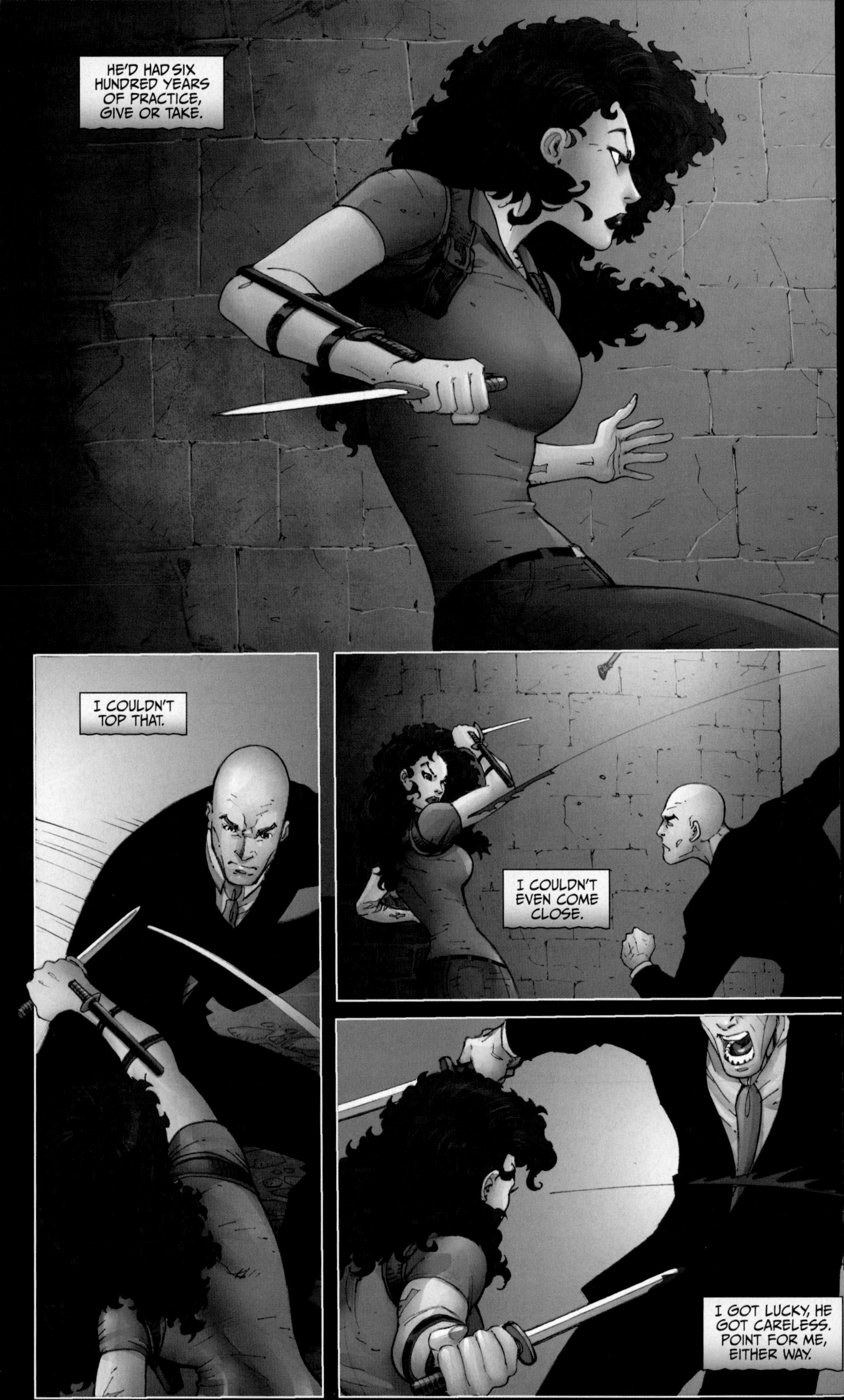
HE'D HAD SIX HUNDRED YEARS OF PRACTICE, GIVE OR TAKE.
I COULDN'T TOP THAT.
I COULDN'T EVEN COME CLOSE.
I GOT LUCKY, HE GOT CARELESS. POINT FOR ME, EITHER WAY.

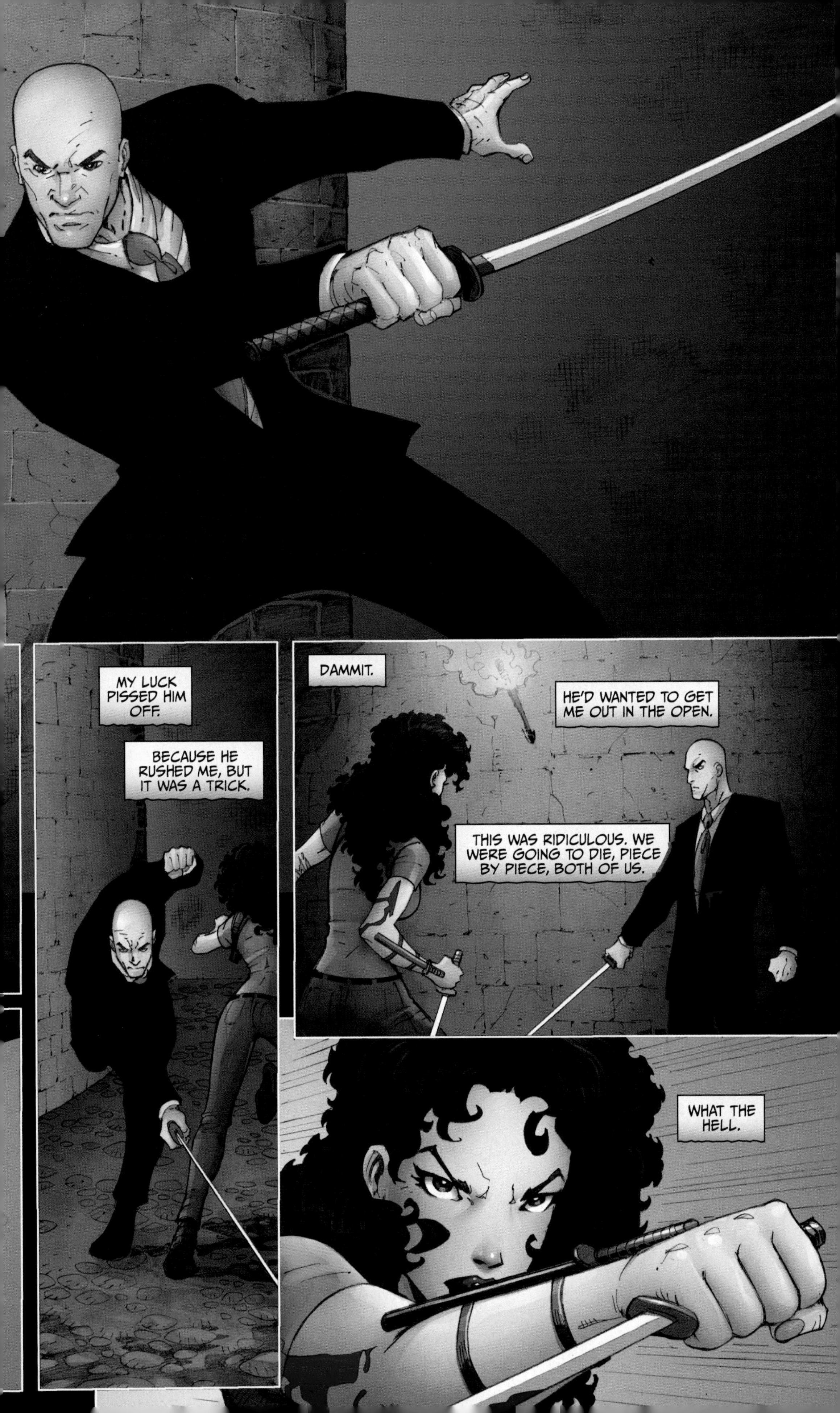
MY LUCK PISSED HIM OFF.
BECAUSE HE RUSHED ME, BUT IT WAS A TRICK.
DAMMIT.
HE'D WANTED TO GET ME OUT IN THE OPEN.
THIS WAS RIDICULOUS. WE WERE GOING TO DIE, PIECE BY PIECE, BOTH OF US.
WHAT THE HELL.

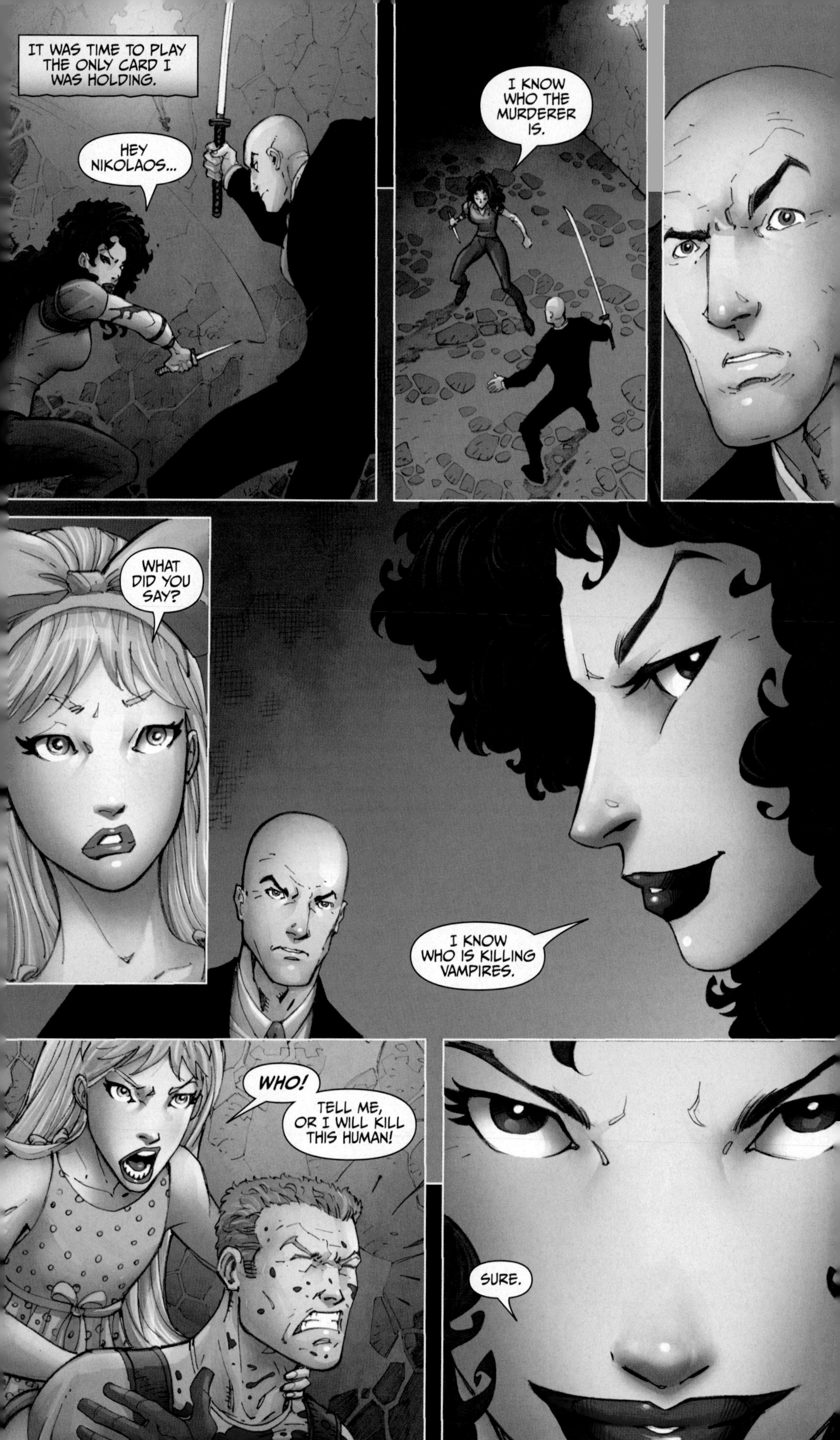
IT WAS TIME TO PLAY THE ONLY CARD I WAS HOLDING.
HEY NIKOLAOS...
I KNOW WHO THE MURDERER IS.
WHAT DID YOU SAY?
I KNOW WHO IS KILLING VAMPIRES.
WHO!
TELL ME, OR I WILL KILL THIS HUMAN!
SURE.

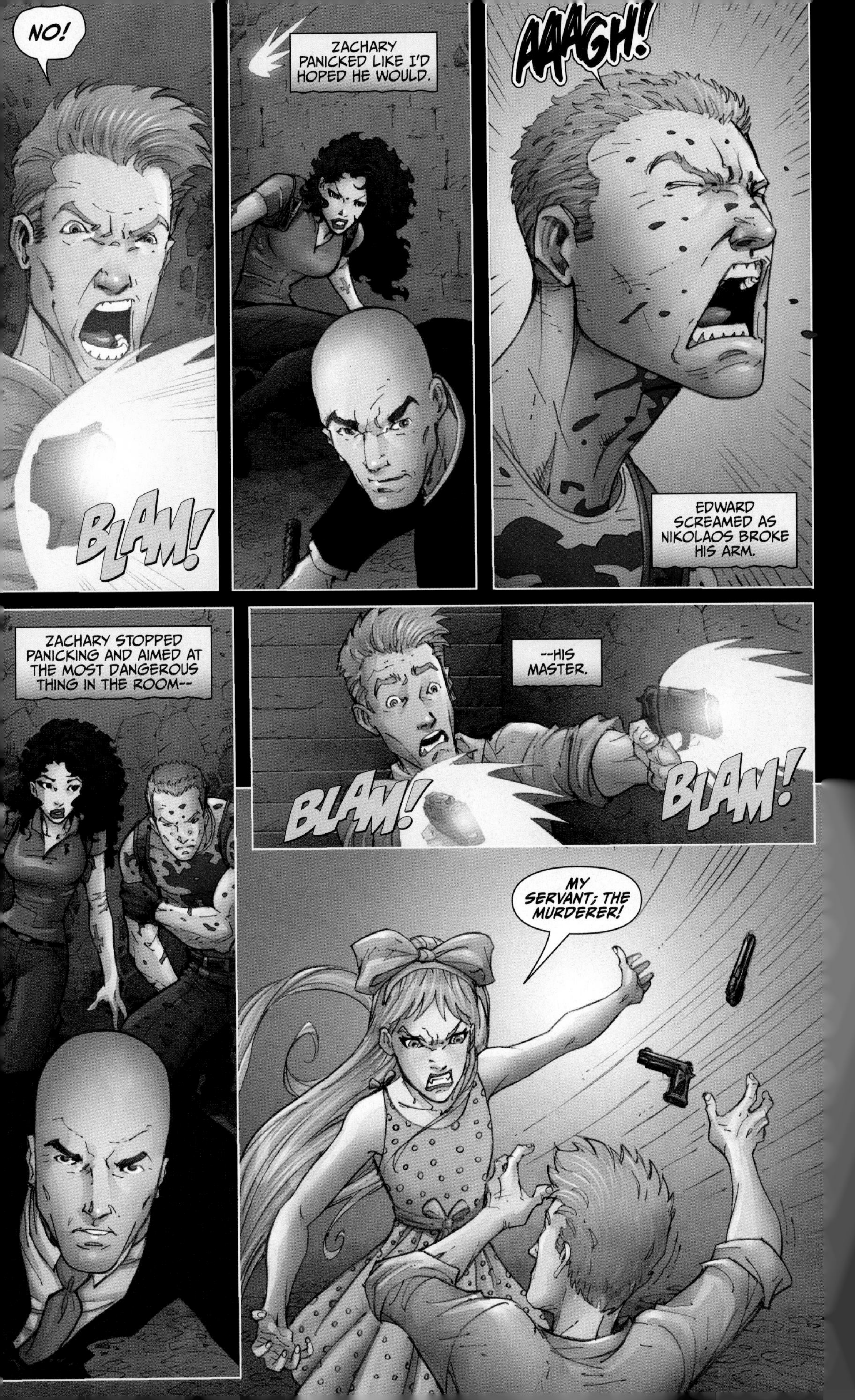
NO!
BLAM!
ZACHARY PANICKED LIKE I'D HOPED HE WOULD.
AAAGH!
EDWARD SCREAMED AS NIKOLAOS BROKE HIS ARM.
ZACHARY STOPPED PANICKING AND AIMED AT THE MOST DANGEROUS THING IN THE ROOM--
--HIS MASTER.
BLAM!
BLAM!
MY SERVANT; THE MURDERER!

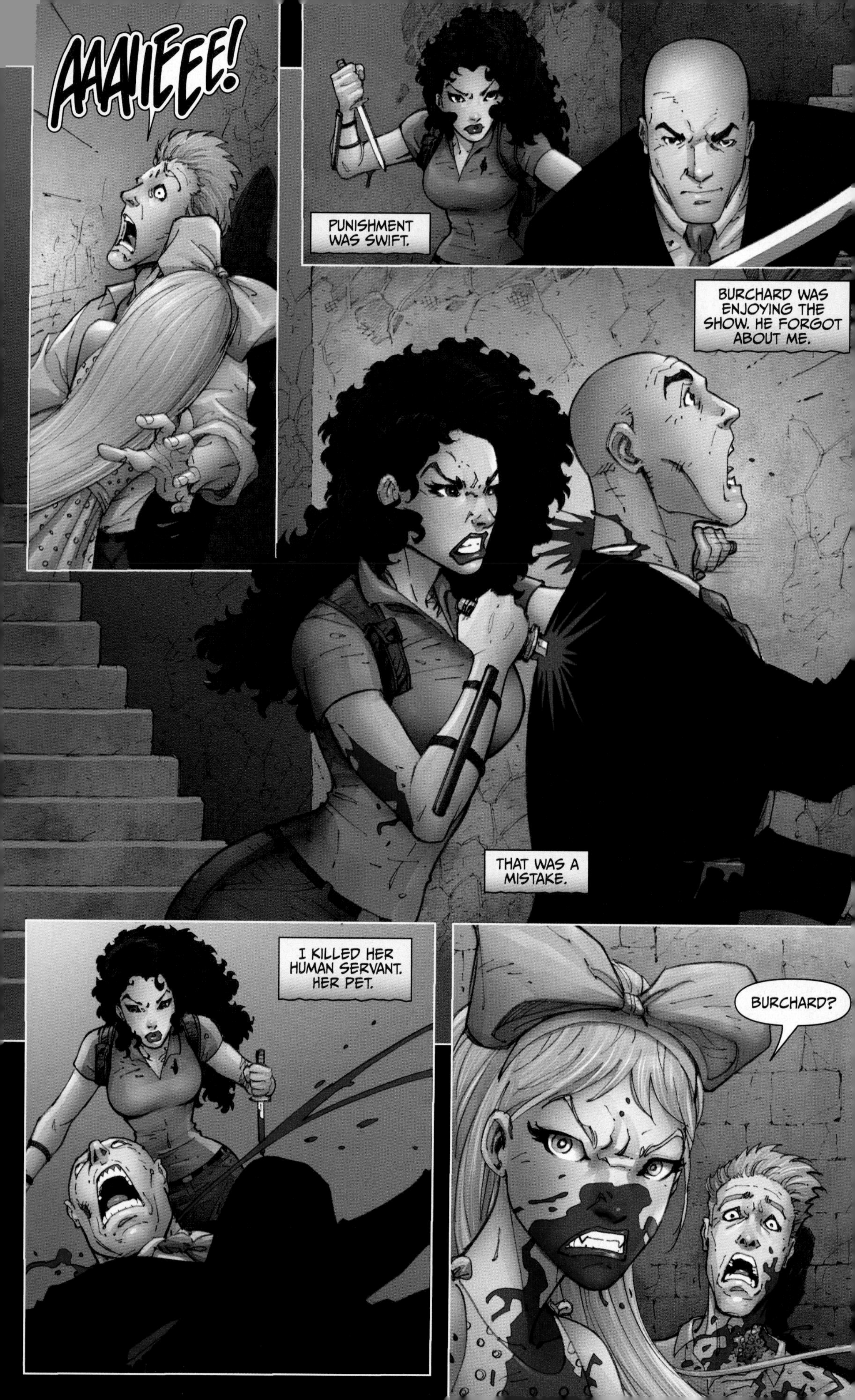
AAAIIEEE!
PUNISHMENT WAS SWIFT.
BURCHARD WAS ENJOYING THE SHOW. HE FORGOT ABOUT ME.
THAT WAS A MISTAKE.
I KILLED HER HUMAN SERVANT. HER PET.
BURCHARD?

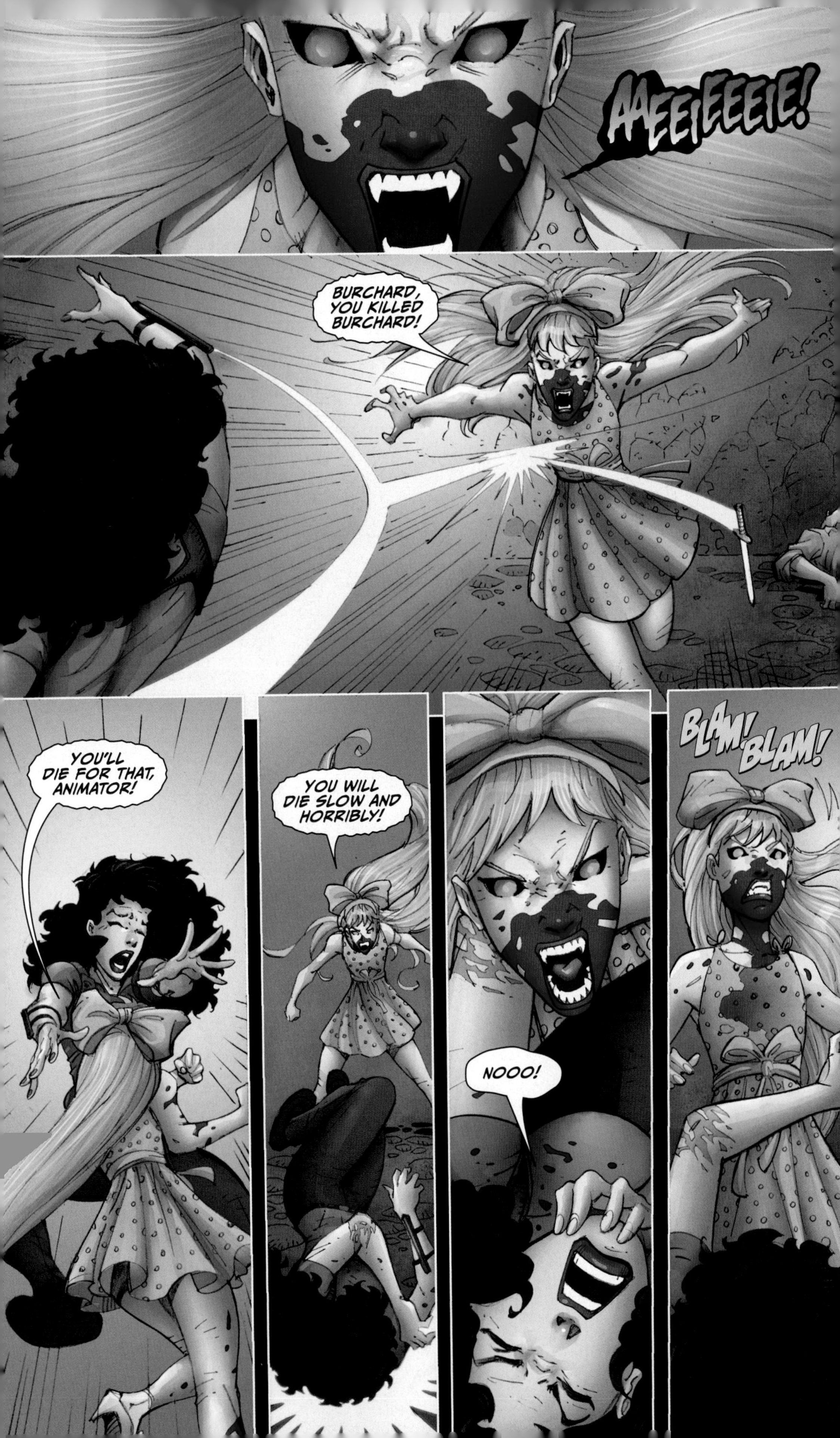
AAEEIEEEIE!
BURCHARD, YOU KILLED BURCHARD!
YOU'LL DIE FOR THAT, ANIMATOR!
YOU WILL DIE SLOW AND HORRIBLY!
NOOO!
BLAM! BLAM!

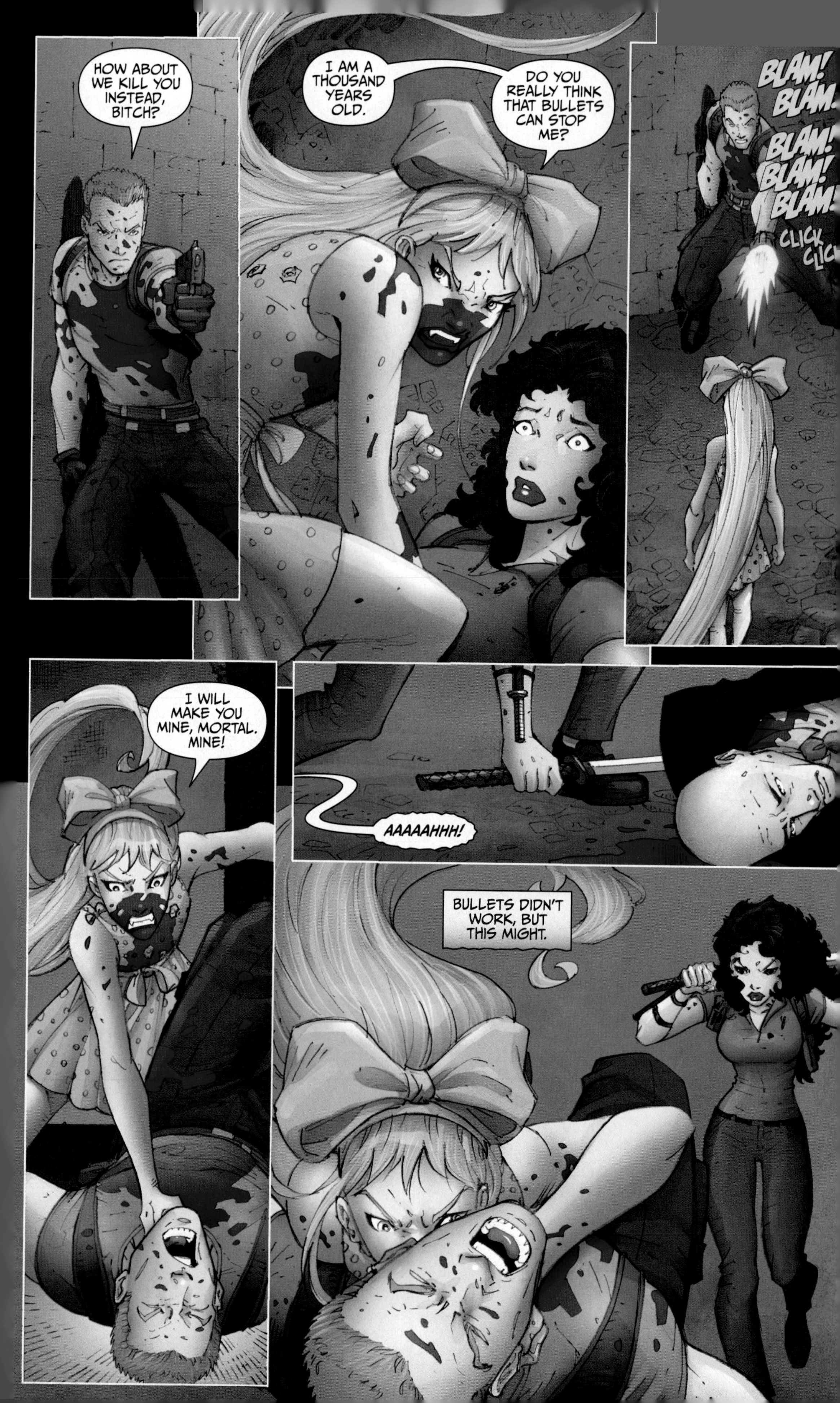
HOW ABOUT WE KILL YOU INSTEAD, BITCH?
I AM A THOUSAND YEARS OLD.
DO YOU REALLY THINK THAT BULLETS CAN STOP ME?
BLAM! BLAM! BLAM! BLAM! BLAM!
CLICK CLICK
I WILL MAKE YOU MINE, MORTAL. MINE!
AAAAAHHH!
BULLETS DIDN'T WORK, BUT THIS MIGHT.

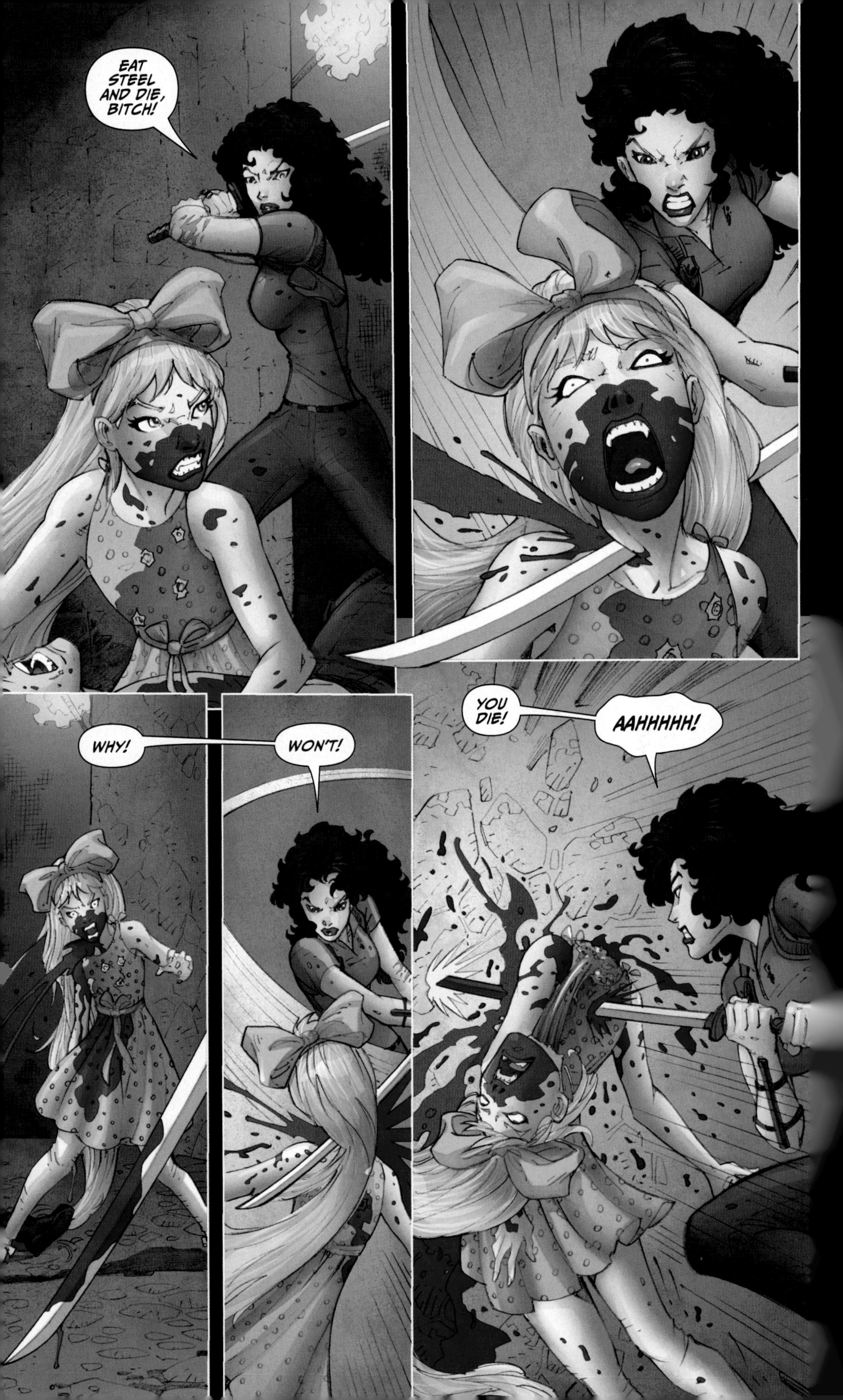
EAT STEEL AND DIE, BITCH!
WHY!
WON'T!
YOU DIE!
AAHHHHH!

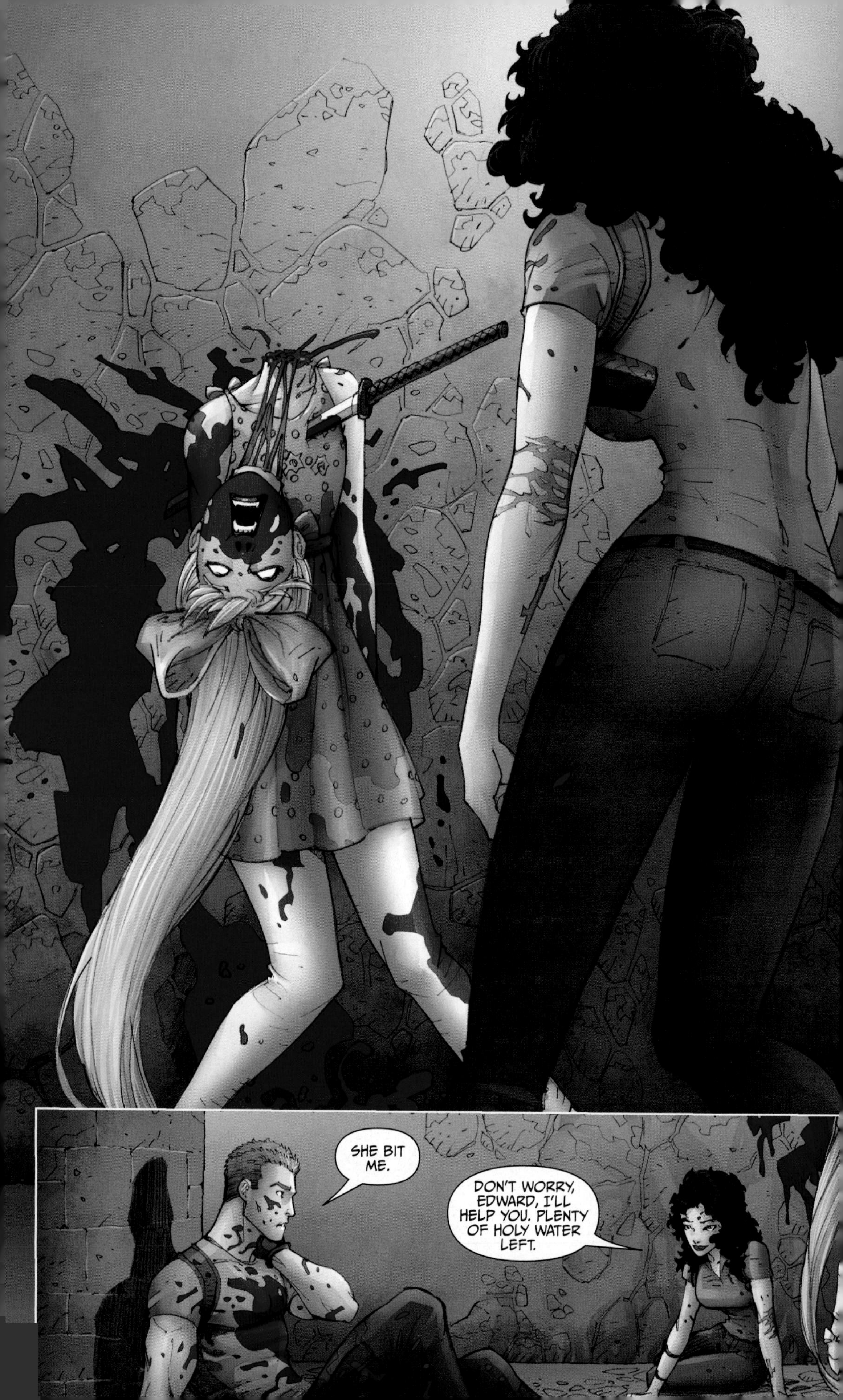
SHE BIT ME.
DON'T WORRY, EDWARD, I'LL HELP YOU. PLENTY OF HOLY WATER LEFT.

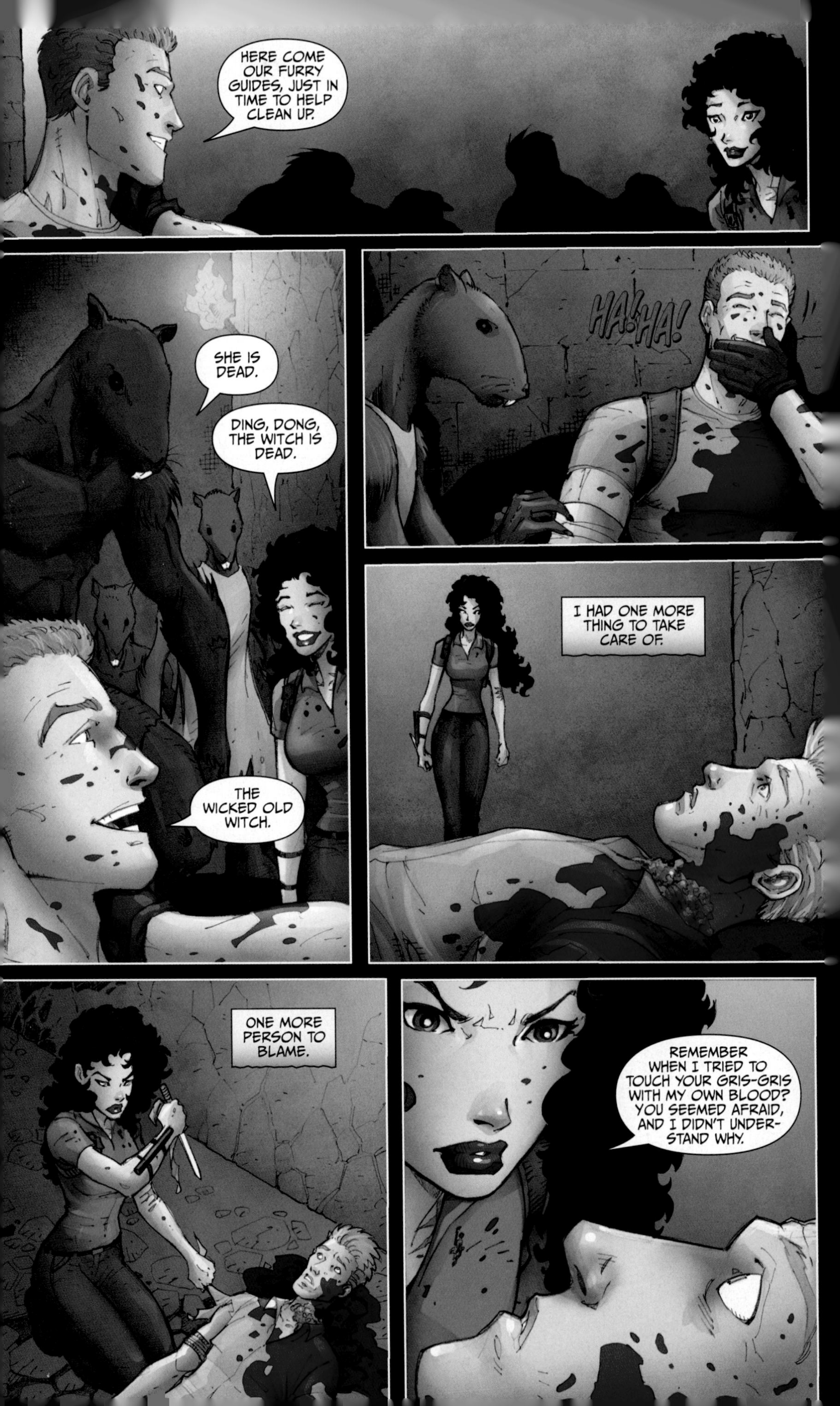
HERE COME OUR FURRY GUIDES, JUST IN TIME TO HELP CLEAN UP.
SHE IS DEAD.
DING, DONG, THE WITCH IS DEAD.
THE WICKED OLD WITCH.
HA! HA!
I HAD ONE MORE THING TO TAKE CARE OF.
ONE MORE PERSON TO BLAME.
REMEMBER WHEN I TRIED TO TOUCH YOUR GRIS-GRIS WITH MY OWN BLOOD? YOU SEEMED AFRAID, AND I DIDN'T UNDER-STAND WHY.

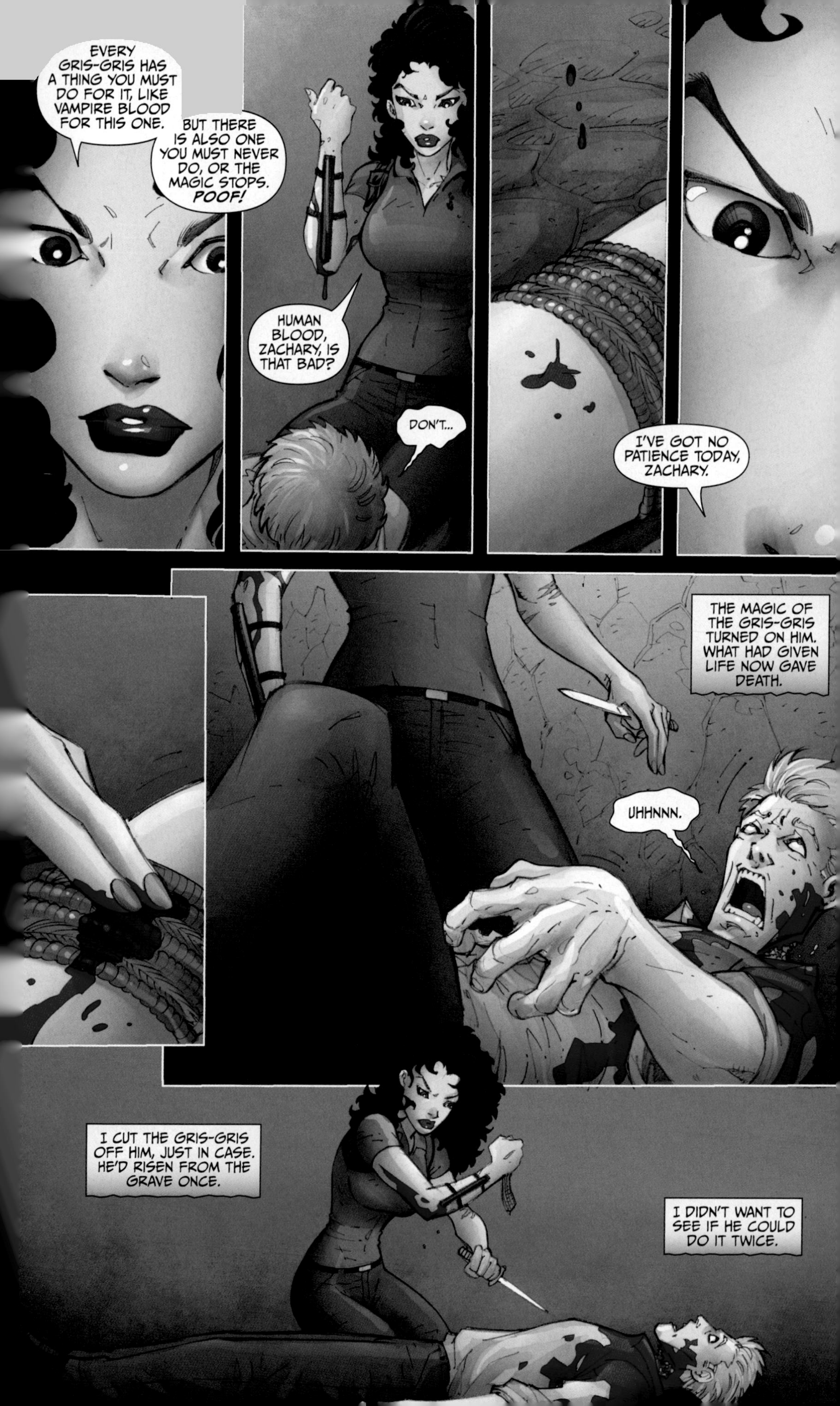
EVERY GRIS-GRIS HAS A THING YOU MUST DO FOR IT, LIKE VAMPIRE BLOOD FOR THIS ONE.
BUT THERE IS ALSO ONE YOU MUST NEVER DO, OR THE MAGIC STOPS. *POOF!*
HUMAN BLOOD, ZACHARY, IS THAT BAD?
DON'T...
I'VE GOT NO PATIENCE TODAY, ZACHARY.
THE MAGIC OF THE GRIS-GRIS TURNED ON HIM. WHAT HAD GIVEN LIFE NOW GAVE DEATH.
UHHNNN.
I CUT THE GRIS-GRIS OFF HIM, JUST IN CASE. HE'D RISEN FROM THE GRAVE ONCE.
I DIDN'T WANT TO SEE IF HE COULD DO IT TWICE.

THIS IS JUST TEMPORARY, YOU'LL NEED STITCHES.

WHERE ARE YOU GOING?

TO GET THE REST OF OUR GUNS.

TO FIND JEAN-CLAUDE. I DIDN'T THINK EDWARD WOULD UNDERSTAND.

I LEFT WILLIE LIKE THAT, TO WAKE WITH THE NIGHT. HE WASN'T A BAD PERSON. FOR A VAMPIRE, HE WAS EXCELLENT.

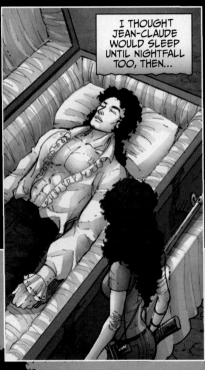

I THOUGHT JEAN-CLAUDE WOULD SLEEP UNTIL NIGHTFALL TOO, THEN...

...HE OPENED HIS EYES.

IT SCARED THE WERERATS AND SURPRISED THE HELL OUT OF ME.

IT'S ALL RIGHT, HE'S SORT OF ON OUR SIDE.

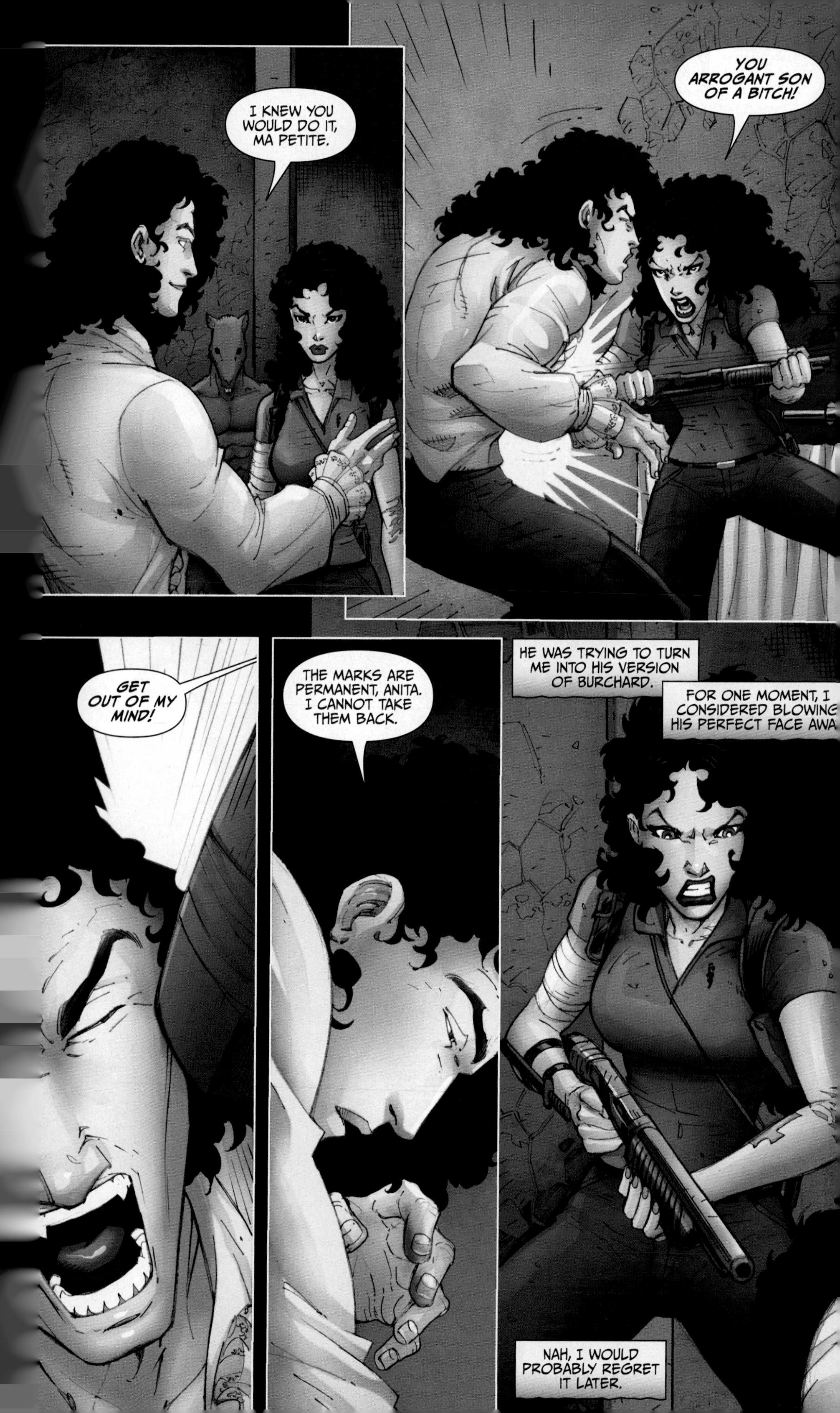
I KNEW YOU WOULD DO IT, MA PETITE.
YOU ARROGANT SON OF A BITCH!
GET OUT OF MY MIND!
THE MARKS ARE PERMANENT, ANITA. I CANNOT TAKE THEM BACK.
HE WAS TRYING TO TURN ME INTO HIS VERSION OF BURCHARD.
FOR ONE MOMENT, I CONSIDERED BLOWING HIS PERFECT FACE AWA
NAH, I WOULD PROBABLY REGRET IT LATER.

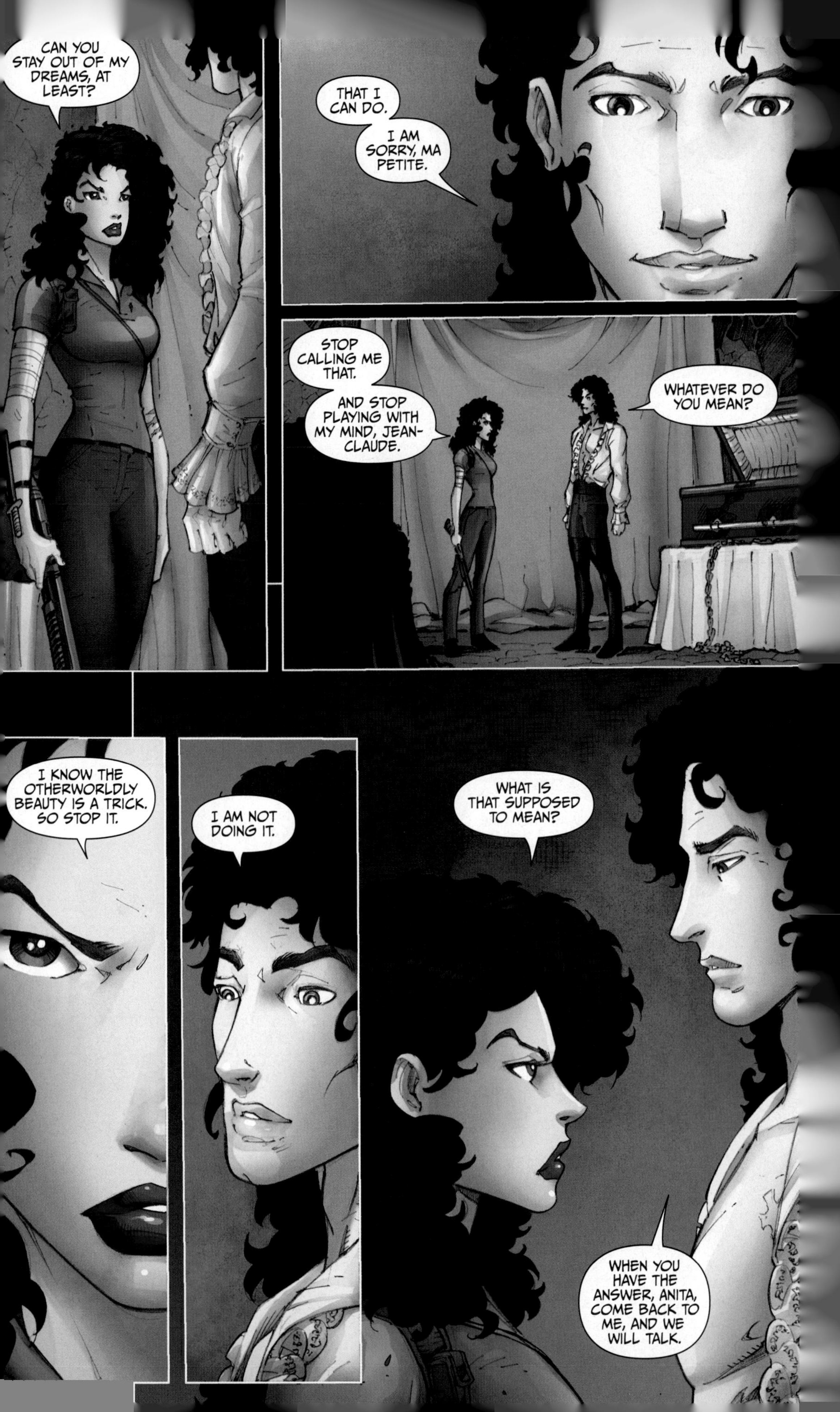
CAN YOU STAY OUT OF MY DREAMS, AT LEAST?
THAT I CAN DO.
I AM SORRY, MA PETITE.
STOP CALLING ME THAT.
AND STOP PLAYING WITH MY MIND, JEAN-CLAUDE.
WHATEVER DO YOU MEAN?
I KNOW THE OTHERWORLDLY BEAUTY IS A TRICK. SO STOP IT.
I AM NOT DOING IT.
WHAT IS THAT SUPPOSED TO MEAN?
WHEN YOU HAVE THE ANSWER, ANITA, COME BACK TO ME, AND WE WILL TALK.

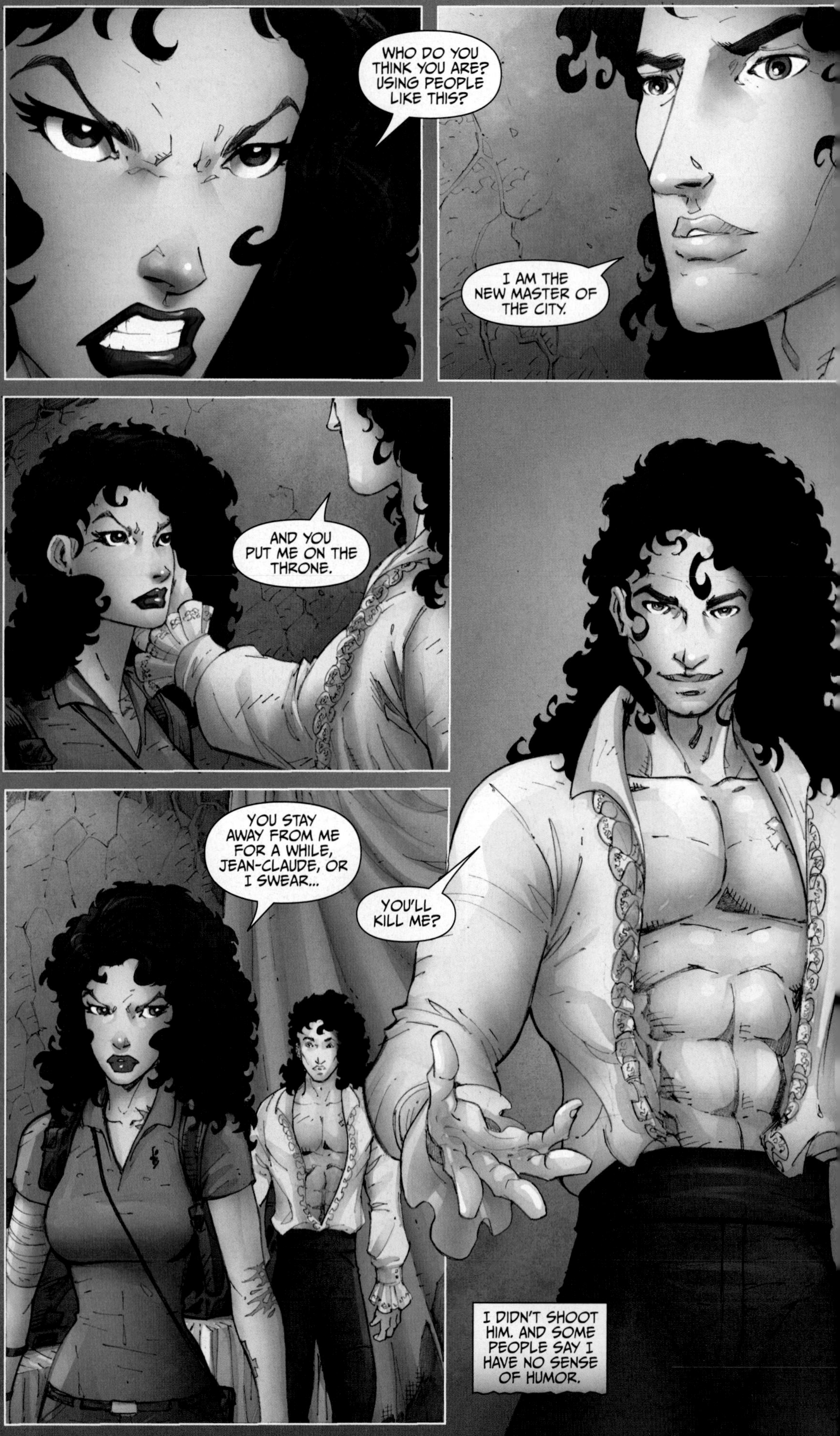
WHO DO YOU THINK YOU ARE? USING PEOPLE LIKE THIS?
I AM THE NEW MASTER OF THE CITY.
AND YOU PUT ME ON THE THRONE.
YOU STAY AWAY FROM ME FOR A WHILE, JEAN-CLAUDE, OR I SWEAR...
YOU'LL KILL ME?
I DIDN'T SHOOT HIM. AND SOME PEOPLE SAY I HAVE NO SENSE OF HUMOR.

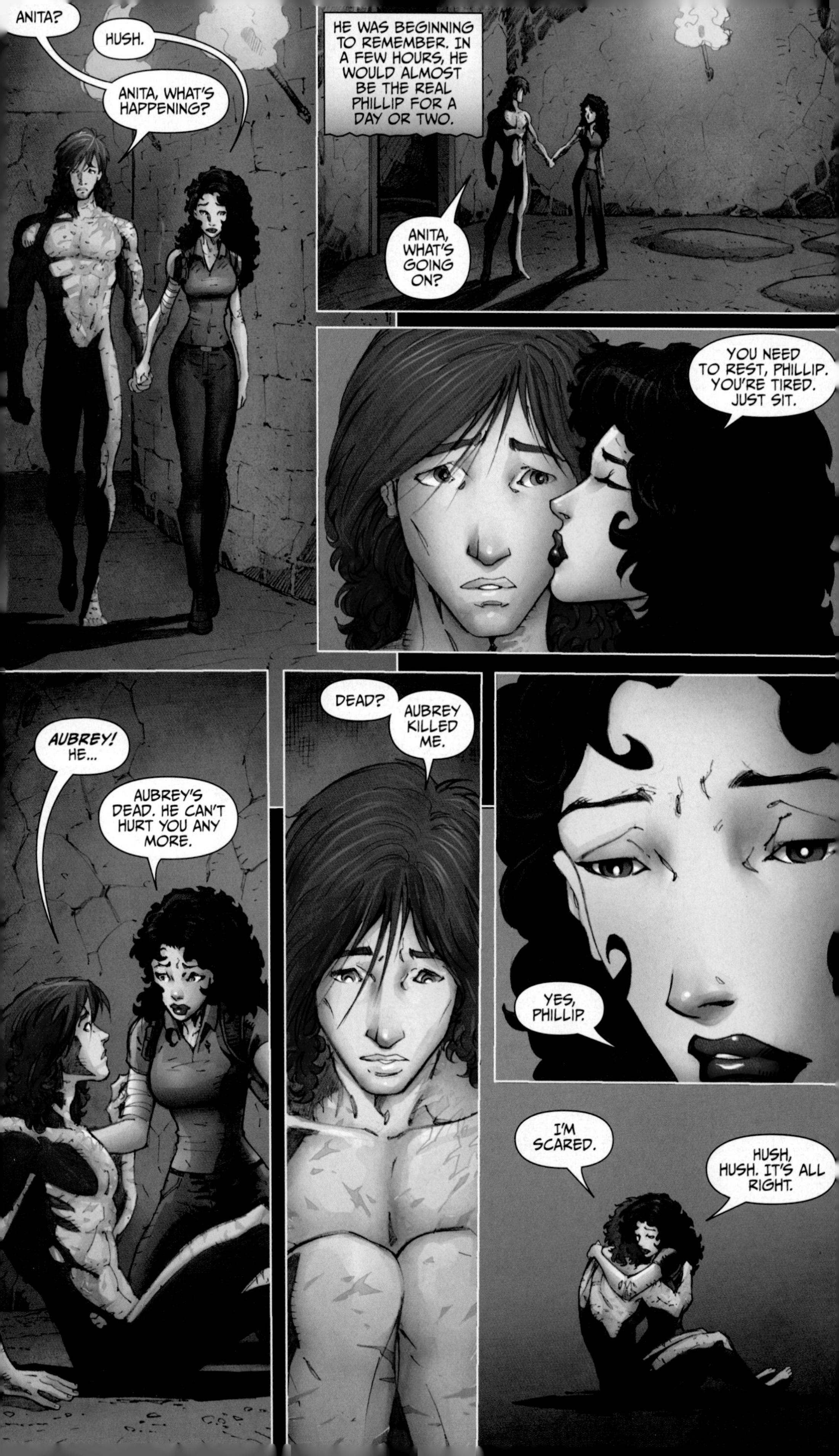
ANITA?
HUSH.
ANITA, WHAT'S HAPPENING?
HE WAS BEGINNING TO REMEMBER. IN A FEW HOURS, HE WOULD ALMOST BE THE REAL PHILLIP FOR A DAY OR TWO.
ANITA, WHAT'S GOING ON?
YOU NEED TO REST, PHILLIP. YOU'RE TIRED. JUST SIT.
AUBREY! HE...
AUBREY'S DEAD. HE CAN'T HURT YOU ANY MORE.
DEAD?
AUBREY KILLED ME.
YES, PHILLIP.
I'M SCARED.
HUSH, HUSH. IT'S ALL RIGHT.

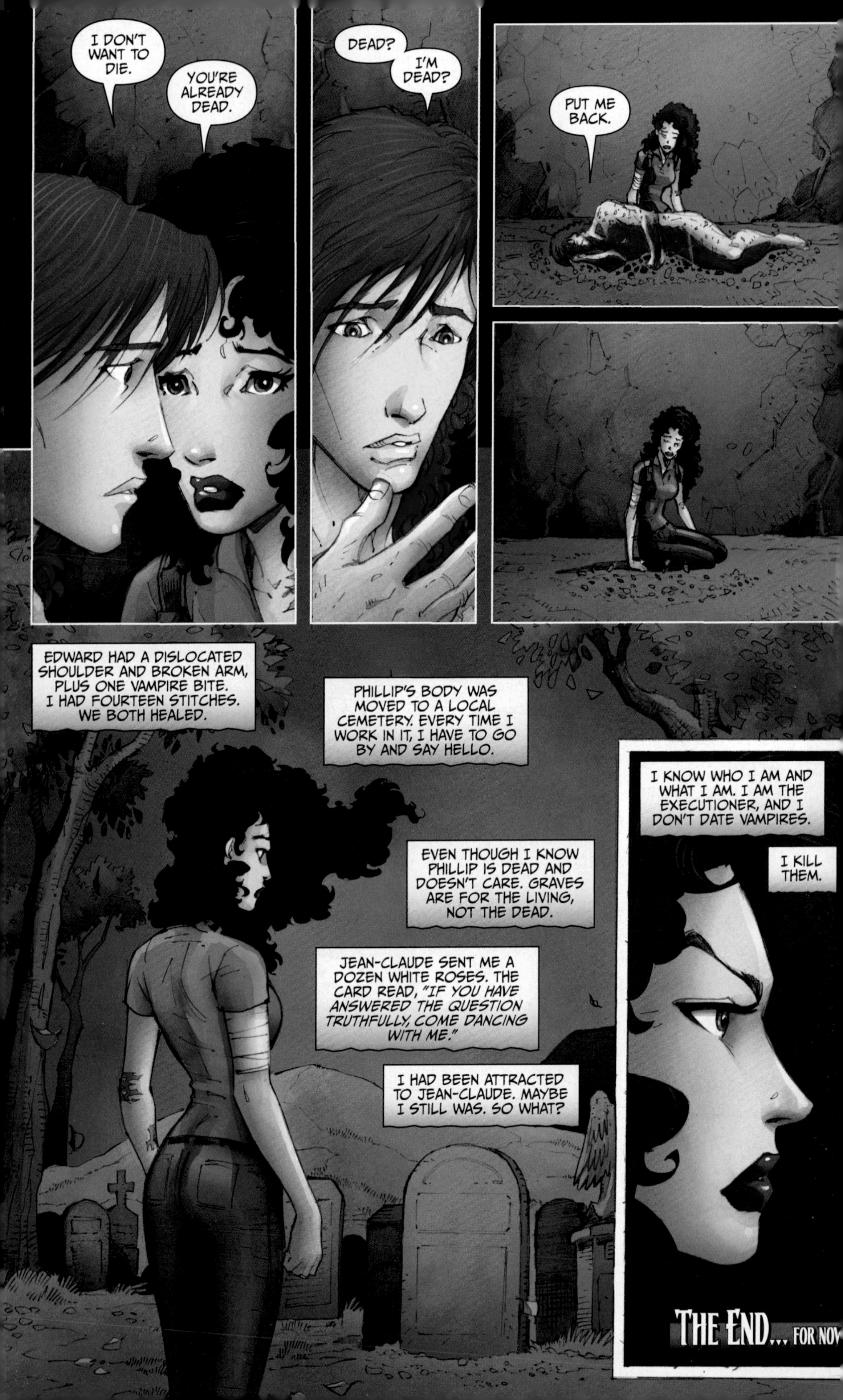
I DON'T WANT TO DIE.
YOU'RE ALREADY DEAD.
DEAD?
I'M DEAD?
PUT ME BACK.
EDWARD HAD A DISLOCATED SHOULDER AND BROKEN ARM, PLUS ONE VAMPIRE BITE. I HAD FOURTEEN STITCHES. WE BOTH HEALED.
PHILLIP'S BODY WAS MOVED TO A LOCAL CEMETERY. EVERY TIME I WORK IN IT, I HAVE TO GO BY AND SAY HELLO.
EVEN THOUGH I KNOW PHILLIP IS DEAD AND DOESN'T CARE. GRAVES ARE FOR THE LIVING, NOT THE DEAD.
JEAN-CLAUDE SENT ME A DOZEN WHITE ROSES. THE CARD READ, "*IF YOU HAVE ANSWERED THE QUESTION TRUTHFULLY, COME DANCING WITH ME.*"
I HAD BEEN ATTRACTED TO JEAN-CLAUDE. MAYBE I STILL WAS. SO WHAT?
I KNOW WHO I AM AND WHAT I AM. I AM THE EXECUTIONER, AND I DON'T DATE VAMPIRES.
I KILL THEM.
THE END... FOR NOW